The Scent of Roses Hung in the Air, Heavy and Seductive

Jonathan's clear amber eyes gazed straight into hers. He made a low growl in his throat, and then his hands were on Millicent's waist, lifting her lightly from the step and pulling her into him.

Jonathan's skin seared her through the cloth of her gown. His tongue traced the meeting line of her lips, and she gasped, surprised at its touch—and at her own intense response to it.

Heat flooded her, racing through her veins. She trembled in his arms. Millicent realized that she wanted to feel his hands on her body. She wanted him to touch her bare skin.

Also by Candace Camp

Light and Shadow
Analise
Bonds of Love
Bitterleaf
Crystal Heart
Heirloom
Rain Lily

Available from
HarperPaperbacks

CANDACE CAMP
ROSEWOOD

HarperPaperbacks
A Division of HarperCollins*Publishers*

HarperPaperbacks *A Division of* HarperCollins*Publishers*
10 East 53rd Street, New York, N.Y. 10022

Cover photograph by Herman Estevez
Cover illustration by Renato Aime
Quilt courtesy of Quilt of America, Inc., N.Y.C.

First printing: July 1991

Printed in the United States of America

HarperPaperbacks, HarperMonogram, and colophon are
trademarks of HarperCollins*Publishers*

10 9 8 7 6 5 4

One

There was a stranger in the yard next door.

Millicent saw him almost as soon as she came out of her own house, dressed in a calico dress, known as a "wrapper" and the old sunbonnet she wore to do her gardening. She stepped out onto the porch and glanced around with pride at the neat rows of flowers growing in front of the house, along the picket fence that surrounded the front yard, and in the rectangular garden on the east side. Then she strolled across the yard, carrying her thick work gloves and her gardening tools, toward the short white picket fence that stretched between the front yards of the Hayes's house and the old Widow Bell's place next door. Her prize irises were planted along this fence, tall and straight, their lovely drooping heads looking almost too heavy for the stalks.

As she neared the flower bed, she glanced across the fence toward the old Bell house, and it was then that she saw the man. It startled her so much to see anyone standing there that she dropped her gloves and tools on the ground and simply stood, staring at him.

The house next door had been vacant for nearly a year, ever since the Widow Bell died, and except for when the attorney's office sent someone out to cut the weeds, there was never anyone there. People said that the widow had only one daughter surviving, who lived in Dallas and had no interest in moving back to Emmetsville. For months everyone had been speculating about what would happen to the house.

The man was much too well dressed, Millicent thought, to be a vagrant or a robber. He was of medium height, perhaps a little taller than the average, and well proportioned. He wore a black hat, and he was turned away from her, so that she could not see his features. She waited impatiently for him to turn around, consumed by curiosity.

He reached up and took off the hat as he bent his head back to look up at the second story of the house. His hair flashed bright golden in the sunlight, mingled with strands of darker blond and light brown. Now Millicent was certain she didn't know him. She could think of no man in this town who had quite that color hair, somewhere between the yellow of corn and the pale gold of wheat—and there were very few people in town that Millicent did not know. In a town the size of Emmetsville, a stranger was always news, and one who was looking at the old Bell place was especially noteworthy.

The man trotted up the shallow steps to the front porch, unlocked the door, and went in. Millicent's interest was now thoroughly piqued. His opening the door with a key must mean that he had gotten it from

Mr. Carter, the widow's attorney and executor of her estate. He must be seriously considering buying or renting it.

Millicent realized suddenly how obvious she must be, standing there staring into the other yard. If the stranger had turned around he would have seen her plainly. The thought made Millicent blush. She prided herself on the propriety of her behavior, and the thought of being caught doing something so rude as gawking was most embarrassing. So she slipped hastily through the side yard to the snowball bush, a spreading tall shrub that at this time of year sported huge round clusters of white flowers. The snowball was the first in a series of intermittent shrubs that lined the boundary between the two back yards. The yards were open to each other in several places, providing access from one back door to the other, a common practice in East Texas where neighborliness was one of the major tenets of life.

Hiding behind the large bush, Millicent was soon lost in intriguing speculation about the stranger and his future in Emmetsville. It would be such fun to be able to tell everyone at the Ladies Missionary Aid Society meeting next week about the possibility of the Bell place changing hands. And just imagine Aunt Oradelle's amazement when Millicent had the news before she did!

Millicent was brought back to the present by the sound of the back door closing at the Bell place. Millicent peered around the edge of the bush. She saw a flash of movement and no more; she wasn't in a direct line of vision to the back porch.

Quickly she left the snowball bush and moved past

the hydrangea and across a gap in the shrubs to the row of bridal wreath bushes, dripping with tiny white flowers. She could see the stranger now, but she was much too obvious, with her head and shoulders showing clearly above the shrubs. She crouched down but discovered that the branches were much too thick to afford a good view of the other yard. In frustration she glanced around, and her eyes fell on the pyracantha bushes just beyond her. They were leafed out, with spreading branches that would afford some protection, but they weren't as thick near the roots as the bridal wreaths. She would be able to see through the tangle of branches into the widow's yard.

Millicent had always been curious, a quality which Aunt Oradelle said was Millicent's besetting sin. She wanted quite badly to see the stranger's face. What good would her news be if she couldn't even describe the man to the other ladies? So, crouching over and holding up the hem of her dress, she scurried to the pyracantha bush and carefully crawled beneath its thorny, drooping branches. She grinned with satisfaction. She had a perfect view of the yard.

The man carried his hat in his hand as he stood on the porch, looking around the deep back yard. He came down the steps and pivoted, studying the house and yard in all directions. As he turned toward her, Millicent could see his face clearly, and she sucked in her breath. He was one of the handsomest men she had ever seen! He looked to be a little older than herself, but not yet approaching his middle years. He had a strong jaw, prominent cheekbones, and a wide, firm mouth. It was a strong face, but there was something about the way laugh lines bracketed his mouth and radiated from the corners of his eyes that indicated that his wasn't a stern face, but one that was frequently visited by laughter and smiles. His light brown eyebrows grew up in a sort of inverted V, giving his face a faintly quizzical, amused expression that added character to a face that might otherwise have been too perfect.

Just looking at him gave Millicent a funny feeling, a curious blending of dread and excitement. She studied the column of his throat, tanned and strong, and his wide hand curled over the brim of his hat, ridged by tendons. Her gaze fell on his chest, then traveled down the long, slender line of his legs. Unconsciously, she leaned forward. What color were his eyes? She couldn't see them well enough to tell. She placed a hand against one of the small branches to steady herself as she craned forward, squinting. Her knee caught in the material of her skirt, pulling her up short, and she almost toppled over. Her hand tightened on the branch, and one of the thorns pierced her skin. She let out a small, unthinking yelp, then immediately clapped her hand over her mouth.

The sound attracted the stranger's attention, and he came a little closer, bending down and peering into the bush. Millicent went perfectly still, partly because she was paralyzed by embarrassment and partly because she hoped he wouldn't see her in the shadows of the branches. He frowned, then his eyebrows went up, and he began to grin. *Oh, Lord!* He'd seen her.

Worse yet, he was walking right toward her! Millicent

scrambled backward out of the bush, but in her hasty withdrawal, several thorns on the pyracantha branches sank into the back of her dress. She felt the tug and stopped. She was caught! She thought of the stranger finding her in this ignominious position, crouched beneath a bush, pinned by pyracantha thorns, and her face flooded with heat. She could not bear that!

He would think she had been spying on him, that she was a nosy, snooping old maid. Well, in all fairness, perhaps she *had* been spying, but she hadn't really meant to! She had simply been curious, that was all, and she had acted impulsively. She could just imagine how Aunt Oradelle would sniff if she heard about this episode.

That thought was enough to give Millicent the impetus to yank away from the bush's grip, despite the scratches and the ominous ripping sound as the thorns reluctantly gave up their hold. She jumped to her feet, and the branches made a last grab, knocking her sunbonnet askew. A breath of air touched her back, and Millicent realized that the thorns must have ripped through the aging material of her wrapper. The thorns had also caught the sides of the sashes and jerked them loose, so that they hung dangling at her side and her waistless wrapper fell loosely down from her shoulders, hiding any hint of her figure. She couldn't imagine why she cared; she had never been particularly vain, and she had resigned herself years ago to being a spinster. But somehow her disarray added the final touch to Millicent's humiliation, and it was all she could do to keep the tears back as she faced the strange man.

He had come up to within a couple of feet of her and was now standing in the gap between the bridal wreath bushes and the pyracantha, regarding her with frank interest. Millicent was sure there was amusement dancing in his eyes, as well, though she was too embarrassed to actually meet his gaze. She looked determinedly at his left shoulder, and her cheeks flamed with color. There was no way to get out of this predicament gracefully. She dared not even turn and run away like a silly girl, for then she would expose the rip in the back of her bodice. She had no idea how long or severe it was or how much it showed of her shift beneath. Any amount was too much! There was nothing for it but to brazen out the situation as best she could. Millicent straightened her sunbonnet and jerked the ends of her sash back into a knot.

She stiffened her shoulders and pulled her features into their coolest, haughtiest expression, forcing herself to look directly into the man's face. Laughter lurked in his eyes. But, oh! what beautiful eyes! It almost made her heart stop to look at them. They were big and brown— no, brown was too common a word for that magical color, a curious blend of gold and brown, almost like the amber her brother Alan kept in his collection of rocks and jewels. His eyelids were rimmed with long, brown lashes so thick that they gave his brilliant eyes a languid, almost sleepy, look. He was even handsomer than he had appeared at a distance, or perhaps it was simply that up close he seemed more real, less perfect and consequently more intriguing. She could see the chiseled cut of his lips and straight nose, the lines at his mouth and eyes that spoke of worldly experience, the tiny scar on his chin.

"Hello," he said, smiling.

She knew he was laughing at her, and it galled her. She was determined to face him down. It was obvious that he was waiting for her to extend her hand to shake, as was courteous, but she wouldn't do it. It was the woman's prerogative, after all, and she could not unbend enough to do that, or she feared she might collapse into embarrassing tears.

"I'm Jonathan Lawrence," he went on. "I'm purchasing the house next door, so it looks as if we will be neighbors."

"How do you do?" Millicent responded primly. "My name is Millicent Hayes. My brother Alan and I live here."

"It's nice to meet you."

Nice for him, perhaps, she thought grimly. Personally, she couldn't remember ever feeling more ill at ease. He bent down as though trying to get a good look at her face inside the tunnel of her sunbonnet. Millicent was grateful for the concealment its long upside-down scoop of a brim provided, and she turned her face a little to make it more difficult to see. She would prefer that he didn't get a really good look at her. If nothing else, she didn't want him to see how embarrassed and flustered she was.

"I was doing a bit of gardening," Millicent said. It was the only thing she could think of that would account for her being down on her hands and knees beside the pyracantha bush—besides the real reason, of course.

She glanced down at her hands and realized that her hands were bare of work gloves and she had none of her gardening tools. They were all in the front yard beside the iris bed, where she had first spotted Jonathan Lawrence. Her cheeks, which had begun to cool somewhat, flamed again. "I was pulling weeds," she explained weakly, then realized how absurd that was. No lady would be out pulling weeds with her bare hands.

"A dirty job for a lovely lady," he responded gallantly.

Well, she thought, at least he was telling as big a whopper as she was. "I enjoy working with my flowers," she replied stiffly, then recalled where she had been when he saw her. "And shrubs."

"It shows. You have a beautiful yard. Your flowers at the front caught my eye as soon as I walked up."

Oh, Lord, did that mean that he'd noticed her there, too? "Thank you."

There was a pause. He took another tack. "Did you know Mrs. Bell well?"

"We visited now and then." *Why didn't the man just leave?* She could not relax, knowing that there was a tear in the back of her dress. Nor could she forget how silly she must have looked peering at him from beneath the pyracantha.

"The house seems to have been kept in good condition."

"To the best of my knowledge she was an excellent housekeeper."

Mr. Lawrence stood for a moment longer, as though he would like to continue the conversation, but Millicent waited him out.

"Well," he said finally, taking a step backward and replacing the hat on his head. "I'll let you get on with your gardening."

Millicent laced her empty hands behind her back, reminded again of how feeble her excuse had been. She nodded to him shortly, knowing that she was being rude, but unable to help herself.

"I hope to see you again, Miss Hayes."

"I hope so, too." Her tone belied her words, and they both knew it.

"And I'll look forward to meeting your brother, as well."

"I—ah, well, Alan doesn't get out much."

"I see." It was obvious that he didn't, but at least he didn't probe any further into the matter. Instead, he doffed his hat, turned, and left.

Millicent turned and ran toward the back door, holding the tear in her dress together behind her. Tears filled her eyes, and it was all she could do to hold them back until she reached the sanctuary of her room. She wished with all her heart that Jonathan Lawrence was *not* buying that property and moving in next door!

Millicent swept down the back stairs and into the wide hallway, pulling on her best black gloves as she went. She rounded the corner and stopped at the door to her brother's room. Alan was sitting up in bed, his back supported by pillows, so absorbed in a book that he did not hear the approach of her heels on the wooden floor. Millicent stood for a moment unobserved, gazing at him.

He appeared small in the massive bed, with its high, thick walnut headboard ornately carved across the top. His head, almost as dark as her own, was bent over the book, and a wayward hank of hair had fallen forward over his forehead. He reached up impatiently to brush it back. His skin, once so browned by the sun, was porcelain pale now after years spent indoors, and his shoulders had taken on a rounded look from constant hunching over his books and rocks and lead armies, all the things with which he occupied his time. The heavy book rested on his legs, hidden beneath the covers.

Poor Alan, came the thought, as it had so many times before, and a familiar sadness compressed Millicent's throat. He had been clever and quick; there had been so many things he could have done with his life. He shouldn't have to spend his life lying there like that. Beneath the pity lay the thorn-prick of guilt, buried with time but never completely gone. He wouldn't be lying there, she knew, if it hadn't been for her.

His long, narrow fingers turned the page of the book, and as he did, he must have caught a glimpse of her from the corner of his eye, for he lifted his head and turned to face her, and a smile spread across his face. "Millicent!"

Millicent smiled in the old, sweet way that she reserved almost exclusively for him. "Good morning, Alan." She made her voice brisk to cover any trace of pity and strode forward to his bedside. "How are you this morning?"

He shrugged for an answer, looking up at her. "Good morning, Millie. My, don't you look elegant this morning?"

"Why, thank you." Millicent made a little pirouette, showing off her outfit to him.

She wore her best dark green skirt, pulled fashionably back into a small bustle, and its matching bodice, trimmed with jet buttons and a design of jet beads around the cuffs. Millicent was well aware of her position as a spinster of good breeding in this town, and she wore the darker colors and plainer styles that befitted that position, but she still had too much love of beauty not to add at least a sober sort of decoration to her clothes. Her dress was, as always, immaculate. No clothes of Millicent Hayes would have dared to show a wrinkle, one of the ladies of the town had once said. Her thick dark hair, parted down the middle and pulled back in wings to a decorous coil of braid on her neck, had not a hair out of place.

She wore her new best bonnet, also dark green, which she had bought just this year to replace the black one she had worn for the past two years in mourning for their father. She shouldn't have bought it, probably; navy blue or black were much more practical choices for a bonnet. However, it was such a fetching little thing, with double, V-notched ribbons trailing down her neck from the back of it, that she had been unable to resist it.

Knowing how much Alan disliked having to crane

his head back to look at someone, Millicent quickly sat down on the bed beside him, facing him. He had been a tall, gangly fourteen-year-old when he fell off the hay-wagon, and even with his ill health since then, his torso had continued to grow, so that he was taller than she when they were both sitting down.

"What's the occasion?" Alan asked.

"I'm going to church, silly. It's Sunday." Alan tended to forget the time and the day of the week, as well. It was only natural, of course, stuck in the house all the time as he was, and even though it was sometimes exasperating, Millicent tried not to let her irritation show.

"Oh, so it is. Stupid of me." He paused. "I suppose that means you'll be going to one of the aunts' houses for Sunday dinner."

"Yes." It was a rare weekend that there was not a gathering of one side of the family or the other at some-one's house on Sunday. Both the Hayeses and the Con-nallys were large, close-knit families who had all lived in the area since it was first settled over sixty years ago. "Aunt Oradelle's house this time. Would you like to come? Everyone would love to see you."

Alan made a comic face and groaned. "Lord, no! Listen to Aunt Oradelle describe every disease or catas-trophe that has struck anyone in the county for the past thirty years? Spare me, please."

Millicent chuckled and reached over to pat his hand. "Come, come, now, it's not that bad."

"Oh, no. I could always watch Cousin Sonny chew

and spit off the front porch or Great-Aunt Nan dip snuff."

This time Millicent laughed out loud. "Alan! You are just terrible." She paused and looked at him, her eyes twinkling with mirth. "But so accurate." She burst out laughing again.

"I think I'd rather stay here and read," Alan went on dryly.

"Then I'll see you this afternoon when I get home from Aunt Oradelle's. Has Johnny been by today?"

"No. You know Johnny. He's late, as usual." There was a trace of youthful petulance in his voice at odds with his face, on which pain had engraved the lines of an older man. In years, Alan was twenty-five, four years younger than his sister. Yet in many ways he could have been a middle-aged man; in still others, he had never quite left the adolescent boy behind.

"I'm sure he'll be here. That's just how he is." Johnny was the son of their cook and housekeeper, Ida Jackson, and he was as slow-witted and lackadaisical as Ida was clever and careful. He did odd jobs for Millicent and her brother, taking care of the heavier garden work such as spading, or mending a broken window. He also lifted Alan in and out of bed when Alan wanted to sit at his table or in his invalid chair that could be wheeled onto the back porch. On Sundays, he stopped by early in the morning and again in the evening to lift Alan in and out of his bed. On weekdays, when he was around the house all day, Alan summoned Johnny by means of a bell pull on the wall beside his bed. But it was sometimes several minutes before Johnny came ambling into the room, and he was often late arriving in the morning.

Alan had frequently complained, but both he and Millicent knew that he would never give the job to someone else. In a way, Johnny and Ida and her daughter Cherry, who cleaned for them in the mornings, were a part of the extended family, not people whom one could simply "let go." Besides, Johnny had "done for" Alan for eleven years and was one of the very few people whom Alan allowed to see his mangled and useless legs; Millicent couldn't imagine her brother subjecting himself to the humiliation of revealing his legs to another human being, no matter how maddeningly slow Johnny was sometimes.

"Ida's still here, isn't she?"

"Oh, yes. She brought me my breakfast ages ago, and I'm sure she'll leave me a tray for lunch before she goes to church. But she can't help me into my chair any more than you can."

Millicent hated it when Alan sounded glum or bitter. It was like a stab to her heart, a reminder of just how much he had to be unhappy about. She glanced toward the window, trying to think of a graceful way to change the topic of conversation. The heavy draperies were pulled back and tied, and the lace sheers had been pushed aside as well. The window was raised, letting in the early summer breeze, and along with it, the sweet scent of the honeysuckle that grew along the back of the house. The long lace curtains, reaching all the way from the top of the ten-foot windows to the floor, stirred in the breeze.

Suddenly a cat sprang onto the low sill from the outside. He stood for a moment, surveying the room, then sat back on his haunches and began to wash a foot in minute detail. Millicent frowned at him, but he ignored her with sublime indifference.

"I see you're still allowing that cat free run of your room," she grumbled to Alan.

Alan smiled at the feline perched on the windowsill. "I like the old reprobate. He's tougher than all of us."

"I have no doubt of that."

He was an ugly cat, she thought, not like her own plump white Persian, Punjab, all stately grace and rich, thick fur. This stray's coat was white and orange striped, and it was all too often matted with dirt or, even worse, dried blood. An ear hung limply, obviously torn in one too many fights, and there were scars scattered here and there all over his face and body. He had shown up at the back porch last winter, and though both she and Ida had shooed him away, he had refused to budge. Finally Millicent had had to slip him a bowl of scraps; she couldn't simply watch any animal starve right there on her steps. It wasn't long before Ida had tossed an old flour sack or two in a pile on the porch for him to sleep on, and after that it was only a matter of time before he managed to slip inside the back door one day when it was opened. He had found Alan's room, and when Millicent had discovered his presence and tried to shoo him out, Alan had insisted she let him stay.

Since then he had come into the house at every opportunity, especially since warm weather had given him easy access through the open windows. Millicent had steadfastly refused to give him a name, calling him nothing more than "Cat" when she had to address him. She disliked the animal on principle; he was too rough, an obvious street cat, and she hated to think of how much dirt he might be bringing into Alan's room. He wasn't at all an appropriate sort of pet in her opinion.

She was careful not to let anyone see the times when she had surreptitiously bent and scratched him behind his ears.

"Hello, Kit," Alan went on, clicking and whistling to the animal. He leaped up on the bed on the other side of Alan, turned around a time or two and lay down, fixing Millicent with his unblinking gaze.

Millicent grimaced back at him. But it was warming to see Alan's hand sink into his fur, rubbing. If Alan wanted it, she knew she'd let two or three worthless old toms in.

She stood up, glancing at the watch pinned to her bodice. "Well, I'd best be going, or I'll be late."

A smile hovered at the corners of Alan's mouth. "Mustn't have that, now. Everyone sets their clocks by when you walk to church, you know."

Millicent made a face of mock annoyance. "All right, you." She bent and gently kissed his forehead. "Goodbye. I'll see you later this afternoon. Take care."

Alan nodded. "Have a good time."

"Listening to a discourse on Mary Sue Grantham's bunions or watching Cousin Sonny spit?" she teased and was rewarded by seeing Alan smile.

With a wave, she turned and walked out of the room.

Two

$\mathcal{M}$illicent took her parasol from the umbrella stand beside the front door before she went outside, for she knew that though the morning was lovely now, by the time she returned this afternoon, the Texas sun would be hot enough to damage her complexion. She stepped out onto the front porch and looked around her. It was a beautiful May day, and it lifted her spirits just to see it.

Her cat Punjab was lying on the railing of the porch, his thick white tail curled around him, and he turned his head to gaze at her with haughty consideration. He was a fat, lazy cat, and his favorite occupation was to lie sunning on the porch or on one of the windowseats. When he was in the mood, he would curl up in Millicent's lap—but no one else's—and *only* when he chose to. It had been obvious to Millicent from the moment she first saw him that he was royalty.

"Hello, Your Highness," Millicent whispered, leaning over to scratch behind his ears. He permitted the caress, closing his round, startlingly blue eyes. "How's my sweetheart this morning?"

Millicent gave him a final stroke and started down the steps. As she did, she glanced up the street. The first thing she saw, of course, was the old Bell place, standing as silent and empty as ever. It was almost possible to believe that the incident in her back yard the other day hadn't really happened. Almost—but not quite.

It had happened. A man was buying the Bell house and moving into it, and she had managed to make herself look like a fool in front of him. It still made her burn with shame to think how impulsively and foolishly she had acted. One would think that by the time a woman was twenty-nine years old, she would have learned a little common sense. Why, even Aunt Oradelle had told her that she was impressed by the way Millicent had matured over the past few years, leaving her flighty ways behind her.

With a sigh, Millicent swung open the gate of the low picket fence that bordered her yard and started down the street. It was too lovely a morning to let the memory of her meeting Jonathan Lawrence spoil her day. She began to hum a little under her breath and even to swing her parasol.

It was still early enough in the year that the air wasn't hot, just deliciously warm, carrying the promise of summer ahead. The trees were leafed out, and roses loomed in the Hathaways' yard, pale pink, vivid red, and fragile white. In the next block was the Morgans's huge old magnolia tree, stretching up almost to the top of the house. Its leaves were a glossy dark green, and here and there perched on the branches were wide, flat white blossoms touched with crimson at their heart.

Millicent had never lived anywhere other than Emmetsville, had never even traveled farther away than Dallas, to which she'd gone with Aunt Sophie and Cousin Susan to shop. But she was sure that there could be no lovelier place than this small town. Emmetsville had always been a prosperous town, even before the railroad had come through fifteen years ago. Long before the war it had been the end of the line for river travel into the state from the Mississippi. Set only thirty miles across the border from Louisiana, Emmetsville had been the shipping point for cotton going out and all kinds of goods coming into the northeast Texas farmland. Unlike much of the state, which was still raw and wild, Emmetsville boasted gas lighting and a bricked Main Street, a downtown area of neat brick business buildings with raised plank sidewalks, and many pleasant, even elegant, residences. There was a park with a bandstand and picnic tables beside the slow-moving river.

But none of these evidences of civilization could match the natural beauty with which Emmetsville had been blessed. Set in the heart of the Piney Woods, its high, graceful pines towered over everything else, filtering the fierce Texas sun through a cooling canopy of green and covering the ground in a soft carpet of needles. Beneath the tall trees grew the shorter, spreading oaks and pecans, the stately magnolias, the mimosas with their fernlike fronds of tiny leaves that closed shyly at a touch, and the delicate flowering redbuds and dogwoods. In the bayou backwaters near the river grew big, knobby cypresses draped in Spanish moss, and quivering stands of marsh grass.

As if inspired by the natural beauty of its rolling landscape, the residents of Emmetsville filled their yards with shrubbery, trees, and bright flowers, so that in spring and summer the whole town seemed to be bursting with rich, fertile growth. Millicent could not have expressed the impact of this beauty on her, and she was far too practical to even try, but she felt it in an uplifting of her heart when she gazed upon the wooded beauty of the town.

When she reached the First Baptist Church, a large, solid white frame structure on the edge of the downtown area, she walked up the steps and marched down to the front to the Hayes's pew. Literally speaking, the pew did not belong to the Hayes family. However, members of the Hayes clan had sat in the same spot for so long and in such numbers that it had become regarded as their spot, in much the same way that everyone knew that the Slocums always sat near the rear of the church on the left-hand side.

When church was over, Millicent lingered to talk to a few people, and by the time she started for Aunt Oradelle's house, most of the other members of her family were gone. Millicent quickened her steps. Aunt Oradelle did not approve of anyone arriving late to her lunches. And everyone knew that Aunt Oradelle ran the family.

Aunt Oradelle's mother had died when most of the children were young, and she, at fourteen, had acted as a mother to the rest of them. Even after her father had married again, she had done a great deal of caring for the babies. Oradelle had, in fact, been such a great help at home that no one had expected her ever to marry herself. She had done so, however, somewhat later in life than was usual, marrying Elmer Holloway, a widower with three small children. Even with her own brood, she had not abandoned her brothers and sisters, and through the years she had continued to direct the Hayes family. Now a short, rather squat white-haired woman of sixty-seven years, she still kept an eagle eye on the entire clan, and there was little that went on in either the Hayes or Holloway families—or, indeed, in the town of Emmetsville—that Oradelle Holloway didn't know about.

Millicent reached the large, impressive brick house where Aunt Oradelle and her family lived, and knocked at the massive oak and beveled-glass door. Camilla Holloway opened the door a moment later.

"Cousin Millicent!" Camilla smiled in the quick, nervous way she had, and brought her hands up as if to hug Millicent, but instead just took her hand, pressing it between her own. Camilla often made short, abortive gestures and sentences, seeming to change her mind in midstream, and her voice tended to die away on the last few words of whatever she said. She was one of the children Mr. Holloway had before he married Oradelle, and she was nearing forty years old, a confirmed spinster residing at home with her father and stepmother. Everyone said that she was a comfort to her parents in their old age, but privately Millicent wondered how much comfort she could be to anyone. Certainly Aunt Oradelle seemed more irritated by Camilla's indecision and nervous ways than comforted.

Millicent had sympathy for Camilla. It couldn't have been easy acquiring Oradelle Hayes as a stepmother. Millicent tried to be especially nice to Camilla, for which Camilla seemed almost pathetically grateful. Once, to Millicent's amazement, Camilla had confided to Millicent that she was her dearest friend. Since Millicent rarely saw Camilla except on family occasions such as this, she couldn't imagine how she could be such a close friend; the fact that Camilla considered her so spoke volumes about how closely Camilla was tied to this house and her parents. Millicent hoped that she would not become the same kind of spinster that Camilla had become. Surely she was made of sterner stuff than that.

"Mama's in the kitchen," Camilla told Millicent unnecessarily. Where else would Aunt Oradelle be but in the midst of things, wearing a spotless white apron and directing all the activity?

Just as she expected, Aunt Oradelle was standing by the huge cast-iron stove, lifting the lids of the various pots and peering inside while one of her daughters-in-law stood patiently by, holding a long-handled wooden spoon. "Gravy looks about done. Best start dishing things up, Ann."

The old lady turned to find another area that needed her attention, and she saw Millicent as she stepped in the door, followed hesitantly by Camilla.

"Mama, Cousin Millicent's—" Camilla began, but

Mrs. Holloway strode forward, impatiently waving away Camilla's words.

"Of course she's here. How are you, my dear? And how is that poor, dear Alan? Why didn't he come with you?" Without giving Millicent a chance to answer, she charged onward, "Why don't you put on an apron and lend Ann a hand?" Then she was off to supervise the setting of the china and silverware on the long dining room table.

Camilla smiled at Millicent apologetically, as though she had done something wrong. "Mama's so active for her age."

"Mm," Millicent responded dryly. "An inspiration to us all." Millicent picked up an apron that had been draped over the icebox and tied it around her waist, then took down a hotpad from one of the hooks above the stove and lifted a pan of peas from the stove.

"Put it in the willowware bowl," Ann directed, nodding toward a large white china bowl patterned with a blue oriental scene.

Millicent complied, knowing that Aunt Oradelle had doubtless decreed which food went into which dish, and woe betide the daughter or daughter-in-law careless enough to put black-eyed peas into a bowl obviously meant for yams. Not that she would fuss. Aunt Oradelle would never make a scene. She would simply frown and sigh, "No, no, no, dear, not the *willowware.*" Or "not Mama's *Spode* dish," as if only a woman with a deficiency in her upbringing would think that vegetable was suitable for that particular bowl. And the incident would become another in Aunt Oradelle's long mental list of debits or credits against the woman's name, contributing to her saying, with a sigh, at some cozy family gossip session, "Poor John, I can't think why he married her; Ann simply doesn't know how to run a household properly."

Millicent carried the steaming bowl through the open doorway into the large dining room. The dining table was long and very dark, made of black walnut, as were the huge sideboard and china closet, and it was covered with an Irish linen tablecloth. Oradelle Holloway liked to remind people that her husband was wealthy and that, though she might have married later than some of the women in her family, she had also married better.

Susan, Aunt Sophie's and Uncle Chub's daughter, was sitting in one of the chairs, folding napkins, while her younger sister and one of Oradelle's daughters bustled around the table, laying out the china, silver, and crystal. She looked up at Millicent's entrance and when she saw who it was, smiled lazily.

"Why, Millie!" Her voice was low and husky, and she spoke in the same languid way in which she moved or smiled or did anything else. Her brown eyes drooped faintly, giving her a sleepy expression. Though she had never been considered a beauty, men had always seemed to find her fascinating, and her husband was as in love with her now as he had been eight years ago when they got married. She had never been flirtatious, however, in the way that Rebecca Connally was; her appeal for men was as effortless and natural to her as breathing.

"How are you? It's been ages!" Susan set aside the

napkins and stretched forward to take Millicent's hand as she approached. "Excuse me for not getting up."

"Heavens, no. There's no reason for you to be exerting yourself." Both of them managed to avoid speaking of the reason for Susan's staying in her chair: she was seven months pregnant, and her rounded stomach pushed out her skirt unmistakably these days, no matter how high she moved the waistline of her dress. Because she was showing so much, she had taken to staying in her house most of the time, going only to a few family functions such as this one. In a week or two, Millicent imagined that she would stop coming even to them, especially now that it was turning hot.

Millicent sat down in the chair beside her, angled so that she was facing her cousin and friend. Only a few months apart in age, they had been playmates ever since Millicent could remember and, next to Polly Craig, Susan was Millicent's closest friend. Since Polly had married a Methodist minister several years ago and moved with him to the hill country of central Texas, Millicent had grown even closer to Susan. Susan had a dry wit, and though she could say some scandalous things at times, she was fun to be around.

"How are you feeling?" Millicent asked her seriously, reaching over and starting to fold the pile of napkins for Susan. This was Susan's third pregnancy and, surprisingly, she had felt worse than she had with the other two.

Susan shrugged, unconsciously running her hand over the curve of her bulging abdomen. "I'm fine. You're too much of a worrywart."

"Well, somebody has to do it for you; you won't do it yourself."

Susan chuckled. "I haven't the time. Little Fannin and Sammy keep me too busy."

"You won't help them any by not taking care of yourself," Millicent scolded. "What would they do if you had to take to your bed?"

"Now, Millie . . . you take things too much to heart. There's nothing wrong. It's just different from the other times, that's all."

"How do you know?"

"I just do." She paused, and a mysterious smile curved her lips, as if she knew something wonderful and secret. "I think it means that this one's a girl." Her drowsy brown eyes glowed. "Wouldn't that be wonderful? I wanted the boys, for Fannin, you know, 'cause a man needs sons. And I love them to death. But they leave you so quick. But a girl, now, a girl is yours forever."

Millicent felt a pang of loneliness. Or perhaps it was just envy, for she knew that she was all too often wickedly envious, even of her friends like Susan and Polly. It seemed as though they had entered a world from which she was excluded, privy to secrets and emotions that she could only guess at. She had adjusted to her lot in life and she was quite satisfied to live as she did, taking care of Alan, but there were moments when she felt sad, knowing she had lost something that could never be replaced.

"Well, I hope it's a girl, for you, then." Millicent looked down at her hands, afraid that something of what she felt would show in her face. Her fingers folded the napkins in quick, efficient movements, doing the simple task in less than half the time it would have taken Susan. It was silly, when you thought about it, how she had spent her life learning to keep a home, to sew, to cook, to clean, to instruct children in the right path, all the things that she would need to do when she married and had children. Yet she would never have the opportunity to use those skills to create the warm and loving, perfect home for a family of her own.

Millicent didn't like the direction her thoughts were taking, and she cast about for something to say. "I have some news."

"Really?" Susan's interest was piqued. "What?"

"Someone's buying the widow's house."

"Mrs. Bell's? Honestly? Who is it?"

Color swept up into Millicent's cheeks, and she wished that she hadn't brought the subject up. She hated to think about that stranger who had seen her in such an undignified position. "I—I didn't recognize him. I don't think he's from around here."

"I wonder who it could be . . . and why would he be moving here? Did he have a family with him?"

Millicent shook her head, and, strangely, her cheeks grew even hotter. "I don't know. He didn't say."

"You mean you talked to him? Why didn't you say so? What did he tell you? Who is he?"

"Who is who?" One of Aunt Oradelle's daughters, Bertie, a short, squarely built woman much like her mother, set a gravy boat down on the table beside them. She had obviously overheard part of their conversation.

"The man looking at the house beside Millicent's," Susan explained.

"Widow Bell's place? Is somebody moving in there?"

"Why, that thing's been empty for ages," Aunt Sophie exclaimed.

"Who is it?" Marianne, another of Oradelle's daughters-in-law asked, drawing closer.

"What's his name?" chimed in Amelia, Susan's younger sister.

Suddenly there was a small cluster of women around Millicent and Susan, drawn by the scent of news, all of them eagerly offering comments and questions.

"Wait. Please. I don't know." Millicent raised her hands as though surrendering.

"What in the world are you all cheeping about in here like a bunch of hens?" It was Aunt Oradelle's voice, cutting crisply across the chatter, and the buzz of voices quieted instantly.

"Millicent says there's someone moving into the old Bell place, Mama," Bertie told her mother.

"There is?" Aunt Oradelle looked surprised and intrigued, and Millicent knew a momentary satisfaction at having information that her aunt did not.

"I think so. I saw him looking at the house, and he said he was buying it."

"You talked to him?" Aunt Oradelle's forehead creased in a frown. "A complete stranger?"

Millicent stifled an urge to squirm beneath her aunt's stern gaze. "I was working in my garden and he was in the other yard, looking at the Bell house. He came over and introduced himself."

"It doesn't sound very proper to me. Is he a gentleman?"

"He seemed . . . " What? Handsome? Intriguing? Different? She remembered his unique brown eyes, alight with an inner laughter, and she could feel a blush climbing up her throat all over again. "He was nicely dressed and . . . and very presentable."

"Presentable!" Amelia exclaimed and made a disgusted face. "Oh, pooh, Millicent, that's not what we want to know. Tell us what he looked like, for goodness' sake! Is he young? Old? Handsome? Fat? What?"

Aunt Oradelle frowned at the irrepressible girl. "You just hush, missy. The important thing is not how he looks, but whether he comports himself as a gentleman."

"Yes, Aunt Oradelle." Amelia cast her eyes down, looking thoroughly chastened, but Millicent suspected that she was looking down so as not to reveal the amusement in her eyes.

"I think he was a gentleman," Millicent said quickly to keep Amelia from getting herself into further trouble. "And he was rather handsome, as well."

"Really?" Amelia's head shot up.

"Indeed?" Even Aunt Oradelle couldn't pretend she wasn't intrigued by that statement. "In what way?"

"Well . . . in every way, I guess. His hair is blond, and his eyes were a most peculiar shade of brown—but not unattractive. His features were even. He was clean-shaven."

"Millie!" Even Susan sounded disgusted. "What a

dry description! Can't you tell us anything more personal than that?"

"Her description was quite proper," Aunt Oradelle decreed. "A lady would not know anything more personal than that about a man she had barely met."

"But we still don't know what he looked like. Was he wickedly handsome or angelically good-looking? Did he smile at you? And was it breathtaking or simply pleasant?"

"Breathtaking," Millicent answered promptly. "That is, I mean, it wasn't pleasant, really. It was . . . mischievous. Almost boyish, though there was too much devilment in his eyes to be that."

"That sounds more interesting." Amelia bent closer. "How old is he?"

"Too old for you," Millicent replied tartly. "In his thirties, I should say, maybe even late thirties."

"That's not too old," Amelia protested.

"Don't be absurd." Oradelle Holloway fixed her with a stern look. "You're barely sixteen."

"Lots of husbands are older than their wives! Why, Mr. Holloway was fifteen years older than you, wasn't he?"

"That was an entirely different matter. No mature gentleman would be interested in a flibbertigibbet like you, young lady. Not unless you mend your ways."

Amelia subsided into a pout, and Oradelle turned her attention back to Millicent. "What was his name? Did he say why he was looking at the house?"

"He said he was buying it and that we would be

neighbors. That was why he introduced himself to me. His name is Jonathan Lawrence."

"I don't believe I know any Lawrences. Although there is a family over by Willow Grove that . . . no, their name is Lawson, not Lawrence. Hmmm." Oradelle tapped her forefinger against her lips.

Millicent felt sure that if Aunt Oradelle had heard of anyone named Lawrence, she would sooner or later come up with the complete name and ancestry, as well as every bit of gossip ever circulated about the person.

"Why do you suppose he's moving to Emmetsville?" Susan's mother asked. If even Aunt Oradelle didn't know him, it was obvious he wasn't from around here.

"You know . . . " Aunt Oradelle narrowed her eyes shrewdly and wagged a forefinger at the others. "I did hear something about a man moving into town. I don't know the name, but Fanny Baldwin told me a couple of days ago that she'd heard someone was buying the newspaper from Fred Gillespie."

"The *Sentinel?*" Millicent named the small weekly newspaper published in Emmetsville.

"Do you suppose it's the same man?"

The conversation bubbled, fact mingling with speculation. Millicent wondered if Jonathan Lawrence was purchasing the town's newspaper. She tried to picture him as a publisher, but couldn't. She thought of a newspaper publisher as a staid, intellectual sort of man, someone wizened and bespectacled like Fred Gillespie. The man in Mrs. Bell's yard yesterday had seemed too tanned and muscular, too filled with life, to spend his days in an office writing about other people.

"But why is Fred Gillespie selling the paper?" Aunt Sophie asked, momentarily halting the speculations regarding the stranger.

"He's sick," Aunt Oradelle replied flatly, giving a decisive nod of her head. "Has been for months. All you had to do was look at him, and you could tell it."

"Why, I saw Lou Ann just a week or so ago, and she never said a word about it."

"She wouldn't. Closemouthed; all those Clintons are."

"Lou Ann Gillespie was a Clinton? Are you sure?"

"Of course I'm sure." Aunt Oradelle gave her sister-in-law a look that would have chilled to the bone anyone less vague and placid than Sophie Hayes. "I was at her wedding. Her father was Jefferson Clinton, and her mother was one of the Bufords from over by Coldwater Creek."

"Oh, that's right!" Aunt Sophie smiled. "Her brother was that nice Dan Clinton. I remember dancing with him at Ruth Tyson's engagement party."

"Daniel went west, you know, and I heard he died in El Paso. Tuberculosis, it was, that got him."

"That's right. I'd forgotten." Aunt Sophie sighed. "How sad."

"The Clintons are notoriously weak in the chest, always have been." Oradelle continued in somber tones, "And Fred Gillespie's not long for this world, either. You mark my words."

Death was one of the subjects dearest to Aunt Oradelle's heart, and her conversations were usually punctuated by predictions of imminent doom or past demises or, frequently, judgments that one or more persons would be better off in that state. Millicent had long been positive that her formidable aunt could list the cause of death for every person who'd passed away in or around Emmetsville in the past fifty years. If she didn't know, the person was clearly unimportant.

"Ah, well." Mrs. Holloway sighed lugubriously and shook her head. "We're not getting anything done standing here talking, and the food's cooling on the table. Bertie, call the men, dear. Millicent, there's still a platter of chicken in the kitchen. Would you get it?"

The knot of women broke up, Millicent going to the kitchen and Bertie stepping around the corner to the library, where the men had gathered, while the other women hastened to set the last chairs and dishes in place. Millicent carried in the heavy stoneware platter of fried chicken and set it down on the table beside the bowl of rich gravy, thick and white and flecked with pieces of batter. The rest of the table was filled with bowls of mashed potatoes, golden corn, black-eyed peas, and candied yams or plates of sliced homemade bread, biscuits, and cornbread, crusty brown on top and crumbly and yellow inside. There were butter dishes and small glass bowls of jewel-colored jellies, another platter of chicken, and a pitcher of milk. A peach cobbler and a white cake sat waiting on the marble sideboard for dessert.

The men began to file into the room, smiling and making compliments about the food that loaded down the table. "Look at that!" "Doesn't that look delicious?" "Mmm, fried chicken." "Peach cobbler! I could smell that all the way down the hall." "Made my mouth water."

The children went into the kitchen to eat at the worktable, and the husbands and wives began to group themselves naturally into sets around the table. Millicent, watching them, felt suddenly distant. She was a member of the family, useful, loved, included in its warmth, and yet . . . She glanced up to see Camilla standing, like her, a little apart. A cold loneliness twisted through Millicent. But she tamped it down and went to an empty chair beside Amelia.

Three

The answers to everyone's questions about the stranger in Widow Bell's yard were soon answered. The *Sentinel* ran an article about the sale of the newspaper to an experienced journalist from Dallas, Mr. Jonathan Lawrence. It was the same man, Millicent thought, reading the article over again. Why hadn't the paper given any important information about him, such as whether he had a family—though of course he must, for why would a single gentleman need a house as large as the Bell place? Still, there had been something about him that simply didn't *look* like a settled family man.

Millicent frowned at the paper. What good was a news article when it didn't tell people the things they wanted to know? No wonder Fred Gillespie was selling the business. With a sigh of disgust, she folded the newspaper up and carried it into Alan's room.

"Here's the *Sentinel*. Want to read it?" She stopped just inside the doorway, holding the newspaper up.

"What?" Alan was sitting in his wicker chair with wheels, bent over his work table, and he glanced up abstractedly. "Oh. No, not right now. Put it down on the bed; I'll get to it later."

"All right." She laid the folded paper down and strolled around the end of the bed. "What are you working on?"

Alan grimaced. "I'm trying to get this hill correct, but I can't seem to do it. It looks like a big lump, not a hill."

Millicent studied the thin wooden board on the table in front of her brother. One of his hobbies was collecting lead soldiers, correct in every detail of uniform and weapon, of various historical armies. There was an older gentleman in town, a West Point graduate and major in the army, later a colonel in the Confederate forces, who shared Alan's interest in military history and also collected the miniature armies. He visited Alan every week or so, and the two of them would lay out the tiny horses and riders, cannons, infantrymen, and even battle standards, arguing endlessly over minute details.

A few weeks earlier Alan had conceived of the idea of making one of the layouts more realistic by adding the actual topography of the battle area. So he had sketched out the area on a large piece of plywood and was trying to mold the landscape on it with papier mâché, a messy and tedious process which often left him grumbling and short-tempered.

"I'm no artist." He sighed and shoved the board away from him impatiently. "I don't know why I even started the thing."

"Now, Alan . . . " Millicent stepped forward to pick up the board and set it aside in the corner of the room.

"You're probably tired. Perhaps you ought to lie down and rest."

"Rest!" He burst out, startling her. "Damnation, Millie, all I ever do is rest! I'm sick to death of resting! How much of my life can I sleep away? There are too many hours in the day, too many days for the rest of my life."

Millicent wished desperately, as she had many times before, that there was something she could do to ease Alan's pain. "If you aren't feeling sleepy, why don't I bring the chess board over and we can play a game? I know I'm not a match for you, but . . . "

"You play well enough, but I'm not interested in it this afternoon."

"Perhaps you could read to me while I do my mending. I could bring my mending basket in here and—"

"Blast it, Millicent! I'm sick of being humored and placated and soothed. Just go away and leave me alone."

Tears sprang into her eyes, but she blinked them away and kept her voice steady, "Yes, of course. I'm sorry."

She turned to walk away, but her brother's voice stopped her, "Ah, Millie, I'm sorry. Wait, don't go. I didn't mean that."

Millicent turned back and gave him a smile, her face softening. "It's all right. I understand."

"No, it's not. I'm an old bear. You're the best of sisters, and I don't know what I'd do without you." He held out a hand to her. "Come here and tell me you forgive me."

"Of course I do." Millicent crossed the room to take

his hand and squeeze it. *"You're* the best of all brothers."

"Get the chess board down, and we'll play a bit." As Millicent reached for the chess board, her gaze went out the window. She went still. "Oh, my!"

"What is it?"

"Alan, look! He's moving in next door."

"Who?" Alan twisted in his chair to look out the window, too. There was a wagon standing in the street in front of the Bell place, piled high with furnishings and trunks, and they could also see the end of another wagon before the Bell house cut off the view.

"The man I told you about. You remember—the one I met in the yard last week."

"Oh, yes. The one Aunt Oradelle thinks bought the *Sentinel.*"

"He did. It's in the paper today. He's moving in."

As they watched, two men approached the wagon and pulled a trunk from it, then carried it into the house. Right behind them came another man. He wore heavy work clothes, and the sleeves of his coarse blue shirt were rolled up past his elbow, revealing muscular brown arms. His head was bare, and the sun glinted off his pale hair. Even though he was dressed differently, Millicent had no trouble recognizing him.

"There he is. That's Jonathan Lawrence."

He pulled a smaller trunk from the wagon, his arms bulging at the weight, and started toward the house. He was looking at the porch of the Bell house, which Millicent and Alan could not see, and a grin broke across his face. A moment later a young girl skipped into view, then turned and walked into the house with Lawrence, talking as they went.

"So he has a daughter." Millicent couldn't imagine why, but the discovery made her feel a little funny in the area of her stomach.

"Mm. A dog, too." Alan pointed at the large white dog that was loping up to the wagon. The dog turned, its tail wagging, when a whistle split the air, and took off at a run toward the porch.

For the rest of the afternoon, the men carried the goods on the wagons into the house. Alan and Millicent watched for a while, then started their chess game. Even after they began to play, Millicent's eyes kept straying to the window where she could see the activity next door, and she had difficulty concentrating on the game. Later, when she went upstairs to do her mending, she took the basket of clothes and her sewing box from the small sewing room into the front guest bedroom. This room, higher and closer to the street, had a better view of Mrs. Bell's house (doubtless it would remain "Mrs. Bell's house" for years to come because things were slow to change in a little country town). From time to time Millicent glanced up from her sewing to see what was going on next door.

It was simple curiosity, she told herself. A new family in town was a thing of interest and her friends and family would expect her to relay to them every tidbit of information she could glean from the Lawrences' moving in.

Throughout the afternoon she watched the laborers go back and forth. Jonathan Lawrence frequently crossed her field of vision, for he continued to help the men. She saw the girl several times, too, darting here and there, usually getting underfoot. Millicent judged her to be about nine or ten. She even saw the dog again and again, sitting in the shade panting or dashing back and forth, barking madly, or simply running in crazy circles. But the one person she did not see all afternoon was a woman. Where was Mrs. Lawrence? He had a daughter; surely he had a wife.

Unless he was a widower.

She felt that silly little flutter in her stomach again at the thought. The sensation irritated her. She wasn't some foolish old maid who grew hopeful every time an unattached male turned up in the vicinity.

He might be handsome, but he was no gentleman, or he wouldn't have stood there watching in amusement while she made that undignified retreat from the pyracantha bush. Just thinking about the way his eyes had danced made her tighten her lips in annoyance. Anyone with a shred of decency would have pretended that he hadn't seen her. No, he was definitely the last sort of man she would be interested in; frankly, she wished that she would never have to see him again.

But Millicent knew that there was no way she could avoid seeing him. They would be neighbors, after all, and they were bound to meet on the street or see one another out in the yard. In those situations, she could get by with a nod and a quick greeting, at least. Far worse would be when she took a covered dish over as a neighborly gesture of welcome. She didn't want to do it, for then she would come face to face with the man;

she would have to speak to him and smile and maybe even chat for a moment.

But she knew that there was no way she could get out of taking him a meal. It was simply part of the Texas tradition of hospitality. Whenever a neighbor was sick or a member of the family died or someone moved in, one brought over a dish of food. If Mr. Lawrence was, in fact, without a wife, he was even more likely to need a meal, for he probably hadn't yet hired a housekeeper. And however rude Mr. Lawrence might be, Millicent Hayes knew and practiced polite behavior. Why, her mother would have considered it a disgrace that Millicent would even think about not taking over a covered dish.

So Millicent ended up late in the day putting on a starched white shirtwaist and dark skirt, sticking her second best bonnet on her head, and taking a pot full of Ida's sweet, thick baked beans to the Bell house. She marched up to the front door, her spine stiff, determined to do her duty.

A sharp rap at the front door brought the sound of footsteps inside, and a moment later, Jonathan Lawrence opened the door. Millicent had carefully rehearsed what she would say to him when she met him, but at the sight of him her well-chosen words were forgotten.

He was handsomer than she had remembered. How could she have forgotten just how thick his lashes were or the precise golden-brown color of his eyes? His sleeves were rolled up past his elbows, revealing muscular forearms, and his skin glistened with perspiration.

His blond hair, too, was darkened with sweat around the hairline, and his face was slightly flushed. He seemed almost overwhelmingly vital and strong.

A wide, white smile flashed. "Ah, a neighbor! How are you today, Miss Hayes?"

"Quite well, thank you," she returned primly. "And you?"

"Tired, a bit," he confessed, though it seemed to Millicent that there was nothing about him to indicate that he felt anything less than energetic.

"I'm sure it's been quite a chore, moving in." Millicent handed the pot of beans to him. "I brought you a little something for dinner tonight. To welcome your family to Emmetsville."

"Why, thank you." He took the pot, breathing in the aroma. "Mmm. They smell delicious. Won't you come in? I'm sure my daughter would love to meet you." He turned his head and called, "Betsy!"

No child came at his call, but the large white dog came pounding around the side of the house and up the steps. He was even larger than he had looked from the window of her house, a white shaggy mutt, his tail wagging so hard it was a wonder it didn't fall off. He whirled around Millicent twice before rearing back and planting his front paws firmly on her chest, almost knocking her over backwards.

"Admiral!" The man roared. "No! Down!"

The dog plopped back on all fours, but looked up at Millicent expectantly, his tongue lolling out of one side of his mouth and his whole rear end wiggling from side to side with the movements of his tail. Millicent looked down in dismay at the muddy pawprints on the front of her white shirtwaist.

"Admiral! Come back!" A girl came tearing around the house in the wake of the dog, and she stopped abruptly when she saw the tableau on the porch. "Oh, no . . . Admiral! You've done it again, haven't you?"

"Yes, he most certainly has. I'm afraid he's gotten our guest muddy, as well as almost knocking her over."

"He's only a puppy," the girl said in excuse.

"A puppy?" Millicent repeated in horror. "My heavens, what will the animal be like when he's bigger?"

Jonathan Lawrence chuckled, as if she had been joking. "Yes, he's big, isn't he? I'm afraid his behavior isn't quite akin to his size, however. I apologize." He looked down at the dog. "Sit, Admiral. Good boy."

The dog sat down, still gazing up at Millicent, panting. He had a smear of black fur around one eye, giving him a slightly cockeyed look, and the tongue hanging out of his open mouth added to his air of silliness. Millicent wondered exactly why anyone would have chosen a dog like this, especially for a girl. Her gaze went back to the child.

She was nothing like Millicent's cousins' little girls, demure in their gingham dresses and white eyelet-trimmed pinafores, with their hair caught at the crown in a wide, flat bow and long fat curls hanging down over their shoulders. This child's reddish-blond hair was in two braids, but much of it had worked loose and hung messily about her face. The bow on one braid had come untied and the ribbon hung down limply; the other braid was completely missing its ribbon and was beginning to come undone. Her sturdy black shoes were scuffed and muddy, and one of them had come untied. She wore a pink and white gingham dress, a trifle too short for her, and the ruffle of her white petticoat showed beneath it. There was a hole in one stocking, and a wide ladder ran up from it.

She was not an especially pretty child; she had too strong a jaw and too wide a mouth for prettiness, and freckles spangled her cheeks and forehead. Her eyes, however, were intelligent and large and shaded with her father's thick lashes, so that Millicent would have accounted them attractive if Betsy had not stared at her with such a bold, frankly curious gaze, utterly inappropriate in a child her age, Millicent thought. Whatever beauty she had was marred by the streak of mud across her cheek.

"Miss Hayes, I'd like for you to meet my daughter, Elizabeth. Betsy, this lady is our new neighbor, Miss Hayes."

"Hello," Betsy greeted her cheerfully.

Millicent blinked. She hadn't even offered a "ma'am" or a "Miss Hayes" or a "How do you do?" Millicent wouldn't have considered it a polite greeting in an adult; from a child, it sounded definitely rude. She glanced over at Jonathan Lawrence. He was grinning down at his daughter as if she were the most delightful child on earth.

"How do you do?" Millicent returned politely. "I'm pleased to meet you." She could at least set a good example for the child; it was apparent that the poor thing had grown up without anyone proper to emulate.

"Are you the one with the cherry tree?"

"Why, yes, we have a cherry tree in the back."

"Did you used to climb in it? It looks like a terrific climbing tree."

"Climb in it?" Millicent's brows shot up at the thought. She could well imagine the look on her father's face if he had ever found her climbing in any trees. "Goodness, no! I didn't climb in trees." She spoke in a reproving tone, hoping the child would take it to heart.

But the girl said only, "Oh, that's too bad." She gave Millicent a look of sympathy. "Papa says nobody should ever grow too old to climb in trees." Her brow wrinkled. "But how could you be too old when you were a girl?"

Jonathan Lawrence had the good grace to look abashed. "Uh, Betsy, I didn't—"

She swung toward him innocently. "But, Papa, isn't that what you said?"

"Well, it was a manner of speaking. But it isn't always polite to . . . ah . . . uh . . ." He stumbled to a halt.

"Ladies do not climb trees," Millicent said decisively. It was clear that Mr. Lawrence had no idea how to handle the matter. "Even when they are girls, for then they should be *young* ladies."

Betsy gaped at Millicent as if she had sprouted horns. "Never?"

"Never."

"I reckon I'll never be a lady then." There was no noticeable regret in the girl's voice.

Millicent's mouth pinched in disapproval. What a thing for a child to say! And to an adult, yet! Millicent would have been sent to bed without supper for speaking thusly at her age. Yet Betsy's father didn't make a move to correct her.

Millicent glanced at Mr. Lawrence. He was looking out over Betsy's head at the yard, his hand over his mouth as if he were stroking his jaw while deep in thought. But Millicent caught the glint in his eyes and the slight shaking of his shoulders, and she realized with a sense of outrage that the man was trying to keep from laughing out loud!

Well, she didn't have to stand here and subject herself to his bizarre sense of humor. "I hope you'll excuse me," she said tightly and swung away, grabbing her skirts and lifting them slightly to navigate the three steps down to the ground. "I must return home now."

"You're going?" Betsy looked disappointed. "But you just got here." She hopped down the steps beside Millicent

"I simply brought a dish over for your supper tonight."

"But aren't you going to eat with us?" She trailed along the walkway with her toward the street.

"I can't. My brother is waiting for me at home."

"Is he little? Or is he old like you?"

The child had managed to insult her again! She looked to be nine or ten years old, yet she seemed to have had no instruction in the social graces at all.

"Alan is an adult," Millicent said shortly, bending down to swing open the gate.

"Oh." Betsy's face fell in disappointment. "I was

hoping there'd be children here. I had to leave all my friends back home."

"I'm sure that must have been very trying for you."

"It was ever so hard. But Papa couldn't come by himself."

"Of course not." Was the child going to follow her all the way home? Millicent turned. "You'd best go back to your father now. I have to go home."

"All right." Betsy suppressed a sigh. "Will you come back to visit again?"

Millicent forced a little smile. "I'm sure we'll see one another again. Now, good day, Betsy."

"'Bye." She stood on the lower crosspiece of the gate, leaning over it and swinging idly back and forth as she watched Millicent stride down the street and into her adjacent yard. Millicent turned and cast a last glance at her, then at the porch where her father had stood. But he was no longer there. She marched up the steps and into the house, closing the door behind her with a thud that made the beveled-glass insets rattle.

Four

$\mathcal{A}$t even the best of times, Millicent did not look forward to attending the monthly meetings of the Ladies Missionary Aid Society. It had been fine when Florence Marshall had been the president of the group; she had been something of a tyrant, but at least she was organized and got things done. Since Emma McMasters had assumed the position of president, it seemed as though nothing was ever accomplished. The meetings had become long sessions of dithering and arguing over which Mrs. McMasters typically had no control.

But this morning Millicent felt even less like going than usual. Not only would there be the usual irritations and vexations, but the news about the Lawrence family moving in next door to her yesterday would be all over town by now, and she would be plagued by questions from all the other members of the group.

However, Millicent was not one to shirk her duty. That was one of the things her father had drilled into her. "You've been blessed with a good family name, a good brain, and enough money that you need never know want," he would say pontifically. "But those things carry with them a duty. You have to set a good example, to be a leader, to give others the benefits of your superior mind and fine moral character."

Certainly, Judge Hayes had believed in following his own precepts. He had been a model [and leader] to others until his dying day, and not just in the area of law, his lifelong work, but in everything he did. And Millicent had always done her best to follow his example, especially since he had died. Her father's name and importance would end with her generation, which left the full responsibility of preserving his memory and carrying on his beliefs to her.

There had been many times when she had thought that she would not be able to live up to the responsibility. But somehow she had managed—at least reasonably well. But duty wasn't a thing one could just pick up and put down, and that meant not only doing the larger things, but the day-to-day tasks as well, no matter how boring or annoying.

The meeting started at 9:30 in the morning, and Millicent left early enough to allow herself ample time to get there. She disliked tardiness in others and refused to allow it in herself.

She walked down the back stairs and through the dining room into the butler's pantry, formerly the short breezeway between the main house and the kitchen. It had been enclosed several years ago after the big black cast-iron stove had made its debut in the kitchen, and the narrow room now held an oak cupboard of pottery and glassware as well as a small old sideboard.

She walked through the pantry in the large kitchen beyond, where Ida was rolling out dough on the large wooden table. She was humming deeply and tunelessly as she worked the rolling pin.

"Ida, I'm leaving now for the Ladies' Aid meeting."

Ida, a woman of few words, nodded her head.

"I shan't return until afternoon." The meeting was at Rose Kincaid's house, and Rose was famous for the repasts which she put on at any meeting or party she hosted. "So don't set out dinner for me. It will be only Alan."

Millicent walked back through the house to the front door, greeting Cherry on her way out, and started down the street to the Kincaid house. It was only a short walk, and she arrived there well before the meeting began.

Rose Kincaid, buxom, smiling, and done up in ruffles and frills, greeted her at the door. "Millicent! How are you, child? Why, it seems like a month of Sundays since I've seen you."

"Mama, she was at church last Sunday," put in Rose's daughter, Isabelle, who was standing by her mother's elbow with a martyred expression on her face. Millicent suspected that the girl had been pressed into helping Rose greet the guests and would much rather be someplace else.

"Well, of course she was. Millicent's always there, aren't you, dear? I just didn't see you. But, say, what's this I hear about the old Bell house? It's been sold?"

Millicent sighed inwardly. This was exactly what she had feared. She hadn't even taken off her bonnet and gloves yet and she was already being pulled into a conversation about Jonathan Lawrence.

"Yes, it has."

"Oh, my, how exciting! But, tell us all about it! Who bought it? Are they from around here?"

Isabelle leaned forward, her eyes sparkling with interest. "I heard it was a widower who moved in. Is that true?"

"I didn't see a woman at the house," Millicent admitted.

"I've heard he's handsome as all get out," volunteered Anna Mae MacAlister, who, spying Millicent, had come up to join the conversation. "Is that true?"

True? It didn't even come close. "Well, he was rather nice looking."

"Ooooh," Isabelle squealed, clasping her hands together. "Tell us all about him."

Millicent resigned herself to having to describe Jonathan Lawrence in detail, and not just to these women, but to everyone she talked to at the meeting. She managed to slip away from her third group of listeners and find an empty love seat in the parlor to sit on. She hoped that at last she would have some peace.

But it was not to be. Only minutes after she sat down, Rebecca Connally made her dainty way to the sofa and seated herself beside Millicent.

"Cousin Millicent." Her teeth flashed in an insincerely sweet smile. Millicent barely repressed a groan. Of all her family, Rebecca Connally was her least favorite member. She wasn't even really family; she had simply married Tyra Connally, who was one of Millicent's cousins on her mother's side.

"Hello, Rebecca." Millicent gave her a perfunctory smile. She couldn't be rude to an in-law, even one as irritating as Rebecca Connally. "How are you?"

Dimples appeared in Rebecca's porcelain-white cheeks as she showed her gleaming teeth again. Her bright blue eyes sparkled. "Why, I'm doing about as well as anyone could expect. I guess you've heard my happy news."

"Of course. Congratulations." The words almost stuck in Millicent's throat. There was something especially galling about Rebecca's bringing up her delicate condition; Millicent knew that she did it primarily to emphasize the fact that Millicent had no children whereas she was about to produce her fourth.

Rebecca was almost the same age as Millicent, only a year younger, and when they were girls there had been a sort of rivalry between them. Rebecca had been pretty in a blonde, china-doll way, and as the only daughter of an older couple, she had been petted and spoiled all her life. She had been jealous of anyone else's popularity, and she had seemed especially to dislike Millicent. Millicent hadn't understood why, since Rebecca was prettier than she was and Millicent could never hope to prevail on her parents to let her wear the kind of elegant clothes to school that the Ordways allowed Rebecca. But Rebecca had been intensely jealous of Millicent's large circle of friends.

"You Hayeses and Connallys and Brashears always stick together!" she had once shouted at Millicent, her delicate features contorted with rage. "I hate you, and I hate them!"

That confrontation, when the girls were about eight, had ended with Millicent yanking one of Rebecca's long blond curls as hard as she could and Rebecca whacking Millicent on the head with her McGuffey's Reader.

As they grew older, the antagonism between them had become submerged beneath ladylike smiles and polite chitchat. However, Millicent was sure that it had afforded Rebecca a great deal of inner satisfaction when she had married before Millicent—and into that same close-knit clan of Connallys, Hayeses and Brashears. It was rare that Rebecca didn't somehow manage to work in a dig at Millicent's unmarried state.

"How is Cousin Alan? Poor thing. I declare, I feel so sorry for him, stuck in bed like that. Such a tragedy." She shook her head sadly. "Why, I think if I were in that situation, I'd rather not live on."

"Alan loves life," Millicent said stiffly. "And we are thankful that we still have him. He has an excellent mind and is able to occupy himself with many pursuits."

It was all she could do to be civil. Rage knotted up in her chest like a fist. How dare Rebecca suggest that it would have been better if Alan hadn't lived! She obviously didn't have a smidgen of sympathy or understanding in her.

"Well, of course you are." Rebecca opened her blue eyes wide in an innocent expression, which only increased Millicent's bad temper. She paused, then smiled archly and continued, "Millicent, dear, I heard that a very eligible widower has moved in right next door to you."

"The Bell place has been bought, yes," Millicent replied stiffly.

"What a golden opportunity!" Rebecca continued, reaching over to touch Millicent's hand in a mockly concerned pose. "Now, you mustn't let him get away."

Millicent wondered if it would cause too much talk if she got up and moved away from Rebecca. "I don't know what you're talking about, Rebecca. I am not in the market for a husband."

Rebecca chuckled. "Come now, every single woman is in the market for a husband."

"Some of us choose not to marry."

"Oh, piddle. That's all well and good for saving face, but just between us cousins, we can speak the truth, can't we? Who ever really *chose* not to marry?"

"I did," Millicent insisted through clenched teeth. No matter how rude it was, she was going to have to leave soon. It would be even more socially unacceptable for her to slap Rebecca's face.

Fortunately, at that moment Emma McMaster finally got up to call the meeting to order. The subject of the meeting was the annual boxed supper the group held late in June to raise funds for the support of missionaries overseas. It was a simple enough affair. The eligible young ladies of the church decorated boxes, often in elegant and beautiful ways, and brought a picnic supper for two in it to the social. There the young men tried to guess who had prepared which box (usually helped along by hints from the young ladies themselves) during the time that the boxes were laid out on display. Afterward, the boxes were bid upon, and the man offering the highest bid won it. But, more than that, he won the company of the girl who had made the meal.

The supper was held in the park and required little more than setting up the tables to display the boxes and finding a man in the church who was willing to act as the auctioneer. It should have been a topic that was brought up quickly and disposed of just as quickly, Millicent thought.

But, of course, it wasn't.

The problem, it seemed, was that James Culpepper, who usually was happy to take the job as auctioneer, was laid up with a "misery" in his back, and no one was sure whether he would be able to perform his duties by the end of June.

"Then let's ask another man," Adelaide Jeffries suggested matter-of-factly. "I'm sure there is more than one man in this town who would dearly love to get up on stage and talk for an hour."

"Oh, but what if poor Mr. Culpepper has recovered by then?" Mrs. McMaster asked, her graying ringlets bouncing as she shook her head, frowning worriedly. "How could we tell him we'd taken the job away from him?"

"That would be embarrassing," another woman agreed.

"If we start asking various gentlemen if they will help us by taking the bids, we might get more than we need who are willing," Mary Lee spoke up. "Then what would we do?"

"There could be hurt feelings."

Conversation buzzed, everyone adding their share. Finally, when Mrs. McMaster suggested that they elect a committee to handle the supper, including the issue of an auctioneer, Millicent could take it no longer and stood up.

"Really, ladies, I hardly think the boxed supper warrants an entire committee." Not to mention all the meetings and discussion and further shilly-shallying that it would cause. "Only one person is necessary to determine whether Mr. Culpepper will be able to be our auctioneer this year and to ask another gentleman if he cannot. As for the rest of it, it only requires appointing a few women to help with the tables and the iced tea and lemonade."

"I agree with Miss Hayes," Adelaide Jeffries said loudly, thumping the point of her parasol down on the floor for emphasis. "And I think we should appoint Miss Hayes to do it."

"Oh, yes."

"Certainly."

"That's a wonderful idea!"

So it was that Millicent was unanimously chosen to be in charge of the boxed supper. With that piece of work out of the way, the room happily settled down to eat the cold luncheon that Mrs. Kincaid's daughters had spread out on the dining table and to discuss the things that really interested them, primarily whether Ruth Harris had ruined her reputation forever by driving out into the country in a buggy with Matthew Slocum— *unchaperoned!*

* * *

Millicent marched into the house, shutting the door behind her with more force than was necessary. *How had she managed to get herself rooked into heading up the boxed supper!*

The fact that she had no one to blame but herself for being elected to the post did little to improve her temper. As Grandma Connally had often told her, she should have thought before she spoke.

She stomped up the stairs to her room, not even stopping into Alan's room to see how he was doing. He would be better off not having to put up with her in this mood, anyway, she told herself. There was only one thing to do when she felt this disgruntled, and that was gardening.

It took only minutes to whisk off her gloves, bonnet, and skirt. The long row of minute buttons down her front, the binding hook-and-eye corset, and the small horsehair bustle apparatus in the back took considerably more time. But eventually she was out of all of them and standing in only her shift, underdrawers, and a few muslin petticoats.

She pulled the shift away from her waist, where it had become wetly stuck from having the corset over it and waved the shift a little, letting air in under it to the marked flesh beneath. Then she stretched her arms up high and bent from side to side and front to back a few times, luxuriating in the freedom from the restraint of the corset. There was no pleasure quite so great as slipping it off. She sat down on the bed to unhook the multitude of buttons up her high-top boots. When she was finished, she slipped them off and wriggled her toes; sometimes the boots felt almost as binding as the corset. Last, she removed her two outer petticoats, the newest and best ones.

In much less time, she pulled on her old calico wrapper (newly mended where she had ripped it) and stuck her feet into a comfortable old pair of shoes. Tying her sunbonnet on her head, she ran lightly down the stairs and out the back door, where she grabbed the trowel, fork, and miniature rake. As she walked back around the veranda to the front yard, she noticed that she was already feeling happier merely at the prospect of digging in the dirt.

It smelled like spring outside, sweet honeysuckle and freshly turned earth. The trees were bursting with buds and new leaves. What a shame it was to have wasted an entire morning at a meeting!

She had been so angry when she came home that she hadn't even glanced at the front yard, but as she crossed the yard now, her eyes went to her flower bed along the side fence. She came to an abrupt halt, her eyes widening with horror, and she gasped.

For a moment, she couldn't grasp what she saw. When she did, she could not believe it. Her flower garden in the front yard, usually so tidy, was an utter mess. Dirt was scattered through the grass surrounding the plot and piled up here and there in the flower bed. There were three holes dug into the soft earth. Several daylilies had been uprooted. And the stalk of her most beautiful deep purple iris was broken, the flower dangling head down.

A small cry of anguish broke from her and she knelt and picked up the hanging flower. It was lost, the stalk utterly ruined. Of course, there would be other years, other blooms; the plant wasn't destroyed. But even so, for now it was ruined. And her daylilies! She picked up one torn plant from a pile of dirt, feeling sick as she looked at its tangled roots. It *was* destroyed. Three of them were ruined, and still another had a crushed flower and stems.

Tears welled in her eyes. She felt violated, hurt in a way that had little to do with ownership and a great deal to do with love.

Anger rose in her chest. She knew who had done it—or, rather, what. It could only be an animal, digging in the damp earth. It could only be that dog.

Millicent jumped to her feet, scanning her yard and that of the Lawrences. "Ohhh! If I get my hands on that animal!"

She flung down her gloves and marched over to the Lawrences' front door. She thundered at the heavy brass door knocker.

The door swung open and Betsy stood in the doorway. "Oh. Hello."

"Come here, young lady. I want you to see something."

"What?" Betsy followed her out the door, her face alight with curiosity. Millicent didn't reply, just strode out through the gate and around to her yard. "Why don't you go over the fence?" Betsy asked behind her. "That's easiest."

Millicent ignored her question and pointed, "Look at that."

Betsy followed her finger with her eyes, and she gasped. "Oh! Your flowers!" She ran to the flower bed and plopped down on her knees beside it. "What happened to them?"

"What happened to them! That dog of yours, that's what!"

"Admiral?" Betsy turned a puzzled gaze up at her. "But why would Admiral want to dig up your flowers?"

"He was probably digging to get at something else. Or to hide something. I don't know what goes on in the animal's mind."

"Well, how do you know it was Admiral?" Betsy came to her pet's defense. "How do you know it wasn't some other dog? Or maybe your cat." She pointed at Punjab, lying stretched out on the porch in the sun.

"My cat does not dig in the dirt. That's absurd."

Betsy's chin came out pugnaciously, and she stood up and planted her fists on her hips. "Well, so's saying my dog did it when you don't know."

"Young lady! That is hardly the way to talk!"

Betsy scowled. "I don't know any other way to talk."

"No doubt that's true. It's obvious that your upbringing leaves a great deal to be desired. But I will not stand here in my own yard and be insulted by a slip of a girl."

"I didn't insult you!" Betsy's eyes flashed at the injustice of her words. "I just said you don't know that it was Admiral that did it, and you don't! It's the truth. What's wrong with that?"

Millicent gritted her teeth in exasperation. "It is hardly becoming in a child of nine—"

"I'm ten!"

"—to dispute an adult's words," she finished. It was true that Millicent had not been around children much, but she had never met a child who spoke back to an adult the way this one did.

"You're not being fair! You don't know Admiral did it."

"I know that nothing ever tore up my flowers before you moved in next door with that dog. I also know that you had better keep that animal out of my yard in the future."

"I will!" Betsy stormed off to her own yard, leaping over the low fence with ease. She whirled around for a parting shot. "Admiral and I don't want to come into your stinky old yard, anyway!"

Millicent felt like shouting something back at the stiff little retreating figure, but she clamped her lips tightly together and knelt beside the bed, venting her anger and frustration on the hapless ground, shoving the dirt back into the holes and tamping it down fiercely. She tried replanting one daylily whose roots did not look too ripped apart, but there was nothing to do for the other flowers. And the Garden Club was planning to meet at her house the very next week!

When she recounted the episode to Alan later, he said, eyes twinkling, "Perhaps you should take her in hand, Millie. I would think you'd feel sorry for the poor motherless child."

"Honestly, Alan. I'm in no mood for your teasing.

There's no question but that she does need someone to take her in hand. However, I don't plan to be the one."

"Probably." Alan couldn't keep a grin off his face. "Lord, I wish I'd been there to see it, though."

"Alan!"

He shrugged. "I have a sneaking sympathy for her. Remember Scamp?"

Despite her disgruntlement, Millicent had to smile. "How could I forget Scamp?" He had been a little black ragamuffin terrier that had taken up with Alan when he was about six. He had been cute and playful, and she and Alan had loved romping with him in the back yard. "I remember thinking it was horribly unfair that you were allowed to have a dog, and I wasn't."

"As I remember, you not only thought it, you were willing to state it to whomever would listen."

She chuckled. "I suppose I did." The smile faded slowly from her face and she sighed a little. "But Mama and Papa were right, no doubt; a dog isn't a proper pet for a young girl. It's too rough."

"I suppose. Although as I remember, you didn't suffer from playing with Scamp."

"Not that I recall." She smiled and reached out to take her brother's hand. "Ah, Alan, you can always make me smile, no matter how disturbed I am. Was I making a mountain out of a molehill?"

"Perhaps." He squeezed her hand and smiled back at her. "But your flowers are very important to you."

"Yes. But I should make allowances for children and pets, shouldn't I? After all, they've only been here a few days. They'll settle down before long."

"I'm sure they will."

Alan was less sanguine the following afternoon when he was awakened from his after-dinner nap by the sound of a ball thumping repeatedly against the side of the house next door, accompanied by childish shouts and the yapping of a dog. Hours later, Millicent found Betsy climbing the cherry tree in her back yard, her movements showering the ground with blossoms and her shoes leaving skinned places along its bark.

The flower incident, Millicent realized, had not been an isolated event brought on by the strangeness of moving or by being in a new place. It was only the first in a series of disasters that would go on as long as the Lawrence family lived next door to her. And she was *not*, Millicent thought determinedly, going to lose the battle to a mere child and a gigantic, clumsy dog!

Five

Millicent opened her eyes and lay for a moment, savoring the early morning stillness. A breeze stirred the lace curtains, bringing into the room the scent of a spring dawn, clean, dewy, and redolent of the last burst of honeysuckle. It was almost the end of May; in a few days it would be Decoration Day, when people across the South traditionally decorated the graves of both Confederate and Union soldiers and families cleaned up their cemetery plots, turning the day into something of a genial picnic. Then would come June and before long the real heat of summer, the steaming days that sapped the strength and seemed to last forever.

But for now it was pleasant outside, particularly in the mornings and evenings. Millicent had sat on the porch last night, gently rocking and listening to the popping of June bugs against the house and the distant croaking of frogs, watching the blinking play of lightning bugs in the dusk. It had been warm and restful, a lazy interlude of peace—until Betsy Lawrence had run shrieking across their back yards, chasing her dog.

With a sigh, Millicent rolled over. Why did she have to remember that? The child was ruining even her most pleasant reveries.

Downstairs she heard Ida's voice as she spoke to the iceman, then the slap of his reins and the creak of his wheels as he drove on down the street. She could hear Johnny, whistling as he carried in wood for the stove. They were familiar, soothing sounds, noises she'd heard ever since she could remember, as much a part of the fabric of her life as her grandmother's quilt, folded across the foot of her bed, which had come to Texas with her as a bride.

An earsplitting yowl ripped across the yard, bringing Millicent straight upright in her bed. Punjab!

Millicent hopped out of bed and dashed to the back window of her room just in time to see the white streak that was Punjab race up the trunk of the mimosa tree and cling to one of its branches, spitting down at the shaggy dog that was barking and leaping around the trunk of the tree. Millicent ground her teeth. It was the outside of enough! This was the fourth time in the past two weeks that that mutt had chased her pampered white Persian across the yard.

Betsy had climbed Millicent's cherry tree again last week, despite the fact that Millicent had explicitly told her not to, and of course the child had broken off one of the limbs. Only two days ago, Millicent had seen her sauntering down the sidewalk, aimlessly dragging a stick along the fences, which set up a dreadful racket. The noise was not as terrible, of course, as the one she had created at the beginning of the week by kicking a can

up and down the street. Millicent had had to take her
to task on both accounts. Betsy had stopped the practice each time, Millicent had to admit, but there was
little relief in that. The girl simply thought up some new
way to irritate Millicent.

Finally Millicent had had to force herself to speak to
Mr. Lawrence about the problems his child was causing,
but he had not been at home when she called on him.
The housekeeper, Mrs. Rafferty, a short, plump, energetic woman, had sympathized with Millicent's problems, adding that she found Betsy to be a "demon" of
a child.

Well, if Betsy was a demon, Millicent knew who the
devil was who created her. It was Jonathan Lawrence.
The man had no business raising a child. Millicent had
not seen Betsy a single time when she had looked as a
young girl should. Her hair ribbons were always dangling or missing altogether, and her hair never seemed
to stay braided. Her stockings either sagged or had runs
in them, often both. Yesterday a ruffle had been partially ripped off one of her petticoats and had hung
beneath her dress, limp and dirty. Her dresses were
often too short, and if she started out the day wearing
a pinafore, she never ended up still wearing it. Worst of
all, she didn't wear a sunbonnet, exposing her fair skin
to the sun, which made the freckles scattered all over
her face multiply by leaps and bounds. No decent, caring father would allow her to continue to look so inappropriate. If he felt incapable of handling the subject of
a girl's clothing (and Millicent suspected that most men
were incapable of that), he could at least have turned

over to some female relative the problem of Betsy's wardrobe.

But those weren't even his worst sins. In the entire two weeks that Mr. Lawrence and his daughter had been living next door to them, he had not once taken the child to church! He hadn't even sent her to Sunday school. It was clear that the man was a heathen and was raising his daughter to be one, as well. If that wasn't bad enough, Millicent had actually seen him last week working in the back yard bare-chested! She had stared, unable to believe it. The man had taken off his shirt and hadn't even had a union suit on underneath. He had been actually naked from the waist up! It was positively indecent. Millicent was of half a mind to tell him exactly what she thought of him and the way he was raising his daughter. It might be forward and impolite, but there were times when principles came before courtesy.

Thinking about Jonathan, Millicent unconsciously glanced toward the house where he lived. She stiffened. Speaking of the devil, he was out in his back yard, finishing the job of cleaning up. And he was once again working without a shirt! Millicent could hardly believe it. Why, even his feet were bare.

It was disgraceful, Millicent thought, propping one hand against the side of the open window and leaning closer to look. Jonathan's blond hair was tousled and uncombed, and there was the faintest hint of a shadow along his jaw that indicated that he had not yet shaved. Obviously he had just gotten up from bed and come out to do a little work at sunrise. Did he sleep that way, too, without anything to cover his chest, not even a night-shirt?

Millicent's fingers curled up tightly against the window's edge. She was suddenly warmer, and there was an odd, twisting feeling in the pit of her stomach. She put her hand to her stomach, rubbing it a little, as though the gesture could erase the funny ache there.

Jonathan brought the two long wooden handles of the pruning shears together, snapping off the thick branch of the shrub, and the muscles in his arms and chest moved with the effort. It was clear that he often went without a shirt in the sun, for his skin was golden brown, and despite the earliness of the hour, it glistened a little with sweat. Reddish-brown hair dotted his chest, narrowing to a thin line down his stomach, and it was beginning to cling damply to his skin.

Millicent's lungs were tight. Her lips were dry, and she smoothed her tongue along them to dampen them. Jonathan reached up to wipe away the sweat from his brow with his arm, not letting go of the shears, and Millicent could see the shifting of his muscles in his chest and side and the ridges of his ribcage beneath his skin. He was taut and lean, with no blurring of fat anywhere on him, and his skin looked as smooth as satin. She could almost imagine its texture beneath her fingertips.

When Millicent realized what she was thinking, she blushed clear up to her hairline. Whatever was she doing? Standing there looking at a half-clad man, even thinking about his skin! Why, it was downright wicked—and it was no excuse that Jonathan Lawrence had the audacity to go around in his yard partially dressed. A true lady would have turned away from the sight in indignation.

She swung away from the window and sat down heavily in the chair beside it. The shock of the sight had frozen her, of course; that was the reason she had remained there, staring at him. She had been so appalled she hadn't been able to move for a moment. Millicent shook her head, as though to clear the bizarre thoughts that had lodged there.

This was really too much to bear! She jumped to her feet on a surge of heated anger. The man was barbaric. A heathen. He should not have charge of an impressionable young girl. Millicent couldn't even imagine how she would be able to live next door to him.

On a wave of righteous indignation, Millicent washed her face and skinned her hair backward, screwing it into an even tighter bun than usual. She pulled on one of her dresses which she had dyed black during their period of mourning for their father. She glanced at herself in the mirror when she was finished and decided that she looked like a skinny black crow, but the image gave her a certain amount of satisfaction. It was an appropriate look for washing day, always a day of hard physical work. But more than that, it was as if her ascetic attire and hairstyle had distanced her even more from Jonathan Lawrence's blatant sensual vitality.

She ate a quick breakfast of cold cornbread and a glass of buttermilk. Then she rolled up her sleeves and set to work helping Ida with the wash. Ida had already heated water on the stove and filled up the large tin washtub, which sat on a worktable in the back yard. The washing was hot work, and it was best to get started early in the morning. Millicent went through the house like a whirlwind, stripping the sheets from the beds and gathering up any other object that needed to be washed. She hauled them outside to the washtub, where Ida had begun her scrubbing, using a strong lye soap.

As Ida finished each piece, she tossed it into another tub beside her filled with fresh rinse water. After the clothes had sat in the rinse water a while, Ida pulled out the items one by one and squeezed the excess water from them, dropping them into a large straw basket. She hauled the tub away, tipped out the now soapy water and refilled it with clean water from the backyard pump. Then she began with another load of clothes. By contrast, Millicent's chores of hanging out the clean wash that sat in the basket and washing the small delicate items such as antimacassars or a lace-trimmed chemise were far less tiring.

Still, her tasks were hardly what one could term easy, and by the time Millicent had finished pinning the wash to the three-rope clothesline, set strategically in the full sunlight, she was perspiring freely and her back ached. The sheets were the most difficult to hang, being larger than her armspan and weighted down with water. Millicent hung them with precision, smoothing out the wrinkles and making certain that an equal amount of cloth fell on either side of the rope. The sheets stretched along the two outside ropes, along with Alan's shirts and her outer clothes. On the inside rope, hidden by the sheets from the view of passersby on the side street or someone in the back yard of the Bell house on the other side, went the more intimate items of apparel.

They were finished by noon, which gave the clothes all afternoon to dry in the bright sunlight.

Ida had already gone inside to throw together some lunch, and Millicent was walking toward the house, stretching her tired back and neck, when Betsy Lawrence came through a gap in the hedges, followed by her dog. Millicent suppressed a groan. She was too tired to deal with the child now. Not only was Betsy regularly falling into one disaster or another, but she seemed peculiarly fond of hanging around Millicent, asking questions about any and every thing. Millicent couldn't understand how one child could be so curious about so many different things.

"Hi! What are you doing?" Betsy called cheerfully.

"I'm going into the house to eat," Millicent replied crisply, hoping without much real expectation that the child would take the hint and leave. "It's time for dinner."

"I know. Papa's home from the paper to eat, too. But Mrs. Rafferty told me to get out of the kitchen and go play until she had the food on the table. She said I was plaguing her to death."

"I can't imagine why," Millicent said dryly, continuing across the yard.

"I don't know either. I was just asking her how the stove worked. Do you know?"

Millicent cocked an eyebrow at her. "Why, because there's a fire in it, of course."

"I know that. But I mean, how come fire makes the

stove hot, but doesn't burn it up like it does wood and things? Or melt it? And why does metal hold the heat? Why doesn't it get cool as soon as the fire goes out?"

How did the child come up with these questions? Millicent hated not having the answers to questions, even when they were as odd and unexpected as the ones Betsy often asked.

"Well, I—I suppose metal would melt, if it got hot enough, but it would have to be really, really hot, much more so than a fire in a stove."

"Like at the blacksmith's?"

"Exactly." Millicent smiled at her quick understanding. Betsy was quite intelligent, really, despite her peculiar ways, and it seemed a shame that she was so neglected. "You see, when the blacksmith gets the metal hot, it turns red and gets softer, so he can bend it. Have you seen that?"

"Yes! And it gets soft 'cause it's melted a little bit?"

"Yes." Or at least she thought so; she wasn't quite sure, but Millicent was a firm believer that one should always speak to a child as if one were certain of their knowledge.

"I see. You're a lot smarter than Mrs. Rafferty."

Considering Mrs. Rafferty, Millicent didn't feel that she could take that as much of a compliment. "That's not a polite way to speak about your father's housekeeper."

Betsy shrugged. "She's not polite to me. Why do children have to be polite and nobody else?"

"Everyone should be polite," Millicent began somewhat pontifically. But it was then that disaster struck, cutting off her words.

Admiral had come trotting into the yard on Betsy's heels, but had been diverted by the need to chase a bird from the grass. As he turned and started back toward Betsy and Millicent, who by now had reached the porch, a breeze touched the drying clothes, billowing out the sheets from the line. The dog, padding along by the clothesline, jumped back from the large thing suddenly whipping out at him. He went stiff as he eyed the sheet distrustingly. The sheet fell back in its place, then billowed out again.

Admiral crept forward, stretching out his head and sniffing at the sheet. Then he bent down in front, and his haunches went up. His tail started to wave back and forth, and he barked invitingly at the hanging sheet. Betsy, seeing him, began to giggle, and even Millicent had to smile at the silly animal's antics.

Until, that is, the wind puffed the sheets out once again, and Admiral sprang forward, clamping his teeth around a corner of the sheet. He lunged back on his hindquarters, tugging at the sheet and shaking his head. Millicent gasped, and her hand flew to her throat.

Admiral jumped forward, then back again, whipping the sheet about. Millicent came out of her frozen state. "No!" she shrieked and started toward the dog. "Those are my clean sheets! Let go of that, you wretched animal!"

"Admiral!" Betsy ran past Millicent to her dog. "Stop it! No! No! Bad dog!" She tugged in vain at the big dog.

Millicent joined the girl, shouting and pulling, but her hands kept slipping off the dog's fur. She was furious, thinking of all her hard work this morning which Admiral was doing his best to ruin.

Millicent let go of the dog and, lifting her skirts almost to her knees, ran to the kitchen. It was obvious that she was going to need a weapon. Inside the kitchen door she grabbed the broom and started back toward Admiral, shaking the broom high in the air.

While Millicent was gone to find the broom, the object of her wrath had managed to pull the sheet loose from its clothespins and drag it to the ground. After a couple of shakes, Admiral dropped the limp sheet and, merrily barking, lunged at the next sheet on the line and clamped his jaws around both sides of the sheet. Growling and twisting, he backed up, pulling down on the clothesline with all his strength.

"Stop it!" Millicent shrieked, goaded into fury by the sight of her clean sheet lying on the ground, punctured with little holes from Admiral's teeth and ripped, as well.

She swiped at him with the broom. Admiral skittered aside, startled, and she missed him. However, when he moved, it was finally too much for the nail holding the clothesline to the house, and it pulled out of the wood. The entire line fell to the ground. Millicent gasped with horror. Admiral took off at a lope, the sheet still firmly between his teeth. The loop of rope tied around a tree limb at the other end, long frayed, snapped at this final jerk upon it, and the entire clothesline of clean clothes followed Admiral and his sheet like a long tail.

"Admiral! No! Stop! Wait!" Betsy took off running after him, shouting and waving her arms.

Millicent wasn't far behind her, brandishing her broomstick. Admiral, the sheet between his teeth and a foolish grin on his face, seemed to be under the impression that this was a new and delightful game of tag, and he darted between the bushes into the Lawrences' back yard and across it. With the child and woman on his heels he pelted into the next yard, also unfenced. There he made a quick turn, and circled the yard, heading straight back where he came from. Betsy fell, trying to make the turn, and Millicent, right behind her, had to jump across her to keep from crashing down on top of her.

Ahead of her, Admiral went for the gap between the bushes that would lead him into Millicent's yard, dragging the line of clothes after him through a puddle of mud. Millicent let out a squeal of pure rage and jumped for the trailing line.

Her knees hit the ground with a thud and she let go of her skirts, but her fingers closed triumphantly around the thin rope. As soon as she caught it, however, Admiral's weight on the other end hauled her forward, and she fell flat on her face. She refused to let go of the clothesline, however, and she scrambled across the grass, trying to hold the dog back and at the same time rise to her feet.

Betsy roared up behind her and grabbed the clothesline, too, hauling back on it. "Admiral!" The dog stopped and looked back at them, his tail wagging. Millicent took advantage of the momentary slackness of the rope to stagger to her feet, and she and Betsy yanked on the clothesline. A tug of war suited Admiral just as well and he dug in, hauling back on the rope, growling and shaking his head.

"Don't you growl at me, you mangy mutt!" Millicent shouted, swept away by her rage. She strained as hard as she could against the rope, her face flushing with the effort.

"We're not playing!" Betsy added.

"Stupid dog," Millicent muttered. She gritted her teeth, digging in her heels. Gradually she and Betsy began to drag Admiral step by step across the yard.

"We're doing it! We've got him!" Betsy yelled.

Millicent let out a shout of triumphant glee.

Then she heard the laughter.

She didn't know why she hadn't heard it before; it was loud enough to wake the dead. It was a man's laugh, and not just a chuckle or even a few guffaws, but a gale of laughter, a paroxysm of deep uncontrollable belly laughs.

Her head snapped toward the back porch of the Lawrences' house. There stood two people. One was the Lawrences' housekeeper, Mrs. Rafferty, and she stood gaping at them, her eyes wide and her mouth open. The other person was Jonathan Lawrence, and it was he who was laughing. He leaned against the column of the porch, clutching his sides, bent over from his merriment.

Suddenly the red fury in Millicent switched to another object: the man laughing on the porch. She threw the clothesline to the ground. "Exactly what do you think you're doing?"

Jonathan looked at her and tried to speak, but nothing but another howl of laughter came out. The anger in Millicent mushroomed. She doubled her fist, aware of a primitive urge to hit that obnoxious man right in his laughing face.

"Papa!" Betsy cried. "Why didn't you come help us? Her voice sounded close to tears. "Look at the mess Admiral's made."

"I—I see." Jonathan drew a shaky breath, trying to quell his laughter, and wiped at the tears of merriment streaming down his face. "I'm sorry, sweetheart. He—he—" He glanced over at the dog, who now stood, with the sheet still in his mouth, tail wagging happily, looking at Millicent with anticipation, ready for whatever new game she wanted to play. The sight was too much for Jonathan, and he went off into another burst of guffaws.

"Oh!" Millicent's eyes narrowed to slits, and she marched toward him. "How can you laugh at that—that infernal hound! He's the terror of the neighborhood! If you had any sense of decency, you'd get rid of him. He's no fit companion for a young girl, anyway!"

"No! Oh, no!" Betsy cried out, terror-stricken, and rushed to Admiral and threw her arms around his neck. Admiral, finally sensing that he had come under the black cloud of disapproval yet again, dropped quickly to the ground, stretching his paws out in front of him and laying his head pathetically on them as he gazed at Millicent and Jonathan.

"Papa, you can't send Admiral away!" Betsy pleaded.

"I won't. But I think it might be a good idea for you and Admiral to pick up Miss Hayes's things, don't you?"

Betsy jumped to comply, quickly rolling up the line of clothes into a large, unwieldy ball. Mrs. Rafferty, sighing, took the girl and the clothes into the house with her. Admiral slunk after them to the porch and crawled into his favorite spot under the raised porch.

Millicent paid no attention to their departure. She was too wound up, too immersed in her rage at Jonathan Lawrence to notice anything else. She planted her hands on her hips. "Of course you won't get rid of that dog. You wouldn't give any consideration to what's right for your daughter. All you care about is what's easiest for you, what gives you the most amusement! You don't deserve to be a parent."

Lawrence scowled at her now, all traces of amusement gone from his face. "You consider yourself qualified to judge another concerning parenthood? No doubt it's your vast experience in the matter that gives you the right."

Millicent flushed at his sarcasm, which hit too close to the mark for her comfort, but she retorted, "I am not a parent, true, but I think I am knowledgable enough in the area of what is and is not decent. You, sir, are raising that girl in a shocking manner. She runs loose about the neighborhood all day, with no supervision at all."

"Mrs. Rafferty is here."

"Mrs. Rafferty is an excellent woman, no doubt, but she is your housekeeper, not a nursemaid or a parent.

I'm sure she's busy enough with household chores without having to pursue a . . . a *hoyden*."

His face darkened at the slight to his daughter, and Jonathan came down the steps toward her. "My daughter's nature and habits are no concern of yours. Besides, she's a ten-year-old girl. *You* may be a stiff, dried-up stick of a woman, but Betsy is a healthy young girl. She needs to be out playing, not sitting neat and prim in some stuffy drawing room. A dog is a fine companion for her, even if he doesn't meet with your approval. And if I hear of you maligning my daughter again—"

Millicent faced him squarely, too heated to be intimidated by his looming over her with a scowling face. "I wouldn't malign your daughter; I'm well aware that she is just a child. It's you who are responsible for her behavior. It's you who allow her to run around like a wild Indian. But, of course, what else can one expect, when you set such a shocking example for her? Going around outside practically in the altogether . . ."

"What!"

"You know what I'm talking about. I saw you this morning out here in the yard without a shirt or shoes. It's positively indecent, and it wasn't the first time, either. I've seen you before."

"Obviously you weren't outraged enough to stop looking, were you?" he said with a sardonic grin.

Millicent blushed to the roots of her hairline. This oaf! This boor! He actually dared to imply that she had *enjoyed* looking at him bare-chested, that she had been so enamored of him that she had kept looking, hoping to see more.

"How dare you! As if I had any interest in viewing you at all, in whatever state of dress! You are a low, crude—" Millicent sputtered, too furious even to articulate the depth of her offense and his iniquity. She broke off and strode back toward her house, rage radiating from every line of her stiff body. A few feet away, she whirled and jabbed her forefinger in the air toward him, like a schoolmarm admonishing a wrongdoer.

"It's precisely that kind of attitude that is ruining your daughter. Levity, no matter how inappropriate to the occasion, is your reaction to whatever happens. What's the child supposed to think except that anything she does, no matter how reckless or unmannerly, is all right because her father laughs at it? A child can't be expected to realize that her father laughs because he's an oaf himself! Perhaps digging up and crushing my prize-winning flowers or chasing the neighbor's cat or romping around in torn and dirty clothes with her hair every which way may seem amusing to you. But I can tell you that it is not to the rest of the world, and if you let that child continue this way, she'll grow up to be an outcast from the polite world."

"The polite world can go to hell! If having Betsy grow up to be a lady means that she'll be like you, then I pray to God that she *never* becomes a lady!"

"If you have anything to do with it, I assure you she won't!" Millicent shot back and stalked off.

She stormed through her own back yard and up the steps, tears of anger gathering in her eyes. The man was insufferable! Rude! She couldn't think of anything else vile enough to describe him, and for once Millicent wished that she hadn't been raised a lady just so she would know a term for him that was as terrible as he was.

She let the screen door bang shut behind her, and almost ran up the narrow back stairs, seeking the sanctuary of her room.

Inside her room, in the long mirror at her vanity, Millicent saw for the first time how she looked. She gaped at her image, dismayed. Several strands of her hair had come loose from her bun during the mad tussle with Admiral and hung in a slovenly manner about her face. The bottom ruffle of her petticoat had pulled loose, and dragged behind her like a tail. There was a smudge of mud on her face, and long streaks of it across her clothes. Her skirt was also liberally smeared with grass stains, and over everything, skin and clothes, lay a coating of dust.

In her anger she hadn't given a thought to how she looked. But all the time that she was lecturing Jonathan Lawrence, she had looked like this! No wonder he had laughed so uproariously. She was a silly-looking spectacle. She was only surprised he hadn't howled throughout her speech. No one, seeing her, could possibly have taken her seriously. Millicent remembered her description of Betsy's ragtag form of dress—and she had been standing there looking like a hoyden herself! Two spots of color appeared high on her cheeks, and she pressed the palms of her hand against them, closing her eyes. Her anger drained out of her in a rush, leaving behind a sick certainty that she had made a fool of herself.

Whatever had possessed her to chase that dog like

that? Worst of all was the way she had grabbed for the clothesline, actually throwing herself onto the ground and then crawling around in the dirt and grass trying to hold on to the thing!

And while she had been doing all that, Jonathan Lawrence had been watching her. He must have thought her an utter fool. As if that weren't bad enough, she had set in berating him about his daughter and the way he raised her. What she had said was true, of course. He wasn't decent and he was bringing the poor thing up like an orphan. But it was none of her business, just as he had said. Even if she could justify her taking him to task as simply expressing proper Christian concern for his little girl, she had far exceeded the bounds of propriety by yelling at him like a common fishwife. And the things she had said! Words that should not pass a lady's lips. Worst of all, she had actually brought up the matter of Jonathan's lack of attire in his back yard. A lady should never mention something like that!

Oh, Lord, what had she done? She had probably earned the enmity of her next-door neighbors for life. Millicent pressed her fingertips against her suddenly hot eyes, and tears seeped from beneath her lids. She could never face Mr. Lawrence again. He must have nothing but contempt for her.

Softly she began to cry.

Six

The following afternoon there was a knock at Millicent's front door, and when she went to answer it, she was surprised to find Betsy standing on the front porch. A basket of neatly folded clothes stood on the porch beside her, and she held a bunch of daisies clutched in one hand. There was no sign of Admiral.

"Miss Hayes?" Betsy began uncertainly, almost as if she did not know who Millicent was. She thrust the bouquet toward Millicent awkwardly. "These are for you. I picked them myself—out of my own yard," she added hastily.

"Why, thank you, Betsy."

"I came to tell you I was sorry about yesterday. Admiral shouldn't have done that, but he's only a puppy. Papa says we must train him better. I—I hope we can."

Looking at the girl's forlorn face, Millicent felt uncomfortable. She thought with a burning shame of her own behavior the day before. "I'm sure you will be able to."

"I should have watched him better and kept him

away from your clothesline." Betsy looked up anxiously. "Will you accept my apology?"

"Of course I will. I—I must apologize to you, as well. I'm afraid I lost my temper yesterday and said some things I shouldn't."

Betsy looked up at her, still frowning a little, but visibly relieved. "Papa sure was mad after he talked to you," she confided. "He said a lot of things he told me to forget he said."

"Oh." Millicent's stomach sank.

Betsy gestured toward the basket. "I washed them myself. Mrs. Rafferty only helped me a little. I couldn't wring them out. And she ironed them. She won't let me iron."

"How sweet of you." Millicent's sense of shame grew. "You needn't have done that; they're in better condition now than they were before Admiral attacked the clothesline."

"Papa said I ought to," the girl confessed naively. "He thought it might soften you up some."

"Oh, did he?" Millicent's mouth tightened for an instant, but then she couldn't help smiling at the girl's honesty. "I suppose it did. Thank you very much for cleaning them."

Millicent bent to pick up the basket and set it inside. They stood, looking at each other awkwardly. Betsy dug at the porch with one toe, gazing down. Finally she said in a muffled voice, "Miss Hayes, do you hate me?"

"What? No!" The girl's words, spoken so softly and uncertainly, pierced Millicent's heart. "Of course I don't hate you."

"Really?" Betsy straightened, looking up at her, and beamed broadly. "Papa said you'd like for me to leave you alone."

Guilt twisted within her. "Well, I—well, frankly, I'm not much used to children being around. Perhaps I am too . . . set in my ways." Millicent hesitated, then went on tentatively, "Would you like to come in and have cookies and milk?"

Betsy goggled at her. "You mean it?"

"Of course I do. I wouldn't have said it, otherwise."

"Golly! I'd love to!"

Millicent barely refrained from wincing at the girl's use of slang. "Good. Then let's go into the kitchen, shall we, and see what we have?"

Betsy bounced along beside Millicent down the hall to the kitchen. The door to Alan's room stood open, and the child glanced inside it and saw Alan, sitting beside the window in his wicker invalid chair, reading a book. Betsy stopped.

"Hello," she greeted him and went over to his open doorway. Millicent glanced at her, surprised, and bit her lower lip anxiously. Oh, dear, Alan hated visitors; she could imagine how he'd feel about an inquisitive child like Betsy.

"Betsy, the kitchen is this way," she said, going back to her.

But Betsy wasn't paying any attention to Millicent. She was gazing with fascination at Alan in his wheeled chair. Alan had looked up from his book at her greeting and was staring back at her in surprise.

"Are you Miss Hayes's brother?" Betsy asked curiously.

"Yes."

"Why does your chair have wheels on it?"

"Betsy," Millicent said firmly, putting her hand on the girl's shoulder. "We were going to the kitchen for cookies, remember? I'm sorry, Alan."

Betsy glanced up at her. "But I don't understand. Why is that chair like that?" A grin flashed across her face and she turned back to Alan. "Can you ride in it?"

Alan blinked, and for an instant Millicent thought that he was going to answer gruffly or simply turn away without speaking. But he said only, "Yes, I ride in it."

"Golly!" Betsy moved further into his room, pulling away from Millicent's hand on her shoulder. "I've never seen anything like that. Does it go fast?"

Millicent went after her, wondering why she'd been foolish enough to bring Betsy inside the house. She might have known that she would see Alan and pester him with her endless questions.

But, surprisingly, Alan smiled. "No. I'm afraid I've never been able to go very fast in it."

"Can I ride in it sometime?" But before he could answer, Betsy's eye had been caught by the battleground Alan had set up on the table, peopled with miniature soldiers, and she swerved toward it. "Oh! Look at this! A whole army! Two armies! And the trees and ground and everything." She glanced over at the shelves along one wall, filled with Alan's books and collections. "You sure have a lot of toys to play with!"

Millicent, knowing her brother's sensitivity regarding his condition, shrank inside. Alan's brows rose, but he chuckled. "Yes, I guess you're right. I do have a lot of toys."

Betsy turned toward him, a puzzled frown on her face. "But why do you play with toys? Aren't you grown up?"

"In some ways."

"I don't understand."

Alan hesitated, and Millicent said quickly, "I'll explain it to you. Why don't we leave Alan alone now so he can read? You and I need to go to the kitchen and get those cookies."

Betsy's gaze shifted from Alan to his sister, obviously unsatisfied. "All right," she said reluctantly and started toward the door into the hall. At the doorway she stopped and turned back toward Alan. "Can I come play with you sometime? We could have a battle with your soldiers."

"I suppose so," Alan said slowly. "All right. Yes, why don't you come visit me?"

Betsy beamed at him. "Oh, good!"

Firmly Millicent turned Betsy around and propelled her toward the dining room. As they walked through the dining room into the kitchen, Millicent bent close to the girl's ear and whispered, "You must not bother Alan."

"Why? What's the matter with him?"

"He had an accident several years ago, and he is unable to walk."

Betsy stared at her, wide-eyed, her mind racing. "Is that why he has that funny chair?"

"Yes. So he can get around from room to room or out onto the porch."

"Can I push his chair sometime? That'd be fun."

"I don't know. Alan likes to be alone. He—he's unused to company, especially children."

Betsy's face fell. "You mean he wouldn't want me to come visit like he said?"

"I'm not sure." Her brother's words had surprised Millicent; he was usually reluctant to have people around—especially a stranger! But he also had seemed to find Betsy more amusing than annoying. "He's often tired, and he's . . . a little shy."

"Oh."

In the kitchen Millicent pulled a large cookie jar out of a cabinet and set it on the table. Betsy removed the lid and was delighted to discover that the jar was filled with gingersnaps and sugar cookies. She happily took two of each and plopped down at the kitchen table to eat them. Millicent poured Betsy a glass of milk and sat down across the table from her.

"Mm. These are sure good. Lots better than Mrs. Rafferty's."

Millicent couldn't suppress a smile. "Why, thank you. I made them myself."

"Did you? Do you know how to do all those kinds of things?"

"All what kinds of things?"

"Cooking and stuff. Sewing, ironing, all that."

"Yes, I do know how to do those things." She paused, then asked curiously, "Aren't you learning how to do them, too?"

"Nope." Betsy shook her head. "Mrs. Rafferty says she doesn't have the time or patience for teaching a 'rattle-about.' That's me."

"Indeed." The housekeeper's words irritated her. It hardly seemed an appropriate thing to call the child one was supposed to be tending. Of course, the phrase fit Betsy, but it was scarcely the child's fault that no one took the time to teach her better manners.

Of course, Betsy's father should marry again; it was a mother's place to teach a girl such things. Millicent wondered, not for the first time, what had happened to Betsy's mother. She didn't dare ask Betsy; not only was it impolite, she was afraid it would bring up unpleasant memories for the child.

Millicent considered, for a brief moment, the idea that she take Betsy under her own wing. Millicent had no doubt that she could turn the girl around and teach her not only to be a lady, but also to run a household. It would not be easy, of course; Betsy had obviously been allowed to run free for a long time. However, Millicent was certain she was up to the task. It would mean having the child around a great deal of the time, and that could be a nuisance, but then, she already hung around Millicent far too much, asking questions and such. At least this would be more constructive.

She could picture Betsy after a few weeks under her tutelage. She would be quiet and well mannered and, most of all, properly dressed. Perhaps she would have a bow in her hair, anchoring a pair of neatly looped braids, straight stockings, clean shoes, and a starched, pressed dress that was long enough for her. She would say "please" and "thank you" and "yes, ma'am" and she would know not to look at one with that bold, frank gaze the way she did now. Millicent smiled a little at her inner image. Betsy would be an attractive girl if she were cleaned up. Her father would be thrilled; no doubt he would thank Millicent profusely and apologize for the terrible things he'd said about her.

It was there that Millicent's bubble burst. She realized that she couldn't possibly train Betsy to be a young lady. Her father despised Millicent, and he would not be happy to learn that Millicent was teaching Betsy anything. In fact, Millicent had the sneaking suspicion that he would regard it as more interference on her part. Besides, he was right when he told her that Betsy's actions were none of her business. Millicent had nothing to do with the lives of Betsy Lawrence or her father. The last thing she wanted was to give Jonathan an opportunity to accuse her again of being a busybody.

No, it was better simply to leave it alone. Let the two of them muddle along as best they could. It was, after all, a relief for her not to have to bother with it.

"What happened to your brother?" Betsy piped up, her agile young mind chasing off in a new direction.

Millicent hesitated. It had been a long time since she had had to talk about it. At first the pain had been so searing, the guilt so deep, that the sympathetic visits of neighbors and her mother's frequent compulsive re-hashing of the accident had been almost more than she could bear. Millicent had done her best to avoid the topic ever since. And since everyone in Emmetsville knew what had happened to Alan, it had not been brought up in years.

Now, at Betsy's blunt childlike question, Millicent's stomach knotted. She clasped her hands together and drew a deep breath. "He fell off a wagon. We were on a hayride, a whole group of us." For an instant Millicent saw again in her mind's eye Alan at fourteen, already tall and lanky, teasing the girls and joking with the boys. How different it all would have been, should have been, except for that one tiny moment. That one foolish instant of inattention.

She felt the pain of that moment again, she turned away and said almost angrily, "He was doing things he shouldn't have done, acting silly—standing up in the wagon, hanging over the side, tossing straw around. And he fell out of the wagon. The back wheel of the wagon rolled over his legs."

Betsy gasped. "Oh, no!"

Millicent stood up and put the lid back on the cookie jar and took it over to the cabinet. She didn't look at Betsy.

Betsy was silent for a long moment. Finally, she breathed, "Golly."

"Everyone kept telling him to sit down," Millicent said bitterly. "Why wouldn't he listen? If he'd only been more careful. . . . If only I'd—" She broke off abruptly and turned around. "Well, it's all old news now. No use talking about could-have-beens."

Betsy sighed. "It doesn't seem fair."

"No. It wasn't." For a moment Millicent felt years older than she was, set in a pattern that would eventually solidify into grimness. But then she gave herself a shake, visibly pulling herself back into the present. "But all one can do is face it." She tried a smile, somewhat unsuccessfully. "Isn't that right?"

"I guess."

"Of course it is." She injected heartiness into her voice. "After all, look at Alan. He faced his affliction and learned to live with it."

"What do you mean?"

Millicent opened her mouth to reply, then stopped. What *had* she meant? It was the sort of thing she said about Alan, but suddenly, examining it in the light of Betsy's question, she wasn't sure of her statement. Had Alan learned to live with it? Indeed, was there any way that a person could accept something that turned his life upside down and chained an active boy to his room, practically to his bed, for the rest of his life?

Millicent frowned. "I—well, Alan is brave about it. He rarely complains. He knows that his life will never be any different, and he doesn't waste his time crying over it."

Betsy took a final gulp of milk and set down her glass, licking away the milk mustache from her upper lip. "I think I'd cry over it," she said honestly. "Wouldn't you?"

"Perhaps . . . in the privacy of my room. But it's hardly fair to inflict one's own misfortune on everyone else. A lady doesn't make a display of her emotions."

Even as she said the words, Millicent remembered the display she had made of her anger the day before, right in Betsy's yard, and she glanced away, unable to meet Betsy's wide, frank gaze. She hesitated, then said, "I was scarcely a model of ladylike behavior yesterday. It was wrong. I should not have lost my composure that way. Usually I do not." What was it about the Lawrences, father, daughter and dog, that brought out the worst in her?

"It's all right. I try people's patience."

Millicent's eyebrows rose. "You don't sound particularly bothered by that idea."

Betsy shrugged. "Papa says that he irritates people, too."

Millicent smothered a smile. She could certainly believe that. Not only had Jonathan Lawrence gotten under her skin, but also, in the brief period of time that he had been publishing the newspaper, he had managed to ruffle several people's feathers. Foremost amongst them was Jonas Watson, probably the wealthiest citizen of Emmetsville and the owner of several wretched houses in the riverfront area which he rented out and which the *Sentinel* had labeled "a disgrace to the town." Personally, Millicent was inclined to agree with Lawrence about Mr. Watson, whom she believed was singularly lacking in proper Christian charity, and she had been appalled to read that her own church, due to a gift in someone's will, was also a landlord in the same area. However, she knew that most people regarded Jonathan's articles as merely an attempt on the part of an outsider to stir up trouble in the town.

"Papa says that if a person goes through life without offending anyone, he hasn't really lived," Betsy went on seriously. "He says that some of us are born to be gad-flies."

Millicent blinked at this unorthodox philosophy of life, so different from her own. "I think it is, perhaps, a belief more appropriate to a newsman than to a lady or a young girl." Seeing the questions already forming in Betsy's eyes, she continued hastily, "Since we've finished our cookies, perhaps we ought to end our little chat. I'm sure we're in Ida's way, and I should get back to work, as well."

As they got up from the table, Betsy glanced hopefully in the direction of Alan's room, but Millicent steered her firmly through the other door, which led onto the back porch. Betsy turned and looked up at her. "I liked talking to you," she said with disarming candor. "Can I come back sometime?"

"May I," Millicent corrected automatically.

"May I come back?"

"Yes, of course."

A grin flashed across Betsy's face, and Millicent realized that she had the same dimpled, charming smile that her father did, in a smaller, more feminine version. She would need it—and more than that, to get through this world with her appalling lack of manners, Millicent thought as she watched the girl hop down the steps to the yard and turn to wave before she took off at a run for her own house. In less than a minute, the girl had made three grievous social errors: She had not thanked Millicent for the cookies and milk; she had made no proper good-bye; and she had boldly asked for another invitation. Millicent sighed and shook her head. Whatever was she going to do with the girl?

She realized what she was thinking and caught herself. How foolish. She was "going to do" nothing with the girl at all. Betsy Lawrence was none of her business.

After supper that evening, Millicent went out onto the front porch to sit, as she often did. As she sat in the white wicker rocker, gently rocking, Mr. and Mrs. Holmes from down the street walked past and nodded to her, calling out a greeting; a child went by, rolling a hoop, and a buggy pulled up at the Andersons' house across the way. Sitting on the porch was a favorite form of evening entertainment in Emmetsville. One could see everything that was happening in the area around them, and people often stopped to chat.

One person whom Millicent did not expect to see, however, was Jonathan Lawrence. She certainly didn't expect him to stroll over to talk to her. But he did.

She watched in amazement as he left his house and strode across his yard, easily stepping over the short picket fence that separated the two houses. She tensed, rising as he reached the steps of the porch.

"Mr. Lawrence."

"Good evening, Miss Hayes." Amusement lit his eyes. "Please don't run back inside the house. I haven't come armed for battle."

Millicent's eyebrows went up a notch, her face falling into the faintly haughty expression she customarily assumed when she was trying to hide her uneasiness. "I had no intention of running inside, Mr. Lawrence. It may disappoint you to learn that I am scarcely afraid of you."

His grin grew, and he came up the two wide, shallow steps to the porch. "It doesn't disappoint me at all. Frankly, I find it refreshing." He paused, then said, "Well, are you going to invite me to sit down, or shall we stand here like two statues?"

"Please sit down." Millicent made a sweeping gesture that included the other wicker chair which sat a few feet away from her, and sat down herself.

But Jonathan perched on the narrow railing of the porch, one foot propped against the floor, directly in front of her chair. Millicent didn't like having him this close nor did she enjoy being forced to look up at him; it gave him a distinct advantage. But she could hardly jump back to her feet.

"Are you here for a particular reason, Mr. Lawrence?" she asked, deciding that she should seize control of the conversation.

"Yes. I came to apologize." He chuckled at her startled expression. "It's impolite to look so surprised that I would do the polite thing, you know."

"I—well, this is rather unexpected."

"Sometimes my temper is too hot, especially where my daughter is concerned. I'm afraid that I spoke hastily yesterday; I said some things that were rude, that I had no right to say. And I'm sorry. It was our fault that Admiral ruined your laundry, and while it was rather . . . um, humorous to see, I'm sure it didn't seem so from your perspective. It's obvious that Betsy and Admiral have caused you a good deal of trouble, and I want to apologize for that, as well."

Millicent's defenses melted away at his candid apology. "I spoke in the heat of anger, too. I was hasty and too critical. I'm sure that Betsy is a charming child." She stopped short of saying that Admiral was a charming dog.

"Thank you." Jonathan smiled, and any last vestiges of resentment or anger vanished from Millicent's heart. He was a well-spoken man, after all. She could hardly blame him for his loss of temper; after all, look at the way she had acted. "You mustn't blame Betsy," he went on. "I have raised her . . . ah, rather unconventionally."

That was certainly an understatement, Millicent thought.

"Her mother died almost five years ago, and I've raised her by myself since then. I've always spoken to her as if she were an adult, an equal. I don't believe in women being treated as if they were inferior creatures. Perhaps I have encouraged her to be a trifle too bold in her speech and actions."

Millicent gazed at him in some astonishment. These were certainly unusual opinions for a man to be espousing. She had read of women (Yankees, of course) who maintained that women were the equals of men but she had never decided what she believed regarding the matter. She was inclined toward the opinion of Aunt Oradelle, who sniffed and said contemptuously, "As good as men! What nonsense. We are *better* than they are, and that's obvious. God knew what he was doing when he entrusted the care of children to women. And who wants to vote and serve on a jury, I'd like to know? The whole idea is ridiculous."

Still, even though she didn't precisely agree with him, it made her warm a little toward Jonathan Lawrence to know that he cared so deeply about his daughter and didn't, as so many men seemed to do, count her second best to a son.

"But," Millicent said, choosing her words carefully, "does it make a woman any less equal to be polite or to act like a lady?"

Jonathan sighed. "You're right. It's difficult for a man to raise a daughter."

"It must be hard."

"Thank you for being understanding. I was afraid that I'd made an enemy for life of you."

Millicent found it difficult to believe that Jonathan Lawrence would worry overmuch about whether he had made an enemy. If he had such concerns, they certainly didn't show up in his newspaper editorials. It was nice, then, to think that he had not wanted *her* to be his enemy.

"No. Of course not. My behavior was hardly well-bred."

"Why don't we blame it all on the heat?" He grinned engagingly. "It's been pretty warm for May."

"Yes, that sounds like a perfectly logical reason." It was impossible not to smile back at him. And there was that funny little flutter in her chest again.

"Well, I must be going," he said. "I have to get Betsy to bed. Thank you."

"Good night." Millicent extended her hand to him

to shake in a gesture of forgiveness, even friendship, and he took it. But instead of shaking it, he surprised her by bending over it in a courtly manner and lightly brushing his lips against the back of her hand. It was an elegant, if somewhat extravagant, gesture, and in any other man, Millicent would have found it faintly pleasant and charming. But when Jonathan's lips touched her skin, she felt it all through her. It was shivery and exciting, and it set up a peculiar melting sensation low in her abdomen. She sucked in a surprised breath. She hoped he didn't feel the sudden trembling in her hand.

Jonathan straightened and smiled at her. "Good night."

He swung off the porch and strode across the yard, jumping lightly over the low fence as he had when he came. Millicent watched him go, one hand clenched against her stomach. She didn't know what she felt—or what she thought about Mr. Lawrence anymore.

Millicent drifted upstairs to her room, thinking about the visit and Jonathan and trying to sort out her feelings. He was the same man who had been obnoxious and rude to her yesterday, yet he was also a man who could recognize his shortcomings and apologize for them. He loved his daughter. His smile could probably charm the birds out of the trees. She could tell from the things he had written in the *Sentinel* that he was a man of talent and principle. Nor was he afraid to go up against even the wealthy and the influential when he thought they were wrong. He was a man who stood by his opinions, and Millicent respected that.

She strolled to her window to close the drapes and

stood for a moment, gazing dreamily out into the night. Next door the house was dark, except for a dim light glowing downstairs. Millicent wondered if that was Jonathan's study. He might be there now, writing something for this week's publication.

She pulled the drapes closed and wandered over to her bed, slowly unbuttoning and taking off her dress. It might be good for her to give the man a second chance. They could start all over. She could show him that she had decided to do so by making a dessert tomorrow and taking it over to them. Millicent smiled. Yes, she liked that idea.

Millicent tossed her clothes across the chair, not folding them neatly and putting them away as she usually did when she undressed, and flopped back onto her bed. She crossed her arms behind her head and lay gazing up at the ceiling, a small smile on her lips, thinking about tomorrow.

Millicent spent most of the next afternoon making her special chocolate cake. By the time she finished it, she had gotten flour, as well as a few other ingredients, on her dress and on her hands and face. She would have to change before she took the cake next door, so she went upstairs and, after some studying of her wardrobe, she decided to put on one of her older dresses. It was a little out of style, but it was a lovely robin's-egg blue and had been one of her favorites when she was younger. She smiled as she put it on and looked at herself in the mirror. It brought out the blue of her eyes, she thought, and the Lawrences wouldn't notice that it was slightly old-fashioned. Nor would they think about the fact that a woman her age shouldn't be wearing such a youthful color.

As she gazed at her reflection, Millicent realized that she had even gotten a spot of flour in her hair. That would never do, of course, so she took down her hair and brushed it out. When she started to put it up again, she thought of the style in which Cousin Susan wore her hair, pulled back into a thick, crisscrossed knot at the back of the head, with a froth of curls framing her face. It was a style, she thought, that would flatter her. When she was younger, she had often worn her hair in curls. And if her cousin, who was a matron as old as she, could wear her hair that way, surely it wasn't an improper hairstyle for Millicent, either.

For the next hour she happily played with her hair, securing the difficult knot with hairpins, then heating an iron and curling her hair around her face. The result, she noted with pleasure, was charming. She revolved slowly in front of the mirror, savoring her image. It was satisfying to see that she was still pretty. Perhaps she was not as sparkling as she had been when she was young, but she hadn't yet dried up into an old hag, either.

She glanced toward the chest of drawers, on top of which sat a wooden box. Impulsively, she stood up and went over to take it down. The box was not large, only about eight inches long and four or five inches across, and it was made of elegant reddish-grained rosewood. Her parents had given it to her on her fifteenth birthday, and she had used it to keep her youthful mementos. But for years now it had sat on top of the tall chest, untouched. For a while, it had been too painful to look at the things inside the box; it had been a sharp reminder of the time of Alan's accident and her own foolishly careless ways.

Millicent held the box for a moment in her hands, her forefinger tracing the delicate carving of a rose that adorned its top. The old pain didn't stab her. Slowly, almost hesitantly, she opened the lid. On top lay a crimson ribbon, stiffened and faded with time. Millicent remembered it; it had gone around the box of chocolates Jimmy Saunders had given her on her eighteenth birthday. She smiled, recalling Jimmy's earnest face as he had given it to her, the tips of his ears turning red as they always did when he was embarrassed. Jimmy had been such a sweet boy; she had rather favored him above her other beaux. He had finally wound up marrying Annabeth McCrae five or six years ago, and they had three children, all boys.

Millicent sat down on her bed and began to pull the items out of the small rosewood box, laying them down on the quilt across the foot of the bed. There was a carved ivory and white lace fan. She had loved that fan and had carried it to all the dances. Beneath it were several dance cards, tied with narrow gold cords, from which tiny pencils dangled. She opened one of the dance cards and glanced over the names written there, some scrawled, some elegant, some formally stating an entire name, such as Davis E. Haskell, and others only a casual and arrogant first name—Alex, J.B., Henry. With a finger that trembled slightly she ran down the names, as if they had texture and substance that she could feel.

Davis had gone on to medical school and was now a doctor in Greenville. Alex Gruenwold had died two years ago in a fall from a grain elevator. He had been such a charming, careless boy, full of high spirits and the most graceful dancer in the whole county. It was hard to believe he was dead. And Henry Clayton . . . He'd had such sweaty palms that Millicent had hated to dance with him, but she'd felt too sorry for him to hurt his feelings by turning him down. He worked in his father's feed store, which he would one day take over, and he'd married Prudence Crum, whose cooking had added at least thirty pounds to his already plump body.

There was a pressed rose, a tiny yellow bow still adorning its long-withered stem, and there was the azalea blossom she'd worn in her hair at the Morgans' dance one summer, brown and brittle now. The wrist corsage Alex had given her, a lacy pink valentine from Jimmy, another one, even more ornate, from Ernie Dalton, one white lace evening mitt with a tiny stain of red punch, and a little net bag of rice from Polly Craig's wedding, tied with a tiny pink bow.

She gazed at the girlish treasures spread out on the quilt, and tears came into her eyes. All the boys were gone from her now, and the time was long dead. But curiously, along with the tears, a reminiscent smile touched her lips. She felt almost hopeful, in fact, as if something long numb were stirring to life inside her.

Millicent stood up, leaving the box and its contents strewn across the quilt, and took down her best summer bonnet, a little straw confection with a delightful cluster of bright red wooden cherries curling down one side. It was late afternoon now, almost time for supper, and she was sure that Jonathan would be home from work. She tied the wide satin ribbons beneath her chin, then ran lightly down the stairs. She picked up her cake plate from the kitchen table and started out the front door. As she stepped out onto the front porch, she glanced toward Jonathan's house. She stopped.

The Widow Woods was going through the gate into the Lawrences' yard. She was dressed up in her best bonnet and dress, and she carried a basket over her arm, covered with a linen napkin. Millicent stood frozen, watching her. Clara Woods was about three years older than Millicent, a round-faced woman with deep-set brown eyes. When her husband had died three years ago, she had determinedly set out to find another husband. So far her efforts had been fruitless, but she had continued to set her cap for practically every eligible widower or bachelor in town. It had become something of a town joke, the way Widow Woods would pursue her targets, dressing up in frills unbecoming to a woman of her age and position and managing to run into her victim at public events or bringing little gifts of jam or candy she had made. Obviously, she had now set her sights on Jonathan Lawrence.

Millicent dropped down on the wicker chair beside the door, her knees weak. She felt sick with shame. Seeing Clara Woods, she had suddenly seen herself. Why, she must appear as foolish as the widow, putting on one of the dresses from her younger days and curling her hair girlishly, then trotting over to Jonathan Lawrence with a cake she had slaved over half the day. Anyone who saw her, including Jonathan Lawrence himself, would think she was chasing him! Millicent was honest enough to admit that maybe they would be right, even though she had been unaware of her intentions.

What an old fool she had been! She'd let his devilish grin and handsome face knock all the sense out of her until she didn't realize how silly she must look, a dried-up old maid trying to be young and pretty again. Heat scorched her cheeks, and tears started in her eyes. Millicent pressed her hands to her cheeks. Thank goodness she had seen Widow Woods and come to her senses in time! She didn't think she could stand to see Jonathan Lawrence gaze at her in a half-amused, half-pitying way, knowing that she had gussied herself up to see him, hoping to snare a man into marriage at last.

She squeezed her eyes shut, and wiped away her tears with short, fierce movements. Well, she wasn't about to become like the widow, despite this temporary lapse. Hell would freeze over before she'd set herself up as a laughingstock in front of the whole town!

Millicent jumped to her feet and hurried back inside the house. She went first to the kitchen, where she put the cake plate down on the counter. Then she ran up the stairs to her room and yanked the pins from her hair and pulled off the blue dress. She put back on the dress she had been wearing earlier, wiping the floury spots from it. She brushed her hair so hard it made her scalp hurt, until she had brushed out all the frivolous curls, and she pulled it back and tightly braided it, twisting the braid into a simple bun at the base of her head.

She glanced toward the bed, where the rosewood box and its mementos still lay. She pressed her lips together tightly. What foolishness! She wasn't a girl of eighteen anymore. It was silly to keep those things, much less to take them out and moon over them. Millicent marched to the bed and stuffed the keepsakes back into the rosewood box, closing its lid with a final click. She opened the lid of the chest at the end of the bed, the chest which when she was young had been her "hope chest" and in which she had stored away her best embroidered linens and her grandmother's quilt, awaiting her wedding day. Nowadays the quilt lay across the foot of her bed and the chest was filled with blankets, afghans, and shawls. Lifting up the corner of the stack of blankets, Millicent stuck the rosewood box under them. She let the blankets fall back on top of it and closed the lid.

Afterwards, she went down to supper with Alan. And for dessert, she cut them each a piece of her cake. Alan was delighted at the unexpected treat, but Millicent just toyed with her slice. She couldn't force even a bite down her throat.

Seven

$\mathcal{M}$illicent saw little of either Betsy or her father for the next two weeks. Now and then, as she was digging or watering or doing one of the other hundreds of tasks in her garden, she would see Jonathan leaving for work in the morning or returning in the evening. When he happened to catch sight of her, he tipped his hat in a polite greeting, and she responded with a nod. Once he walked up to the fence and asked how she was doing. She responded that she was fine, but could think of nothing to extend the conversation, and after a moment, he nodded again and left.

Millicent discovered, to her surprise, that she vaguely missed Admiral and Betsy. They had been aggravating, but she realized now that they had made her days interesting. Now everything was as predictable as ever. Millicent wondered why she hadn't noticed before how uninteresting her days were. Even the club meetings and the preparations for the boxed supper were not enough to fill her time. In the past her father had let her do work for him, looking up cases, writing correspondence, filing and organizing his material. But since his death, she had nothing except housework, her garden, and her clubs. Frankly, she was often bored. She must be, if she was missing Betsy and that scamp of a dog!

One evening in the middle of June, an hour or so after supper, Millicent and Alan were sitting in his room, reading in companionable silence, as they often did after Johnny had put Alan into his bed for the night. Suddenly there was a loud knock on the front door, and Millicent glanced in surprise at her brother.

"Who could that be at this time of night?" she wondered, and Alan shrugged.

"Probably one of our innumerable family members," Alan said dryly. "No doubt we haven't reported in to Aunt Oradelle this week. Whoever it is, I'm sure I have no desire to see them."

Millicent sighed and, laying her book aside, walked out of his bedroom and down the hall toward the front door. Before she reached the door, there was another knock, even more thunderous than the first, and Millicent's mouth tightened in irritation. She hastened her steps to forestall yet another banging on the brass door knocker and swung open the door. Her mouth fell open in astonishment.

Betsy Lawrence stood directly in front of the door, her body taut and her face white. Behind her stood her father, carrying a woman's limp body.

Millicent stared. The scene was so unexpected, so bizarre, that for a moment she could not absorb it.

"Let us in! Please!" Betsy said urgently, reaching out to take Millicent's arm. "You have to help us."

"What? Oh! Of course!" Millicent recovered her wits

and stepped aside quickly so that Jonathan could bring his burden inside. "Right down the hall on the left." She pointed toward the open doorway of the front parlor.

Jonathan carried the woman into the parlor, and Millicent and Betsy followed on his heels. "Put her on the sofa. What happened? Who is she?"

"I don't know." Jonathan laid her down gently on the sofa and stepped back. "She showed up on my doorstep a few minutes ago, asking for work. She fainted right there."

"My goodness." Millicent bent over her. The woman—no, the girl; she looked too young to be called a woman—had a thin face, exceedingly pale, as if all the color had drained out of her. Her hair, drawn back into a single braid, was light blond, and her eyebrows and lashes were only a few shades darker. Everything about her was so pale that she gave the impression of almost not being there, as if she could fade into the background at any moment. Millicent had never seen her before.

Millicent patted her cheek gently. "Miss . . . miss . . . can you hear me?" She spoke to Betsy without turning her head. "Betsy, can you run into the kitchen and bring me back a glass of water? There's a pitcher on the counter."

Behind her she heard Betsy's rapid footsteps across the floor. Millicent knelt on the floor beside the sofa and reached down to pick up the girl's hand and feel her pulse. It was then that she noticed for the first time that the girl was pregnant. In her astonishment, she hadn't seen the girl's condition. She stared for a moment at her rounded stomach, absorbing this information and she revised the girl's age upward; she was simply thin, even frail.

"I brought her here because I thought she might need a woman's help, especially in her condition," Jonathan explained behind Millicent.

Millicent felt the heat begin to rise in her cheeks at his casual reference to the stranger's pregnancy. Jonathan Lawrence had a more blunt way of talking to a woman than any man she'd ever met. Most men would have avoided the subject, knowing that her condition was obvious.

"I'm sorry to bother you," Jonathan went on, "but Mrs. Rafferty had gone, and I didn't know what else to do."

"Of course you did the right thing. Don't apologize." Millicent felt the woman's pulse. It was pumping steadily, though a trifle faintly. The woman's hand was cold as ice, and Millicent rubbed it between her hands. The woman stirred and moaned. "Good. I think she's coming around."

Betsy returned on the run and handed Millicent a glass of water. Millicent dipped her handkerchief in the water, then gently wiped it across the woman's face and throat. The stranger moved her head from side to side, and her eyes fluttered open. They closed, then opened again. She stared at Millicent blankly.

"What—who . . ." she asked in a faint, confused voice as she tried to sit up.

"Shhh. There, now, lie quietly. It's all right. You

fainted, that's all, and Mr. Lawrence brought you to my house."

The woman licked her lips and blinked. She looked beyond Millicent to Jonathan, and recognition sparked in her eyes. "Oh. It's you. I remember—I'm so sorry." Huge tears gathered in her eyes.

"It's all right." Jonathan's voice was kindly and reassuring. Millicent hadn't heard this tone from him before. "There's nothing to be sorry about. *You're* the one we're concerned about."

"Perhaps you should fetch Dr. Morton," Millicent told Jonathan.

The girl's eyes filled with panic, and she struggled to sit up again. "No! No, please! I'm fine! I don't need a doctor. Truly."

"But perhaps there's something wrong." Millicent's eyes dropped significantly to the girl's stomach.

The girl covered her protruding stomach protectively with both her hands. "No, really. I'm sure. I—ah—was just tired. I should have sat down and rested."

Millicent stood up. The girl did look tired but it was clear that she was not taking proper care of herself. Still, it seemed to Millicent that the prudent thing to do would be to let a doctor see her. Millicent glanced uncertainly at Jonathan. He raised his eyebrows in an expression of confusion, then turned back to gaze thoughtfully at the girl.

"How long has it been since you last ate?" he asked shrewdly.

Millicent stared at Jonathan. It hadn't occurred to her that the woman might be faint from a lack of food.

She glanced at the woman and saw that Jonathan's words had brought a trace of color to her cheeks.

"I don't know," she admitted in a low voice, looking down at her hands. "Maybe a day, or two."

"Two days!" Millicent was shocked. "You haven't eaten in two days? Why, you have to eat! It's not good for the baby."

"I know, ma'am." Millicent could hear tears in her voice. "I know I should, but I—I didn't have the money."

Pity shot through Millicent. No wonder the girl was so thin. Once again Millicent exchanged a look with Jonathan. "Well, we'll have to change that right now."

She bustled off to the kitchen and returned minutes later carrying a tray on which sat a tall glass of milk and a plate of bread, ham, and cold black-eyed peas. She set the tray down on the woman's lap. The stranger picked up the glass and drank greedily from it. Afterwards, she bolted down almost half the bread in three bites. It wrung Millicent's heart to see the way she gulped down the food. If she really had eaten as recently as a couple of days ago, Millicent suspected that she hadn't eaten well.

Halfway through the food, the girl glanced up at the other three, all standing watching her. She looked embarrassed. "I'm sorry. You must think I'm awful, the way I'm gulping this down. It's just so good, ma'am, and I was right hungry."

"No, please, there's no need to apologize." Millicent frowned with concern, and she lectured her sternly, "But you shouldn't be tramping around like this, going without food. I—you should be at home, resting and eating well and. . . ." Her voice trailed off. Clearly, this woman had had no home to go to, or she wouldn't be sitting where she was right now, eating so fast that Millicent was afraid she would make herself ill.

"I haven't got a home, ma'am," the girl assured her. "Honest. I don't want to hurt the baby, but I don't know what else to do. I have to find work, or we'll starve, the both of us. And I—" Her eyes filled with tears, and a sob escaped her. "I'm sorry," she mumbled, wiping at her eyes.

"Please, don't be upset." Millicent reached out and placed her hand awkwardly on the girl's arm. "It's all right. Finish your food; then we'll talk."

Millicent became aware of Betsy standing to the side, wide-eyed, taking in the scene. She suspected that what they would talk about now might not be appropriate for a young girl to hear. "Betsy," she began brightly, turning toward her. "Why don't you go into Alan's room and visit with him? I'm sure he would love to see you. You'll be interested in what he's done with his soldiers; he's been setting them up like mad the past few days."

"Really?" Betsy looked torn. Normally she would have sped off to Alan's room with alacrity, but she was reluctant to leave the strange young woman who had caused all the excitement.

"Really." Millicent's voice was firm.

With a sigh, Betsy left the room, casting back one last, wistful glance. Millicent turned back to the young woman on the couch. She realized that she wasn't sure how to begin. What could she say to this woman, really little more than a child herself from the looks of it, and quite pregnant, without anything to eat and no home to go to? What could she do with her?

She took a breath. Well, one thing Millicent Hayes had never done was shirk her responsibility. Obviously it was her duty to take charge here. "I don't mean to pry. But I would like to help you. I'm sorry, I haven't even introduced myself. My name is Millicent Hayes. Mr. Lawrence, on whose porch you fainted, is our neighbor, and he brought you here, quite correctly. Obviously this is a delicate situation."

The girl gazed at her frankly. "My name is Opal Wilkins, ma'am. I'm terribly grateful to you for letting me come into your house this way, and for feeding me and everything. You're a generous lady; I can see that." She looked down and to the side, avoiding Millicent's gaze. Her voice dropped so low that Millicent had to strain to hear it, "But you may not want to have anything more to do with me. I—you see, I ain't got a husband." She raised her face and met Millicent's eyes a little defiantly. "I'm not married."

"I see." Millicent had suspected as much from her pitiful circumstances, although of course it was always possible that her husband might have died or that he was simply a wretch who would not take care of her properly. It was scandalous and wicked, of course, and Millicent could not condone what the girl had done, but neither could she harden her heart against Opal's plight. There was the poor unborn child to consider, as well. "But haven't you any family you could go to?

Someone who would take you in? You shouldn't be working in your condition."

"I got no family. I'm an orphan, you see. My ma died when I was six, and I didn't have a father or no one who was willing to claim me. So I was put in an orphanage. When I was older, I was sent to live with a family, but I left there soon as I could when I was fourteen. I started hiring out as a maid or a cook or laundress, whatever I could find. But," she added proudly, straightening her spine and looking Millicent squarely in the eye, "I always made my living honest. I never stole or did anything wrong. I wasn't . . . " She glanced at Jonathan uncomfortably, then back at Millicent. "I wasn't one of them kind of women."

Millicent felt heat touch her cheeks. It was a most indelicate thing to talk about, especially with a man sitting with them. "Of course not," she said hastily, wishing to close the subject. But she had the uneasy feeling that there was no way she could do that, not with the woman sitting there so obviously pregnant. Why didn't Jonathan do the gentlemanly thing and excuse himself? But, of course, it would be foolish to expect that of Jonathan.

"Then I went to work for the Johnstons." Disgust laced Opal's voice, and her face turned hard and bitter. "They weren't good people, but I didn't know that at first. I could tell soon enough that *he* was a wicked sort of man. He would look at me funny and sometimes he'd do things, say things, that, well, that he shouldn't be doing or saying. And his wife right there in the house, too! I should have left then." Tears filled her gray eyes, and she clenched her fists tightly together. "But I needed the money, and I reckoned that I could avoid him. So I decided I'd hold out to the end of the month, when they'd pay me, and then I'd go on. I never thought that he'd do what he did, not with his missus there. But one night, he—he came to my room behind the kitchen and he—he had his way with me," Opal finished in a rush.

Millicent blushed, but her embarrassment at hearing such a thing in the presence of Jonathan Lawrence was far secondary to her horror. As Opal had talked, she had felt a creeping presentiment of what the girl was about to say, but even so, the bald announcement of fact was shocking. She gasped, one hand flying to her mouth, and with the other she reached out instinctively to Opal. "Oh, my dear! You poor girl! I—I—" She fumbled for something to say, but she realized that there was nothing that was adequate.

"I didn't want him to. I swear it!" Opal looked at her pleadingly, her eyes swimming with tears and her face contorted with the remembered horror. "He made me. I fought; I truly did. But he was too big and too strong. Please, you have to believe me!" She looked to Jonathan, then back to Millicent, her big eyes begging.

"Of course I believe you!" Millicent patted her hand comfortingly. How could anyone not believe the terror and disgust that were so plainly written on Opal's face?

"Honest?" Opal's hand curled around Millicent's, clutching it tightly. "Do you truly? Oh, ma'am." Her voice broke. "Thank you. You're such a good, kind woman. *She* didn't believe me. His wife. I went to her the next morning; I'd cried all night long in my bed. I told her what happened." Her voice dropped to a flat whisper. "She didn't believe me. She slapped my face and called me a liar. She said I must have led him on, enticed him. She turned me out of the house, didn't even give me my pay. I went as far away as I could get. I got a job, but I kept getting sick to my stomach, and they let me go, thinking I was sickly. I knew what was the matter, but I didn't dare tell them. I got another job, scrubbing floors and such, but after awhile I couldn't hide my condition anymore. As soon as they found out, they sent me packing. They said they wouldn't have no wicked woman in their home."

She began to cry softly, and she brought trembling hands up to hide her eyes, but she couldn't hold back the stream of words that poured out of her, driven by pain. "Nobody would take me in. They'd see how I was and ask me where was my husband, and that'd be the end of it. That was a month ago, and no one will hire me. Sometimes a nice woman like you will give me a bite to eat before she sends me on my way. But they won't let me in their house. They reckon I'm loose, or at least that I won't be strong enough to do my work. I don't know what to do no more! How'll I take care of my baby? I'm afraid for it. I'm so scared."

"Oh, no, don't cry." She moved quickly to the sofa beside Opal and curled an arm around her shaking shoulders. "It will be all right. We won't let you starve. I'll see to that."

"Of course not," Jonathan added. He had remained silent throughout Opal's sad story, not wanting to add to her humiliation by reminding her that a man was witness to her shame. But now he crossed the room to the couch and squatted down in front of it. "Don't worry. You'll be all right now, you and the baby. You'll both be safe."

"Yes," Millicent agreed firmly. "You can spend the night here. I think the first thing you need is to rest, now that you've gotten some proper nourishment."

To her amazement, Opal began to cry even harder. Millicent exchanged a look of bewilderment with Jonathan. "I—I'm sorry," Millicent said stumblingly. "I didn't mean to make you more unhappy. I wanted to help. Did I say something wrong?"

"Oh, no!" Opal uncovered her face and grasped Millicent's hand with both her own, her expression horrified. "No, miss. You didn't say nothing wrong. I ain't unhappy. It's just that you're so kind and so generous, and—I don't know, I guess I was mostly crying from relief. I'm so tired, and it's hard to believe that I've finally found good people who're willing to help a nobody like me."

"You're not a nobody." Jonathan looked thunderous. "And neither will your baby be one."

Opal tried to smile. "Thank you, sir. I don't know how I'll ever repay you, either of you."

"Don't worry about that."

"Well, then, that's that," Millicent said briskly, standing up, eager to deal with the practicalities. "There's a room downstairs. It's rather small and oddly shaped. It's tucked in under the back stairs and into part of what used to be the walkway between the house and kitchen. But it is downstairs, and that would be better for you than climbing up and down the staircase."

The area, one of the many nooks and crannies of the big old house, had once been a large storage closet and one of Millicent and Alan's favorite playing places when they were children. After Alan's accident, their father had had it cleaned out and turned into a small bedroom for the attendant who had helped nurse Alan. It contained only a narrow bed, a single chest of drawers, and a chair, but Millicent doubted that Opal had many possessions to put away anyway, and it fulfilled the primary need, which was that the poor girl get some rest.

"I'll put on some clean sheets, and you can go right to bed."

"I can put them on, miss." Opal looked horrified. "You needn't be putting yourself out for me."

"Nonsense. It's no trouble. I've made a bed many times before, I can assure you, and you're in no condition to be doing anything but resting."

Opal still looked troubled, but Millicent swept out of the room without giving her a chance to protest. She trotted up the stairs to the linen press and pulled out a set of clean, ironed white sheets. She carried them and a dust rag downstairs to the narrow room that opened under the stairway. She found Jonathan standing in the hall.

"I thought you might need help."

Millicent couldn't imagine a man being of much use in making up a bed, but she said only, "I suppose you could turn the mattress."

She lit a kerosene lamp and went into the small room. It was narrow, and the ceiling sloped bizarrely, but it was quite cozy. She set the lamp down on the chest and while Jonathan flipped over the feather mattress, she flicked a dust rag over the few simple pieces of furniture. There was no place in Millicent Hayes's house that went uncleaned, but this small room was swept out and dusted only once a month. She wasn't about to let anyone, even a total stranger, sleep in a room that showed dust on the furniture.

It was strange to be standing together with Jonathan in as intimate a place as a small bedroom, doing something as ordinary and commonplace, yet as tinged with sexual overtones, as preparing a bed to be slept in. Millicent watched the movement of Jonathan's arms as he turned the mattress. She watched his large hands smooth it down, the fingers sliding, widespread, across the ticking. Her mouth went dry. Millicent realized with a start that she had been staring at him. Self-consciously she turned and dusted the top of the chest, although she had already cleaned it once.

"Millicent . . ." Jonathan began, his voice a little tentative. "Thank you for taking the girl in."

Millicent turned to look at him. "I could hardly turn her away, could I? Poor girl, such a sad story."

"A lot of people would have. I think you're quite kind under that starchy demeanor."

Starchy demeanor! What did he mean by that? That she was a prig, she supposed; naturally that would be what a man like Jonathan Lawrence would think of her. Still, it hurt to hear him describe her like that.

It's no more than what any Christian woman would do," she replied stiffly, returning to her task.

"No. Not any Christian woman. A lot of 'good Christian' women have already turned her away."

"No doubt they didn't realize how bad her situation was." Millicent picked up the sheet and whipped it out over the bed, keeping her eyes on it to avoid having to look at Jonathan. She was surprised when he reached out and smoothed the other end of the sheet down and tucked it neatly under the mattress. She glanced up at him in amazement, and he chuckled at the expression on her face.

"I am capable of doing a few simple chores," he told her, amusement quirking the corners of his mouth. "Actually, I made my bed every day of my life, at least until I was married. Even then, I did it when Elizabeth was pregnant." He saw shock widen her eyes, and he amended hastily, "Sorry. In the family way, I mean." He cocked an eyebrow. "Is that acceptable?"

There was an amused tolerance in his eyes that made Millicent want to double up her fist and hit him. But all she allowed herself was a cold, "Yes, it's fine."

There was a pause and Jonathan asked, all hint of laughter gone from his voice, "What do you plan to do about Miss Wilkins? Will you give her a job?"

Millicent frowned and began to gnaw at her lower lip. "I don't know what to do. She shouldn't be doing physical labor. She's small and delicate. I'm afraid she'll hurt herself or the baby, or both."

"Will you send her on her way?" His voice was carefully neutral.

Millicent's head snapped up and she glared at him. "Of course not! How could you say such a thing? I couldn't turn her out! I'll have to think of something. Perhaps the church could do something for her. . . . "

"I wouldn't depend on that."

Millicent put her hands on her hips pugnaciously. "I realize, Mr. Lawrence, that you have some sort of aversion to religion, but you are entirely wrong."

"Do you mean to tell me that your church ladies would raise money for this young woman to live somewhere and eat and bring up her baby? Isn't it more likely that they'd send her to a home for wayward young women, where she would have to agree to give up her child in return for care and food? Where they'd sing hymns and preach at her all day for her 'wickedness' in having a baby out of wedlock, even though it was no fault of her own?"

Millicent hesitated. For once, she wasn't certain. She didn't know where Opal would have to go to have her baby. She thought that there were societies who took care of such as she, but Millicent honestly didn't know what their policies were. However, she was acquainted with the women in her own church well enough to know that there were several who would react just as the women Opal had described. There were those who would say that what was happening to her now was a just punishment for the sin she had committed. Even those who were sympathetic were likely to agree that the girl should be sent to a home for wayward women.

Whether or not Jonathan was correct in his supposition of what her life would be like in that home, somehow, having seen Opal and listened to her story, Millicent could not bring herself to send Opal away. There was something about the girl that was honest and good, so strong despite all her past troubles, that Millicent wanted her to have a better life than being stuck in a dreary house with women of largely questionable morals. Surely, after what had happened to her, she deserved better treatment than that.

Jonathan saw her wavering, and he pressed his point. "Opal Wilkins is a proud girl; I could see that in her. It would shame her terribly to be in such a place. And she needs a job, not charity; she has to feel that she's earning her own way. She has too much character to live on charity."

"I don't know why you think you know so much!" Millicent said crossly, her irritation covering her own uneasy feeling that he was probably right.

"Because I know that kind of place. I know the kind of life Opal Wilkins has led. I was an orphan, too, and I was raised in an orphanage, just as she was." He gave a crooked smile. "That's where I learned my bed making skills, by the way. I was farmed out, too, to people who needed physical labor, not a child to nurture. The difference was that when I was thirteen, I ran away from the last home they sent me to, and by sheer luck I went to the city and got a job hawking newspapers on the street. An editor there saw potential in me, and he took me under his wing. When he found out I was sleeping in the streets, he and his wife took me in. They fed and clothed me and sent me to school. They taught me everything important I ever learned. But most of us, like Opal, never got that kind of chance."

Millicent's chest ached with sympathy as she listened to his story. She looked away, not knowing what to say. Her heart was so full that she thought she might begin to cry if she tried to speak.

"Will you let her stay here? Give her a job?" Jonathan asked. "I'll pay her wages myself. It's just that I can't have her living and working in my house, not with me being a widower and her being young and unmarried and pregnant, too. It would cause an unholy scandal, and I can't subject Betsy to that."

"Oh, no! That would never do," Millicent agreed wholeheartedly. It demonstrated more good social sense than Millicent would have credited Jonathan Lawrence with having; she was glad that he had enough concern for Betsy to think of the proprieties. "Of course she can stay with me. But I'll pay her wages." It rankled that he didn't think her kind enough to keep Opal unless he paid her wages. "I'm well aware of my charitable obligations."

Jonathan's mouth twitched, and Millicent had the feeling that she had, yet again, amused him somehow.

Millicent went back into the parlor, where Opal sat. Worn out, the girl had fallen asleep sitting up, her head resting against the back of the sofa. She looked defenseless and frail sitting there, her hands loose in her lap, shadows beneath her eyes and her cheeks too thin and pale.

"Poor thing," Millicent murmured. "I hate to wake her even to get her to bed."

"Don't. There's no need to. I'll carry her. She's light—too light for how far along she is, I'll warrant."

She must be growing inured to Jonathan's frank references to Opal's condition, Millicent thought, for this time she didn't even blush, merely nodded in agreement at his assessment. Jonathan bent and lifted the girl easily off the couch. She opened her eyes in bewilderment for an instant, then closed them and nestled her head against Jonathan's shoulder like a trusting child. He carried her down the hall and into the tiny bedroom, with Millicent following. He paused beside the bed, and Millicent hurried forward to turn down the covers so that he could lay Opal on it. She curled up on her side, still not waking, and Millicent bent down to remove the girl's shoes. She pulled the covers up over Opal, and they tiptoed out of the room.

Outside the bedroom, Jonathan turned and reached out to take her hand. Millicent's nerves jumped at his touch. His skin was warm and rough against hers, and it seemed as if every nerve ending in her body were centered in her hand. Millicent gazed up into his face, and her eyes touched his mouth, wide and firm; his sculpted cheekbones; his eyes, the amber color shadowed by thick lashes, mysterious and sensual. Suddenly she thought about him kissing her. Bending down and pressing his lips into hers, gentle and passionate. Hot.

Heat flooded her face, and Millicent hoped that Jonathan could not guess what she was thinking just by looking at her.

"Thank you," Jonathan said softly. He squeezed her

hand, not letting go of it. "You're a kind woman. There's more to you than I realized. My apologies."

"Perhaps . . . " Millicent began breathlessly, "perhaps I've misjudged you, too."

He looked down into her eyes, and for a moment they simply stood there, unmoving. Then Betsy opened the door to Alan's room and stuck her head out, breaking the silence. "What happened? What are you going to do?"

Millicent jumped, and Jonathan released her hand. He turned away from her. "Miss Hayes is going to hire Miss Wilkins. She'll be living here now."

Betsy beamed. "I knew it! It'll be wonderful! Can I come visit the baby when it's born? I'll be extra careful, I promise."

"I—why, I suppose so."

"Come along, sugar," her father said, going to Betsy and taking her hand. "We'd better get home. I think it's past someone's bedtime."

"Oh, not tonight, please. . . . " Betsy began to plead as they started toward the front door.

"You can go out the back, if you want," Millicent offered. "It's closer." Going from back door to back door also implied a friendship and acceptance that had not existed between them before.

Jonathan looked at her. "All right," he said and turned, walking past Millicent to the back door. He opened the door, hesitated for a moment, then nodded a good night and left with his daughter.

Millicent turned and went to her brother's room. She knew that he was probably burning to know what had happened, for whatever information Betsy had given him would have been tantalizingly incomplete.

She related what had happened, skimming embarrassedly over some parts of Opal's story and hoping that Alan would be able to read between the lines and not ask questions.

"She's so pitiful, Alan," Millicent finished. "She's much too thin, and she barely looks old enough to be out on her own, let alone in her condition. Yet at the same time, there's an odd, old expression to her face, as if nothing could surprise her anymore. Of course, perhaps that's true, with the things that have happened to her."

"You're sure she hasn't just taken you in?" he asked, a concerned expression on his face. "That she's an honest person?"

"Oh, yes. I'm positive. You will be, too, when you see her."

"I'll be interested to meet her."

Millicent glanced at him, surprised. Usually Alan was not interested in seeing anyone.

He saw her look and shrugged, smiling a little sheepishly. "I confess, I'm curious. I can't help but wonder what she's like."

"Well, you'll get a chance to meet her tomorrow." Millicent stood up. "But right now I think that what you and I both need is some sleep. I'm feeling very tired all of a sudden."

Alan nodded, and she bent over to kiss him on the forehead. Alan took her hand and squeezed it. "This girl is very fortunate that she found you."

Millicent smiled at him fondly. "I believe you might be a little bit prejudiced."

She picked up the kerosene lamp by his bedside and carried it with her out into the dark hallway.

Eight

Opal slept soundly through the night and into the next morning. Indeed, she slept so late that Millicent began to worry about her. Finally, she tiptoed to Opal's door and opened it to peek in. She watched Opal long enough to make sure that her chest rose and fell in steady, if slow, breaths before she closed the door.

She went in to visit with Alan, and when she left his room, she peeked in at Opal again. Still the girl slept on, so Millicent went upstairs to her sewing room. Every thirty minutes or so, Millicent stopped pumping the foot pedal of her sewing machine and crept softly down the back stairs to check on the sleeping girl, unable to quell the nagging worry that something must be wrong with her.

Finally, when the morning was almost gone, Millicent stuck her head inside the door of the small room and found Opal sitting up in bed, eyes open, gazing slowly around the room. Opal spotted Millicent, and a wide grin split her face. "Oh, Miss! Am I glad to see you! I was thinking maybe I was in a dream. Only if I was,

I didn't want to wake up." She took another long look around the tiny room. "Isn't this pretty? It's the nicest room I've ever slept in."

Millicent, who had been about to apologize for the room's smallness and simplicity, clamped her mouth shut over the words and pasted on a smile. Opal's delight in the room brought home to Millicent how hard Opal's life had been.

"I can see that your rest has helped you." Opal's skin had a healthier color, and her eyes were clear and alert, without the tired dullness that had clouded them yesterday evening. "You're looking much better."

"Am I?"

"Yes, indeed. See for yourself." Millicent gestured toward the small mirror that hung on the wall above the table. She had set a washbowl and pitcher on the table to serve as a makeshift washstand.

Opal noticed the mirror for the first time and gave a cry of delight. She jumped out of bed and ran to peer into it. Her cheeks were tinged with rose and with the sunny smile spreading across her face, she looked almost pretty.

"Oh, Miss Hayes!" Opal clasped her hands together and swung around to gaze at Millicent with shining eyes, then turned back to the mirror, unable to pull her eyes away from it for long. "I never had a mirror all to myself before! This is lovely! You're too, too kind."

Tears glittered in the girl's eyes, and Millicent looked away, embarrassed by Opal's gratitude. "Well, I'll let you get dressed now. Ida set aside some biscuits and bacon for you in the kitchen, if you're hungry."

"Thank you. Yes, ma'am."

Millicent withdrew from the room, leaving Opal to delight in her surroundings in private, and went up to her sewing room where she finished stitching up the seams in a dress she was making. Then she began to monogram a set of linen napkins for a cousin who was getting married in the fall. Concentrating on the small, delicate handwork, she hardly noticed the passage of time until her stomach reminded her that it must be time for dinner. Laying aside the napkin, she trotted down the stairs. She glanced out the front door, standing open to admit any stray bit of breeze that came along, and caught sight of Opal wiping a cloth down the outside of the glass panel beside the door.

As she watched, Opal bent down, picked up a tin bucket and walked across the porch to the bay window of the front parlor. Millicent grimly marched out onto the front porch. "Opal!"

The girl started and turned around. At the sight of Millicent standing there frowning at her, her hands on her hips, Opal's face paled and her hands dug nervously into her skirts. "Miss Hayes? I'm sorry. Did I do something wrong?"

"Wrong? I should say so. What in the world are you doing? You're in no condition to be washing windows and carting heavy buckets around."

Opal's lower lip began to tremble despite her best effort to keep it firm. "But, Miss . . . I thought, last night when you let me stay . . . I figured that meant you were going to let me work for you. Do you want me to leave?"

"No, of course not." Millicent paused and drew a

breath. "I'm sorry. I should have made myself clearer. I want you to live here until you have your baby and get back on your feet and all. But I didn't intend for you to work."

Opal blinked. "You mean—you mean, you're only giving me a place to stay, not a job? But I can't live off of you, without doing anything in return. That wouldn't be right."

Millicent could see the hesitation in the girl's face, the hurt pride, and she remembered what Jonathan had said last night. Opal was too proud to accept charity; she wanted to earn her way. She knew, looking at Opal, that Jonathan had been right, and she moved quickly to amend the situation.

"I am giving you a job. But it isn't wise for you to be lifting things like that bucket."

"Oh, I'm strong, Miss. You'll see."

"You have to think of the baby now," Millicent reminded her. "You don't want to do anything to endanger it. Besides, I have plenty of lighter tasks that you can do. The dusting, for instance. The peas are about ready to be picked, and I'll need help shelling and canning them. After that there'll be okra and squash and tomatoes. Those are the things I'm really going to need help with."

"Oh." Opal absorbed this information, then smiled a little shyly. "All right, Miss, that's what I'll do."

After Millicent went back into the house, Opal stood for a long moment, looking at the doorway where she had been. Opal's chest felt tight and funny, and she wanted to cry. She couldn't remember when anyone had ever worried about her well-being before. Miss Hayes, she thought, must be an angel in earthly disguise. Opal turned and looked out across the yard. That Mr. Lawrence was another one, even if he was as handsome as Lucifer himself. He had treated her with kindness and respect, something she was unaccustomed to from anyone, let alone a man.

Opal ran her hand down the slender column of the porch. It would be a joy to clean this house; it was so lovely and grand. She picked up the bucket and strolled across the veranda, following it as it curled around the corner of the house and back to the rear porch. She poured the soapy water out of the bucket, then put it and the rags away in the small mop closet at the back of the kitchen. Ida was in the kitchen eating, but Opal wasn't hungry, having less than an hour ago devoured the biscuits and bacon.

Instead, she took the feather duster and a dustcloth and went to clean.

She started on the elegant front parlor. Next she did the smaller, less formal parlor across the hall, where she had come out of her faint last night. She dusted the wainscoting and wiped the expanse of the closed mahogany pocket doors with her cloth. Then she pushed the two doors back into their concealed "pocket" in the wall and stepped into the next room, fully expecting it to be another room for entertaining guests.

She stopped with a gasp when she saw that she had inadvertently entered a bedroom and there was a man sitting up in bed, staring at her with amazement. "Oh!

Oh, I'm so sorry, sir. Forgive me. I was just going to dust, and I—" She blushed, mumbling, "I didn't realize you were sleeping. I'll come back later, when you get up."

He gave a short laugh. "You'll wait till the sounding of the Last Trumpet then, if you wait for me to arise."

His words confused Opal, and she simply stared at him.

He patted his legs beneath the quilt. "My legs don't work. I can't get up. I'm a cripple."

Opal's pink face turned crimson as she realized that her mistake had been worse than waking a man trying to take an afternoon nap. She had barged into his bedroom without even a knock and then had caused him embarrassment with her clumsy words. "Oh! I'm terribly sorry, sir." She clutched her skirts, wishing that she could magically disappear. "I didn't know. I—Sister Anne-Marie always did say my mouth moved before my brain did."

To her surprise, he chuckled. "Sister Anne-Marie? Who's Sister Anne-Marie?"

"One of the nuns, sir, at the orphanage. Beg pardon, I haven't even introduced myself. I'm Opal Wilkins. Miss Hayes hired me to help around the house."

"Yes, I know. My sister told me. I'm Alan Hayes, Millicent's brother." He paused. "Obviously she didn't tell you about me."

"No, sir."

"Well, it doesn't matter. Come in." He gestured her toward him. "You'll have to learn to clean around me."

Alan didn't want her to leave. Opal intrigued him.

She had ever since she'd arrived last night. A little while earlier, he'd caught a glimpse of her as she walked past his window on the veranda, but she'd gone by too fast for him to get a good look. It had only increased his curiosity.

Now that he had a chance to study her, he could see that she looked younger than he had expected. He didn't know exactly what he had thought she would look like, but it hadn't been small and delicate, with a complexion as white as a porcelain doll or hair the color of cornsilk. She seemed too awkward and shy, too fragile, to have lived the kind of life she had.

She came further into the room, sliding the doors together behind her. "If you don't mind, I should do the footboard," she began tentatively.

She had big, solemn gray eyes, and from this close Alan could see in them a certain sadness. There were lines of strain around her mouth and eyes. Last night when Millicent had talked about Opal, he had wondered if his sister had been taken in by a clever minx, but now he knew that she hadn't. He doubted that Opal Wilkins knew how to lie.

"Of course, go ahead. You won't bother me." He pretended to return to work on the collection of rocks he had spread across the tray on his lap, but surreptitiously he watched Opal as she wiped the footboard of his bed.

She moved a little awkwardly, hampered by her protruding belly. He wondered how far along she was and felt faintly embarrassed at his thoughts. Alan had rarely been around pregnant women. He couldn't help looking at the curve of her stomach beneath the loose dress even though he was afraid that his interest must be prurient, some licentious remnant from the youth that he had never really gone through.

He made himself focus instead on the collection on the tray. Gradually he began to relax, almost to forget Opal's presence, for she moved quietly. Even when she began to hum a low tune as she wiped off the chest of drawers, he didn't mind.

"Oh, my!" Opal exclaimed, startling Alan out of his contemplation of his newest piece of quartz.

He glanced up, slightly alarmed. "What? What's the matter?"

"These little soldiers!" She was standing beside his table, where he had begun to lay out the battle of Antietam. She bent down to examine them more closely. "They're so cunning. So small—and yet look at all the little things they have on them!"

"They're supposed to be correct down to the last detail."

"Really?" Opal glanced back at him and smiled. "They're wonderful. What do you do with them? Oh, I'm sorry, I'm disturbing you, aren't I?"

"No. It's perfectly all right," Alan replied quickly. "I'm setting them up in battle formation. I'm trying to recreate certain battles of the war. This one is going to be the battle of Antietam. See that large book open on the table? That's one of the maps I'm working from."

"Ain't that something?" Opal wondered admiringly, peering at the map. "I can't make heads nor tails of this. You must be awfully smart."

Alan let out a dry laugh. "No. I've simply spent a lot of time doing this. It's not that difficult to become an expert when you have nothing else to do."

He realized suddenly how self-pitying his remark must seem. Was that usually the way he sounded? Did the bitterness and pity seep into everything he said?

But Opal didn't seem to notice anything because she just smiled knowingly and glanced toward his shelves of books and boxes. "Oh, no, I can't believe that. With all those books sitting there? You have to be smart. I couldn't ever get through that much reading." She shrugged self-consciously. "I never was much good at school."

"I was a terrible student, too," Alan confessed, and his green eyes lit up with amusement. "If my teacher could only see those books, she'd never believe it. I hated to read . . . well, to study anything, actually."

"Honest?" She cast him an astonished look. "I wouldn't have reckoned you were a slackard at school. I bet you could have been anything you wanted. A doctor or a lawyer."

"Those were my father's wishes."

Opal wandered over to the shelves. "What's over here, anyway? What's in all them boxes?"

"A variety of things. I have several collections besides the miniature soldiers. That's the biggest, of course, but I also have various rocks and minerals and—"

He stopped, snapping his fingers as a thought struck him. "Say!" He pushed himself up higher against the pillow, his face suddenly animated. "Do you know what you're named after?"

"Opal?" She looked puzzled. "I'm not sure."

"It is a jewel. A semiprecious stone. Have you ever seen an opal?"

"No."

He grinned. "Good. Bring me that box that's just above your head."

Opal quickly brought it to his bed. Alan took the box and raised its lid. Frowning, he perused the contents, then reached down and plucked out a small stone. Laying it on the palm of his other hand, he held it out to her.

"There. That is an Australian opal."

Opal bent closer to see it, her usual shyness dispelled by her curiosity. There, in the cupped palm of his hand, lay an oval-shaped stone. It was milky white, yet streaked through with iridescent colors that glimmered in a rainbow fire. Opal sucked in her breath. "Ohhh! It's beautiful. How can it be so pale and yet so . . . so flashing with color?"

"It's lovely, isn't it?" Alan gazed down at the opal with her, lost again in the wonder of its beauty.

Opal reached out a finger toward it, then snatched it back guiltily, glancing at him. "I'm sorry."

"That's all right." Her obvious vulnerability touched him, and for the first time in a long while Alan found himself feeling sorry for someone else. "You can touch it. You want to hold it?"

"Could I?" He nodded, and she stretched out her hand, plucking the stone delicately from his palm. She turned a little so that she could get a better light on the gem, and she bent over it, her face rapt with wonder. Alan watched her, surprised to find a kind of delight inside himself at observing her pleasure.

Opal stroked a forefinger across the smoothly polished surface of the stone. "I never realized . . . I reckon my mama must have loved me to name me after something this beautiful."

"I would think so." Injuries came in all sorts, Alan thought as he looked at her. He remembered his own childhood; it had never occurred to him that there was any possibility that either his mother or his father might not love him. He had had fourteen years of a carefree life before his accident; that was almost as many years as Opal had lived. He'd never thought of himself as lucky before.

A little reluctantly Opal laid the stone back in his hand. "Thank you." She smiled at him, her gray eyes aglow. She took the box and set it back on the shelf, then began to dust the shelves.

Alan watched her, the tray on which he'd been working lying forgotten on his lap. When she finished, Opal picked up her cloth and duster and started for the hallway door. She paused in the doorway and turned, bobbing a little curtsey toward him. "Good day, sir. Thank you again."

"No, please, stop calling me 'sir.' Or 'Mr. Hayes.' I expect my father to appear when you do."

She smiled. "All right, s—that is, well, what should I call you?"

"My name is Alan."

She nodded and smiled again and hurried away, as if he might take back what he'd said if she lingered too long. She entered the dining room and attacked the china cabinet with energy, determined to make sure that neither of the Hayeses regretted—ever—taking her in. Why, she'd work so hard, she'd be so good, that they would wonder how they'd ever gotten along without her.

Millicent bent over the tomato plant, searching for a sign of a fat green caterpillar clinging to the stem, looking deceptively like a curled-up leaf. She was in constant warfare with the tomato worms. Her concentration was interrupted by a rude squawk close behind her. She jumped, startled, and turned to frown at a fat, smug mockingbird. The mockingbirds were another one of her enemies. They constantly preyed on her cherry and peach trees. She erected scarecrows in the backyard to scare them off, but the arrogant birds were prone to jeer at the lifeless hats and dresses she hung on the sticks. They even made life miserable for Punjab, swooping down at him with their sharp beaks whenever he was making his slow, majestic way across the yard.

"Shoo!" Millicent said, waving her arms at the mockingbird, but he continued to sit on the mimosa branch, his bright eyes turning from side to side. "Looking for more mischief to get into," Millicent muttered beneath her breath and watched with a jaundiced eye as the gray bird made a lazy flutter to the ground.

Out of the corner of her eye, she noticed a low shape move in the grass, and she turned her head slightly. It was Alan's cat, creeping through the grass on its belly, its gaze fixed unwinkingly on the mockingbird. Millicent had to press her lips together to keep from giggling. The tabby looked like a tiny tiger as it moved noiselessly through the grass. The mockingbird twisted its head from side to side, then began to trill one of its many shrill songs, oblivious to the doom creeping upon him. Then the cat sprang, its legs stretching out, and came down with one white paw on the bird's distinctive scissor tail. The mockingbird's song ended with a squawk, and the bird zoomed upwards. It lit on the rose of Sharon bush and cursed the cat roundly. The cat sat down and began to preen, as though it had had nothing to do with pouncing on a mockingbird a moment earlier.

Millicent began to laugh. She wasn't sure which looked more foolish, the embarrassed cat or the outraged bird. "Kit, you silly animal."

She didn't know when she had stopped calling him "Cat" and had started using the name Alan had given him. Somehow it had just slipped out. The cat cast her a haughty look, then stood and padded over to her to rub up against her skirts. "Ah, looking for some comfort, eh?" She stroked a hand down the cat's back, glad that Alan couldn't see her. He would tease her to death.

"You're getting fat, did you know that?" she asked the cat, scratching behind its ears. He closed his eyes and leaned his chin on her leg, a look of ecstasy on his face. "That's why you didn't catch that silly bird."

Only yesterday evening, she had found Opal sitting on the back steps, surreptitiously giving Kit bits of meat saved from her supper. It was no wonder he was gaining weight. Poor Opal had looked so guilty when Millicent found her that she had had to laugh and confess that she, too, was in the habit of slipping food to the once-stray cat.

Millicent smiled to herself, thinking about it. Opal was a sweet girl. She hadn't regretted for a second taking her in. She was hardworking; the only problem Millicent had with her, in fact, was trying to keep her from working *too* much. Best of all, Alan liked her. Millicent had worried at first that he would dislike this intrusion of another person into their house, and the first day that Opal was there, Millicent had dropped by later to make sure that she hadn't bothered Alan. But Alan had been anything but upset; he had seemed unusually cheerful, and he told her with a grin that Opal's chatter hadn't bothered him, that they talked about his collections and he'd enjoyed it.

Millicent would have hired three new girls if she'd thought they would improve his mood the way this one had. He hadn't sunk into sullenness once this past week. It was funny the way he'd fallen into this quick friendship with Opal when usually he regarded strangers with horror. But Millicent wasn't about to question her good fortune. Alan had even pushed his chair into the informal parlor yesterday, where Opal was darning stockings, and had sat with her while she worked.

Had it been anyone other than Opal, of course, she might have worried that Alan would fall in love with her and break his heart. But thin-faced, pale Opal, with her protruding stomach, was not exactly a siren beauty to whom Alan would be fatally attracted. Nor was Opal the conniving sort to try to win his heart in order to better her position in life.

Millicent returned to her hunt through the tomato plants, creeping forward on her knees and bending every which way to peer all over and under the plants. She had a good crop of tomatoes this year, big and round and still green. They were just right for making her chowchow; she'd have to pick several before she went in and do that tomorrow. The tomatoes left on the vine would ripen into a deep red, and then she would start canning them in earnest. She, Opal, and Ida had already been shelling and canning peas for two days, and tomorrow they would start on the squash. The work went far faster with Opal helping; she was a quick, efficient worker, though Millicent worried about her being on her feet too much. She had seen Opal sitting on the back porch last night, shoes off, rubbing her feet wearily.

Suddenly a shriek split the air. Millicent's head snapped up and she looked around. She could see nothing that had caused the noise, so she jumped up and hurried around to the front of the house. Shading her eyes against the setting sun, she scanned the street. In the next block, two boys were scuffling. As Millicent watched, one of the boys reached back and sent his fist crashing into the other's face.

It was then that Millicent realized that one of the boys was not a boy at all, but was wearing skirts. Not only that, it was the girl who had just punched the boy in the eye. And that girl was Betsy Lawrence!

Nine

Millicent didn't even stop to think as she picked up her skirts and ran across her front yard. She threw open the gate and raced down the street, not caring how she looked to anyone who might have happened to see her. She had been a fast runner as a child, and she hadn't entirely lost the ability. It was fortunate, however, that she had taken off her corset before she went to work in the garden, or she would have fainted before she'd run half the distance.

As it was, she arrived panting but still able to stand upright at the spot where the two children were now rolling on the ground, wrestling, kicking, and swinging at each other, for the most part ineffectually. Reaching down, she hooked both hands into the collar of the one on top, which turned out to be Betsy, and yanked her to her feet. Betsy twisted, still swinging, and her fist slammed into Millicent's hip.

Betsy froze in horror, her mouth open, as she realized what she had done and whom she had just hit. "Oh, no!" she wailed. "Miss Hayes, I'm sorry! I'm sorry! I didn't know it was you."

The boy whom Betsy had been pummeling seized the opportunity to jump to his feet and start to run, but Millicent was too quick for him. One hand lashed out and caught him by the collar as well and jerked him around.

"Jefferson Stillwell! Just where do you think you're going?"

The boy swallowed, shoved his hands in his pockets, and stared at the ground. He had had dealings with Millicent Hayes before, having once been caught trying to tie a can to her cat's tail. It wasn't an experience he cared to repeat.

"I cannot believe such shocking behavior. What would your mother think, Jefferson?"

He knew what she would think, that Miss Hayes was a nosy old busybody; she'd said so the last time. But he didn't dare offer that opinion.

Millicent's question was entirely rhetorical, and she charged on. "Fighting with a girl! Where are your manners? Where is your chivalry? I'm sure your father has taught you better than that."

"She hit me first!" Jefferson retorted hotly, stung by the unfairness of her criticism.

"She is a young lady, and she should be treated as one."

"Well, she doesn't act like one!"

"Agreed, but that doesn't excuse your misconduct. And your parents will hear about it, believe me."

The lad sighed. "Ah, please, Miss Hayes! Papa'll switch me for sure. I didn't mean to do anything wrong.

Honest. What else could I do when she swung at me like that? I think she broke my nose!"

"Nonsense, she hit you in the eye. That's obvious." It was red all around his right eye and already swelling.

"Well, she hit me in the nose, too!"

"That's 'cause you can't fight!" Betsy declared, no sign of repentance in her voice. "You're a sissy, as well as a liar!"

"I ain't a liar!"

"I am not a liar," Millicent corrected. "Now, Jefferson, I suggest that you get yourself home immediately and see to that eye. Then spend some time thinking about the role of a gentleman and exactly how little you resembled one this afternoon."

Millicent released him, and the boy scuffed away. Behind him Millicent rounded on Betsy. "Betsy Lawrence! I cannot believe what I saw! Your behavior was absolutely shocking. Young ladies do not—"

"But he lied! He was saying awful things about Papa! He said Papa was a scalawag and probably a Yankee, too! I couldn't let him say that kind of thing about him!"

"I see." She might have known. Not only had Betsy gotten into a fight, her father had been at the root of the problem. Millicent sighed, her anger giving way to a kind of weary resignation. "What else did he say?"

"He said that Papa had made everyone in town hate him with the lies that he printed in his newspaper. But that's not true! He'd never put a lie in his paper. He wouldn't!"

"I'm sure he wouldn't." Millicent put a hand on her

head, looking down into the girl's defensively set face. "Your father isn't the kind of man who would lie. Nor is he a scalawag, and as far as I know, he isn't even a Yankee. However, he does have a way of saying things in a rather blunt manner in his newspaper, and these things aren't always matters on which everyone agrees with him. In fact, a lot of them are practically guaranteed to make certain people dislike him."

"But, why, if they're the truth?"

"People don't necessarily always want to hear the truth. Sometimes we'd rather keep on believing a comfortable lie."

"Huh? I don't see how that could be." With her outthrust chin and determined expression, Betsy carried a strong resemblance to her father.

"Well, let us say, just suppose now, that everything that Jefferson Stillwell said about your father is true."

"It isn't!"

"Of course not, but let's pretend that it is. So even if it were true, you wouldn't want to hear it about your father, would you? You'd rather be able to go on believing what you already believe about him."

"Oh."

"That's the way most people are. They don't like to read bad things about themselves or the people they know and like, even when they're true. So often they simply assume that whoever said those things must be lying. I imagine that Jefferson has heard his father say that something Mr. Lawrence printed in his newspaper was a lie because it was something he didn't want to be true. Jefferson believed his father, which is only natural," Millicent continued.

"Well, it isn't fair," Betsy said mulishly, her mouth drawn into sullen lines. "And I hate Jefferson Stillwell! If he says it again, I'll punch him again."

"No, you will not," Millicent replied firmly, taking Betsy by the arm and turning her toward home. "We are going to march right home and have a talk with your father about your deplorable behavior this afternoon. You shouldn't even be playing with a boy like Jefferson Stillwell. He's far too rough."

"Rough! Hah!" Betsy sneered. "I could whip him any day of the week. He swings like a girl."

"My dear Betsy, girls don't swing their fists at all. Obviously that's something you haven't learned yet."

"Papa always told me I had to be able to look out for myself, that there wouldn't always be a grown-up around to protect me."

"And I'm sure you need protection, since he also taught you to say whatever misguided thing comes into your head."

Betsy scowled. "Don't you like Papa, either?"

Millicent hesitated. "Like? Well, I don't know; I hadn't thought of it exactly that way." He made her furious. He shocked her. He made her tingle all over when he smiled at her. He touched her heart with his kindness and concern for Opal. "Like, I think, is a rather lukewarm word for the feelings your father inspires in people."

Betsy giggled. "Mr. Hargrove used to say that, too. He owned the newspaper where Papa used to work. Do you know that one time a bunch of men gathered in front of the house, yelling and calling Papa horrible names, and the police had to come and everything?"

Millicent suppressed a smile. "I'm not surprised. And what did your father do on that occasion?"

"He came out on the porch with a shotgun in his hand and he said he'd be happy to de—uh,—debate with any of them anytime, but that his daughter was sleeping, so would they kindly leave? 'Course I wasn't. I woke up and was listening at my window. One of them started ranting and raving and said he bet Miz Elizabeth—that was my mama—was glad she was dead so she wouldn't be humiliated in front of the whole city of Dallas by having a . . . a something Papa said I must never say . . . for a husband. Papa looked so mad, I thought for sure he was going to shoot him."

Millicent's eyes widened expressively. "I see."

"That's when the policeman came, and the men left." She shrugged. "They never came back."

"I'm glad." What a rough-and-tumble life Betsy's father had put her through! No wonder the girl was the way she was. It was all very endearing for Jonathan Lawrence to admit his blame for Betsy's lack of manners, but it didn't really help matters. The fact was, the girl needed a guiding hand—a *firm* guiding hand.

"Why were you playing with Jefferson, anyway?"

Betsy shrugged. "There's nobody else. He's the only child I've met here." Betsy sighed lugubriously. "Emmetsville's an awfully small town."

"It isn't that small. There are plenty of other children."

"Where?"

Millicent thought. Jefferson was one of the few children who lived within a block or two of Betsy's house. But there were plenty of other children who lived within walking distance. But of course Betsy hadn't been able to meet them. It was summer, and school was out, and she couldn't even meet them at church because her father never took her there. Millicent mentally added that to her list of grievances against Betsy's father.

"I'll introduce you to some. I have plenty of cousins, and they have plenty of children. I'm sure there must be one among them that you'd like."

"Really?" Betsy's face brightened.

"Yes, really."

"I know I'd like one of your relatives. Papa said the other day that he thought you and I were 'kindred souls.'"

"Kindred souls!" Millicent stared at the girl. "Whyever would he think that?"

Betsy shrugged. "I don't know. That's just what he said. He said you were feisty like me. That you'd stand up for what you believed in. That's the way he is, too."

"Well, I . . ." Millicent wasn't sure whether to be flattered or insulted. It was nice to hear that someone, even Jonathan Lawrence, thought she stood up for her principles. But to say she was like Betsy! Sweet and endearing as the girl could be, she was also quite pigheaded and quick-tempered, and she didn't know the first thing about proper deportment. "Those are good things to be," Millicent said carefully. "However, it isn't proper for little girls to punch little boys in the eye.

There are better ways of solving your disputes. There are also better ways of expressing your opinions."

"Papa says that, too!" Betsy exclaimed with delight. "He told me that he used to get into fights a lot until he learned that he could make a point better with words on paper. Golly! You two must be a lot alike! No wonder Papa likes you."

"He—he does?"

"Oh, yes. He must. Otherwise he wouldn't have said you and I were alike. 'Cause he likes me a lot. I'm the most important thing in the world to him. He told me so. When Mama died, he told me I was the only thing that kept him from falling apart."

"I see." Millicent didn't know quite what to think. "Well, I'm sure you are very important to your father. And that is why we need to talk to him about your fighting. Immediately."

"Oh." Betsy looked disgruntled, but she went along to her house with Millicent without having to be led. When they reached the Lawrence house and turned in at the gate, she said, "Papa's not home now, you know. He's down at the newspaper office."

"Oh." Millicent checked, nonplussed. She had thought he would be home by now. It seemed to her that Betsy should not be staying with Mrs. Rafferty so much of the time; her father should be with her more. "Well, then I will go to see him there. This is too important a matter to wait. You go on in the house, Betsy, and clean up. Then I suggest you sit down and think about what you did and whether it really helped either you or your father."

"All right." Betsy looked downcast. She turned her gaze up to Millicent's face. "Miss Hayes . . ."

"Yes?"

"Don't you like me anymore? I mean, because I was fighting."

Millicent's face softened. "No. Of course I still like you. You simply made a mistake, that's all. In fact," she added, surprising even herself, "I've missed having you around lately."

"Good. 'Cause I like you, too." She started toward the house, walking away from Millicent, then stopped and turned. "I like you better than anybody, except Papa and my mama. And Admiral."

"My goodness, that's a lot."

"I know." Betsy turned and ran up the steps to the house, calling good-bye back over her shoulder.

Millicent stood for a moment, looking after the girl. Her chest felt warm and funny, and she knew she was smiling like a fool at nothing. But she couldn't seem to stop.

She turned and marched back to her house to get her bonnet and gloves. She was determined that she was going to talk to Jonathan Lawrence right now.

There was a high counter at the front of the newspaper office, and behind that were two desks, with a young man seated at one of them. He was bent over a sheaf of newsprint, scribbling madly, but he glanced up when Millicent walked in.

"Hello, ma'am." He jumped to his feet and came to the counter. "May I help you?"

"I'm here to see Mr. Lawrence."

"Oh. He's back in his office." He nodded toward an open door in the wall behind him. "I'll get him for you."

"That's quite all right." Millicent wasn't about to be put off or stalled, and she was quite sure that Jonathan was capable of either. "I'll go on back."

She slipped through the section of counter that swung back and marched across the small front room to Jonathan's door. He was reading something, a blue pencil in his hand, and his head was propped on his hand, his finger thrust back into his thick hair.

Looking at him like this, there was something faintly vulnerable about Jonathan. But Millicent stiffened herself against giving in to that appeal. She spoke up in a clear, no-nonsense voice, "Mr. Lawrence."

"Why, Miss Hayes!" Jonathan stood up, smiling. "I never expected to see you here. Come in."

"I haven't come on a social visit."

"Mm. Indeed not." His eyes began to twinkle. "I can see by the schoolmarm look on your face. Am I about to receive a lecture? Shall I close the door?"

Millicent glanced at the door. She hadn't thought about that. It would not be exactly proper for her to be alone with him behind a closed door, even in his office, but neither was what she was about to say the sort of thing that an employee should be listening in on. She frowned. "I—yes, I suppose so."

"Uh-oh." He came around from behind the desk and closed the door. "Now. We're safe from prying ears. Please, sit down." He gestured toward a padded leather chair in front of his desk, and Millicent perched stiffly on its edge, her reticule clutched on her knees. Jonathan walked over to the front of the desk and sat casually on its edge, his long legs braced on the floor in front of him. "All right. We might as well get it over with. What sin have I committed now?"

His joking attitude irritated Millicent. "It's very easy for you to jest, Mr. Lawrence, but, personally, I don't find Betsy's future a laughing matter."

"Neither do I, I assure you." He sighed. "So you're here about Betsy? I thought the two of you had reconciled your differences. And I cautioned her not to bother you so much."

"Oh. Is that why she hasn't been by lately? Well. I—that's very thoughtful of you, but I really don't have a problem with Betsy. She can be a sweet child once one gets to know her. I don't mind her coming over to the house sometimes."

A smile spread across his face. "I'm glad to hear that." He paused, looking puzzled. "Then what's the matter?"

"I found Betsy fighting with Jefferson Stillwell this morning."

"Who? Fighting? What about?"

"About you, that's what. That's why I'm here."

"About me!" He looked astonished.

"Yes. Because of those inflammatory articles you write."

"Ah, yes." His brow cleared. "Stillwell. He owns a few of the riverfront shanties. I presume you're talking about his son."

"Yes. Jefferson apparently told Betsy that you

printed lies in your newspaper, and Betsy felt compelled to stand up for you."

A faint smile touched Jonathan's mouth. "Good for her. Betsy's no coward."

"Mr. Lawrence! You can't mean that you're pleased that your daughter gave a boy a black eye!"

Jonathan let out a bark of laughter, then quickly clamped his lips together in an attempt to hide his amusement. "*She* gave *him* a black eye?"

"I might have known that you would have this attitude," Millicent said exasperatedly. She stood up, her back stiff. "It's obvious that it's useless to say anything to you about Betsy's situation. No doubt you'll find her alienation from the entire town of Emmetsville equally amusing."

"No, wait! Don't go. You fire up too easily. I apologize for laughing. Please, sit back down."

"To what point? You find it funny that your daughter takes a swing at someone when she dislikes what he says. Worse than that, you're proud of her."

"But I don't encourage her to fight, at least not with her hands. I've spoken to her about it before."

"You think it doesn't encourage her when you laugh to hear that she's blacked a boy's eye? She's bound to realize that you don't regard it as a serious infraction."

"I don't laugh in front of Betsy. I was talking to you, not her. I wasn't aware that I had to censor my words or my laughter in front of everyone, even adult friends. Or should I not consider you my friend?"

"Well, of course I am. That is, I mean, I hope I am speaking to you in Betsy's and your best interests."

"Precisely what are we talking about?"

"Betsy's conduct! The way she talks and acts. The way she thinks! She isn't like other children. What's worse is that she has no preparation for her future. Why, do you know that she doesn't know how to sew or how to cook even the simplest things? I'm sure she hasn't any idea how to can or preserve or clean a house. How is she going to take care of herself when she grows up? I presume that you don't expect her to have servants to wait on her hand and foot, do you?"

"No. Of course not." Jonathan shook his head, looking at her with appealing masculine helplessness. "But what am I to do? I can't teach her much about any of those things, and since her mother died . . . well, housekeepers aren't that interested in teaching a child things. It's not the same as growing up with a mother, learning to do what she does."

Millicent didn't respond that he should marry and give Betsy a mother, though that was the obvious answer. "It's understandable, of course. But that's not the only problem Betsy has. There's her manner of dress, of course. Her dresses are often too short; she's obviously outgrown many of them. Her stockings are an absolute disgrace. Her hair is rarely braided. Those things, too, are understandable, but really, children notice them, and it will make her stand out when she starts school in the fall. They're all too likely to say something cruel to her or even to cut her out because she's different. And that's only the difference in appearance!"

Jonathan sighed heavily. "I assume there's more."

"Yes. Your newspaper articles and editorials have

offended many people in town. You seem to go out of your way to make yourself unpopular." He started to interject a statement, but Millicent held up her hand peremptorily. "I realize that *you* care nothing about that, but what about your daughter? A child cannot grow up without friends."

"What would you have me do? Suppress the truth? Not publish what I believe? Ignore the wretched state of the property by the river that these upstanding citizens own? Or do you, like the others, think I'm wrong in what I say? That it's all right for Jonas Watson and Frank Stillwell to get enormous returns on their properties by not making basic, necessary repairs, by charging excessive—"

"No," Millicent interrupted. "Of course not. I am obliged to agree with you that the state of that property is a disgrace to Emmetsville and that no one should have to live in that way. It's just that, with Betsy so new in town, couldn't you have given her a little time to make friends and learn to fit in before you set about making enemies out of half the community? And some of the ideas you have instilled in her are so—so unusual." She frowned. "I hate to see her become an outcast among the other children."

"I do, too," he replied, his expression for once grave. "But I can hardly bring her up to think that it's all right to allow other people to get away with misdeeds just so that you will have friends. That isn't what you believe, either, is it?"

"No, of course not!"

"Then what are you proposing I do?"

"Couldn't you temporarily moderate your stand? Couldn't you let her establish a few friendships first?"

"Moderating my stand is just death by degrees. I have nothing against Betsy having friends, but until school begins, it's a little difficult for her to make them."

"Well, she might make some if you ever took her to church!" Millicent snapped.

"You advocate attending church to make friends?" he asked sardonically.

"You twist whatever I say. I simply said that she would have an opportunity to make friends if she attended church. The reason why she *should* go there is so that she won't grow up to be a heathen like—" She stopped abruptly.

"Like her father? Is that what you were going to say?"

"Well . . . yes! It was. How can the child acquire a proper set of values when she never darkens the door of a church? How can she be expected to understand how she should behave? Or what's right or wrong?"

Jonathan's face shut down, and he replied shortly, "I have no desire for Betsy to learn a lot of nonsense."

"Nonsense!" Millicent gaped. He obviously wasn't a very religious person; she had long ago realized that. But she hadn't expected him to be actively opposed to religion.

"What are they going to teach her there?" he asked, rising from his lounging position on his desk and beginning to pace. His voice was laced with anger and bitterness. "That God is fair? And good? I learned long ago, Miss Hayes, that nothing in life is fair, which makes it a little difficult for me to believe that it was created by a fair Being. As for goodness—well, I knew only two truly good people. One of them was the editor who took me under his wing, and he died a painful, lingering death, coughing up his lungs and wasting away. The other one was my wife, who was young and beautiful and had everything in the world to look forward to, and she died, along with my infant son, trying to give birth to him."

For an instant, Millicent thought that she saw the glimmer of tears in Jonathan's eyes, but he turned away too quickly for her to be sure, and when he faced her again, his eyes were as dry as his face was stony. "When Elizabeth died, I said I wouldn't go inside a church again. And I'm certainly not going to send Betsy to something I don't believe in just so I will look better to people."

Millicent didn't know what to say in the face of his intense emotion. She had never dreamed that such sorrow and anger lay behind his not attending church; she had assumed that it was primarily laziness and a lack of moral training. He was wrong; she was certain of that. But she didn't know how to convince him of that, and she had the suspicion that any attempt to do so would only infuriate him. She looked down at her hands.

"I—I'm sorry. Obviously you loved your wife very much."

Jonathan released a long breath. "She was the best thing that ever happened to me," he said quietly. He smiled a little. "You would have liked her. She was everything that I was not. Sweet, good-natured, proper. I don't think I ever heard her say a thing against anyone.

A perfect lady. I'd never known a woman like her before; I certainly never thought I would marry one. When she learned she was going to have another child, I was the happiest man alive. I was hoping for a son this time, to balance it out." His mouth twisted. "Instead I lost her, the baby, everything."

"But you mustn't let it make you so bitter," Millicent put in softly. It created a funny little stab of pain in her chest to hear him, but she refused to think about that. "I don't think she would have wanted you to feel that way. Do you?"

He shrugged, his face still giving nothing away. "She was unfailingly kind and forgiving. Unfortunately, I am not." Jonathan made an impatient move and strode around his desk, flopping down in the chair behind it. "None of this is getting us anywhere regarding Betsy. What is it you want me to do about her? What are you proposing?"

"Well, I think . . ." she started to reply, then hesitated for a moment. Finally she shook her head. "No, it's probably silly."

"What?"

"I—you might not like it."

"Why don't you ask me and see?"

"It occurred to me that perhaps I—I could help Betsy a little."

"How?"

"She has seemed very interested in what I'm doing. I thought I might let her help me. We've started canning some of the vegetables, preserving cherries. She could come to my house and watch us. She could even do some of it herself. I could teach her some things that might help her. I could make suggestions about her hair and—and clothes and manner. She's a bright child and quite interested in everything. I'm sure she could pick up a lot of things rather quickly. Sewing or cooking. She seems interested in such things." Millicent looked at him a little hesitantly. It was an expression he hadn't seen on her face before.

Jonathan studied her for a moment. "I must confess, you've surprised me again. Thank you. That's a very kind and generous offer. I am sure that Betsy would love to visit you, and I have no objection to your teaching her whatever you two care to do."

Millicent smiled, feeling relieved. She hadn't even thought of suggesting this when she arrived at the office, yet somehow, instinctively, she must have wanted to. "Good. Thank you."

"It is I who should be thanking you. This is far more than I could ask of you."

Millicent blushed a little at his thanks. "You're welcome. It won't be a problem. Betsy and I will get along well, I think. And I have a large number of children in my family. I could introduce Betsy to some of them. She might like them."

"I'm sure she would." He reached out and took her hand. "Miss Hayes, you're a godsend."

"Hardly that." His hand on hers made her feel unaccountably silly and giggly. She had the most inappropriate urge to slant a look up at him through her lashes and smile in the way that had always turned Jimmy Saunders to putty.

She backed up, pulling her hand from his, and took a death grip on her skirt. "Well, that's settled, then."

"Yes. I'll tell Betsy this evening." He smiled. "I'm sure she'll be over first thing in the morning."

"Good. I will look forward to seeing her." Strangely enough, Millicent found that she actually meant it. "I, ah, good-bye, then."

"Good-bye." He smiled in a way that sent a frisson of excitement all through her.

Millicent turned and fled his office. Afterwards, she would be filled with embarrassment at her awkward departure. But right then, all she knew was that she had to get away from Jonathan Lawrence before she did something irreparably foolish.

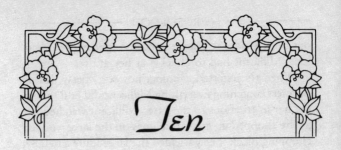

Ten

$\mathcal{M}$illicent wasn't surprised the next morning when Betsy knocked on their front door only moments after they had finished eating breakfast. It was still several minutes before the time Millicent had told her to come, but Betsy must be eager to get started.

Betsy's hands and face were scrubbed clean, and her hair was pulled back into two clumsily woven braids. Millicent was surprised by the sudden impulse she felt to reach out and hug the child to her.

She smiled at the child, unaware of how her features softened, and reached out to take Betsy's hand to lead her along the hall toward the kitchen. "You're right on time," she lied cheerfully. "Let's put an apron on you and get started."

Millicent tied a full-length pinafore-style apron on herself, knowing well how messy this job could be, and wrapped one of her half aprons high around Betsy's chest beneath her arms. Betsy giggled at the way it looked on her and twirled around, holding the apron out on the sides so that it appeared even more ridiculous. Millicent had to chuckle at her antics.

When they started canning, however, Betsy was all business, watching everything Millicent did and following her instructions to the letter. Millicent watched her as she chopped up green tomatoes on the large wooden chopping block. Betsy wielded the large knife carefully, using both hands, her tongue clamped between her lips in concentration. Millicent found that Betsy was quick to catch on, and though her fingers were clumsy and slow on the unfamiliar tasks, she persisted until she was able to do them. Millicent was also surprised to find that it was rather enjoyable teaching someone else to do things. There was excitement in seeing Betsy catch on, and pride in handing down knowledge that she herself had learned from her mother and aunts.

It was a hot day, another in a string of many that summer, and it was even hotter in the kitchen with the stove blazing for the canning. By the time they finished, both Betsy and Millicent were dripping with sweat and exhaust. Millicent had made Opal give up the hot work several hours earlier.

Millicent was too hot and tired to want to eat supper, and after Betsy went home, she dragged up to her room. The only thing that seemed appealing to her was to immerse herself in cool water. She thought with longing of the days many years earlier when she and Alan would go to the pond not far behind their house, and jump in. Their mother scolded Millicent whenever she found out about it, but the summer swims had been worth it. It would be heavenly to jump in that water again, right now. But Millicent never went to the pond anymore, and she certainly wouldn't think of undressing and jumping into it in only her shift.

She unfastened her dress and pulled it off, then peeled her camisole, damp with sweat, away from her body and shook it, fanning her skin. She looked at the door thoughtfully, gnawing at her underlip. It wouldn't be exactly proper, of course, but it was so terribly hot.

Millicent went to the closed door leading into the hallway and turned the key to lock it. She whipped her camisole off over her head and pulled down her petticoat and underdrawers. She stretched, feeling a little guilty at being naked; it wasn't the act of a lady to strip off all her clothes and stand there boldly nude, no matter how hot it was and no matter how alone she was in her own bedroom. What was worse was how wonderful it felt to be naked. A faint breeze stirred the curtains at the windows across the room and she could feel the movement of air against her bare flesh.

She took the wide china washbowl from the washstand and stepped into it carefully. Holding the pitcher of water up, she poured it over her shoulders. It sluiced down her body, both front and back, wonderfully cool. She closed her eyes, luxuriating in the sensual pleasure. It was almost as good as plunging into that pond. The curtains billowed out again, and the breeze blew against her skin, almost cold upon the dampness.

Millicent opened her eyes and glanced in the other direction, toward her image in the mirror. Her figure was still good, she thought. Her waist, reddened and chafed by her dress in the heat, was slender, and her legs were still shapely. Her hips were slightly larger than they had been when she was young, but so were the high, round globes of her breasts. She hadn't begun to sag or wrinkle.

Droplets of water clung to her bare skin. One trickled down her chest and onto her nipple. The brownish pink bud puckered under the cooling touch of the air. Millicent raised her hands to her chest and smoothed them down over her breasts, skimming the last drops of water from them. She paused, her hands cupping her breasts, and gazed at her reflection. Undefined sensations stirred within her, vague and restless, as she stared into the mirror.

Suddenly she came out of her trance with a start. A blush spread up her throat, and she looked quickly away, dropping her hands to her side. What in the world was she doing? Whatever had she been thinking of? The water was refreshing in the hot evening, certainly, but that didn't mean she had to stand there staring at herself. She stepped out of the bowl and grabbed a soft towel, wrapping it around her. She dried off quickly and took out a nightgown and dropped it over her head. It was the coolest one she had, sleeveless, with a scoop neck, and made of snow-white cotton, but even its light touch on her skin felt heavy after the moments of freedom.

She sat down in the rocking chair beside the window and took down her hair. She brushed it out with long strokes, one hundred of them, as she had done every night since she could remember. She rocked and watched the sun sink in blazing red glory over the horizon. There wasn't a cloud in sight.

After sundown Millicent went to bed, but she couldn't sleep. It was too hot, and she was unable to relax, despite her exhaustion. She tossed and turned, and finally, after two long, sleepless hours, she got out of bed. She walked to the window and looked out. The moon had risen. It was huge and round, casting a pale wash of light over the landscape. It was too bright to sleep, she thought. Too hot. She stirred restlessly.

She thought of going down to the back porch. There was something about the hot, humid night that drew her. Suddenly she didn't think she could bear to stay inside another moment. Without bothering to pull on a robe over her cotton nightgown, she slipped out of her room and down the narrow back stairs. She unlatched the screen and went outside, easing the screen door shut behind her so that she wouldn't awaken Alan. On tiptoe she crossed the porch and sat down on the edge, her feet on the step below her. She leaned against the post supporting the small porch roof and gazed up at the bright silvery-white moon.

She heard a faint noise, and she glanced across the yard, mysterious and strangely foreign in the pale moonlight, broken by unfathomable shadows. Something moved in the shadows near the boundary of the Lawrences' property. Millicent jumped, and her heart began to race wildly.

"I'm sorry. It's only me," a man's voice said softly, and a figure detached itself from the shadow of a bush and moved into the light. It was Jonathan Lawrence. "I didn't mean to scare you. I couldn't sleep and was out watching the stars. Then I saw you come out. I didn't say anything; I didn't want to disturb you." He moved closer. "Couldn't you sleep, either?"

Millicent shook her head, unsure of her voice. Her heart was still pounding from the fright, but there was another feeling unsettling her, too.

Jonathan wore trousers and a shirt, but the shirt hung outside his pants and was unbuttoned against the humid heat, revealing a wide swath of browned skin all the way down his chest. Millicent swallowed. She was very aware of the fact that she was sitting there clad in nothing but her nightgown. And it was the middle of the night. It was far too intimate a situation; if anyone knew about it, it would be a scandal.

But no one would know. They were by themselves, wrapped in the hot, secret darkness of night.

A shiver ran through Millicent. She made no effort to move back into the house as Jonathan came nearer, stopping a few feet away and slightly below her in the yard. His eyes were shadowed, his fair hair whitened by the moonlight. His hands were on his hips, fingers spread wide, and Millicent thought how strong they looked, how large. His fingers were long and big-knuckled, the palms wide, and the backs of his hands were ridged by thick tendons. She realized that she was staring at his hands, and her eyes slid back up to his face.

"No, I couldn't sleep," she said, a little breathlessly. "It's too beautiful a night." But his eyes were on her, not the night.

Millicent's hair was out of its usual tight bun and

flowed freely down her shoulders and back like a dark cape. It reached to her hips, a sensuous, silky cloak of femininity. The straight line of her lips had softened; indeed, her whole face had, and her eyes were huge and dark in the moonlight.

"I have thought many things about you since I moved to Emmetsville," he continued in a soft, almost meditative voice. "But this is the first time that 'beautiful' has been one of them. Interesting, yes. Irritating, definitely." He grinned. "Strong of character, even warm—though I think you try your best to keep that hidden. Intriguingly full of undercurrents." He paused. "But why have I never noticed before how very lovely you are? How huge your eyes are. How soft your skin."

His eyes moved downward. She was wearing only a loose white cotton nightgown, and concealing as it was, it hinted of a soft woman's body beneath it, of a night spent wrapped in sweetness and pleasure.

Millicent's breath caught in her throat. She couldn't move, couldn't speak. The air was thick with the scent of the roses growing beside the back porch, heavy and seductive. Millicent felt almost dizzy with it.

"Why have you never married?" Jonathan asked softly.

A heartbeat passed before Millicent replied, trying for light amusement, "Don't you know it's not polite to speculate on the reasons for a woman's lack of popularity?"

Jonathan smiled in his slow way that invited one to smile with him. "I can't believe that you haven't married because you haven't been asked. You're far too pretty for that. So?" he prodded when Millicent didn't answer. "Can you honestly tell me that no one ever pursued you?"

Millicent smiled secretly, not meeting his eyes. "Yes, there were those who pursued me."

"That's what I thought. I bet your dance cards were filled with names," he hazarded, and when her face softened, he was sure that he was correct. Suddenly he could clearly see in her the girl that Millicent had once been, pink-cheeked and laughing, light dancing in her eyes. His voice dropped, rich and intimate. "They flocked to you as if you were honey, didn't they?"

"I didn't exactly have to fight them off."

"No? Only 'cause your daddy was the judge. Am I right?"

A giggle escaped Millicent. "Come on, now, you're exaggerating."

She flashed a glance up at him, and it was at once so flirtatious and young and entirely natural that it almost took his breath away.

"I think not." He came forward, gazing steadily into her eyes. "Why didn't you marry one of those adoring boys, Millicent? What happened?"

"Is it so strange that a woman could choose not to marry?" she retorted sharply. "Why is it that men always presume a woman would like nothing better than to give up her name and subject herself to his whims?"

"I don't think you dislike men. At least, not then. Did someone hurt you? Betray you?"

Millicent rolled her eyes, struggling to pull back on her mask of pinched and cynical spinsterhood. "A very romantic thought, Mr. Lawrence. Perhaps you should write novels, not newspaper articles." He said nothing, just waited, arms crossed. Her gaze shifted from his and finally she said softly, "It was nothing so dramatic, I assure you. I was a starry-eyed girl, full of silly romantic dreams. But such things fall by the wayside when . . . when something important and hard happens. The fact is, my brother Alan met with an accident. He was injured, crippled for life. Not long afterwards, my mother died. She was a delicate woman, and I think her grief over my brother hastened her end. So there were my father and brother, with no one to look after them but me."

"You stayed to take care of them? You gave up a husband, a family of your own? A life of your own?"

"I have a life!" she flared, her eyes lighting with anger. "I have a family."

"Not children out of your own body, created by a man's love for you."

His husky words set up an ache deep in her loins, and Millicent had the awful feeling that she might begin to tremble all over. She clasped her hands tightly together.

"You have no right to judge me, to value my life worthless."

"Not worthless. Never that. But it's the life of a martyr."

"You exaggerate. There was no man whom I really wanted to marry. And I enjoy my life. It's quite full."

"I have no doubt. Full of joyless activity." She glared at him, and he continued, "Tell me, do you really think it's fair that you should have to sacrifice your life because your brother was crippled?"

"I love my brother."

"I don't question that. But what you did was more than love. You've buried yourself alive for him."

"You know nothing about it!" Millicent responded heatedly. "*Some* people believe in doing their duty, in fulfilling their obligations. I love my family, and there's nothing I wouldn't do for them. For Alan."

"I'm sorry; you're confusing me. Which are you talking about, duty or love?"

"Both! A person isn't put on earth only to enjoy himself, to do whatever he pleases, whenever and wherever he likes. Our purpose is to try to understand what is right and do it; it doesn't matter if it's unpleasant or difficult. There's an order to things. There are rules of behavior, no matter what you believe. People have obligations and responsibilities. My brother is my responsibility. What kind of a person would I be if I simply tossed him aside so I could run off and have fun?"

"No one's suggesting that you should have been a selfish, uncaring monster. But don't you think you have an obligation to yourself, too?"

"Do you really think that I could marry someone and walk away, leaving Alan alone in that condition?"

"No. I know you could not; you're far too kindhearted, however much you try to hide that fact from the world with your prickly ways. But it's pretty obvious that the two of you were not left destitute. You have a housekeeper, a gardener. It isn't necessary for you to care for your brother yourself. You could hire someone to look after him."

"To cook and clean for him, of course. Johnny lifts him in and out of bed whenever he needs it. But that isn't the same as caring for him. That wouldn't satisfy a person's need for affection and companionship, for love. Who would talk to Alan and tell him the gossip if I were not here? Who would play chess with him and laugh with him and recall the times when we were young? Who would hold his hand when he feels lonely or weighted down by fate? Or sit at his bedside and worry when he has a fever? Alan couldn't purchase love. Only I can give him that."

"Only you? Are there no other women in this town? Is there no one with a kind heart and a loving nature? Someone that he could be a man with and not just a little brother?"

"Jonathan Lawrence!" Millicent's jaw dropped in shock. "Are you suggesting that Alan marry?"

"It does happen. Is your brother so unlovable?"

"Of course not! He's a wonderful man, intelligent and good and brave. Uncomplaining. But . . . but he's an invalid."

"You mean he's incapable of—"

"Mr. Lawrence, please!" Millicent blushed. "This is hardly an appropriate topic for us to be discussing."

"That's true; it's a matter private to your brother. But I can assure you that there are women who would be happy to love a man without having to share his bed."

"Really! You're being quite . . . vulgar."

Jonathan shrugged. "I've been accused of that before. I prefer to think that I'm honest and realistic."

Millicent could not even imagine thinking of her brother in that way. Such topics were not fit things for a lady to think about, anyway, let alone discuss. "Alan is an invalid," she repeated firmly. "He was still barely more than a child when his legs were crushed, only fourteen. He doesn't know any women other than me and my aunts and cousins. He stays in his room most of the time, and he never leaves the house. He's quite shy and retiring. He is at a loss around strangers, especially women. There's no possibility of his marrying."

"Then you're saying that the two of you are buried in the same coffin."

Millicent came to her feet abruptly. "You are the rudest, most insufferable man I've ever met."

"So you've told me."

"Well, obviously, it didn't sink in. Let me assure you of one thing, Mr. Lawrence. You don't need to feel sorry for me. I am quite happy as I am. And my life is no sacrifice. I have many fulfilling activities."

"Such as?"

"Such as . . ." she spluttered, her mind wildly, willfully blank for an instant, "such as the Garden Club! And my church work. The WCTU. I'm in charge of the boxed supper for the Ladies Missionary Aid Society, and I—" She stopped, furious to see that the obnoxious man was actually laughing. "I'll have you know that my life is full! It has order and structure and—and decency!"

"Tell me something, *Miss* Hayes." His tone made a

mockery out of her title of respect. He moved forward slowly, his hands on his hips, his eyes boring into hers as he said huskily, "Have you ever, in your entire life, done anything spontaneous? Or wild?"

"I should certainly hope not," Millicent retorted, but her voice was shaky. In the heat of their dispute, she had forgotten about the state of her attire, but suddenly, with his eyes on her like that, she remembered all too well that she was standing before him clad in nothing but a light summer nightshift. She could feel the coolness of the cloth against her nipples, suddenly turning hard and pebbly, and the folds of the material as it fell past her thighs. Her blood was racing and hot, but somehow the anger that had made it so had fled, leaving only the pulsing heat behind.

"Haven't you ever done anything for no other reason than that you wanted to?" He was standing at the base of the steps now and his words were little more than a whisper. She was standing only one step above him, and their faces were almost on a level. Millicent could see his eyes, dark and intent; indeed, she could see nothing else at the moment.

Jonathan reached out and slid his finger slowly, lightly down her cheek. Millicent could not stop the tremor that ran through her at his touch. His thumb inched across her bottom lip. "Have you never acted on impulse, out of sheer, uncontrollable desire?"

Millicent closed her eyes. She was weak in the knees, as if she might fold up and fall to the ground, limp as a rag doll. She could not even manage to shake her head in answer.

But she did not need to answer. Jonathan was not listening. His entire focus was on the soft curve of her lip as he traced it, the satin-smooth texture of her skin. He leaned forward and his lips touched hers, gentle and brief, without pressure. Millicent swayed forward, her hands going to his shoulders to steady herself, and her fingers dug unconsciously into his shirt.

He made a growl low in his throat, and then his hands were on her waist, lifting her lightly from the step and pulling her into him, and his mouth pressed deeply into hers. He kissed her long and lingeringly, and he wrapped his arms around her, squeezing her into his hard body. Millicent's breasts were flattened against his chest; her arms wrapped around his neck. She clung to him, trembling, shaken by the storm of feeling that flooded her. She had never known this kind of heat, this desire. She wanted to moan, to cry. She wanted the kiss to last forever. His lips dug into hers, and she kissed him back, wanting only more of his mouth. His arms. His hands.

She could smell him, feel him, taste him. It was as if he surrounded her; she was drowning in him. Yet she wanted more.

Jonathan's skin seared her through the cloth of her gown. His tongue traced the line of her lips, and she gasped, surprised at its touch—and at her own intense response to it. His tongue came into her mouth. Millicent had been kissed a few times when she was younger by some beaux who were more audacious than the others, but she had never known a kiss like this one. It was demanding, possessive—and it was delicious and exciting, bringing up such a tumult of sensations inside her that Millicent felt as if she might explode.

Heat flooded her, racing through her veins and pooling heavily in her loins. She forgot to breathe. She trembled in his arms. Millicent realized that she wanted to feel his hands on her body. She wanted him to touch her bare skin. An ache started between her legs, throbbing and unfulfilled. And she knew that she wanted to feel him *there*.

The thought shocked her. She stiffened and jerked out of his arms, stumbling against the step. She grabbed at the porch post to keep from falling and faced him. Jonathan gazed back at her, his eyes glittering; she could almost feel the heat emanating from him. His hands curled up into fists at his sides, the tendons standing out against the flesh of his arms.

Jonathan had made her own body a stranger to her, awakening urges that she would never have dreamed she could feel. It was exciting, like standing on the threshold to a wonderful new world. But it was also terrifying. For a moment they simply stared at each other. Then Millicent broke away, letting out a small cry, and her hand came up to her mouth, pressing against her lips as though she could hold something inside. She turned and ran back into the house, leaving Jonathan outside.

In the room at the back of the house, Alan lay awake, staring at the ceiling high above him. The back and side windows both stood open, and, as awake as the others on this hot, restless night, he had heard everything that had been said on the back porch. He had heard, too, the muffled sounds as Millicent and Jonathan had come together in a kiss, including the soft noise Millicent had made at the end before she ran back into the house and up the stairs to her room. He did not have to see the scene to know the war that raged inside his sister. It had been clear in every word, every sound.

She wanted the life every woman should have—a loving husband, children, a home of her own. She wanted Jonathan Lawrence. Alan wanted that for her; he loved his sister, and he knew she deserved whatever she desired. But even more desperately, he wanted her not to leave him. The thought of the rest of his life spent in this house by himself stretched bleakly in front of him; he couldn't bear it. Millicent, because of her strong commitment to him and to duty, would not leave him; that was the other force inside her.

Alan hated Jonathan Lawrence at that moment, though he'd never met the man. More than that, Alan hated himself. Only a coward, he thought, would sacrifice his sister for his happiness. And that was what he was.

Hot tears welled in his eyes, and he threw his arm across them. He had grown older all these years, he thought, but he had never become a man. He was a cripple, he knew, and not just his legs.

Eleven

$\mathcal{M}$illicent was humiliated. Safe in the sanctuary of her bedroom, she sat in her rocker, palms pressed against her hot cheeks, and thought about what she'd just done. She was aghast. She had never been kissed that way, never acted that way. Never felt that way! What was happening to her? Was this something that happened to spinsters as they turned thirty? Did these strange, erotic thoughts and sensations bubble up in them until they felt so confused and distraught they didn't know what to do? Millicent had always been in control of her life and herself. Even when she was young and lighthearted, her life a succession of parties, dresses, and girlish chatter, she had been sure of herself and what she should do. She hadn't felt wild and on the verge of losing control. She wouldn't have dreamed of allowing a man to take such liberties with her—much less enjoy it so!

Millicent squeezed her eyes tightly together, wishing that she could block out the image of Jonathan kissing her, his body hot and hard against hers. She shivered again just at the thought of his lips on hers, his tongue invading her mouth. Even now it made her go hot and weak. Despite the shame she felt at her improper behavior, she couldn't deny that there was also a thrumming excitement inside her, or that her heart hammered wildly. She knew that she would delight in having his kiss again, right now.

She felt as if she were standing on the threshold of some dark, deep secret place, that beyond her lay the mysteries of womanhood, of passion, love, and men. It was a world cut off from her by fate, at once frightening and intriguing, a bubbling cauldron of heated emotions and sensations unknown to her, and curiously living inside her, as well. She wanted to cry. She wanted to laugh. She wanted to flop back on the bed and shriek out her frustration.

Millicent spent a long, wakeful night. Her mind ran on relentlessly, trying to bring some order and rationality to what had happened. She couldn't understand herself, and that fact disturbed her more than the turmoil of her emotions.

Nor could she understand Jonathan Lawrence. Why had he taken her in his arms and kissed her so fervently? She was too old and faded, surely, for him to be interested in her. She would be foolish to let that kiss mean anything. The whole incident had been disturbing, but all she could do was put it behind her. There simply was no place in her life for quivering desire or a handsome blond man with a devil-may-care smile. It was impossible; nothing could, nothing *would* happen between them. A lady didn't have such feelings; a lady didn't act that way. That moment with Jonathan on the back porch had been a temporary aberration, that was all.

The only problem, unfortunately, was that Millicent found it difficult to banish the kiss from her mind. She thought about it when Betsy came over to help with the canning. She thought about it when she saw Jonathan leaving or entering his house. She thought about it at night when she was going to sleep and her wayward mind was floating aimlessly where it wanted to. She thought about it when she should have been working on the boxed supper charity for the church. She thought about it, in fact, until she thought she would go mad.

The annual boxed supper took place the following Saturday. Millicent had, with her usual efficiency, made the arrangements ahead of time, but she had to call on several of the flightier of the young women to make sure that they remembered their commitment. Few of them were in any danger of forgetting; it was a social event that they looked forward to with great hope and excitement. It exasperated Millicent that most of the young women considered it only a social event and seemed both unknowledgeable and unconcerned about the charity for which they were raising money.

On Saturday afternoon she sat at a table she had had set up in the park not far from the bandstand and collected the boxed suppers from the girls who had made them. As each one gave Millicent her elaborately decorated box, Millicent checked her name off the list in front of her. One of her cousins on her mother's side,

Hannah Redfield, sat with her, fanning herself desultorily against the heat, and chatting between the arrival of boxes. Millicent would have preferred to have had Susan helping her, but Susan was showing too much nowadays for her to go to something as public as this supper. She rarely even came to family functions now.

Others stopped by to chat and move on. Millicent and Hannah knew almost everyone in their church—or, for that matter, in the whole town—by name. One of Millicent's cousins sat down for a few minutes to talk breathlessly, mostly about her fiancé and their wedding this fall. But when she saw Aunt Oradelle bearing down upon them like a steamship, her timid stepdaughter Camilla in her wake, she murmured "Un-oh," under her breath and quickly escaped.

Millicent would have liked to do the same, but she was trapped at the table. She was grateful that Hannah didn't disappear, also.

"Honestly, Millicent, I can't imagine what you think you're doing!" Aunt Oradelle said crossly in place of a greeting and sat down with a thump on the stool beside the table. "It's a disgrace!"

Guiltily Millicent's mind flew to the other night with Jonathan Lawrence, and a blush crept up her neck into her face. How in the world could her aunt have found out about that! Then she realized that, of course, her aunt could not have known. She was talking about something else.

Millicent drew a breath and responded calmly, "Good evening, Aunt Oradelle. How are you?"

"How am I?" Oradelle repeated, her massive bosom

quivering with indignation. "How should I be, with the stories I'm hearing about you buzzing around this town? You're everyone's favorite topic of conversation this afternoon."

"Oh, surely not," Hannah protested lazily. "People always love to find fault, but no one could have handled the church's boxed supper social better than Cousin Millicent."

Aunt Oradelle fixed Hannah with a piercing look. "I was not referring to the boxed supper, as you well know, Hannah Connally Redfield."

Millicent sighed inwardly. Her aunt was even more upset than she had imagined; it always meant she was blowing at a full gale when she started calling people by their full names.

Having taken care of Hannah's impudence, the matriarch of the Hayes family turned her sights once more on her primary target. "I'm talking about the foolishness going on at your house, Millicent. I couldn't believe it when Bertie told me what you'd done."

"What?"

"Don't play the innocent with me, young lady. You know exactly what." She lowered her voice, leaning secretively closer. "Hiring that trashy girl, that's what. Ruby or whatever her name is."

"Opal. Her name is Opal Wilkins."

"Opal. Ruby. What does it matter? The point is," her voice sank to a piercing whisper, "she's in a family way!"

"Yes, I know." Millicent laid down her pencil and folded her hands together calmly, facing her aunt.

Aunt Oradelle's face flushed with anger. Calm in the

face of her disapproval was something she could not abide. Hysterics, fear, even defiance, all confirmed her control over the family, but that coolness on Millicent's face was as good as telling her that her opinion didn't matter.

"Yes, you know! That's all you have to say for yourself? Yes, you know?"

"Well, Aunt Oradelle," Millicent responded calmly, "what else am I supposed to say? I realize Opal's condition, but there's nothing I can do about it."

"There most certainly is, and it'd behoove you to do it this instant. Get rid of the girl!"

Millicent's mouth tightened. She had been determined not to let her aunt get her goat tonight, as she so routinely did, but it was difficult to hang onto the calm demeanor she had decided to adopt.

"No," she said shortly.

"No?" Aunt Oradelle's eyes bulged alarmingly.

"Now, Mrs. Holloway," Hannah tried to soothe the older woman. "There's no need to get your dander up."

"I never 'get my dander up,' to use your vulgar expression." Oradelle Holloway cast a contemptuous look at Hannah. Hannah was not her concern, thank goodness; she came from the Connally side of the family, and everyone knew that the Connallys were often too lax in their upbringing. But Millicent was another matter; she was a Hayes and fell under Oradelle's domain. "I am simply expressing my disappointment. I never thought Millicent would be so careless of the family name."

Millicent clenched her jaw, then forced herself to relax it. She picked up the straw mat fan in front of her and began to fan her face slowly. "I haven't been careless of the Hayes name, Aunt Oradelle."

"I don't know what else you'd call it, when you've set the whole town gossiping by hiring some poor white trash girl from God knows where and installing her right in your house. Why, what about your poor brother? If you won't think about the rest of us, won't you consider him?"

"Alan likes Opal, just as I do."

"Of course he likes her!" Oradelle opened her own black lace fan with a snap and proceeded to flutter it beneath her chin in a quick tempo to match her nerves. "He's a man, after all. What else can you expect? That's precisely the problem. He may come to like her altogether too much."

"I don't think there's any need to worry about that. Opal would never try to—"

"Oh, pish-posh." Aunt Oradelle dismissed Millicent's opinion with an airy wave of her fan. "A lot a young girl like you knows of life. That's exactly what she would try to do, a girl like that."

"A girl like what?" Millicent snapped, stung out of her calm. "There's nothing wrong with Opal." Her aunt cast her a speaking look. "There's not! You're judging her without knowing the least thing about her! It isn't her fault that she's pregnant!"

Aunt Oradelle gasped, and both Hannah and Camilla, sitting silently behind her stepmother, looked shocked. "Millicent Anne Hayes! A little propriety, please!"

"I'm sorry." Millicent knew it was an indelicate thing

to say; she had been shocked when Jonathan had bluntly said the same thing. Still, that was what Opal was, after all. It seemed far simpler to say it, as Jonathan had, instead of beating about the bush with vaguer terms, when everyone knew that was what you meant.

"I don't know what's come over you." Aunt Oradelle sounded as if her niece had suddenly developed a hopeless, baffling illness.

"Oh, I think I do," said an arch voice behind Millicent. She whirled around. Rebecca Connally!

"What are you doing, Rebecca? Eavesdropping again?" Hannah asked scornfully.

"Why, no, sister dear," Rebecca replied in a silken voice, gliding up to stand beside their table. She was a vision in pink, and she held a lacy parasol, resting it against her shoulder and twirling it now and then in a coquettish manner, even though it was almost sunset and there was little danger from the sun's rays even for her fair skin. Millicent knew that Rebecca simply liked to use it as a frame for her pretty face. "I was coming over to pay my respects to Mrs. Holloway, and I happened to overhear what you-all were saying. Of course, I suspected what you were discussing; everyone's talking about it tonight."

Aunt Oradelle's eyes narrowed. "Talking about what?" she asked Rebecca coldly. Oradelle felt that she had a perfect right, of course, to chastise her niece, but she wasn't about to let outsiders say anything derogatory about a member of her family. And Rebecca Connally, connected to Alan and Millicent on their mother's side and only by marriage, at that, was definitely an outsider.

"Why, Millicent and that handsome new man," Rebecca responded. "Jonathan Lawrence? You know, the one who bought the *Sentinel?*"

"I am aware of who he is. I fail to see any connection between that odious troublemaker and my niece."

"You mean you didn't know that he had moved in next door to Millicent?"

"Of course I knew that. Everyone does."

"Or that Millicent has practically adopted his little girl?" Rebecca glanced at Millicent, her eyes malicious, but more than a little curious, as well. "I've heard she's over at Millicent's house all the time these days."

"Alan enjoys her company. She takes his mind off things," Millicent commented stiffly. She hoped she didn't look as guilty as she felt. What if any of these women knew what had happened on the back porch the other night? That would really make a scandal.

"Well, people are saying that you have other reasons—that you're hoping her daddy will make you officially her mama."

"What utter nonsense!" Aunt Oradelle put in crisply. "Rebecca, you always did have more hair than wit."

Rebecca's eyes widened, and she sucked in an indignant breath, but Oradelle plowed ahead ruthlessly, not giving her a chance to speak. "However, that's what gossips feed upon, credulous and foolish people like yourself. I do hope that you've had the sense not to spread the story around outside the family, at least. It is so easy to get a reputation as a jealous person."

"Jealous!" Rebecca's outraged look said clearly that the last person she would be jealous of was Millicent Hayes.

"Oh, yes." Aunt Oradelle looked at Rebecca significantly. "Folks have long memories."

Hannah didn't bother to hide her chuckle, and a pink flush rose in Rebecca's cheeks. All of them knew that Oradelle was reminding Rebecca that Millicent had been more popular than she until Alan's accident, that she hadn't really achieved the distinction of being the most popular girl in Emmetsville so much as taken it by default.

Aunt Oradelle's tactic worked. "Of course I wouldn't think of repeating rumors about one of my own family," Rebecca stated coldly, rising from the seat she had just taken. "I simply thought Millicent should know what people are saying about her. She ought to be more careful about what she does. As you pointed out, it's terribly easy to get a reputation."

With that, she turned and stalked off, her back rigid. Hannah turned to Mrs. Holloway with a chuckle, part amusement and part admiration. "I think that's the fastest I ever saw anybody get rid of Rebecca Ordway." Rebecca's husband was Hannah's brother, and it was well known among their families that the women of the Connally family disliked Rebecca heartily.

Oradelle sniffed. "That little snippet. I've known her since she was a baby, and I don't believe I've ever heard a good word from her about anybody." But Rebecca's interruption wasn't about to distract Aunt Oradelle from her mission. She swung back to Millicent, raising a forefinger in admonition. "But you best let that be a lesson to you, missy. People gossip, and you are laying yourself open for it. You think I haven't heard about you taking Mr. Lawrence's girl under your wing?"

"Aunt Oradelle, honestly!" Millicent slapped her stiff fan down on the table in exasperation. "You'd think I'd brought Betsy in to live with me, the way everybody talks! The child is lonely and comes by the house all the time. She amuses Alan, and she's one of the few people he likes to see. What am I supposed to do, tell the poor little motherless thing to get out?"

"Motherless—that's the point. Her father's a widower and living right next door to you. He's a fine-looking man, but not necessarily a gentleman, by any means, or he wouldn't keep writing those inflammatory articles. He's no respecter of persons, that's obvious. I don't think he's the sort that a lady should see."

"I don't 'see' him. I hardly know the man. All I've done is allow his daughter to help me can some squash and tomatoes! Surely that isn't a crime."

"No. But it gives people ideas."

"I'm not responsible for their ideas!"

Oradelle's eyebrows vaulted up at this heresy. "A lady," she said firmly, punctuating her words with little jabs in the air with her folded fan, "does nothing which could give rise to the wrong ideas about her."

Millicent ground her teeth together. Aunt Oradelle usually justified her opinions with sweeping pronouncements of what a lady should or shouldn't do. Millicent found the habit even more irritating today than usual. However, she knew from long experience that it was worse than useless to argue with her aunt. The best one could do was simply let Aunt Oradelle run out of steam or hope that she would be distracted by some other subject.

"This . . . this *menagerie* of people you've taken under your wing is bound to give rise to speculation. What is a man to think when you start mothering his daughter except that you are interested in him? And when you've taken loose women into your house, what's he to think except that you're loose, too? I tell you, Millicent, you are dangerously encouraging unwelcome advances from this man."

"Maybe they aren't unwelcome," Hannah teased, flashing a smile at her cousin. "I've seen Jonathan Lawrence, and he's wickedly handsome."

Red washed up Millicent's face. Her cousin, in teasing, had hit dangerously close to the truth. If only she knew exactly *how* welcome Millicent had found Jonathan's advances the other night, she would be shocked, Millicent was sure. Everyone thought that she was a model of propriety. No one would suspect the licentious yearnings that had bubbled up in her. Certainly Millicent herself had never suspected that they existed until she'd met Jonathan.

"Wicked is right," Aunt Oradelle put in emphatically. "No man should be that good-looking. It's positively indecent. Especially for a widower with a child to raise."

Millicent wasn't sure what Jonathan's wife's dying

had to do with his looks, but she knew it was better not to ask. At least it had sent Aunt Oradelle chasing off after another topic, that of Jonathan Lawrence's short-comings, instead of her own niece's failings.

Millicent relaxed in her chair, picking up her fan again and wafting it languidly, while she half listened to her aunt and Hannah discuss Jonathan Lawrence, his looks, and the stir created by his newspaper's editorials. She glanced out across the park. Tad Barnhill, who had agreed to do the auctioneering this year, had arrived and was up on the bandstand. In front and to one side of the stand were several young women, talking to each other and giggling, frequently glancing around the park with great interest. They were the girls who had pre-pared the boxed suppers that would be auctioned off; Millicent was sure they were checking to see if the young men they hoped would buy their suppers had arrived yet.

With a pang, Millicent remembered standing in just that way, Susan and Polly beside her, trying to conceal her nerves with bright chatter, all the while wondering who would bid on her box and how high the bidding would go. It seemed absurd now, the way she had wor-ried whether some young man would bid more for Re-becca Ordway's boxed supper than another boy did for hers. She wouldn't go back to that age for anything; she had no desire to experience once more the trembles and terrors, the pounding pulse, the heart leaping into her throat. And yet . . . she couldn't help but feel a sort of wistful nostalgia for that time, as well. How easy and simple everything had seemed then, how clear. One just waited and flirted, and one day a man would come along and sweep one off one's feet, and then would come marriage and children and a happy life, as surely as night followed day.

It was a dream world, of course, and she had been a child, selfish and unknowing. But there were moments, like now, when she looked at those fresh young girls, bright as daisies in their pastel dresses, and she couldn't stop the ache inside her chest for what she had once been and for the dreams that had died when Alan went tumbling from the top of the wagon.

"Speak of the devil," Hannah said in a suddenly lowered voice that drew Millicent's attention. Hannah reached out and tapped Aunt Oradelle on the wrist with her fan. "Here he comes now."

"Who?" Oradelle, interrupted from her long monologue regarding all the reasons the *Sentinel* was wrong, blinked in confusion.

"Jonathan Lawrence, that's who," Hannah hissed. "He's behind you, coming straight toward us!"

"What?" Millicent couldn't keep herself from turning her head. Sure enough, there was her next-door neighbor, strolling across the grass toward the table where they sat. He smiled at her and tipped his hat in greeting.

"Miss Hayes," he said as he drew near.

"Mr. Lawrence." Millicent jumped to her feet. She hadn't seen him face to face since the night he had kissed her, and she was seized by confusion and embarrassment. "I, uh—it's nice to see you." Why did he have to walk up and speak to her right now, right here? What would her aunt and cousin think, after what they'd been discussing? "Ah—may I introduce my aunt to you? This is Mrs. Elmer Holloway, my father's sister. And, uh, Mrs. Richard Redfield, my cousin. Aunt Oradelle, Cousin Hannah, do you know Jonathan Lawrence?"

"No, I'm afraid I haven't had the pleasure," Hannah said, extending a hand toward Jonathan. "How do you do, Mr. Lawrence?"

Aunt Oradelle gave him a frosty nod. Millicent could see from the amused twinkle that sprang into Jonathan's eyes that he knew precisely how her aunt regarded him. She hoped he would attribute it to his articles and editorials and not guess that her aunt viewed him as a rake intent on seducing her innocent niece.

"Well, ladies, are you enjoying the picnic? Looks like you have quite a few boxes to sell." He nodded toward the table where the boxes sat.

"Yes, we have a good turnout," Millicent said primly, putting herself in her proper role as organizer of the event.

"Are you here to purchase a boxed supper, Mr. Lawrence?" Hannah asked with a lift of one eyebrow.

Jonathan chuckled. "No. I'm afraid I'm here to get the facts for an article for Saturday's edition."

"Don't you have reporters for that sort of thing, young man?" Aunt Oradelle's tone strongly suggested that it would be beneath the dignity of a proper gentleman to report on a social event.

"Yes, ma'am." The corners of his wide mouth turned up in that mischievous way of his that managed to suggest, no matter what the occasion, that Jonathan had inside knowledge of some magnificently wicked fun. "Unfortunately, I've found that only the owner has to work on Saturday evenings."

Aunt Oradelle made a noncommittal noise that could have been a grunt or a sound of approval. It was her usual response when she couldn't come up with a retort.

Jonathan turned from her to Millicent. "I understand that you're in charge of this."

"Yes, I suppose I am. It isn't a terribly difficult thing."

"I'm sure you are being too modest."

"Of course she is," Hannah agreed, and Millicent glared at her cousin.

"Excuse me," Millicent interrupted. "I have to take these boxes to the bandstand." She stepped around Jonathan and began to pick up several of the suppers.

"Allow me to help you." Jonathan reached out to take the boxes she had piled up. His fingers grazed hers as he took the boxes from her, and a tingling warmth curled through Millicent's abdomen.

"Thank you." Millicent tried to appear nonchalant, but she was afraid Jonathan could see the faint trembling in her fingers as she added a few more boxes to the ones in his arms. She scooped up several of the suppers herself and turned, managing to avoid looking at Jonathan.

She set out toward the bandstand, walking as quickly as she dared on the slightly uneven ground. Jonathan fell into step beside her. Really! Why did he have to pick this moment to be gentlemanly? After what Aunt Oradelle and Rebecca had told her, the last thing she needed was for half the church to see them together at the supper. Now the tongues would really be flying.

She didn't know how to act around him. Between what had happened between them the other night and the gossip that was circulating about them, she was too embarrassed to talk to him or to even look at him. What if the wild sensations she had experienced when he kissed her showed in her face whenever she looked at him? What if everyone could tell what had happened just by seeing them together? What if he could see how much he disturbed her tranquillity? Millicent was uncomfortable and uncertain, and as always when she felt that way, she was irritable and sharp.

"Which of these lovely concoctions is yours?" Jonathan asked lightly, indicating the decorated boxes he carried.

Millicent glanced at him, forgetting, in her astonishment, to be embarrassed. Was he joking? "None, of course."

"You mean, you bully those other women into making these elaborate boxes of food, and then you don't contribute?" He tsk-tsked mockingly, shaking his head. "Really, Miss Hayes."

He must be making fun of her, she decided. Surely it was obvious even to a man that an old maid offering a boxed supper would be holding herself up to ridicule. Coldly she said, "It would hardly be appropriate, Mr. Lawrence. It is an event in which young women participate. I'm afraid my boxed supper days ended long ago."

They had reached the bandstand, and Millicent set her load down on the table and turned to go back for the remainder of the boxes. Tears stung her eyes, but she blinked them away exasperatedly. She was *not* going to allow Jonathan Lawrence's jesting to hurt her feelings.

"Miss Hayes!" Millicent heard his voice behind her, but she strode on determinedly. "Miss Hayes, wait."

Jonathan had had several more boxes to put down, and it had taken him longer to get rid of his burden, but he caught up with her and clamped his hand around her arm, pulling Millicent to a halt.

Millicent whirled around. "I beg your pardon!" She cast a fulminating look at his hold on her arm, and he dropped it.

"Millicent, please. I'm sorry. Did I offend you? Truly, I didn't mean to."

His voice sounded sincere. Millicent gazed up into his face. A puzzled frown creased his brow, and his golden-brown eyes were clear and concerned. He saw her wavering, and he pressed his case, "Please. Tell me what I did, what I said. I didn't mean to upset you. I was simply making conversation. What did I do to make you stomp off like that?"

"Oh, don't be obtuse!" Millicent snapped, exasperated. "I was attempting to close the topic without having to get into embarrassing explanations."

"I'd rather be embarrassed than uninformed. Now, would you please tell me why you were angry?"

"I wasn't angry. I was hurt," Millicent admitted.

"Hurt? But, why? I don't understand. What did I say?"

"You were joking about the suppers and my having one of them, when everyone knows I'm far past doing that. I don't like being ridiculed," she finished in a rush and turned to go.

Once again he took her arm, holding her there. "Just a minute. You're too quick out of the chute. I assure you, I was not ridiculing you. I simply asked you which supper was yours; I assumed since you were in charge of this that you had contributed a supper as well. Why wouldn't you?"

"Really, Mr. Lawrence!" Millicent's cheeks blazed with color. "This is a charitable function, but it's part of courtship, as well. It's a way for a young man to single out a young woman as—as the object of his affection. It's for marriageable girls, not old maids."

"That's what you consider yourself?"

"Of course it is. What else would I consider myself?"

Jonathan gazed at her for a moment, nonplussed. "I—I don't know. It obviously wasn't that apparent to me."

Millicent swept him with a look of scorn. "Are you telling me that you thought I was one of them?" She nodded toward the knot of giggling young women in front of the bandstand. "Honestly?"

A grin spread across Jonathan's face. "Of course not. You have far too much sense. But neither would I have characterized you as 'old' or 'unmarriageable.'" His eyes took on a twinkle. "At least, given a husband who doesn't dislike a few thorns among his roses."

Millicent's pulse sped up. Was Jonathan Lawrence flirting with her? No. That was absurd. She hadn't flirted with anyone for years. Even if he had kissed her the other night, it hadn't meant that he was interested in her in any but the most basic way. She hadn't thought for a moment that he was going to court her, to come calling or flirt with her in public. No matter what he said, anyone could see that she was past her prime. Couldn't they? Jonathan couldn't mean that he found her attractive or that he was interested in her. Could he?

She found that the palms of her hands had begun to sweat, and surreptitiously she wiped them against her skirt. "Mr. Lawrence, I really don't see the purpose of this conversation."

"Must every conversation have a purpose?" he countered. "Can't one simply talk to you because one enjoys it?"

"I'm not sure what you find enjoyable about our conversations, given the fact that we usually wind up arguing."

Jonathan chuckled. "I like a little spice in my conversations. Don't you? It's like gorging on cake icing to talk to one of those dewy-eyed maidens over there for long." He nodded toward the girls who had donated the boxed suppers. "Personally, I'd rather spend my greenbacks on a meal that will give me an hour's worth of entertaining conversation rather than an hour's worth of simpers and giggles and 'I declare's.' "

He rolled his eyes so comically as he affected a young girl's speech that Millicent had to laugh. "Perhaps we should have set up a category of boxed suppers for men such as yourself, then." She paused, then added teasingly, "Are there any such creatures?"

Jonathan pressed a hand to his heart. "You wound me." Then he grinned. "Perhaps you are right."

Later Millicent realized that she should have foreseen what would happen, given what he had said, but at the moment she did not. She simply felt lighthearted, even happy, as Jonathan walked with her back to the table and helped carry over the last load of suppers to the bandstand. Afterwards, he asked her a few reporterly questions about the supper and the charity to which the money went, and they parted.

Before long the auction started, and Millicent, sitting at her table with a small strongbox before her, happily took the young men's money when they won a bid for a box, and jotted down the price beside the corresponding young woman's name on her sheet. The auctioneer, a jovial man, made several joking comments to people in the crowd in front of the bandstand, ribbing this man for his parsimony or that one about which box he wanted to buy. Millicent paid little attention to him until she heard him call out the name Jonathan Lawrence. Then her head snapped up and she looked at the people gathered there. Jonathan was standing toward the front and to one side, grinning up at the auctioneer, his arms crossed across his chest.

"Come on," Tad was coaxing. "You haven't bid on a single box all evening, Mr. Lawrence."

"Ah, but you haven't had the one box I'm interested

in bidding for," Jonathan replied, his smile stretching wider.

Millicent laid down her pen, her interest thoroughly captured. Whose boxed supper was he interested in? She leaned forward, craning her neck to see what boxes remained on the table behind Tad. There were only three. One she recognized as the gaudy creation that Beulah Dorsey had brought; surely Jonathan wasn't hoping to acquire Beulah's company. For that matter, why would he want any of the three? What had happened to his fine words earlier this evening, when he'd claimed he wouldn't want to have to listen to any of the simpering girls who had donated boxes? Of course he hadn't meant what he'd said; that was just like a man. He had simply been flattering her. And she, like a fool, had fallen for it.

Her eyes went to the girls beside the bandstand, narrowing as she tried to make out the features of the small, pale girl beside Beulah. Who was she?

"Well, now, and which one is that, Mr. Lawrence?" Tad went on, making a gesture toward the table where the boxes sat. "There are three mighty fine meals here, I bet, and three mighty pretty girls to share them with."

"I'm sure that's true. But, unfortunately, there is no contribution there tonight from this particular young lady."

Barnhill's eyebrows rose. "No? Are you telling us you're set on somebody who ain't here tonight? Why don't you pick another one? You won't regret it."

"She's here tonight, all right," Jonathan went on.

"She simply didn't see fit to put her picnic supper up there."

By now everyone in the crowd was staring at him curiously, wondering who he could be talking about. A cold lump began to form in the pit of Millicent's stomach. He couldn't mean . . . no, he couldn't be talking about . . .

"Well, now, who might that be?" Tad asked, leaning forward. "I reckon she'd be happy to bring her own supper basket up here right now if you was to make a bid."

"Is that right?" Jonathan reached into his pocket and pulled out a gold coin. "Well, let's see, shall we? I'll offer twenty dollars, gold, for Miss Millicent Hayes's supper."

Twelve

$\mathcal{J}$onathan turned and looked straight at Millicent, a challenge written clearly on his face. Millicent stared back at him, dumbfounded. A ripple of gasps ran through the crowd. Twenty dollars was far more than had been paid all evening for any of the baskets—in gold coin, too! And for Millicent Hayes, whom everyone knew had been an avowed spinster for years!

Almost as one, everyone in the park turned to gawk at Millicent. Heat flooded up her neck and into her face. She felt as if a thousand eyes were watching her. She'd never been so embarrassed in her life. She thought about crawling under the table, or jumping up and fleeing from the park. Or perhaps simply putting her head down and bursting into tears.

But none of those things were real possibilities. Not for Millicent Hayes. After all, she had a position in the community; she had to retain whatever shred of dignity she had left after Jonathan had publicly embarrassed her.

She rose slowly, her legs trembling beneath her. She

made herself bend down and pick up the wicker basket she had filled with a small supper for herself for this evening. She refused to think about the thoughts that must be going through everyone's heads, the speculations about her and Jonathan that would be made, then enlarged upon. With feet like lead, she started to walk toward the bandstand. She would be calm, she thought; she would be so cool and above-it-all that no one could think anything wrong about her or about Jonathan's presumptuous offer.

Millicent held the basket up to Tad, saying in a clear, steady voice, "Of course, Mr. Barnhill. If Mr. Lawrence wants to pay twenty dollars for a few deviled eggs and some biscuits, I'll be happy to let him have it."

Then she turned and walked away, keeping her pace even and her back straight. She refused to look as if she was running away. She sank on her chair and stared down at her hands, clenched tightly together in her lap. "Is everyone still staring?" she whispered to Hannah.

"No. It's fine. Cousin Millicent! Why didn't you tell me about this?" Hannah leaned forward across the table, her voice low and throbbing with curiosity. "Why didn't you tell me Mr. Lawrence has an interest in you?"

Millicent's head snapped up. Hannah's eyes were gleaming, and she smiled broadly. Aunt Oradelle, on the other hand, was gaping at her in shock.

"He doesn't have an interest in me! He did it to annoy me. He's the most obnoxious man I ever met."

"Why would he pay twenty dollars to be obnoxious?" Hannah countered reasonably. "Anybody can be that for free."

"Miss Hayes." Jonathan came up to the table, carrying her wicker basket, a smile on his face.

"What?" Millicent snapped, scowling at him.

"I believe it's customary for the person who made the meal to sit with the one who bought it."

"Oh!" Millicent jumped to her feet and swept around the table. She stalked past Jonathan and walked quickly through the park, avoiding the places where other people were gathered, although she retained enough of her calm not to go completely out of their sight. She could imagine how that would set the tongues wagging!

She stopped beneath a tree and whirled to face him. "How could you do that to me?" she demanded.

Jonathan shrugged innocently. "Do what? Pay an exorbitant amount of money to your charity for a meal that didn't even have one of those adorable pink bows and lace decorations on it?" His eyes danced as he set the basket on the ground and flopped down beside it.

Millicent glared at him. "You know exactly what. Don't try to squirm out of it by being clever. You embarrassed me in front of practically everyone I know."

"Embarrassed you! What's embarrassing about receiving the highest fee for your supper when it wasn't even entered in the auction? It seems quite a compliment to me. I would have thought you'd have been pleased. Proud, even."

Millicent felt foolish looming over Jonathan as they talked, so she sat down and primly curled her legs under her, making sure that her skirt covered her legs down to her high-top boots. "My aunt told me that she'd heard gossip about us because Betsy visits me. There's nothing this town loves like gossip. Tonight you added fuel to the fire by paying that ridiculous sum for my basket, and for absolutely no reason. It'll be all over town tomorrow. We won't either one be able to walk down the street without people starting to whisper. Don't you care?"

He shrugged. "Should I? If I let my life be ruled by what others said about me, I'd have been out of a job long ago. The only person I have to be responsible to is me, and as long as I can look at myself in the morning while I shave without being ashamed, then I don't worry."

"Well, perhaps *you* don't care about what other people think. Perhaps *you* can make your way through life gloriously alone and indifferent to opinion. But what about me? What you did affected me, too. Why did you do it?"

He paused, considering her question. "I'm not sure. I think because my mind kept running over what we talked about earlier, and I thought what a silly and antiquated notion it is that a woman is an 'old maid' simply because she doesn't marry by the time she's twenty. Why should a woman have to jump into marriage the first time she's asked, or even the second or the third? Or ever? Some women are far more beautiful and interesting at thirty-five or forty than most silly girls of seventeen. Why should they retire into the shadows because they haven't married? And why should a man have only immature girls to choose from?"

Millicent looked at him oddly. "That's simply the way things are."

"But why? And why do things have to remain the way they have been? I meant what I said: I'd far prefer having a conversation with you to sitting with a simpering young girl for an hour. You're an attractive woman; any man would enjoy looking at you. Logically, you should be sought after as a dinner companion. The only reason your boxed supper wasn't up there was because of this outmoded social custom of banishing an unmarried woman to the back rooms after a certain age."

"Really, Mr. Lawrence, don't you think you're getting carried away? I have hardly been banished to the back rooms. As you pointed out yourself, I organized this whole event."

He made an airy gesture. "I was speaking figuratively, not literally. What I meant was that you were taught that you should blend into the walls if you remained a spinster, that you should become part of the furniture. You should no longer wear bright or pastel colors, but should transform yourself into some sort of plain brown sparrow of a woman. It's an idiotic convention."

"A woman doesn't wish to make a fool of herself by pretending to be younger than she is," Millicent countered stiffly.

"Why pretend to be older? Or more rigid? You know, I think there's more to you than you want anyone to guess. You pretend to be all sternness and propriety."

"Pretend? Really, Mr. Lawrence, I think you're being absurd. I believe it was you who told me I—"

"And it was you—" he plowed on determinedly,

"—who let a question-asking, troublemaking ten-year-old girl tag around after her despite the fact that the girl is lacking in social graces and has a disruptive mutt of a dog and a shocking father. It was you who took in a poor, friendless young woman whom any 'proper' woman would have sent off immediately to a home for wayward girls. Those were acts of kindness and charity, not propriety. They show a good heart, no matter how many layers of lace and crinoline you try to smother it in. They also show, I think, a disregard for social convention. There's far too much independence in you ever to be really happy living by other people's rules."

"You seem to know a remarkable amount about me for someone who's talked to me only three or four times."

"It doesn't take a long time to penetrate some disguises. What I can't figure out is why you wear it."

"I am hardly disguised. I am what you see."

"I don't think so." He paused, then smiled. "But I do think that you believe that. You've tried very hard to *be* what you appear. Fortunately, I don't think you've been quite successful."

"Really, Mr. Lawrence. You're talking utter nonsense."

Jonathan shrugged. "Perhaps." He opened the wicker basket and peered inside it. "Hum. You weren't jesting about the few deviled eggs, were you?"

"Of course not. I was planning to feed only myself tonight. I'm sure you'll be quite hungry."

He looked up at her, his eyes dancing with mirth. "Oh, please, you mustn't be concerned about me."

"You know I'm not."

"Why, Millicent, you wound me," he mocked and popped a deviled egg into his mouth. "Mmm. Delicious. I can see that the quality of your food will make up for the lack of quantity."

"I don't recall giving you permission to address me by my first name," Millicent responded frostily, struggling to retain a hold on her anger and not give in to his teasing charm.

Jonathan gazed at her for a moment, not saying anything, and a slow smile, laden with sensuality, spread across his face. His eyes turned dark and warm with meaning. Millicent knew that he was thinking about their kiss the other evening. She felt heat creeping up into her face, but she wasn't sure whether it was a blush of embarrassment or the flush of desire. "My," he said slowly, licking the last bit of deviled egg from his fingers, "we're very formal tonight, aren't we?"

"Jonathan . . . " She began almost pleadingly, then realized that she had just used his given name and stopped, embarrassed.

He chuckled. "See how easily it comes out?"

She was positive she was blushing now. Millicent looked away. "I'm sorry. I wasn't thinking." He was right; his name came easily to her tongue. Too easily. She was afraid it bespoke how often she thought of him—and on what intimate terms.

"There's no need to apologize. I don't mind. I like to hear you say my name. I like to say yours. Don't you think we're familiar enough with each other to drop the formal address?"

Millicent looked at him. His golden eyes were serious now. Her mind went to the other night on her back porch. She could taste his lips on hers again, feel the searing heat of his skin. Yes, they were familiar with each other, familiar in a way that she had never been with any man.

Her eyes dropped. "I—I suppose we are."

"Good." She heard him rustling around in the basket again, and he held out a deviled egg toward her. "Won't you have some of your own food? It's delicious."

"Thank you." Millicent took the half egg from his fingertips, and her fingers grazed his in passing. She hated how trembly it made her feel. Lord, she hoped that she was not going to make an utter fool of herself over this man. She was sure that many women before her had.

She ate the egg in quick, dainty bites, not in the least bit hungry for it, but not knowing what else to do with it. She had never met anyone who could put her in such a turmoil as Jonathan Lawrence.

He lay on his side, reclining on one elbow in the grass, and made a production of searching through her basket again. Millicent watched him through her lowered lashes.

"There isn't *that* little there," she snapped finally, her mouth twisting with irritation.

He glanced up at her innocently. "Did I say anything?"

"You didn't have to."

Jonathan grinned. "My dear Millicent, I believe you

must feel a trifle guilty about foisting this basket on me."

"I didn't foist it on you! It never occurred to me that you would be foolish enough to purchase it—and for that price!"

"I've always had my head turned easily by a pretty woman." He fished another half of an egg out of the basket and popped it in his mouth.

"Do you enjoy being irritating?"

His eyes twinkled as he grinned at her. "Actually, I have to admit to feeling a certain wicked enjoyment in watching you fire up. It makes your eyes uncommonly blue."

Millicent glared. "I am not taken in by flattery."

"Flattery? It isn't flattery if it's the truth. Do you always slap down compliments that way?"

"I don't know what game you think you're playing, but I can assure you that I do not wish to participate in it."

"You're a damned prickly woman, Millicent Hayes. Has anyone ever told you that? No, I doubt they'd dare. However, it's the truth. You see insults and slights where there are only compliments, treachery and games in a simple attempt to make conversation. I merely wanted to spend a little time in your company, to talk with you, yet you persist in thinking that I have some kind of devious motive."

"It doesn't make sense."

"What doesn't?"

Millicent waved her hand vaguely. "All this. Your

buying my basket. Our sitting here together. The things you say. I don't understand you."

"It isn't hard." He gazed at her soberly. "I am not as devious or subtle as you think. I bought your basket for the reasons I told you. And one other—I wanted an excuse to spend time alone with you. It's not hard to understand; it's the same reason any man buys a lady's boxed supper. He wants her company."

Millicent's breath caught in her throat. "I am past the age of believing in fairy tales," she managed to say, but her voice shook on the words.

Jonathan grimaced. "There you go again. Do you really find it that hard to believe that a man might wish to have your company? That he might find you attractive?"

"I am almost thirty years old. I'm a spinster."

"You hold your spinsterhood in front of you like a shield. What are you afraid of?"

"I'm not afraid of anything," Millicent retorted scornfully.

"No?"

"No."

"Then why do you try so hard to convince yourself and everyone else that you are plain? Why do you dress like an old woman in dark, dull clothes and yank your hair back into a tight knot? You looked beautiful the other day, you know, with your hair down."

Millicent glanced at him; she couldn't keep from doing so, though she knew even as she did that it wasn't wise. Jonathan was gazing at her with those slumberous pale brown eyes, and his mouth was heavy with sensuality. Her chest tightened. All she could think about was their kiss. She could almost smell the roses beside the porch, almost feel his arms sliding around her again.

This man was dangerous. Millicent looked down at her skirt, pleating it between her fingers in an effort to still the trembling in her hands. She could not let him do this to her. She was too old, too wise, too calm. "I hardly think that's an appropriate thing to discuss," she told him shakily.

"Perhaps not. But I'm often accused of being inappropriate."

"I can imagine."

"I'm also accused of being persistent," he went on in the same low, steady voice. Millicent suspected that he would go on until he got the response he wanted out of her. "Cynical retorts rarely deter me; neither do other people's standards of conduct."

"I don't understand why you're doing this," Millicent said in a rush, avoiding his eyes.

"Doing what?"

"You know what. Saying these things, doing what you did the other night—"

"You mean when I kissed you?"

Millicent nodded, her face flaming with embarrassment.

"I kissed you because you were beautiful. Because I wanted you. I suppose I'm here now, saying these things, for the same reasons."

"This is absurd," Millicent protested breathlessly. She felt as if her nerves were sizzling all through her body. Every muscle in her body was clenched tightly, as if she struggled against something, though she wasn't sure what it was.

"Absurd?" Jonathan's voice sounded puzzled. "It's absurd that a man wants you? Surely you have been the object of other men's desire."

"That was long ago. It's over. I am not the foolish girl I once was." Millicent started to get up, to move away from him, but Jonathan reached out and encircled her wrist with one hand, holding her in place.

"Is that what you're afraid of? The girl you once were? Is that what you're denying in yourself?"

"I am denying nothing!" Millicent retorted fiercely, scowling at him. "Except your crazy accusations! I don't understand what you're doing. Are you trying to make a jest of me?"

"No." His clear eyes gazed straight into hers; Millicent could feel them almost like a physical touch. "Never that."

"Then what? Do you think that I'm an easy conquest because I'm a spinster? That I am so panicky at the approach of age that I would let you sweet-talk me into—" She stopped, spluttering, unable to think of a genteel way to express it.

"Making love?" he suggested bluntly. Then he sighed and sat up, releasing her wrist. "No, I don't have any wicked designs on your virtue. I am not in the habit of luring unsuspecting females into sin. I won't deny, though, that I have desires and impulses like any other man. Nor will I deny that I felt desire for you the other night. That I could easily feel it again." He looked at her. "Isn't that the way it usually is between a man and a woman?"

"I wouldn't know," Millicent replied shakily. "I haven't had much experience in that area."

"I'm sure not, the way you run from it."

"Jonathan, honestly . . ." She forced herself to look him in the eye. "I am not a loose woman . . ."

"I never said you were," he cut in. "But I do know that you are passionate, however much you may try to hide it. I felt it in your body. I tasted it on my lips."

His low words sent tingles of desire through her. She could feel the heat rising up her throat. She glanced around them a little furtively. It seemed to her as if everyone must know what they were talking about, must see the intensity of Jonathan's eyes and feel the heat emanating from him.

"Jonathan, please, you mustn't talk like this. It's not fit."

"Why not?"

She stared at him. "Are you serious? We're in the middle of all these people and, why, it's still daylight."

Jonathan chuckled. "They can't hear us. And is what a man and woman feel for each other something that can only be talked about in the dark? I'll admit, I wouldn't mind being alone with you in the nighttime. It's something that could be arranged."

"Jonathan! Really! It's not appropriate to talk about anytime. And I certainly don't plan to 'arrange' anything with you, at night or any other time. You must have a poor opinion of me, indeed, if you think that I would agree to some sort of clandestine meeting."

"I never expected you to. And my opinion of you is not poor. I have the highest regard for your morals, your abilities, your face, your form." His voice softened on the last few words. "Millicent, I enjoy teasing you. I enjoy watching the sparkle come into your eyes and the pink into your cheeks. But I'm being serious now. I like you. I have no idea what, if anything, might ever happen between us. I don't know if I will ever love another woman or marry again." He grinned. "I don't know if you and I could be together for longer than five minutes without fighting. But I do know that I enjoy your company. I want to see you, to be around you. I think we should find out what might happen with us. Why not let things take their natural course? I'd like to dance with you at a party. Sit with you at an ice cream social."

Millicent simply looked at him, unable to speak. Was he really serious? Was he talking about courting her?

"I suppose I'm asking permission to come calling on you," he went on. "What would you say, Millicent?"

Millicent drew in a sharp breath. She looked away. Her heart wanted to say yes. She wanted to sit with him on the front porch or in the parlor and talk. She wanted to hear his laughter and his voice, to watch the expressions move across his face. It would be heavenly to step onto a dance floor in his arms or to go for a walk with him in the cool of the evening. Heavenly, but dangerous.

She could so easily lose her heart to him. From the first time she saw him, she had tried to fight her attraction to him. But Millicent knew that deep inside she was drawn to him. She had trembled with desire when he kissed her. And no matter how much she squabbled with him or disapproved of what he did, it didn't change the excitement that rose in her when he was around, the warm rosy glow that permeated her body when he smiled at her. It would be easy for her to be foolish where he was concerned. And what would happen to her if she lost her heart to him?

Millicent knew the answer to that. She would be miserable. For, whatever Jonathan might think, she knew that there could be no future for them. He might enjoy her company, might even desire her, but she couldn't imagine that he would actually want to *marry* her. It was absurd.

Even if he did crazily want to marry her, it wasn't a possibility for Millicent. She couldn't abandon her brother and her duty just because she had met a man whose heavy-lidded eyes sent heat rippling through her. It would not be as easy to give up Jonathan as it had been to give up her former beaux; for whatever reason, he aroused feelings and sensations in her that were far stronger than anything she had ever felt before.

Her strong, elemental desire shamed her; she couldn't imagine how she could have suddenly developed the low, even primitive, appetite. It was not what a lady should feel. She was sure that none of the ladies she knew experienced such passions. And Millicent was determined that she would not allow her finer instincts to be overmastered by her base desires. She would do what everyone, including herself, expected of her; she would look after Alan.

The bizarre feelings that Jonathan awoke in her were not love, she told herself. However, she was afraid that they would turn into that or that it would hurt just as much to refuse them as to rip love for him out of her heart. She could not afford to grow close to him. She could not let things develop naturally between them, as he suggested. It would be risking too much. Of course, Jonathan couldn't be expected to understand that. He would not be at the same risk.

"Well, Millicent?" he prodded, reaching out and turning her chin up so that she had to look into his eyes. "Will you let me come calling?"

"Jonathan, this is silly. We're far too old to be engaging in such things."

His eyebrows rose in amusement. "Too old? To be attracted to a member of the opposite sex? Not I, my dear, and I think not you, either."

"Everyone would talk." Millicent grasped at the first excuse she could think of. After all, she could hardly tell him that she was afraid of feeling too much for him, of falling in love and being left with a broken heart.

"No doubt," he agreed cheerfully. "I don't know of anyone whom gossip has killed yet."

"It wouldn't hurt you," Millicent agreed tartly, pulling her chin out of the grasp of his thumb and forefinger. "It is always the female who suffers. I am the one who would be a laughingstock."

"For keeping company with me? My dear Millicent, you wound my pride."

Millicent grimaced. "They would say I was making a

fool of myself, setting my cap after such an obviously marriageable widower."

"I hadn't realized that the people of Emmetsville held me in such high regard."

Millicent rolled her eyes. "Such false modesty. Surely you must realize how handsome you are."

He smiled. "It's much nicer hearing you say so."

"I'm simply stating the obvious," Millicent retorted freezingly. "A handsome, unmarried man, owner of the town's newspaper—of course you would be considered eligible. Far more so than I would be. They would say I was riding for a fall, and 'mark my words, that Millicent Hayes'll get her come-uppance shortly.'"

"Are you that tied to the opinion of a few small-minded, small-town gossips? What other people might say about you is more important to you than how you feel or what you want? I would have thought you were made of sterner stuff."

"As I told you before, it's easy enough for a man to say that," Millicent snapped back at him. "It's the woman who's held up to ridicule or shame. It's I who would have to face my family and everyone else in this town, knowing that they were all whispering about me behind my back. What does a woman have except her reputation?"

"Happiness?" Jonathan suggested, lying back on the grass, his hands crossed behind his head, looking at her. "Laughter? Love?" Millicent said nothing, just looked away, chewing nervously on her bottom lip. "You know," he continued in a more gentle voice, "I'm hardly asking you to throw your reputation to the winds and become my mistress. Nor am I asking you to make a fool of yourself over me."

"I know." Millicent's voice was low. She felt close to tears. There was no way she could explain to him the dilemma she was in, how much she wanted to see him yet knew that ultimately they were doomed. He would only present her with a dozen more arguments to prove that she was wrong. And her pride would not let her reveal how frightened she was of losing her heart to him. "Jonathan, please . . . I know I'm making the right decision. It would be far better if you didn't come calling on me. It's easier to end this now, quickly and cleanly."

"End 'this'? End what? Nothing's happened between us." He sounded angry, and Millicent couldn't bring herself to look him in the eyes. She felt miserably sure that he would dislike her now and that she would probably cry her eyes out over it tonight alone in her room. But what else could she do? She could not forsake her duty, could not forget her promise to her father and Alan and God Himself. She had sworn to take care of Alan, and she could not let even Jonathan Lawrence sway her from that oath.

Finally, when she said nothing, Jonathan sighed and rose to his feet. "All right, Millicent. I'll leave you alone. I won't importune you any more. And I hope that you will be happy with your safe position in society. You know what you remind me of? Rapunzel, locked in her tower. Except that it was the witch who trapped her there, whereas you are the one who's imprisoned yourself, with your own fear."

Jonathan turned and strode rapidly away from her.

Thirteen

Alan was sitting up in his bed when Opal came in to clean his room. A frown pinched his forehead, and there was an almost petulant set to his mouth. Opal smiled cheerily at him, but he merely grunted in reply. Opal hesitated. First Millicent had been decidedly silent and irritable yesterday evening after the boxed supper, and now Alan seemed to be angry. She wondered a little fearfully if she had done something to offend them.

"I'm sorry," she said softly. "Did I come at a bad time? Would you like for me to leave? I can return later."

"No, it isn't you. Come in, Opal; don't mind me." Alan sighed, and his mouth twitched in irritation. "It's that da—darn Johnny. I rang the bell for him at least ten minutes ago, and he still hasn't put in an appearance. I wanted to get up and sit in my chair; there's some work I need to do at the table. Where could he be? How could it take any human being ten minutes to walk in here from the back yard?"

"He isn't in the yard. Ida sent him down to the grocer's to get a sack of flour. And he was going to stop by the post office and mail something for Miss Millicent, too. It'll probably be a while before he gets back."

"Wonderful." Alan's mouth settled into a sullen line. He turned his face away, not wishing Opal to see him this way. "I'm sorry. You must think I'm a thoroughly spoiled, selfish man to expect everyone to be at my beck and call all the time."

"No. Of course I don't!" Opal went to the side of his bed. "Truly. You're not spoiled or selfish, either one. It must be awfully hard to have to wait for someone just because you want to get out of bed. It'd be enough to make anybody out of sorts."

Alan managed a small smile. "Thank you. I can always count on you to give me the benefit of the doubt. More than I deserve, I imagine."

"Maybe I could help you get up," Opal suggested. "I'm pretty strong, you know, a lot stronger than I look."

Alan looked horrified. "I should say not! In your condition? It's out of the question. Why, even if you weren't—ah, in that condition, you wouldn't be able to support me." He didn't add that Johnny did more than help him; he literally picked Alan up and sat him down in the chair, as one would a child. That was too embarrassing to admit to Opal. "It's all right. Don't worry. I'll simply wait till Johnny returns home. It won't be that long."

"Well, if you're sure . . ." Opal hesitated. "But I could help you. Honest." She turned away and began to dust.

Alan watched her as she went around the room,

quickly and efficiently wiping her rag over the surfaces of the furniture, even bending down to clean the front and sides of the chest of drawers and the legs of his bed. He frowned. "Are you sure you should be doing that kind of work? It seems a bit difficult to me. I mean, for someone who's, well, you know, expecting."

Opal straightened up, using the bedpost to help her rise from her bent position, and cast a smile toward him. "Lord, no, it ain't hard. The fact is, it's way too easy. I feel like I'm cheating you and your sister."

"Oh, no," Alan interrupted hastily. "Don't think that. You're a great help to Millicent, I'm sure."

"I can't think why," Opal replied frankly. "But I'm awful glad she's been kind to me. And you, too."

Alan glanced down, embarrassed by her gratitude. It didn't seem to him that either he or his sister had done that much for Opal. He didn't think she should be working at all in her condition. She should have a husband who pampered and cosseted her. She was so sweet and pretty, so fragile, and such a kind, warm-hearted person, too.

Opal turned away again to work, then hesitated, and swiveled back slowly. "I was thinking . . . I hope you won't think me too bold or anything. . . ."

"Of course not," Alan assured her when she paused again. "What is it?"

"Well, one of the homes that the orphanage gave me to, there was a man in it, an uncle, and he'd been wounded in the war when he was young. Anyway, both his legs had been amputated right above the knee. He had this contraption rigged up from the ceiling so that he could pull himself in and out of his bed." She stopped, searching Alan's face for his reaction.

Alan looked at her for a moment. Strangely, at her words, he'd felt a cold sensation, almost like fear, steal through his torso. But that was silly. What was there to be afraid of? "Contraption?" he said finally. "What do you mean?"

Encouraged by his question, Opal came closer. "Well, he was an independent ole cuss, see, and he hated having his nephews or his sister's husband help him in and out of bed. He had this chair by his bed where he could sit and look out the window, and he'd sit there practically the whole day, whittling. He had his brother-in-law hang a piece of knotted rope from the ceiling above his bed. He'd reach out and grab it, and he'd kind of scoot across the bed and swing out of it, using the rope, and he'd sit down right in this chair. He did it every day. 'Course they had to lower the bed so the chair wouldn't be so much below the bed. They sawed off the bottoms of the bedposts."

"I see." Alan paused. He wasn't sure what to say. "And you think I should try the same thing?"

"Oh, I'm not saying you *should*. But I know you don't like having to wait for Johnny to come. I reckoned you didn't like feeling, you know, like you had to depend on someone else."

She was certainly right about that. He hated it. But he had always looked upon it as something he had to put up with. He had never thought of it as something he could change.

He had been very sick after his accident; it had almost cost him his life, not just the use of his legs. For the year or two after that, he had continued to be weak, catching every cold that came his way, it seemed. From the first, Johnny had lifted him out of his bed and put him back in it, taking care of him like a baby. Millicent and his mother had babied him, too, always hurrying to fetch whatever he asked for or to bring him something they thought might please or entertain him. They had spoiled him unmercifully; he supposed that Millicent still did. And he had tried to accept his lot in life and not rail and complain about it, to live with the fact that he was an invalid, not capable of doing for himself.

"But I—" He tried to smile to mask his humiliation. "I am not a strong person. The accident left me weak. It's unlikely that I would have the strength required to lift this dead weight in and out of bed.

"Oh. I'm sorry. I guess it's just that I don't ever think of you as being in delicate health." A blush began to spread over her face. "You look fine, you know, but I should have realized. I didn't think." She turned away in embarrassment.

Alan found that he didn't want Opal to think of him as sickly. One of the main reasons he had liked her was that she didn't treat him as an invalid, but as a man. She hadn't pitied him or talked down to him, hadn't acted as if he were still a child, which Millicent and his other relatives were prone to do. With Opal, he hadn't felt so much like a freak or so useless. Why, she had looked up to him, thinking that he was smart and kind. Now, he thought, with a sense of dread, she would realize that he wasn't anyone special; he was just a bedridden man who was too weak to take care of himself, a man who had to depend on others to do everything for him. She would see him as he was, just a cripple.

Opal left the room quietly. Alan leaned his head back against the heavy headboard of his bed and closed his eyes. He ached inside, ached in a way he'd never known before. It wasn't bitterness or sadness or even the familiar despairing desire to do any of the things he had once done. He didn't want to be the boy he had been. All he wanted was to be able to act like a man.

It was some time before Johnny came silently into the room, interrupting Alan's somber thoughts. "Mr. Alan," he said, coming around the side of the bed.

Johnny was tall and as thin as a knife edge, but Alan knew that his slender frame was deceptive; he was capable of lifting Alan bodily from the bed. He moved slowly. Yet Alan remembered when they had been boys that Johnny had been able to run like the wind. Alan had never been able to catch him. Everything about Johnny was at odds. His quiet voice and slow, almost dull-witted manner of talking contrasted sharply with the frequent humor and insight that lay hidden in his words.

"Johnny," Alan said, looking up at him, "would you tell me something? Truthfully?"

Johnny's smooth brown face didn't move a muscle. "Tell you something? Why, sure, I tell you. You worrying about something?"

Alan shook his head. "No. It's just—how weak do you think I am? I mean, if I had something rigged up to hang from the ceiling, could I pull myself up with it? Or would it be too much for me?"

Johnny gazed at Alan for a moment, then looked up at the ceiling. After another long pause, he turned his head back to Alan. "What you mean, rigged up? How we going to do it?"

"I'm not sure. But if we did, would I be able to pull myself up with it and swing over into a chair?"

Johnny blinked at him. He glanced at the wheeled chair sitting a little distance from the bed. "What you want to do that for? I help you."

"Yes, but I don't want to be helped. That's my point." Alan grimaced. "All I want to know is, could I do it? Am I too weak?"

Again the unwinking stare was fixed on him for a long moment. "You mean, is your arms strong enough? Can you pull yourself up by something?" He frowned, shaking his head a little. "Now, that I don't rightly know. You was always a strong one when you was little but your muscles been lazy too long. I think they pretty weak. I ain't sure you could haul yourself out of this bed that way. Leastways right now."

Alan slumped. It was the answer he had been expecting.

"Only . . ." Johnny began slowly.

"Yes?" Alan prodded. "Only what?"

"Well, strength, that's something you can get back. That's what I think. It ain't like using your money and it's gone. If you was to work at it, you be able to do it 'fore too long."

Alan brightened. "Work at it how? What could I do?"

Johnny looked blank. "Well, now, I don't rightly know. I never thought much about it." He paused. "Lifting something? Something small-like, but heavy, like a rock, or a brick."

"Yes. I could start out with a small one and get bigger stones as I get stronger." *If* I get stronger.

Alan wasn't at all sure he could do it. After all, he hadn't done any kind of physical activity in ten years. On the other hand, he didn't think he could bear to have Opal think of him as weak and useless. But if he failed he would have to face that fact. He could still taste the shame he had felt when he had had to admit to Opal that he was too weak to do the things that other men could; the last thing he wanted was to have to own that shame for the rest of his life.

Alan drew a shaky breath. He couldn't remember the last time he had taken a risk. Well, really, the last time had been when he was cavorting on the side of that wagon and had fallen off. A final, disastrous risk.

He thought of Opal's wide gray eyes and the way they had shone with admiration as he explained something to her. There were times, he thought, when not risking was even more foolhardy. More painful.

Throughout the rest of the afternoon, after Johnny had lifted him into his chair and wheeled him over to the table, Alan's mind kept returning to the possibility of strengthening his arms. It wasn't as if he had no strength. After all, he had used them all these years to push the wheels of his chair; they weren't entirely unaccustomed to work.

And why would his arms be weak just because his legs had been mangled? There really wasn't any reason for him to be a complete invalid, he thought. His health had been good before the accident, and though he had been a mere stripling of a lad, he had possessed a certain wiry strength. He had chopped wood, ridden horses, climbed trees. He had been a good swimmer, the fastest boy he knew at crossing the pond.

If he had started lifting himself in and out of bed from the very first this probably wouldn't be that difficult for him. His muscles would have grown in strength, not decreased. Why hadn't he tried? Why hadn't anyone made him try?

He thought of his parents' and Millicent's love and how they had wrapped him in it, doing everything for him, trying to make up to him for the fate that had been dealt him. It had been so easy, so pleasant, so comforting for him in his loss and turmoil. They had made his world safe. And that had been what he wanted. But now—now he found that he felt smothered.

It would be wonderful to be able to haul himself in and out of bed. It would be a way of recapturing some measure of independence. He felt a heady sense of freedom at the thought of it.

He could begin, he thought, by taking down a couple of his books and lifting them up and down. If he did that often enough each day, he would be able to at least see if it increased his strength or aggravated his ill health. Alan rolled his chair across the room to the bookshelves and picked up the long-handled clamp that Millicent had ordered for him through the mail. He raised it to the third shelf up and maneuvered it until he could clamp it around a book. Then he pulled the book out and brought it down to his lap. He did it several more times until he found two books that seemed to weigh approximately the same and were a size he thought he could handle.

He began to lift the books up and down, over and over again, until his arms ached. He sat for a moment resting, wondering how he would ever manage to strengthen his arms enough, when he heard a young, bright voice behind him.

"Hi! What are you doing?" Betsy was kneeling on the veranda outside his window, her folded arms propped on the windowsill.

"I'm not sure at the moment. What I'm trying to do is exercise my arms."

"Why? How?"

Alan smiled. They were Betsy's two favorite questions. "I—" He hesitated, reluctant to reveal what he was doing to anyone. Something inside him wanted to hide his effort until he found out whether or not it worked. But Betsy was too curious a child to give up without an answer. "Well, I'm conducting an experiment with these books."

"An experiment? Really?" Betsy leaned closer, her eyes growing big with interest.

"Yes. I want to find out if I can make my arms stronger."

Betsy frowned, wrinkling her nose. "But how can you tell that from books?"

"I'm going to use them. See, they're easy to hold, and they're heavy. If I lift them for a while, my arms should get stronger, and then I can try lifting heavier books and so on."

"Oh, I see! But why do you want to do that?"

"Because I hope that if I get strong enough, I could have Johnny hang something from the ceiling so that I could pull myself out of bed. Then I'd be able to get in and out of my chair whenever I wanted and not have to have someone help me."

Betsy nodded sagely. She was close enough to childhood to understand the desire to be able to do things oneself without any help from others. "What are you going to put on the ceiling?"

"A rope. I was thinking I'd put a small wooden bar at the end of it—I could grab the bar and use it to swing over the side of the bed and into the chair."

"Golly! That'd be fun!"

Trust Betsy, Alan thought, smiling. "You think so? I hope it is. But first I have to get strong enough to lift myself up."

"I reckon you better get to work, then," Betsy decided, jumping up. "Can I help you do anything?"

"No, thank you. I think, if you don't mind, that I'd rather try it out alone."

"All right." Betsy understood that; it was always easier to do something the first time without anyone hanging over your shoulder watching. And, unlike many adults, she was not offended by his frank admission that he'd like her to leave. She leaned into the room and said in a low, conspiratorial tone. "Is this a secret?"

Again, she made him smile. "Yes," he whispered back. "I think it is, at least for the time being."

Betsy nodded and put her index finger to her lip. "I won't say a word. Cross my heart." She solemnly made the gesture, then skipped down the veranda and was gone.

Alan gripped the books in each hand and began his lifting exercises again. He lifted the books in every position he could think of, trying to use each muscle in his arms. By the time he was through, he was sure he must have used them all, for it certainly felt as if every one of them ached. He wondered briefly if it was really worth the pain, but he knew that it was. For the first time in years he was going to accomplish something on his own.

It had been a long time since Alan had had the nightmares. But that night they came again, the demons that stabbed his legs with pain that was at once both hot and icy, the monsters that chased him toward the cliff and suddenly he was falling endlessly. Screaming.

"Alan!" the hissed whisper came, and a hand shook his shoulder. "Alan, wake up, you're having a nightmare!"

He pulled out of the darkness and opened his eyes to see Opal bending over his bed, her forehead knotted in a worried frown. He sat bolt upright, his heart pounding crazily. His nightshirt was soaked with sweat.

"Oh, thank God!" she exclaimed. "I was worried to

death. I heard you moaning in here, and then you hollered." She smoothed his hair back from his forehead in a maternal gesture. "Are you all right?"

Alan nodded. His heart was still pounding, but he was himself enough again to feel like a fool.

"I'm sorry." Alan pulled back from her touch. It felt too good; it made him want to lean against her, to seek the comfort of her arms. He wasn't about to let her see any *more* of his weakness.

"That's all right."

"No, it's not. I awakened you, and I—I'm sure you need your sleep." Alan knew it was impolite, but he couldn't keep his eyes from sliding down to her protruding stomach. There was something mysterious, even forbidden, about a pregnant woman. It seemed that no one should see her except her husband, the one man who knew her body. That thought made him feel embarrassed.

But Opal seemed unperturbed by his oblique reference to her pregnancy. She smoothed her hands over her rounded abdomen, smiling to herself. "No, it's no problem. It's getting hard to sleep the night through now anyway. I'm getting so big it's uncomfortable. I wake up all the time. That's why I heard you."

"I hope I won't disturb you again." He looked away from her. "I don't have nightmares often anymore."

"That's good." Opal reached behind him to plump up his pillows. "There now," she said soothingly. "Why don't you lie down and go back to sleep? My goodness! Your nightshirt's all damp. You must have been having the night sweats." She bustled away. "We better get something dry on you, or you'll catch a cold."

"No, don't worry. It's far too warm to catch a cold." Alan flushed, grateful for the relative darkness of the room.

"I don't know about that. It ain't—" She stopped, gave him a shy smile and corrected herself, "I mean, it isn't good to sleep with something wet on, no matter what the weather's like. I've heard tell of folks that caught terrible things like diphtheria or pneumonia even in the summertime. You don't want to risk that."

"I'm not as frail as you think."

The bitterness in his voice made Opal pause and turn toward him. "I didn't mean that! I'm sorry, Mr. Hayes. I didn't mean anything bad by it." She came back to the bed, her pale face wrinkled in consternation.

"I know, I know." He waved a hand to stop her worried explanation. "It's me. I'm a grouch. Ask Millicent; I'm often bad-tempered. I don't mean to be."

"Oh, no . . ." Opal laughed a little. "You aren't bad-tempered. Not at all. You should have known some of the people I have. Then you'd know what bad-tempered is. Besides, you'd have to be a saint, not a man, to be patient and good-tempered all the time." She turned away and went to the chest. "Now, where's a fresh nightshirt for you to put on? Aha, here they are."

She whipped out the long cotton garment triumphantly and returned to Alan's bed. "Here, let's get you out of that thing and into a dry one."

Alan hesitated. It embarrassed him to take off his

nightshirt with her in the room. It seemed almost indecent. But Opal was standing there waiting patiently for him to do it.

He reached down and yanked the thing up, pulling it from under his legs, careful not to let the quilt slide down below his waist. Opal held out her hand to take it. Fingers touched as he handed it to her, and his stomach jumped at the contact.

Opal tossed the old nightshirt aside and held the other one up, stretching on tiptoe to put it over his head. Alan put his head and arms into it, and she let it drop down. He felt shame at her helping him as if he were a child. Of course, that was doubtless how she thought of him, as a child. Certainly not as a man. She probably assumed that he was impotent as well as crippled.

Well, God knows he was still capable of being aroused. He let out a shaky breath. She was so close to him, and she wore only her nightgown, her pale blond hair hanging in a thick braid down her back. He felt confused, hungry, shamed, awkward. He didn't know how to act, what to say.

Hide it, of course. That was the thing to do. Pretend that his heart didn't speed up when her hand touched his or that his blood didn't heat when he glanced down from Opal's face and saw the dark circles of her nipples beneath her nightgown. Let her continue to assume that he was some kind of eunuch. Otherwise, he was sure, she would stay away from him completely.

"There," Opal said with satisfaction, taking a step backward. "That's better, isn't it?"

He nodded. "Yes."

Opal picked up the old shirt and spread it across the back of the chair to dry. She came to the foot of his bed and wrapped a hand around the thick bedpost, lingering. "I used to have bad dreams a lot, when I was little. Afterwards I'd be scared to go to sleep for fear they'd come back. I was glad the other girls were there. Kind of big now, I reckon, to feel scared."

"I don't know about that." Alan lay back against the plumped-up pillows, crossing his arms behind his head, and gazed at her. "It seems reasonable to me."

Opal leaned against the post, resting her head against its smooth, cool wood. "Sometimes I wonder how I can do it. How can I take care of a baby? Your sister asked me if I was going to put it in an orphanage, let it be adopted. Maybe she's right; maybe I wouldn't be able to look after it and work and all. And—and maybe some nice rich couple would adopt it. Some folks want a baby awful bad, and they could give it the things I couldn't." Her face contorted. "But I don't think I could live with myself, knowing I put my baby in one of those places. What if nobody wanted to adopt it? What if it grew up like I did? I can't bear the thought. I want to keep the baby. I want to love it and—oh, Mr. Hayes, you're a smart man." Opal edged forward toward him. "Tell me, am I doing wrong? Should I give it up?"

"Of course you're not!" He sat up, leaning toward her earnestly. "You're the baby's mother. Where else could it be better off? She stood uncertainly at the edge of his bed, looking so forlorn that Alan reached out and took her hand, forgetting his usual self-doubting reticence in his desire to comfort her. "No one could doubt that you would make an excellent mother. It's only natural that a mother would want to raise her baby, don't you think?" That was a subject on which he had no knowledge, but surely it must be true. "I'm sure Millicent didn't mean that you ought to give the baby up; she was only suggesting it, if you wanted to. But maybe you shouldn't work, at least not so much."

"But how can I afford a place to live and food to eat and the clothes and everything?"

"You have a place here with us. Don't you like it?"

"Of course I do! It's been the most wonderful time of my life. But I can't ask you and Miss Hayes to keep on putting me up."

"It's not charity. You work, probably harder than you should right now. And it might be nice to have a baby in the house. I've never been around one. Millicent would probably spoil it dreadfully. She'd like that, I think."

"She's good with children. Look at how nice she is to that little neighbor girl."

The mention of Betsy brought back to Alan's mind the conversation between Millicent and Jonathan Lawrence that he had overheard a few weeks ago on the back porch. Millicent did like Betsy. She more than liked Betsy's father. Once again Alan felt loneliness and fear touch his heart.

"Yes, she is," he said, and his voice turned distant and tired. Of course Opal would want to move on, to meet a man and marry, provide a father for her child.

That was what she deserved, too. "Naturally, you'll want a real home for yourself."

Opal looked at him uncertainly, thrown by the change in his voice. "I—I'm sorry. You're tired, and here I am, keeping you up talking about my problems. You go on to sleep now, Mr. Hayes, and if you need anything, just call, and I'll come."

Alan nodded without saying anything, and she slipped out of the room. With a sigh, he lay back against his pillows. Pale moonlight lit the room eerily through the sheer lace curtains and he stared at the strange, shifting patterns of light on the high ceiling, thinking about his sister and his life, about Opal. Sleep was a long time coming that night.

Betsy often came over to the Hayeses' house during July. Sometimes she visited Alan in his room. Millicent wasn't sure what they did, but she knew they were involved in some sort of secret. Alan and Betsy were apt to grin conspiratorially at each other, though they firmly denied that anything was going on. Alan's door was often closed these days, and his face held new life and interest. Opal was as in the dark as Millicent about the secret, but neither of them cared. It was too wonderful to see Alan looking well and happy.

Most of the time Betsy was there, however, she helped Millicent. They weeded and watered the garden. They picked vegetables, and Millicent taught the girl to clean, cut and can them. Betsy helped pick the cherries from the tree in the back, climbing up into the high limbs to get the fruit that Millicent couldn't reach standing on the ladder. They washed and pitted the fruit until their fingers took on a seemingly permanent red stain, and they made cherry pies, tarts, and preserves and canned the rest (all that they didn't eat or give away).

Millicent found herself growing more and more fond of the girl. Betsy learned things quickly, and she rarely repeated a mistake. She soaked up all the information Millicent could give her about anything. She seemed eager to learn, and Millicent was surprised to find out that Betsy even had an interest in looking better.

"Oh!" she exclaimed when Millicent parted her hair sharply down the middle and plaited it into two neat braids. "You did that so pretty! I can't manage to make it come out like that at all. How do you do it?" She twisted and craned, trying to see herself from all angles in the mirror.

"Well, I've been doing it for a long time. Here, I'll show you." She began to undo Betsy's hair.

"No!" Betsy cried in horror, clutching the sides of her head. "Don't undo it! I like it!"

Millicent chuckled. "It'll look the same next time, honest."

She took it down and showed Betsy how to part it precisely with a comb, having the girl practice it over and over until she was able to do it. Then she showed her step by step how to braid it tightly, so that stray ends didn't come slipping out all the time. Betsy was inordinately proud of herself when she finished.

"It looks grand, doesn't it?" she bragged innocently. "Almost as good as when you did it."

"It certainly does. And with practice you'll get better and better. Now, all we need to work on is your clothes."

"Really?" Betsy beamed. "Can you fix them, too?"

"Well, of course." Millicent was surprised that Betsy had even realized that her manner of dress was wrong. "If you want me to, that is."

"Oh, yes." She turned to Millicent seriously. "I'd like to look nice, Miss Hayes. I really would. It's just that I don't know what to do. I don't want to complain to Papa; then he'd feel bad. He tries so hard to take care of me right. Sometimes he gets real sad and says he's not raising me well. I don't want him to think that. But I can't make a dress myself." She looked down at her attire. "Mine are too short, aren't they? And sometimes my sashes come off. But I don't know how to make a new dress. I sew on the sashes, but they don't look good."

"I'll help you. I'll teach you how to sew, and we'll make you some new dresses together. Would you like that?"

"Oh, yes!" Betsy's eyes lit up. "That'd be so nice. Oh, Miss Hayes, I love you!"

Impulsively she threw her arms around Millicent and hugged her. It startled Millicent so much that for a moment she didn't move. But then, her own arms went around the child. It felt so good and right to hold her this way. Her chest began to ache, and tears picked at her eyelids. Instinctively, she curled down over Betsy.

"I love you, too," Millicent whispered. Amazingly enough, she realized that she did. Somehow Betsy had wormed her way into her heart. It hurt a little, but it felt glorious, too.

As much as Betsy was at the Hayes house, Millicent noticed that her father never showed his face there. Millicent saw Jonathan in his yard a few times, and once she met him on the street as she walking to the millinery shop. They said hello briefly, with only a nod to the other, and went on their ways. Other than that, there had been no contact between them since the evening of the boxed supper social. Millicent was relieved that Jonathan had honored her wish that he not come to call on her. It made the situation much easier. Still . . . she couldn't help but think that he had given up awfully easily.

And, though she would never have admitted it to a soul, she couldn't deny that she missed him.

One evening in the middle of July, Millicent was sitting in the parlor with Alan and Opal. Millicent was catching up on her correspondence, her portable writing box on her lap, and Alan was holding a skein of yarn between his hands for Opal, who sat on the couch across from him, rolling the yarn into a ball. Suddenly there was a loud clang outside which disturbed them all.

Millicent glanced up. "What in the world was that?"

She exchanged glances with Opal and Alan. Alan shrugged. "I'm not sure. It sounded like something hitting metal."

"Maybe the wrought-iron fence next door?" Opal suggested.

"Perhaps," Millicent agreed, "but who would be out

pounding on the fences at this hour?" She laid her pen down, frowning. "If that little terror Jefferson Stillwell is out hitting the fences at this time of night . . ."

"I don't think that's it." Alan looked faintly troubled. "It sounds . . . funny."

Millicent had to agree. There had been more noises outside as they talked, muffled thuds and scrapes as well as some other unidentifiable sounds. Millicent thought she heard a voice, though she wasn't able to distinguish the words. Whatever the odd noises were, they left her with an uneasy feeling. She walked over to the parlor window and pulled aside the curtain, peering out into the dark night. "I can't see a thing."

Millicent turned and went out of the room and down the hall to the front door, pulled by the vague sense of dread which all of them felt but could not identify. Alan followed her in his chair, with Opal right behind him. As Millicent opened the door and stepped out onto the porch, she heard another thud and an odd, low groan. The hair on the back of her neck stood up, and goosebumps rose over her flesh.

"Who's out here?" she called, stepping to the edge of the porch and peering out into the darkened street. "What's going on?"

"What is it, Millie?" Alan asked as he and Opal came out onto the porch.

"I'm not sure." Millicent trotted down the steps and along the walkway toward the fence. Her eyes were adjusting to the dim light, and now she could see the dark forms of men in the street in front of the Lawrence house, two or three of them, bunched together in a strange way. "Who are you?" she called again in a peremptory voice.

The forms became more distinct as the men shifted and turned toward Millicent. There was one man standing with his back toward Millicent, and in front of him was a lumpy mass that resolved itself into three men, the two on the outside holding up a third man between them. The man standing alone and the two on the outside all swung around, startled, to look at Millicent.

Millicent gasped and took an involuntary step backward. The men were faceless! It was a moment before she realized that the three had something dark pulled over their heads to mask their features, giving them a blank appearance. In that instant she knew that whatever they were doing had to be wrong, and she also knew that they were cowards, to be concealing themselves thus.

"Here!" she commanded crisply, whatever fear she had felt swept away by her outrage. "Just what do you think you're doing?"

She hurried to the gate and flung it open. Behind her she heard Opal gasp, "No!" and her brother say, "Millicent, don't! Dammit, Millie, come back!"

She paid them no attention, for the two men who had been holding up the third dropped him, letting him sink to his knees on the ground, and started to run. The other masked man was right on their heels. Millicent saw as the man in the middle dropped to the ground that he alone was unmasked. His face was bloody and discolored, but Millicent recognized him immediately. It was Jonathan Lawrence!

Fourteen

"**J**onathan!" Millicent cried out and ran forward, not thinking of the danger to herself or, indeed, of anything else except the fact that Jonathan was hurt. The three men turned and ran as she approached. Millicent didn't even glance at them. She flung herself down on the ground beside Jonathan, reaching out to grasp his arms as he swayed unsteadily.

He groaned and struggled to raise his head. One eye and the side of his face was puffy and reddened, already beginning to bruise, and his lips were swollen and cut. Blood trickled from his mouth and from another cut high on his cheekbone. His arms were pressed against his stomach in pain. His eyes wavered on Millicent's face for a moment before they focused. His lips twitched, trying to form into a grin.

"Now you're rescuing *me*, I see," he whispered haltingly.

"Oh, hush!" It was all Millicent could do not to throw her arms around him and squeeze him to her; she could feel tears starting in her eyes, and she had to blink to keep them from falling. She was *not* about to break down in the midst of an emergency, especially not in front of Jonathan Lawrence. Her fear quickly transformed itself into a saving anger. Exasperation and irritation were things she could deal with far more readily than that awful bone-chilling fear. She scowled at Jonathan and snapped, "What in the world have you gotten yourself into this time?"

He shook his head a little and looked past her. "A whole team of saviors," he murmured. "Lord help us."

Millicent looked over her shoulder. Alan had wheeled down from the porch using the ramp beside the steps, and he and Opal were hurrying toward them. Alan held a tree branch across his lap, obviously having grabbed the only weapon he found at hand as they followed Millicent.

"Well, if that isn't just like you," Millicent exclaimed. "To make fun of the very people who've just saved your hide. Those men were beating you, weren't they?"

"Yes." The smile disappeared. "I'm not making fun, Millie, just—" Jonathan grimaced in pain. "Just trying to keep from disgracing myself in front of you."

"What claptrap. Here, let me help you up. I need to get you into the house and look at those wounds."

"I'm all right." Jonathan shook his head. His voice was still thin and breathless with pain.

"Poppycock. What are you planning to do? Go into your house looking like that? Do you want to scare your daughter out of seven years' growth? Now get up and come in the house and stop acting like a . . . a typical man!"

Jonathan half groaned, half laughed. "Ah, Millicent, must you strip me of every bit of pride? Dammit, I can't stand up!"

"For heaven's sake!" Millicent snapped. "We'll help you." She looped her arm through one of his, and on the other side, Alan and Opal reached down to grasp his other arm.

All three of them pulled, and, with a muffled groan and curse, Jonathan stumbled to his feet. He looped an arm around Millicent's shoulder and leaned upon her as she guided him back into her yard and up the walkway to her house, with Opal and Alan hovering behind them.

Millicent walked Jonathan down the hall and into the kitchen. She released him at the kitchen table and helped him into one of the chairs there. She brought an oil lamp from the counter and lit it, setting it down on the table in front of him. In its light, Jonathan looked even worse than he had outside. His face was pale except for the streaks and smears of blood, and his jaw and eye were red and swelling alarmingly. Millicent's lips began to quiver, and she turned away quickly to hide it. She gripped her hands together, willing herself to be strong.

She strode briskly to the sink and pumped water into a bowl, then returned to the table with the bowl and several rags. Jonathan was leaning forward over the table, his head propped up on his hands and his elbows braced against the table.

"All right, look at me," Millicent instructed, unaware of how her voice had softened.

Slowly Jonathan raised his head, his hands falling away, and he sat back against the chair. Millicent wet a rag and carefully applied it to his face. He winced, but didn't move away, and she continued to wipe the blood from his skin as gently as she could.

Alan and Opal stood watching silently from the doorway of the kitchen. As Alan looked at his sister tending to Jonathan, he remembered the night that he had overheard the two of them on the back porch. His stomach tightened. He glanced at Opal, and she turned to him, smiling, her eyebrows going up significantly. Alan knew that she, too, had guessed that there was an attraction between Jonathan and Millicent. She reached over and squeezed his shoulder, then nodded toward the dining room, indicating that they should leave.

Opal wanted to encourage whatever tender shoot of feeling was developing between Jonathan and Millicent. That was the difference between Opal and him, Alan knew. Alan wasn't sure he wanted to encourage it. He glanced back at the kitchen table. Millicent was still softly dabbing at Jonathan's face.

But just then Opal bent down to whisper in his ear. "Let's go finish the yarn," Opal suggested, and turned and walked into the dining room. Alan followed her.

Millicent hardly noticed Opal's and Alan's departure, any more than she had noticed that they had come into the kitchen with Jonathan and her. She was too intent on his wounds.

Nothing looked too serious, she was relieved to discover. His injuries were no doubt painful, but the cuts on his face weren't deep, no matter how bloody, and none of his bones appeared to be broken. Gently she felt along his jaw and cheekbone to make sure. Jonathan let out a quickly smothered exclamation at her exploration.

"Just checking for broken bones," she explained and dropped her hands. "It seems as if everything's all right."

"That's what you think," Jonathan grumbled. "You should be inside it."

"Thank you, no." Millicent dropped the bloodied rag into the bowl of water, then wrung it out and continued cleaning his face. When the blood was all wiped from his face, she laid the rag aside and went to the icebox. Squatting down beside it, she opened the door to the storage compartment for the ice block. The block had been melting all day and was only a fraction of its former size, but there was enough there for her to chip out several chunks. She wrapped them up in a thin dishtowel and held it against Jonathan's cheek. He winced, but he laid his hand over the towel and held it there. "Why were those men beating you? What happened? Who were they?"

"I haven't the slightest idea. Didn't you see their faces? They wore dark hoods, with only the eyeholes cut out. I didn't recognize them."

"I didn't, either," Millicent admitted. "But I hoped you might have gotten a better look at them."

Jonathan shook his head. "I didn't. But it hardly matters, anyway. They're only hired hands."

"What do you mean?"

"I mean, I'm sure they weren't simply two readers

who took exception to one of my editorials. They were hired to inflict damage on me. A warning, so to speak."

"A warning?"

"Yes. Of what might happen if I didn't stop writing my opinions in my newspaper."

Millicent's jaw dropped. She hadn't thought of that possibility. She had assumed that the men had been robbers. "They were threatening you? Trying to intimidate you into not writing something?"

Jonathan shrugged, then grimaced at the pain caused by his unthinking movement. "I would imagine so. Others have tried."

"And did they succeed?"

Jonathan cast her a sardonic glance. "What do you think?"

"That you behaved as foolishly then as you will now. Why is it that men have this unreasonable need to prove that they can't be scared away?"

"I have a very reasonable need. I am upholding the rights of a free press."

"Very noble of you, I'm sure."

He sighed and closed his eyes. "Millicent . . . I don't feel up to quarreling with you right now."

A pain stabbed Millicent's chest. He looked so tired, so uncustomarily vulnerable, with his eyes closed and his face bruised and swollen from the men's blows.

"Oh, Jonathan . . ." Millicent's words were barely above a whisper. She sank down into a chair across the table from him. Her knees were suddenly too weak to stand, and she realized that she was trembling. Without thinking she reached across the table and placed her hand on his. "I was so scared."

Jonathan opened his eyes and looked at her, surprise registering in his eyes. "Why, Millicent, is that concern I see in you?"

Millicent's mouth tightened. "You needn't be sarcastic. Is it any wonder that a woman would be frightened at seeing a gang of ruffians attack someone?"

"I'm not being sarcastic. I'm simply a little amazed. And pleased. I don't think that you're feeling exactly what you'd feel if it had been another man attacked. Are you?"

Millicent felt a flush rising up her throat. She turned her head and would have pulled away her hand, too, but Jonathan had laced his fingers through hers, holding her there.

"Tell me the truth. Were you frightened for me?"

"Of course I was. Anyone would be if they had an ounce of sensibility."

"I'm not talking about sensibility. I'm talking about personal concern."

She knew she should lie, or at least sidestep the issue, but somehow her mouth would not form the words. "All right," she replied at last in a choked voice. "Yes. Yes! I was concerned about you. I was frightened for you." She looked up at him then, and her gaze turned pleading. "Jonathan, please, you have to be more careful. You mustn't expose yourself to danger."

"When you look at me like that, somehow none of my aches seem to hurt as much." He smiled crookedly, and his thumb stroked up and down Millicent's thumb.

"Don't be foolish," she retorted breathlessly and tried to tug her hand from his, but he refused to release it.

"No. Don't pull away from me. Not again. Not now. I—" He paused and glanced away. When he went on, his voice was low and hurried. "I need you right now."

Millicent simply sat for a moment, stunned by his admission. It was not the sort of thing she would ever have expected to hear Jonathan Lawrence say. She was too full of sudden emotion to speak, so she pressed her fingers against his hand more tightly. He laid his head down upon their linked hands, pressing his forehead against her skin.

"You feel so cool. So good," he murmured. "Ah, Millie, sometimes I wonder if I'm crazy for doing what I do, for writing what I think. It'd be easier to go along."

Millicent would have liked to smooth his pale hair back from his head, to stroke his forehead and whisper soothing words. Her chest ached with a sad-sweet pain. "I can't imagine you doing that. Can you?"

Jonathan looked up. Millicent was smiling faintly at him in a sort of fond resignation. A smile twitched at his lips, too, but it hurt too much to do it, and the smile fell away. "No," he agreed, "I can't."

He sighed. Finally, he rubbed his thumb across her hand, then released her fingers. "I better go. The longer I sit here, the harder it's going to be to leave." He stood up, stifling a groan. "My muscles are tightening up already."

Millicent looked at his face, swollen and even more

splotched than earlier. She felt a sympathetic tightening of her own muscles. "Why don't I help you walk back?"

He glanced at her. "Would you?" The brief smile flickered again on his face. "I wouldn't turn you down."

Jonathan came around the end of the table, and Millicent met him. She looped her arm around his waist, and he put his arm around her shoulders, holding her against his side. He didn't lean on her as he had when he'd first staggered to his feet, simply held her close to his side. Millicent felt strangely comforted by his nearness, even though logically it should be he who was in need of comforting. She glanced up at him, wondering if Jonathan received the same sort of comfort from having her body nestled against his.

They walked through the kitchen door and out onto the porch, making their halting way down the back steps and across the yard toward Jonathan's home. The night air was muggy and hot, so thick one could almost stir it, and the night insects whirred and hummed. In the distance, Millicent could hear the sound of frogs croaking by the pond, and it seemed a peaceful, homey sound. It was hard to believe that three men had attacked another on a night like this, no matter what the reason.

Unconsciously Millicent's hand tightened on Jonathan's waist. "Will you at least promise me that you'll be more careful in the future?"

"That I will. I usually am, in fact, but tonight I was distracted, just strolling around the yard, looking at the moon and thinking, not paying any attention to anything. They were upon me before I even saw them. I'll be more alert from now on, I can assure you. This is not a pleasant way to feel."

"Good." They reached his back porch and walked slowly up the steps.

A little reluctantly Millicent released Jonathan and stepped back. "Well . . ." She linked her hands awkwardly behind her back. "I'll leave you here. If you're sure you can make it, that is."

"Yes, I'm fine. Or I will be in a few days."

"Good," she repeated. Millicent took another step back. "All right, then. I—perhaps I'll stop in to check on you tomorrow."

"I'd like that."

They looked at each other for a moment longer. Jonathan reached out and put his hands on her shoulders. Then, wordlessly, he pulled her to him and wrapped his arms gently around her. With a sigh, Millicent relaxed against him, letting her arms encircle his waist and leaning her head upon his chest. She could hear the rhythmic thumping of his heart beneath her ear, feel the warmth and strength of his body. It felt so good and soothing, so right somehow, that she closed her mind to all thoughts, all doubts and fear and for the moment just let herself soak in the feelings. There was a terrible hunger inside her, not of the body, but of the soul. It had been there for years, covered up and ignored, but tonight it came bubbling up out of her depths. In Jonathan's arms there was satisfaction and surcease. She did not want to leave.

He buried his lips in her hair, breathing in her scent. "Thank you," he murmured. Jonathan stroked his hand down across her hair and onto her shoulder. He paused for a moment, his head bent to hers, his hand lingering on the curve of her shoulder. Then his hand dropped away and he pulled himself back. "Good night."

Millicent looked up at him.

"Good night," she replied softly. "Promise me you'll take care of yourself."

"I promise."

She tried a little smile, but she knew that she was about to break into tears. She whirled and ran down the steps and across the yard, hurrying back to her home.

Millicent awoke when the first ray of sunlight drifted across her face. She smiled up at the ceiling, then bounced out of bed. She was unaccountably happy this morning, and she didn't pause to wonder why. She went to the window, humming as she brushed out her hair, and watched the landscape turn from the bluish tone of dawn into the full gold of morning. Her chest felt full, as though she could burst into trills like one of the birds outside her window. The world was full of color today, the cardinals redder than red, the hydrangeas great balls of blue and pink, the leaves of the trees a deep, rich green. It reminded her of the way things looked fresh after a rain, with all the dust and grime washed away.

She searched through the dresses in her wardrobe, rejecting all her newer ones. She had been out of mourning for her father for a while, and she wondered why she had continued to wear such drab colors. Jonathan was right; the fact that she was unmarried didn't mean she had to look like a crow all the time. She pulled out the blue dress with black ribbon trim that she had almost worn to take Jonathan the cake a few weeks ago and held it up in front of her, looking at her image in the mirror.

Millicent smiled. Yes, this one would look much better. It would do until she bought some material and made a new dress or two. A deep blue might be nice, she thought, or maybe even a lavender. She had seen a lovely calico print in a rose shade a few weeks ago at Hunter's Mercantile. Perhaps she would go shopping there today.

She dressed and pulled her hair up on top of her head in a soft bun and added a pair of jet earrings. She moved her head a little, setting the dangling oval beads to dancing, and she chuckled to herself. Lightly she ran down the stairs. Ida was in the kitchen; she could smell the biscuits baking and the bacon sizzling in its pan, but Millicent didn't turn that way. Instead she crossed the hall to the front door and stepped outside onto the wide veranda.

It wasn't what one could call a lovely day. It was already hot, the kind of day the people of Emmetsville termed a "scorcher," and the air was thick with humidity. By noon the town would have fallen into a somnolent, static heat, the insects droning and the leaves of the trees not even stirring. But to Millicent the golden wash of the landscape was beautiful, the torpid heat not even a nuisance. She went down the steps and leaned over to smell the roses growing beside the front steps. She strolled across the shaded yard to the bed of daylilies. The iris blooms had ceased long ago, but the other flowers still added sunny color to the yard.

Millicent glanced across into the neighboring yard. She wondered if Jonathan was still in bed. She would go over after breakfast and see how he was doing. It would be too early to check on him now; he needed sleep. But, at that moment, much to Millicent's surprise, the front door opened, and Jonathan emerged.

He was dressed in a suit, his hat in his hand, and he walked down the steps and along the walk to the gate, carrying himself carefully. His face was swollen on one side and garishly splotched with purple and blue bruises. Only one eye was truly open. Yet he was obviously going to work.

"Jonathan Lawrence!" Millicent exclaimed in dismay.

He stopped in surprise and turned toward her. A smile perked up half his mouth. "Why, Millicent. I didn't expect to see you." He started across the grass to meet her at the fence.

"And I certainly didn't expect to see you!" Millicent planted her fists on her hips pugnaciously. "Just what do you think you're doing?"

"Walking to work. I'm afraid I have to leave a little early; it'll take me longer to get there today."

"You should be home in bed."

"In bed? Why? Lying there sulking won't help my bruises."

"You can't possibly feel up to walking to your office and sitting at a desk the whole day. You should give yourself a chance to recuperate."

He shrugged. "Maybe, if all things were equal. But I can't afford to. I have a newspaper to put out by tomorrow, you see."

"Couldn't someone else do it?"

"Not as well as I." The familiar cocky grin was on his face, eerily distorted by his injuries. "Besides, I have something to prove, other than printing what I intended to print. If I stayed home, there are some people who might assume that they had frightened me, maybe even defeated me. I have to make sure they realize that they haven't."

"Honestly!" Millicent's tone was exasperated, but she couldn't quell the rush of pride that swelled up inside her. Jonathan Lawrence was no coward. He would never let a bunch of bullies intimidate him. "Men are so stupid sometimes."

"Come now." His voice dropped and he reached out to take one of her hands in his. "You wouldn't really want me to be any other way, would you?"

Millicent grimaced and jerked her hand away. "Oh, all right! I suppose not. But it scares me."

"Thank you. I'm pleased that you care enough to be scared. But there's no need to worry, I won't be careless again."

"You can't guarantee that you'll be safe."

"No. But being safe isn't the same thing as living."

"You say the most peculiar things."

"I think you understand them." He took her hand again, and this time Millicent did not resist. He brought it to his lips and kissed it softly. "Thank you for what you did last night."

Millicent drew in a shaky breath. Her knees went idiotically weak when he did that.

"You know," Jonathan went on, "I took you at your word. I've stayed away from you. Have you noticed?"

"Yes." She glanced away.

"But last night I realized that I was being foolish. My pride was hurt because you turned me down. But I don't want to give you up. Especially not because I was hurt that you could do without me so easily. That you counted me less than other people's opinions."

Millicent's eyes widened. "Oh, no, I didn't mean that!"

"I hope not. Last night, I thought . . . I felt . . . it seemed to me as though you might feel something more for me. I—" He shook his head and looked away. "I rarely have this much trouble expressing myself. Being unable to talk is not one of my faults." He drew a breath. "Millicent, there was something between us last night. Not just physical attraction, though God knows I feel that for you, as well. But I took comfort from you last night; I drew strength from you. I felt as though we *touched* one another. I don't know when I've felt that way about a woman. Maybe never. But I don't want to lose it. I won't lose it."

Millicent's breath fluttered in her throat. "I'm not sure I know what you're talking about."

"I plan to pursue you. That's what I'm saying. I won't be put off or dissuaded this time."

"Don't I have anything to say in the matter?"

"I think you said what was important last night."

"I don't remember saying anything about—about you and me."

"Not in words. I saw it in your eyes when you looked at me. I felt it in your hands when they wiped the blood off my face. I knew it when I held you in my arms. I felt such . . . such possibility that it was almost frightening. It's also something I want quite badly. Enough to try to break down those barriers you've constructed around you."

Millicent couldn't find words to reply. She realized, with some amazement, that she didn't even know she felt or what she should say. She thought of the sunniness inside her when she woke up this morning, the airy, bright feeling that equaled the day outside. Her heart hurt at the thought of losing that feeling. "Perhaps," she said slowly, "perhaps there aren't quite the barriers you believe."

Jonathan grinned. "I'll take that for encouragement."

Millicent smiled back, feeling reckless and perhaps a little foolish and suddenly bubbling with excitement. She wasn't thinking of the consequences of her action. She *wouldn't* think of them.

"Then perhaps I will see you at the dance next week."

"The dance?"

"At Miller's barn."

"Oh. Oh, yes." There was a dance in the big barn every summer, usually in July before the harvesting began, but Millicent had not gone in years. "I hadn't thought about it. I don't know whether I'm going or not."

"Well, plan to. And plan to dance with me."

"All right."

Afterwards, Millicent was amazed at herself for agreeing so easily, so quickly. She told herself that she had been a fool. She told herself she would not go. Her decision at the boxed supper had been the right one. It would be silly of her to attend the dance, and she'd make a laughingstock of herself if she danced with Jonathan. But every time she thought of it, anticipation flamed up in her. She thought of dressing up, of looking pretty, of whirling around the room in Jonathan's arms, and she wanted to go to the dance so badly it was like a physical hunger within her.

On Sunday, at Aunt Sophie's house at dinner, when the conversation drifted to the barn dance the following Friday, Aunt Oradelle turned to Millicent and said, "I presume you aren't going to the dance this year either."

Her tone was not approving. She thought it was Millicent's obligation as one of the spinsters of the family to sit with the older women against the wall and help chaperone the marriageable girls. Millicent had let her aunt push her into it once or twice, but she had been thoroughly miserable the whole time and had vowed not to go again. She had always loved to dance, and it was horrible to have to sit there and watch others dance, her own feet twitching all the while to get out on the floor herself.

"Yes, I think I will," Millicent replied.

Aunt Oradelle stared at her. She started to speak, but before she could say anything, Aunt Sophie piped up, "Why, how nice, dear. Perhaps you'd like to go with Chub and Amelia and me."

"Thank you, Aunt Sophie. I'd like that," Millicent replied quickly, before Aunt Oradelle could stick her oar in.

Aunt Oradelle frowned. It wasn't often that her sister-in-law beat her out. Millicent's more proper place would have been with *her* family, since her own parents were dead. And Millicent would have been good company for Camilla, whose silly chatter distracted Oradelle from her primary goal of keeping an eagle eye on everyone on the dance floor to make sure that no one committed any indiscretions, such as leaving the barn with a boy.

"But why have you decided to go this year?" Aunt Oradelle asked. "You've never wanted to before."

"I'm not sure," Millicent replied, somewhat less than honestly. She knew that the reason for her going to the dance was tall and blond, though she would never have admitted it to anyone. "Perhaps I ought to get out more. After all, we've been out of mourning for Papa for quite some time now."

Oradelle continued to frown, but said nothing else. Millicent was sure that her aunt would maneuver it so that Millicent sat close to her at the dance. That way it would be easy to watch her like a hawk. Millicent smiled blandly back at Aunt Oradelle. Let her watch, she thought. She had no intention of doing anything reprehensible. There was nothing wrong with watching people dance—nor with chatting with Jonathan Lawrence, should he come over and engage her in conversation. She wouldn't dance, of course; she was too old for that. But that didn't mean that she couldn't enjoy herself. And for once, Millicent thought defiantly, she intended to do just that.

Fifteen

$\mathcal{W}$hen Millicent returned from her aunt's house, she set straight to work cutting out a dress from the pink cloth she had bought in Hunter's Mercantile the week before. It was a simple dress, but it looked lovely on her. The wide sash around her waist emphasized its smallness, and the pink lent color to her face. With her hair pulled up and secured with another rose ribbon and cascading down in a waterfall of curls, as she wore it the night of the dance, she thought she looked rather pretty.

Her opinion was confirmed when her uncle and aunt came to take her to the dance. Uncle Chub's eyes widened when she opened the door to him, and he exclaimed, "Well, bless my soul, Millie, you're looking awful pretty!"

"Thank you, Uncle Chub." Millicent smiled, dimpling, and sailed out onto the porch. From the open buggy she could hear her aunt's soft exclamation and Amelia's less restrained squeal.

Millicent put her hand on Uncle Chub's arm and walked with him to the buggy where her aunt and cousin waited. Cousin Amelia leaned out eagerly as they approached, saying, "Cousin Millicent, you are beautiful." She stretched the last word out into at least four syllables.

"I agree," Aunt Sophie added in her slow, languid way. "I haven't seen you in such good looks in years. I wish Susan could see you."

"How is Susan?" Millicent asked as she climbed up into the buggy and sat down on the back bench seat beside Amelia.

"As well as one can be." Aunt Sophie's voice lowered. "Her time is almost any day now." She sighed. "I do worry so about the child."

Her aunt's placid face appeared anything but worried. Millicent couldn't remember a time when Aunt Sophie had seemed disturbed by something.

Uncle Chub pulled his rotund form up into the front seat and picked up the reins, slapping them and clucking to the horses to move forward. Uncle Chub was a jovial soul, as full of chatter and laughter as his wife was quiet and calm. He was the youngest of the Hayes brothers, and Millicent had once heard her father remark that he thought Chub had lived so long under their oldest sister's thumb that he had gone out as soon as he was old enough and married the most different woman from Oradelle that he could find. Privately, Millicent thought that his choice of Sophie was as much because she gave him no competition in talking as because she was unlike Aunt Oradelle.

True to form, Uncle Chub kept up an almost non-stop stream of conversation all the way to the Miller's barn, but Millicent hardly heard a word he said. She was too busy with her own thoughts—and the churning in her stomach. She kept thinking about Jonathan Lawrence and wondering if he would really be there. How would he look? She hadn't seen him in several days, but when she had last seen him, his face was still marked with yellowish bruises, though at least it was no longer swollen.

Most of all, she wondered if he had really meant the things he said to her. Or had she colored his words with her own hopes?

She was hoping that when they arrived at the dance, she would be able to arrange things so that she didn't have to sit close to Aunt Oradelle, but she soon found that she wasn't to be so lucky. Her aunt, Uncle Elmer, and Camilla had arrived before them, and as soon as Oradelle saw them, she imperiously beckoned them over to where she and Camilla sat against the wall as rigidly as if the wall were held up solely by their straight backs.

"Millicent. Sophie." Oradelle's voice carried plainly above the hum of other people talking. There was no ignoring her.

Millicent thought she heard a soft sigh from Sophie before her aunt put on a pleasant smile and waved back at Oradelle. "Come along, girls, let's say hello to Oradelle. Then we'll get some punch. I'm dying of thirst."

Glad that Sophie was preparing an escape plan, Millicent followed her and Amelia toward the Holloway women. Amelia didn't care whether they visited Aunt Oradelle or not, she would be out dancing the whole evening. By the time they reached Aunt Oradelle, Amelia had already been approached by two young men and asked to reserve a dance for them. Millicent could remember those times, when she never had to worry about being stuck by some boring old woman or a harping relative all evening and the only problem she had was the possibility of filling up her dance card before a favorite swain arrived to claim a dance.

"Hello, Oradelle, how are you this evening?" Sophie asked, remaining standing. Dutifully Millicent and Amelia chorused their hellos behind her.

"Hello, Sophie. Millicent. Amelia." Aunt Oradelle inspected each of them with sharp eyes as she greeted them. "My, but you're in excellent looks this evening, Sophie. And you, Millicent." It was obvious that the woman couldn't tell whether to approve or not of the way Millicent looked. It was always gratifying to see that the Hayes women were the prettiest group at the party. However, Oradelle wasn't sure whether she really liked Millicent taking such trouble with her dress and hair tonight. The girl had been acting peculiarly lately, and Oradelle was afraid of what it might indicate. At the very least, it seemed an affront to her as the head of the family that Millicent hadn't made her privy to the reason behind this sudden change.

"Thank you, Aunt Oradelle." Like Sophie, Millicent remained standing.

"What about me, Auntie?" Amelia asked coquettishly, drawing her mouth up into a playful pout.

"Of course you look pretty, Amelia. There's no need to try to cozen a compliment out of me. You know how you look as well as I. Sophie's children have always turned out attractive."

"Why, thank you," Sophie commented, ignoring the unspoken barb in her sister-in-law's comment that implied that they hadn't turned out as well in other ways. "I'm rather proud of them myself."

"How is Susan?" Oradelle went on in a suitably lower voice.

It occurred to Millicent that everyone spoke about Susan as if a death had occurred or something unseemly had happened to her. It was always that way when the subject of pregnancy was brought up, and though Millicent had never paid it any attention before, she found now that it irritated her. Everyone acted as if having a baby were something to be ashamed of, yet they were deliriously happy whenever one was born into the family. Babies were always cooed over and petted in her family. For the first time in her life Millicent wondered why pregnancy and childbirth were embarrassing topics, why one didn't discuss them around children or men. And why must everything that was said be couched in ambiguous terms? She thought of Opal and her impending childbearing, of the easy way she spoke about it. Somehow it seemed more natural.

Aunt Sophie began to relay the same news that she had given Millicent earlier about Susan, bending down to talk more quietly.

"Sit down, Sophie," Oradelle commanded crisply. "I'm getting a crick in my neck staring up at you."

"No, we really can't. We were on our way to the punch bowl." Sophie pulled out her prepared excuse for not staying with Oradelle. "I declare, the ride made me so thirsty."

"Nonsense. No need to trot over to the punch bowl." Oradelle glanced around and found one of her sons lounging not far away, talking to a young lady, and she crooked her finger imperiously at him. "Donald, go and fetch the ladies some punch. Where are your manners?"

"Yes, Mama." Donald raised an eyebrow in exasperation, but started off obediently toward the refreshment table.

"Here, Millicent, sit next to me." Aunt Oradelle patted the chair beside her.

Millicent could do nothing but smile and accept the offer of the seat with as much grace as she could muster. She should know by now, she thought as she sat down beside Oradelle, that she could not outmaneuver her aunt.

She half listened to her two aunts talking beside her while she glanced around the room, surreptitiously taking stock of who was there. On the other side of her, Camilla stirred and said quietly, "It's nice to see you again."

Millicent turned toward her and smiled. "Thank you. It's good to see you, too."

"You look awfully pretty this evening," Camilla went on.

"Why, thank you." Millicent could not in truth return the compliment. Camilla seemed to have done her best to fade into the woodwork, wearing a brown dress with a high neck and little ornamentation and pulling her hair back in a modest bun low on her neck. "It looks to be a lively dance tonight, don't you think?" Millicent said to keep the conversation alive, hoping that she could at least avoid some of her aunt's questioning that way.

"Yes, it does." Camilla's voice was a trifle wistful as she looked around the room. "Look, there's Dan and Rebecca and their little boy."

"Mm-hm," Millicent replied noncommittally, glancing at her cousin and his family.

"I wonder if he's happy with her," Camilla remarked.

"I don't know. Rebecca is a pretty woman, and no doubt she shows a better side to her husband than she does to the rest of us."

A faint smile curved Camilla's lips. "I hadn't realized she had a better side."

Millicent chuckled. "It's well hidden."

"Mother always says men are blinded by a beautiful face."

"Perhaps. But don't you think some men could be different? That they could like a woman for her wit instead of her youth? There must be men who want more substance in a woman."

Camilla turned her head to look at Millicent, her expression intrigued. "Millicent? Are you talking about someone in particular? Is there—are you keeping company with someone?"

Millicent was irritated to feel a blush rising in her cheeks. She glanced away from Camilla's curious eyes. "No, of course not. I was just thinking, that's all."

"I see."

But she was certain that Camilla didn't believe her. Why had she blurted out something like that? Sometimes it seemed as if she hardly knew herself these days.

Millicent was pulled from her self-recriminations by the sound of her aunt's voice on the other side of her. "Well, would you look at that! He's at the dance, and looking like he does!"

Millicent's head snapped up and she looked toward the door, certain that she knew about whom her aunt was talking. Sure enough, it was Jonathan. There were still traces of yellowish bruises around his eye; she supposed that was what aroused Aunt Oradelle's indignation. But even those could not hide his handsomeness or dim the mischievous twinkle in his eyes.

Her heart began to pound. Jonathan was glancing around the room. Millicent wondered if he was looking for her. She knew she was crazy to feel this way, but she couldn't seem to stop it. Her cartwheeling emotions overran her control these days. She gripped her fan tightly in her hands, waiting for his gaze to fall on her.

"He's obviously a brawler," Aunt Oradelle went on disapprovingly. "Why, a decent man wouldn't have had the gall to appear in public the way he's looked the past week. He's hardly the kind of person fit to be publishing a newspaper—influencing public opinion."

"A brawler!" Millicent turned toward her aunt, righteous wrath welling up inside her. "He's no such thing. It was scarcely his fault if three men—three, mind you—set upon him in his own yard and dragged him out to the street to beat him up!"

Aunt Oradelle gaped at her, for a moment too stunned by her niece's answering back to even speak. "Millicent Hayes! What in the world do you know about a common street fight?"

"I saw it! I heard it. I could hardly avoid it, as it happened right outside our house. Alan and Opal saw it, too. There were three men attacking him, and they ran off when we came outside. That's scarcely his fault. And what would you have him do? Cower in his house until the bruises went away? Bad as he felt, he had to go to his office to show them that he couldn't be intimidated into not expressing his opinion."

Her aunt stared at her. "You certainly seem to know an awful lot about this, missy! And I'd like to know what you're doing, defending the man."

It was a serious mistake, Millicent knew, to have given her aunt even a hint of any connection between her and Jonathan Lawrence. Now she would be in for a long and tiresome interrogation. But she was not about to back down from her statement or apologize for defending Jonathan. Millicent set her jaw pugnaciously and stared back at her aunt.

"The man is my neighbor, and I am appalled whenever I encounter brutality and suppression of free speech."

"Free speech!" Aunt Oradelle echoed in disgust. "What would you care about something like that!"

On the other side of Oradelle, Aunt Sophie looked on with interest, and Millicent was sure that more than one head was turning toward them at Aunt Oradelle's loud tone. But Millicent couldn't find it in her to care.

She was too determined to face Aunt Oradelle down, too tired of years of holding back and maneuvering around her aunt simply because she was the spokeswoman of the family.

"You forget that I am the daughter of a judge," Millicent replied stiffly. "I was raised to believe in certain principles. My father was a fair man and one who believed in the Bill of Rights."

Aunt Oradelle's eyes bulged alarmingly, and an angry flushed suffused her face. She started to deliver a long and withering dressing-down to her niece, but before she could say a word, a man's voice interrupted her. "Good evening, ladies."

Millicent's head snapped around. It was Jonathan, standing there before them. He had taken off his hat and left it by the door, and without the shadow of the hat brim the fading bruises on his face were glaring. He had addressed the women sitting there in general, but his eyes were on Millicent, and they were bright with amusement—and with something else. Millicent wasn't sure what his look meant, but it made her stomach begin to perform furious somersaults.

"Jo—Mr. Lawrence." Inwardly Millicent cursed herself for the slip of her tongue.

Aunt Oradelle turned her gaze on Jonathan and coolly nodded her head. The look in her eyes would have felled an elephant at twenty feet, but Jonathan Lawrence merely smiled without a trace of embarrassment or intimidation.

"How are you this fine evening?" he continued placidly.

"Fine, thank you." Camilla spoke up and was silenced by a look from her stepmother.

"Enjoying the dance?"

"Yes. And you?" Millicent's voice was a little breathless; she hoped it didn't betray too much of the excitement within her.

"I'm sure I will enjoy it if you will be so kind as to dance with me, Miss Hayes."

Millicent felt as if her heart were suddenly bouncing around in her chest. She hadn't intended to dance with him. Frankly, she hadn't really expected Jonathan to ask her. She had thought he might sit with her and talk or they might take a stroll through the crowded room to the refreshment table. Dancing with him probably wasn't the proper thing to do. Certainly, Aunt Oradelle wouldn't think so. Out of the corner of her eye, Millicent saw her aunt turn toward her, and her expression was pointed.

Millicent opened her mouth to decline the dance, but she heard herself say, "Why, yes, Mr. Lawrence, I'd love to."

Ignoring one aunt's astounded look and the other one's hastily smothered giggle of delight, Millicent stood up on feet that scarcely seemed to belong to her. She held out her hand, and Jonathan took it to lead her out onto the dance floor.

Millicent felt as if she floated through that dance in Jonathan's arms. He held her expertly, his hand light but firm upon her waist, his other hand curled warmly around hers, and he danced not just competently, but with a kind of joie de vivre that was rare.

"I think your aunt was less than pleased," he commented with a smile, nodding his head toward where Aunt Oradelle sat, watching them with a thunderous expression.

A giggle escaped Millicent. Whirling about the floor in his arms, she felt as young and carefree as a girl. "I think you're right."

"I take it she doesn't approve of me."

"I don't think she approves of me *dancing* with you." Millicent paused, then added honestly, "Actually, I don't think she approves of you, either."

"And I thought you said I was such a marvelous catch in this town," he joked.

"Aunt Oradelle is an exception to the general rule. For one thing, she doesn't have a marriageable daughter. For another, her husband is Jonas Watson's banker."

"Ah, it's becoming clearer to me."

"She is also a pillar of the First Baptist Church."

"Which owns some of the riverfront property. Mm. I can see I'm sinking deeper and deeper."

"Add to that my impertinence and disobedience, and . . . "

Jonathan threw back his head and laughed. "You? Miss Millicent Hayes, the very symbol of ladylike propriety? You have been impertinent and disobedient to your aunt?"

"You needn't laugh," Millicent retorted sharply, but then she couldn't help but chuckle herself.

"You have to tell me what you've done that was so sinful."

"I took in Opal, for one thing, and when Aunt Oradelle told me how improper it was and decreed that I must get rid of her, I refused. Nor does she like my seeing Betsy so much."

"Betsy!" His brows drew together. "Opal is one thing: I find the fact abhorrent, but I realize that most ladies would consider her beyond the pale. But a ten-year-old girl? How can she be a wicked influence?"

"Oh, she's not a wicked influence. It's just that her being with me will make people talk. They'll think, you know . . . " Millicent glanced down, her voice suddenly faltering in embarrassment.

"No, I don't know. They'll think what?"

She looked up at him, surprised, and saw that his eyes were dancing in merriment. "Oh, you!" A blush rose in her face. "You know what they will think it means about you and me!"

"Tell me." His thumb moved caressingly on her hand.

Millicent jumped; it felt as though lightning had darted through her hand. "Stop. You're trying to provoke me."

"No. I'm trying not to kiss you right here in front of everyone."

Millicent's breath caught in her throat. She stared into his eyes, no longer twinkling, but suddenly hot and searching. She could think of nothing to say in response.

"When you look at me like that, it makes it all the more difficult," he murmured.

Millicent tore her eyes from his. Her insides were like hot wax.

"No, don't look away," he protested. "I'm perverse enough to enjoy the torture."

"You're teasing me. I—I don't know how to respond to you."

"I'm teasing myself, perhaps." His voice was low. "I wasn't reared a gentleman; it isn't bred in me to want a woman, yet keep the desire leashed. I enjoy being with you; I even like the hunger I feel. But it's difficult sometimes not to let my need overwhelm my judgment."

Millicent drew a shaky breath. "I've never met a man who talked as you do. I think it's probably disrespectful."

"Not disrespectful. Never that. Can you not respect a woman and desire her, too? Isn't it showing respect that you tell her the truth?"

"I—I don't know. You confuse me. You're very persuasive." She smiled at him, dimpling. "I think that makes you dangerous. I shouldn't feel safe with you."

The dance ended, and Jonathan reluctantly released her. "Will you give me another dance?"

Millicent wanted to tell him she'd dance with him all night, but of course that was impossible. It would be improper to dance more than two, at most three, dances with him. If she danced with him several times, tongues would be clacking all over the room; it would be a scandal. Reluctantly she told him, "Perhaps another one later."

"Then could I bring you some punch?"

"Yes, that would be nice."

He walked with her from the dance floor to the refreshment table and picked up glasses of punch for them both. They drank them, chatting. Millicent felt as if every eye in the place were on them. It was exasperating, really, the way everyone in Emmetsville made it their business to know everything that was going on with everyone else. She would have thought that people had more to do than sit around calculating how much time one woman spent with a certain man at a dance.

Millicent knew that such thoughts were heresy here. She had lived with the unwritten rules of behavior all her life; most of the time she followed them without question. But now she examined them and wondered what their value was. And why was it that the Aunt Oradelles of the world were the ones who were given the right to dictate behavior to the rest of them? Why were they any better judges of morality than she?

She was somewhat amazed by the thoughts she was having. She could well imagine what Aunt Oradelle would say about them. But she could not deny her own logic. In fact, she could not understand why she had never thought of these things before.

When they finished their punch, there was no reason to delay any longer returning to Aunt Oradelle's side. Millicent gritted her teeth and walked back to her aunt with Jonathan. She hated the prospect of sitting and listening to Aunt Oradelle's scolding for the rest of the evening. So she was pleased when just after she sat down, before Aunt Oradelle could get started on her tirade, William Butler walked up and asked Millicent to dance.

Millicent jumped up and accepted his invitation under the astounded gaze of her aunt. After she danced with William, she was surprised to be asked to dance three more times in a row. Of course, two of the men were widowers old enough to be her father, and the other was one of her cousins, a man who was terribly shy around most women. Still, it had been years since she had done anything but sit with the chaperones at a party, and she enjoyed the dances thoroughly. She couldn't understand why suddenly she was a popular dance partner.

When she walked back to her aunt's side after the third dance, her skin was glowing, her eyes vivid. She was unaware of how pretty she was or of how different she appeared from the restrained, even colorless image that had been Millicent Hayes for several years past. Aunt Sophie was beaming at her, and Camilla was watching her with a secretive, eager joy. Aunt Oradelle was frowning, but Millicent decided to ignore her. She felt too good to let her aunt infuriate her again.

"Millie!" Aunt Sophie leaned across the massive expanse of Aunt Oradelle's bosom and patted Millicent's hand. "You looked beautiful out there! I'm so happy to see you coming out of hiding after all these years."

Hiding? Millicent didn't understand, but she smiled back anyway.

"Happy? Hmmph!" Oradelle shot a look of scorn at her sister-in-law. "You never did have any more sense than a peahen, Sophie."

"Oh, pooh!" Sophie waved her fan airily, dismissing Oradelle's remark. "You're just disgruntled because Millicent's done something without you arranging it. Be happy for the girl. She's doing what she should have been doing for years now. She's enjoying herself."

"That's just like you. As if enjoying oneself were what's important."

"Well, it is what's important at a party. A dance is no time for doom and gloom. It's all fine and well for you and me to sit around discussing Edna Rundberg's misery in her bones, but Millicent's young. She should be having fun, and I, for one, am glad to see her doing it."

"She can have fun without making a spectacle of herself," Oradell retorted heatedly and shook her folded fan at Sophie. "You mark my words, she's going to regret her behavior this night!"

"My word, you're like an old crow. That's exactly the way you are, Oradelle, sitting here casting gloom over everything."

Millicent could hardly keep from laughing aloud. In all the years that she had known her, Aunt Oradelle had carped at and needled Aunt Sophie, but never before had Millicent heard her placid aunt take Aunt Oradelle tó task for it. "The worm turns," she murmured under her breath, and beside her Camilla smothered an unladylike snort of laughter.

Aunt Oradelle stared in shock at her brother's wife. "Why, Sophie Cortland! You talk as if I didn't want Millicent to be happy! As if I didn't care about her!" Oradelle's chins quivered in indignation. "You know that isn't true! Who was it that sat up with her all night when she had the fever when she was a little girl and her mama was down with it, too? And who, I'd like to know, helped her through her poor father's funeral?"

"It was you, Oradelle, we all know that. I certainly am not trying to say that you don't have a caring heart or that you don't love Millicent. There's no one who is more a tower of strength than you are whenever there's trouble in this family. Everybody knows that."

It was true, Millicent knew. Aunt Oradelle, for all her exasperating ways, loved her family above everything else, and she was always ready to help. In fact, Millicent thought that Aunt Oradelle never enjoyed life as much as she did when there was a crisis to be managed or a tragedy to be weathered.

Oradelle gave a short nod, somewhat mollified by Sophie's words.

"But I don't see," Sophie went on calmly, "why loving Millicent gives you the right to decide how she should live, or to squelch her whenever she starts to have a bit of fun."

Oradelle blinked. Millicent was unsure whether she was actually considering Aunt Sophie's words or simply silenced by amazement at her continued defiance.

Oradelle swung her head around to look at Millicent. "Is that what you think of me, Millicent?" she asked her in tones of awful politeness, her wounded feelings vibrating beneath the surface. "Do you think that I am like Mary Ada?" She named the sour-faced great-aunt who had for years cast a dismal shadow over everyone around her. "Always criticizing? Always bemoaning everything that's been lost?"

Millicent felt her usual twinge of guilt at the hurt look in her aunt's eyes. Aunt Oradelle was good-hearted, which was more than one could say for Aunt Mary Ada, and she had done so much for everyone else in the family. "Of course not, Aunt Oradelle," she replied quickly. "You aren't like Aunt Mary Ada. You know that."

"Oh, Oradelle, stop putting words in my mouth," Sophie flashed. "I never said you were like Aunt Mary Ada. Good Lord, that woman was raised on sour milk and paregoric. But I don't see why it's so blamed wrong for Millicent to dance and have a good time. The poor child deserves it."

"There's a world of difference between having a good time and acting like you haven't got good sense." Oradelle fixed a doleful look upon her niece. "I'll tell you this, young lady, you set your sights on a man like that, and you're setting yourself up for a world of hurt."

"I am not setting my sights on anyone, least of all Jonathan Lawrence!" Millicent retorted, stung.

"No?"

"No! I'm just dancing. And I'm enjoying it. And I don't think there's anything wrong with that!"

Aunt Oradelle's mouth tightened in irritation. "It isn't proper for a woman your age to be out whirling all over the floor, especially with a man as questionable as that Jonathan Lawrence. It doesn't look right. Why, what would your father think?"

Millicent wavered for a moment. Her aunt had

touched upon her weakest point. Was what she had done tonight disgraceful? Would her father have been ashamed of her if he could have seen her tonight?

"I don't know," Millicent answered honestly. She drew a shaky breath and continued, "And, frankly, I don't see how that has anything to do with this. My father isn't here, and he never will be again, and all I can do is rely on my own judgment." She stood up. "Now, if you'll excuse me . . ."

Millicent turned and strode rapidly away from them.

Sixteen

$\mathcal{M}$illicent wound her way through the crowd of people, not sure where she was going. She knew only that she had had to get away from Aunt Oradelle before she managed to strip her of this evening's happy glow. The barn was packed with people, and the noise and heat were stifling. Millicent decided that she would get a breath of fresh air.

She slipped out the side door of the barn, open like all the other doors and everything else that could possibly be opened to admit the cooler outside air, and strolled across the side yard. The Miller home was lit up, and several women were walking from it toward the barn, carrying a tub of punch. On the porch of the house sat several young girls playing jacks. Millicent hesitated, unsure where to turn. She didn't want to see anyone, so she couldn't go toward the house, but she wasn't about to walk around behind the barn, where the rowdier boys and young men tended to congregate at a dance. There were several men down by the corral, talking and passing a bottle among them, which eliminated that direction, as well.

As she stood there, a masculine voice behind her asked, "Out for a bit of air, or did your aunt drive you away?"

"Jonathan!" She recognized his teasing voice immediately and whirled around. "What are you doing here?"

"I could say, the same thing you are, cooling off; but the truth is, I was watching you and I decided to follow."

"Oh." Somehow, standing here with him in the dim light spilling out from the barn made Millicent feel breathless.

"Don't you know that it isn't proper for you to be out here alone?" he added, his grin flashing in the darkness.

"Well, it certainly isn't proper for me to be out here with you."

He chuckled. "No doubt that's even worse. Which is a good reason to move away from the barn." He took her arm and propelled her around the barn toward the other side.

Millicent had to laugh, and she did not resist his pressure on her arm. They passed another couple leaning against a wagon and talking in front of the barn, as well as two men out for an evening's cigar. They nodded to them, and Millicent wondered if they would tell everyone that they'd seen the Hayes girl outside *all alone* with that Lawrence fellow.

Jonathan's thoughts must have run along the same lines, for he asked, "Will the word be all over town tomorrow that you and I left the barn together?"

"More likely it will be all over by the end of the dance tonight." Millicent chuckled. "I remember once when

I was seventeen, Teddy White and I slipped out of a dance at Mrs. Crawford's house and went walking in the back yard. Papa was furious—mostly because my great-aunt heard about it and gave him a proper lecture about letting me run wild."

Jonathan smiled. "Why, Millicent!" He tsk-tsked, trying to sound grave. "I can't imagine you indulging in such scandalous behavior."

"It was worse, only thank heavens Papa and Aunt Mary Ada didn't know about all of it. Teddy kissed me behind the pecan tree, too."

He glanced at her, his eyebrows shooting up in an amused way. "My, my, my, the things I'm discovering about you. And here I thought you were the gravest of young ladies, the epitome of virtue."

"Hush." Millicent rapped her fan sharply against his arm. "Stop making fun of me."

"Me? I wouldn't do that. But you have to tell me about this wicked kiss you received." They had left the barn behind and were strolling along the edge of the wagons and buggies bunched in front of the barn. Jonathan stopped and leaned back against the side of a wagon, pulling Millicent around to face him. "Did you enjoy it?"

Millicent gazed up at him. The moon was barely a sliver, leaving the night illuminated by the pale starlight. Jonathan's eyes were in shadow, his shock of blond hair a light streak in the dimness. He seemed a stranger, looming and unknowable—and exciting, as well, like the dangerous beauty of a dark bayou.

"Enjoy what?" Millicent's voice came out barely a whisper. She couldn't pull her eyes away from his face.

His smile was lazy and sensual. "The kiss, silly. The one outside the dance with Teddy Whatever."

"White." Millicent swallowed. Her stomach was dancing crazily. She couldn't keep her gaze from going back to Jonathan's mouth. His lower lip was full, seductive, the upper one sharply cut. She remembered the taste of them on her own lips weeks ago. "Well . . ." she began shakily. "I don't remember much."

"What a blow to Mr. White." Jonathan's voice fell even lower and softer.

"It was my first kiss. All I was concerned about was its happening, not how it felt."

"Your first kiss." His hand came up to her face, and Jonathan lightly traced her lips with his forefinger. His voice was husky. "I wish I'd been there. I wish I'd been the man."

"Then I wouldn't have forgotten," Millicent replied without thinking, and when she realized what she had admitted, she blushed furiously. "Oh, no, I'm sorry. I shouldn't have said that."

She started to step back, but Jonathan grabbed her arm and stopped her. His hand was fiery hot even through the cloth of her dress. "Oh, yes. Yes, you should. It's exactly what I wanted to hear."

He took hold of her other arm, too, and tugged her gently closer. Millicent moved will-lessly forward, until her body was only a fraction of an inch from Jonathan's, so close that she could feel the heat of his flesh and see the glitter of his eyes.

"You are beautiful tonight," he murmured. "When I saw you, I nearly came out of my skin, you looked so good. It was hard as hell to keep my hands off you while we were dancing. Even harder to let you go."

His words shot through Millicent like wildfire, lighting up every part of her body. A heavy, pulsing heat started low in her abdomen. She felt softer, as if she were malleable, as if she couldn't stand on her own. She swayed a little, and her body touched his.

She heard him pull in his breath sharply. His arms went around her, hard and tight, pulling her into the furnace of his body. He curved down over her, pressing her flat against him all the way up and down, and his mouth sought hers. Millicent tilted her head up to meet him. There was no coyness in her, no genteel protestation, only a hunger to feel his mouth on hers again, to melt into his heat.

He kissed her deeply, and this time when his tongue came into her mouth, she did not jerk away. Her heart skittered in her chest, and she curled her hands into the lapels of his coat, hanging onto him in the storm of sensation that whirled through her. Her skin sizzled everywhere she was flattened against him, and her breasts were strangely full and achy, yearning in the same way as her loins. Jonathan's breath was hot upon her cheek. The sharp scent of his flesh filled her nostrils. His tongue possessed her mouth, demanding, consuming. She was surrounded by him, inundated, yet it wasn't enough. Millicent pressed up into him, wanting more, and her tongue twined around his.

Jonathan's breath shuddered out. One hand slid

down to her hips and pushed her tightly against him. Millicent felt the hard ridge of his desire even through the layers of her clothing and she sensed its meaning. She went up on tiptoe, rubbing her body against his as she did, and wrapped her arms around his neck, holding onto him for dear life. It was all she could do to swallow the moan that rose in her throat.

Jonathan groaned, echoing her own hunger, and tore his mouth away from hers to wildly kiss her neck and face. He turned, pinning her against the wagon, and he took her mouth once more. His hard body crushed the air from her, but Millicent hardly noticed, too wrapped up in her clamoring need to care. She dug her fingers into his hair, delighting in the contrast of his silky hair and the hard bone of his skull. She wanted to taste him, to touch him. Oh, Lord, she wanted to feel his hands on her body.

A whimper escaped her, and Jonathan shuddered at the sound. His lips dug into hers, his tongue raking her mouth, and his hands slipped in between their bodies, sliding upward. He felt the pillow softness of her breasts, and his hands covered them, savoring the points of her nipples against the dress. It was all he could do not to rip at her dress to expose them to his hands and mouth.

The feel of his hands on her breasts was shockingly delightful to Millicent. She had never dreamed that anything could feel like this, that she could want the things she wanted, that her senses could be so filled. It was crazy. Stunning. She was lost in the new, wild sensations, unable to pull together any threads of her lost control.

"Millicent. Millicent." He mumbled her name as his lips moved across her face to nibble at her earlobe. His breath rasped in her ear, sending shivers through her.

Beyond them, near the open front doors of the barn, a man's laugh rang out, and then there were the higher pitched tones of a woman, calling good-bye to a friend. The sounds penetrated the haze of Millicent's and Jonathan's desire, jerking them back into the realm of the real world.

Jonathan froze, fighting a fierce internal battle. With a gusty sigh, he buried his lips in her hair and stood for a moment, willing his taut muscles to relax. Millicent wanted to cry out to him not to stop, but she knew as well as he how impossible their situation was. She bit her lip to hold back her protests. They were standing so close that she felt his muscles gradually loosen. He stepped back.

"I'm sorry. I—I will remember next time how easily you affect me." He raked a hand back through his hair and gave her a shaky smile.

Millicent gazed at him gravely, not knowing what to say; she wasn't sure she was yet capable of speech. She had always thought that it was men who were the prisoners of their raw desires, but certainly at this moment it was she rather than Jonathan who was unable to function normally.

"Ah, Millie, don't look at me like that," he told her huskily, "or I'll forget myself all over again."

Millicent glanced away from him. "I'm sorry."

"No. I'm the one who should apologize. I—normally

I am not quite this impulsive." He glanced at her uneasily. "I hope I haven't . . . offended you."

Despite the turmoil inside her, Millicent had to giggle. She felt as wild and tumbled, as thrumming with desire, as the loosest of loose women, yet he asked if his actions offended her!

Jonathan relaxed, chuckling with her. "That's my Millicent." He reached out and smoothed his finger down her cheek. She could feel the faint tremor in his flesh. "I knew beneath all that starch you weren't prim at all. God, but you're a woman to treasure."

Millicent blinked, surprised by his statement. She would never have thought of herself in that way. The women whom men treasured were delicate little creatures, frail and lovely, women like her mother had been, not healthy, dependable sorts like herself. She was more likely to be termed a "hard worker" or a "good woman" than a treasure. Yet Jonathan looked perfectly serious, without the usual twinkle in his eyes.

"I—uh, thank you."

He drew a breath and let it out slowly. "We should return now."

"Yes. We should." Neither of them moved.

"Damn. This shouldn't be so difficult." Jonathan frowned. "I thought I'd gotten over this sort of thing years ago."

"What sort of thing?"

"Being unable to part with a woman. Wanting to linger here and watch you, talk to you, just keep you with me. I feel like a schoolboy."

A warmth swelled in Millicent's chest at his words.

She knew what he was talking about. There was some-thing in her that felt the same way. She didn't want to leave him, didn't want to return to the dance. She wanted to laugh and talk with him all night. But that was impossible.

Millicent sighed and turned her head. She was a sensible woman now, not a flirtatious girl. She had to act sensibly. "But we must go back."

"You're right." He turned, and they walked toward the barn. The nearer they grew, the more their steps slowed, and finally, just beyond the yellow rectangle of light coming through the open barn doors, they stopped entirely.

Millicent looked at Jonathan. "I'd better go in by myself."

"All right." He reached up and smoothed back a stray lock of her hair.

Millicent blushed, remembering suddenly that she was probably in disarray from the time she had spent in Jonathan's arms. She brushed down her dress with her hands and repinned the loose strands of her hair. "Do I look all right?"

Jonathan smiled slowly. "You look lovely."

Pleasure spread through her, and she glanced away in embarrassment. "No. I mean, is everything in place?"

"Completely."

Well, her hair and clothes might be back to normal, but Millicent suspected that nothing could get rid of the new glow in her cheeks or the sparkle in her eyes. "Good night."

"Good night." Jonathan took her hand for a moment, and there was a wealth of unspoken promise in his touch. Reluctantly he released her hand and stepped back.

Millicent turned and walked away from him, back to her family.

Every day after Opal had suggested that Alan get himself in and out of bed, he had struggled to increase the strength in his arms. He worked until the sweat stood out on his brow and his muscles were sore. Often his long-unused muscles protested painfully. He became disheartened at his slow progress. There were days when it seemed to him that he was accomplishing nothing except making himself hurt all over. He should quit, he told himself, give up and go back to the life he had lived for so long.

But something inside him refused to give up. Whenever he thought about it, a steely refusal rose up in him, and he would push onward. He had to do it; he would do it. No matter how long it took, no matter how much it hurt, no matter how frustrating it was, he was determined to see this through to the end.

He didn't tell anyone except Betsy about his plans. She sneaked in bricks and rocks when his books were no longer heavy enough. She asked eager questions and encouraged him, and Alan was sure that he would never have made it without her childish enthusiasm.

After some weeks of his work, it became obvious to Alan that he would never be able to gain enough strength in his arms unless he began to try to lift his own weight from the bed. He would have to install the bar he had envisioned above his bed. Once he did that, everyone would know what he was trying to do. Then they would be watching and waiting to see what happened. Everyone would know if he failed. Opal would know. He hated the thought of it, but there was no other way.

One morning he called Johnny into his room and explained how he wanted the bar hung from the high ceiling of his room so that it dangled just above him on one side of the bed. Johnny listened, nodding his head, moved Alan into his chair and pushed it to the far side of the room, and set up a ladder to begin work. It took him some time to get the ropes and bar set up just as Alan wanted them, but eventually he did and was able to move Alan back into his bed.

Scared and eager, Alan took hold of the bar for the first time and began to pull himself up by it. He couldn't do it. He paused, letting his arms lie still by his side. Then he flexed his fingers and tried again. He strained upward, trying desperately to pull his weight at least a little off the mattress. At last his fingers slipped from the bar, and he fell back, panting from the exertion.

He felt like screaming. Frustration knotted his stomach, and he cursed under his breath.

"What?" Opal asked, coming into the room, a stack of linen in her hands. She stopped and stared at the contraption Johnny had rigged to the ceiling. Her mouth dropped open. She tore her eyes away from the equipment and stared at Alan. "You're going to try it?"

She sounded breathless with amazement and happiness, and a brilliant grin spread across her face. "Oh, Alan! That's wonderful! Do you think you can do it?"

She hurried over to the side of his bed, a hundred questions already forming in her mind. The angry expression on Alan's face stopped her. "What—what's the matter?"

"I can't do it, that's what's the matter." Alan's eyes blazed with rage and frustration. "Dammit!" He slammed his fist back into the heavy wooden headboard. He hit it again and again, emphasizing each word, "I cannot do it! I'm useless!"

"No! Please don't say that. You're not. Not at all." She put down her load of linens on the bed and reached out to take his hand solicitously in hers. She felt his hand twitch beneath hers, and he jerked it away.

"Stop it! Stop humoring me. Do you think I don't know it? I do! I can't do anything. I'm not worth anything. I'm nothing but a millstone around Millicent's neck."

Opal stared at him, appalled. "No! I'm sure she doesn't think that."

"She may not think it. She's too good. But if it weren't for me, she would be married now and have children. She'd—she'd be with *him*—" he jerked his head in the direction of the Lawrence house "—instead of here with me. How can she be fulfilled? How can she be happy when she's sacrificing her life for a crippled brother?"

"Millicent loves you."

"I know. That's why she's given up her life. And for what?" He ran his hands roughly up his face and back through his hair, as if he could somehow physically remove the pain and despair raging through him. "It would have been better if I'd died when I fell off that wagon. I wish to God I had."

"No!" The normally quiet, even timid Opal surprised them both by grabbing his shoulders and digging in her fingers, shaking him with all her strength. "Don't say that! Don't you dare say that! I thank God that you're alive! You were given a great gift. How can you despise it? There are so many people who would have given anything if they had been spared, if they had been able to go on living. You should be grateful!"

Alan stared at her, shocked into silence by her changed manner.

"What would have happened to me if you had died? Or to my baby? You and your sister wouldn't have been here to take me in and give me hope and . . . and kindness." Tears glittered in her eyes. "What about what you've done for Betsy? Haven't you seen the change in that child? How much happier she is now that she has you and Millicent as friends?"

"I haven't done anything. Both those things were Millicent's doing, not mine."

"She wouldn't even be living here if you had died! She would be married and living in her husband's house. Or perhaps she would still be single because she was never able to recover from the tragedy of her brother's death. But then she'd be living with her aunt or some other relative, without even a house of her own. Besides, it wasn't only Millicent's doing. Do you honestly think that she would have let me stay if you had objected to taking me in? What about your kindness to me, the way you treat me, as if I was a lady and not some girl from the gutter?"

"You're not 'some girl from the gutter.'" He scowled.

Opal shook her head fiercely. "I am. I've never felt like I was anything, leastways until I came here. You and Miss Millicent have been good to me." Tears filled her eyes and she had to swallow hard before she could continue. "You've never thrown my past up at me or treated me like I was cheap."

"Good Lord, whyever would I?" Alan gaped at her.

Opal smiled, blinking the moisture from her eyes. "That's what I mean. You're such a nice man, such a gentleman that you wouldn't even consider taking advantage of a woman who was beholden to you."

"No! Don't misspeak yourself. I won't allow it."

"Thank you. You make me feel—I don't know, so much better than I am. Like I'm as good as anybody else."

"Opal . . ." Alan took her hand in his and squeezed it, his anger and frustration melting away in concern for her. "That's the way you should feel. That's the way you are. You *are* quality. Its shines out of you."

Her cheeks flushed. "Oh, Mr. Hayes . . . "

"Alan."

"Alan."

His name, murmured in her soft, low voice, sent a shiver through him. He thought about lifting her hand to his lips and kissing it. He thought about holding it against his heart. His breath quickened, and his skin turned warm. He released her hand awkwardly and looked away.

"I—I'm sorry I spoke so harshly earlier." He tried to pull his mind away from where it wanted to go.

"There's no need to apologize."

"Yes, there is. Sometimes I'm an ungrateful wretch, I know. I have a great deal to be thankful for; I am alive. But it's hard to accept my inabilities. When you mentioned that idea the other day, about me pulling myself in and out of bed, I wanted so much to do it, and . . . " He breathed out a sigh of disgust. "Oh, hell! I've been working on it for days, and I tried today to pull myself up. It was futile."

"But, Alan," Opal said earnestly, leaning forward and putting her hand on his arm. "You can't expect to do that right off. Today's the first time you've tried to lift your body. Your arms simply don't have the strength. But if you keep working on it, you will. I mean, I'm sure nobody could do it the very first time he tried."

Alan smiled crookedly. For the moment he believed her. When Opal smiled at him, trust and admiration beaming out of her eyes, it was impossible for him not to believe her. After she left his room, Alan reached up to the bar and wrapped his hands around it to try again. This time he clung firmly enough to the bar that his fingers didn't slip from it when he tried to pull himself up. He strained upwards, his arms aching, and this time he actually moved. It wasn't much, probably no more than an inch off the bed. But it was something, and when he let go and flopped back against his pillow, he was smiling.

Over the course of the next few days, he tried time and gain to pull himself up. His muscles ached from the constant testing, but he refused to give in to the pain. He kept at it every day, several times each day, and in between the times he was trying to pull up at the bar, he was using heavier and heavier weights to exercise his arms. As he made progress, he began to realize that perhaps he actually could do it. For the first time in years, he was flooded with hope.

Before long he lifted himself enough that he could bump his way clumsily across the bed and back. It wouldn't do for the swing out into the chair, but it was an accomplishment, and Alan was filled with pride. Millicent, who had been watching her brother's progress with a combination of anxiety and pride, was amazed, then thrilled. Opal was gratifyingly pleased by his progress, though there was none of the surprise in her that he saw in Millicent. Alan realized that Opal had been sure from the start that he would be able to do it. Her belief in him warmed him through and through.

Opal grew heavier and slower every day, and finally Millicent was able to persuade her to stop trying to work. Her time was near, Alan knew, and he worried about her. She looked tired even though she had stopped working. She had told Alan that she had trouble sleeping at night, often waking up and sometimes spending long sleepless hours tossing and turning, trying to find a comfortable position. Alan dreaded her birthing, afraid of what might happen to Opal. So many women died. He knew little about childbirth; he'd never had cause to think about it before, and it certainly wasn't a topic anyone was likely to discuss with him. All he'd had were the hints gleaned through the years and the example of the various animals they had owned. He had heard bits of hushed tales of the awful pain involved. He couldn't bear to think of Opal in pain. Just the idea of it turned his blood cold.

He tried to keep his mind off it, to ignore the fact of Opal's rapidly approaching childbearing. Instead he concentrated on pulling himself out of his bed and into the invalid chair beside it. The first time he bumped and wriggled his way to the edge of the bed and looked down at his chair, it seemed as though a deep chasm lay between them. Just thinking of swinging free out of the bed and dangling above the chair filled him with fear.

Rationally, he knew that the space that separated his bed from the chair was only a few inches; it was his anxiety that made it appear enormous. But it was obvious that his bed was far too high above the chair. He couldn't possibly drop into the chair from that level. He remembered Opal saying that the crippled veteran she had known had had a low bed. The next day he had Johnny search the attic for an old bed and cut the legs down until it sat only an inch or two above the height of the chair arms. Once the new bed was installed in his room, Alan pulled himself over to the edge of the bed and looked across at his chair.

It still looked impossible.

He knew that his arms were strong enough to hold

him as he swung his body out from the bed and into the chair. What held him back was fear.

Then the nightmares began to return. Alan wondered if he was crazy for putting himself to this test. But the thought of Opal's faith in him kept Alan going.

One morning he woke up resolutely determined that this would be the day he did it. Before he could think and worry or waylay himself with fear, he reached up, grabbed the bar, and swung himself over to the edge of the bed. He glanced down at the chair beside his bed, wrapped his fingers tightly around the bar, closed his eyes, and swung himself out.

He couldn't let go, and the momentum of his swing brought him back against the bed. All at once his fingers slipped from the bar, and he fell, half sprawling over the chair. It knocked the wind from him and one of the arms of the chair bit cruelly into his side. For an instant he lay there, stunned. Then he realized that he was out of the bed and into the chair—after a fashion. Forgetting about the pain, Alan began to squirm and wriggle until he was fully in the chair, using his arms to pull him up and then to turn his body around.

When he was sitting upright in the chair at last, he flopped back against its high wicker back. He had made it. He had gotten out of bed under his own power, and he had managed to get into the chair, no matter how clumsily. He wiped the sweat from his brow and smiled. He had done it. And he knew that from now on it would get easier and easier.

The door opened a few minutes later and Opal came into the room, carrying a tray of food, saying, "Ida says

Johnny'll be late, so I thought I'd—" she came to a dead stop and her voice dwindled away "—bring you your food." She stood staring at him for a moment, then said, "Alan! You're in your chair!" Alan nodded. A grin burst upon Opal's face like sunlight. "You did it!"

She set the tray down on the bed, the food forgotten, and hurried around the bed to his chair. "I'm so proud of you! This is wonderful!" Impulsively she bent down and hugged him, her cheek pressing against his.

It was all Alan could do not to grab her arms and hold her there. She smelled so sweet and fresh and felt so good. It was like a glimpse of heaven to feel her hands on his arms and her face against his for that brief moment. He looked up at her smiling face.

He knew that everything it had taken to be able to leave his bed was worth it.

Seventeen

Alan came slowly awake. He blinked in the darkness, foggily wondering what had pulled him from his sleep. Then he heard a sound, faint but disturbing, and he knew it was this that had penetrated his consciousness.

But what was it? He sat up, listening. There was only the surrounding stillness of night. He heard nothing but the steady thump of his heart. Finally, it came again, a low-pitched moaning sound, quickly cut off. Even before he realized what it was, what it meant, it sent a shiver through him, and he began to move instinctively toward the edge of the bed. It was Opal.

For an instant he froze. Then he grabbed the bar and swung out into his chair, not even thinking about an act that had seemed such an accomplishment yesterday. He had no thought except Opal. Her time must have come, and she needed help.

Releasing the stop on his chair, Alan wheeled around his bed and out into the hall, rushing toward the little room that lay beneath the stairs. Opal's door was closed. Alan didn't even knock, just yanked it open.

—311—

"Opal?" His voice came out too loud in his fear, bouncing around the small room.

He stopped. Opal was sitting up in her bed, leaning against the side wall. Alan could barely see her in the dim light, but her distress was obvious in the way she huddled against the wall. "Opal?" he repeated, moving closer.

"Yes." Her voice came out constrained and faint, and her fast, ragged breathing was loud in the dark.

"What's the matter?" Alan could see the boxy shape of the low chest of drawers, and he wheeled his chair to it. He took the kerosene lamp in his hand and pulled the chimney off, then felt across the top of the chest until he found the matches. He lit the wick, adjusted it, and replaced the chimney. He turned back to Opal. "Is it the baby?"

Opal nodded. In the lamplight he could see her taut, sweat-dampened face; her eyes were stark with pain and fear.

"I think so," she told him, her voice unsteady. "I'm having pains. Every few minutes I get another one. The last one's over, but—but it won't be long now."

Alan wet his lips nervously. He was completely at a loss. He wanted to take the pain away from Opal, but that, of course, was impossible. He had no idea what needed to be done. He rolled over to the door and called up as loudly as he could, "Millicent! Millicent!"

It was only seconds before he heard his sister's feet flying across the hallway above him and down the stairs. "What? Alan?"

Millicent dashed down the last few steps and into the

hall. She was wearing only a nightgown. Her feet were bare, and her hair hung in a thick braid down her back. Her face was contorted with anxiety. She stopped abruptly when she saw Alan, leaning out from his chair into the hall. She looked confused for an instant. Her expression cleared. "Oh, my Lord!"

She ran to Opal's room. As she stepped inside, Opal let out a muffled groan. Alan swung around, and his insides iced up. Opal bent over, clutching the bed-clothes beside her, and her face twisted in pain. Alan clenched his hands around the arms of his chair in frustration and empathy. He looked toward his sister. "Millie! Do something!"

"I'll go for the doctor," Millicent said decisively.

"No," Opal protested feebly. "Please, you'll wake him up. It's the middle of the night. I'm sure he wouldn't want to be pulled out of his bed for this. It'll be a while yet, I think. Sometimes it takes hours."

"Hours!" The blood drained from Alan's face. Opal was to be in this pain for hours?

"Don't be silly," Millicent replied stoutly. "You don't know for sure how long it will take. I certainly don't. We need the doctor. And if he didn't want to be rousted out of his bed in the middle of the night, he shouldn't have become a doctor." Millicent put an end to the matter with a decisive nod of her head, once again in charge of the situation. She whirled around and sailed out of the room, calling back over her shoulder, "I'll fetch Dr. Morton. Alan, you stay with Opal."

Alan nodded. He had no intention of going any-where else. He rolled his chair over next to Opal's bed as Millicent's feet thundered up the steps above their heads.

"It'll be all right now," he told Opal reassuringly. "She'll be back with the doctor before you know it. And Dr. Morton's good. He pulled me out of it, you know, years ago when I had my accident. Nobody was sure I'd live, but he managed to patch me up."

Opal nodded and tried to smile, but it was a failure. Her face was utterly devoid of color, and her eyes were huge and dark with fear and pain. "Alan?"

"Yes?"

"I'm scared."

His own fear gushed up in him, but he pushed it aside. He couldn't let her see that he, too, was scared about what might happen to her. It would only make it harder for her. "Opal, no!" He took her hands in his. "Don't be scared. Don't worry. Dr. Morton's the best."

"I'm so alone."

"No, you aren't. I'll be with you. I won't let anything happen to you." It was what he wanted, what he felt for her, though he wondered inside what he could possibly do to stop her pain or keep death away from her.

"What if I die?" she whispered. The bluish circles under her eyes made them look even larger than they were, and her hands were small and frail in his. Alan's heart clenched.

"No! Don't say that! You won't die. I told you, the doctor will be here soon, and he'll take care of you."

"A doctor can't make your baby come right if it isn't meant to. Sometimes it just comes your time, and there's nothing anybody can do about it."

"Stop talking that way. It isn't your time," Alan insisted. "Look, Opal, once you told me I was the smartest man you knew."

Opal nodded faintly. "You are."

"Then believe me. I know what I'm talking about. You aren't going to die." He squeezed her hands more tightly and stared deep into her eyes, trying to infuse his gaze with all the confidence and calm he possessed. He had to make her believe him. He didn't know nearly as much as Opal liked to give him credit for, but one thing he was certain of: The doubts and fears Opal was feeling would only make her delivery more difficult; she might not struggle hard if she kept thinking that perhaps it was her turn to die.

Opal smiled faintly. "Really? Are you sure?"

"Positive." He hoped she wouldn't ask him how he knew.

She didn't. Instead she tensed, and he could see the anguish begin to build again in her face. Alan would have liked to jerk his hands away and speed as far away as he could get from the pain that would rack her body. He didn't know how he could bear to watch her suffer. But he couldn't leave. Opal needed him, and the only thing he could do to help was to stay and offer her calm reassurance, to last out her agony with her.

Opal's fingers tightened around his, and her breath came in gasps. Sweat beaded on her forehead. She dug her fingers deeper and deeper into Alan's hands as she struggled to hold back a groan. She could not stop it, however, and she groaned. Afterwards, when the pain receded, she whispered, "I'm sorry."

"Sorry? For what?"

"I must sound like an animal. I'm sure you never been around anything like this."

"No, I haven't," he admitted. "But I know one thing, there's not anybody that wouldn't moan or cry out when they're in pain. Men are probably the worst; that's what my sister tells me, anyway."

"I'm sure you never—"

"Me? Hah! When I had my accident, I hollered to beat the band. Did it lots of times throughout the years. Just ask Millicent; she'll tell you." He paused. "Don't worry about embarrassing yourself. You won't. Scream. Cry. Whatever you feel like. Nobody will think any less of you."

The next pain that hit her, Opal dug her fingers into him again, and this time she didn't try to restrain her moan of pain. When it passed, and she could relax slightly, panting and spent, she opened her eyes and looked at Alan. "What would happen to my baby if I died?"

"I told you not to think that way."

"I know, but what if it should happen? What then? That's what scares me. I could face dying; I really could. But who'd take care of my baby? How would he get by?" Tears welled in her eyes and spilled over onto her cheeks. "Oh, God, Alan! What would happen to him?"

"Don't worry about it. Nothing bad would happen to it, I promise. I'll see to that. We'd take care of it, Millicent and I. We'd see that it wouldn't want for anything. There's no need to think about it."

"Really?" Hope filled her face. "Would you take care of it, honest?"

"Yes."

"And you wouldn't send it to an orphanage, like me?"

"No!" he responded fiercely. "Never. I'd take care of it as if it were my own. I swear."

"Oh, thank you!" Tears poured down her face. "Thank you!" She pulled one of his hands up to her lips and kissed it. Hot tears splashed onto his skin.

"Please. No, Opal, don't. You make me feel so ashamed. I don't deserve this kind of gratitude."

Opal held his hand against her face, oblivious to his words. But then the pain hit her again, harder than ever, and she jacknifed forward, crying out.

"Oh, God." Alan felt the sweat crawling down his sides. Her agony was like a knife thrust into him. But he could not escape it, could not pull away from her. He could only hold on and help her to bear it.

"That one seemed quicker," he said when it had subsided and Opal went slack, lying back down on the bed.

She nodded wearily. "They're coming closer together now. The awful—the awful thing is, you can't make them stop. I keep thinking: All right, I give in; take me away from this; I can't stand it no more. But nobody can do that. I have to stand it. There's nothing else to do." She looked at him. "Thank you for staying with me."

"I'll be here as long as you want. As long as you need me."

It seemed to Alan as if hours passed before Millicent came back with the doctor. The pains gripped Opal more and more often, until he didn't know how her slight body could take any more of it. She dug her fingers into his hands so hard her fingernails scratched raw streaks across his skin, but Alan didn't notice his own pain, he was too full of Opal's.

Finally he heard the front door open and the sound of footsteps in the hallway outside the room. "Alan! Opal! We're here." Millicent almost ran into the room.

"Thank God!" Alan exclaimed, turning toward his sister. "What the devil took you so long!"

"I ran all the way there!" Millicent responded heatedly. "But it took forever to rouse Dr. Morton. Then I had to wait for him to dress." Millicent rolled her eyes. "He's outside now, tying up the horses and getting his bags. I never realized before how slow that man is!" She broke off as they heard the doctor's stately tread on the boards of the hallway.

Dr. Morton stepped into the room and stopped, taking in the scene before him. "Alan. How are you?"

"I'm fine. It's Opal who—"

A faint smile touched the doctor's austere countenance. "I realize that. Miss Millicent explained it to me in some detail." He walked over to Opal, and Alan released her hands and moved out of the way to give the doctor room. Dr. Morton picked up Opal's hand and felt her wrist, smiling down at her in his dignified way.

"Well, young lady, I understand that we are about to witness a blessed event. That's a wonderful thing, a new life coming into the world. Perhaps it may not seem so to you now, but later you'll rejoice in it." His expression was both grave and kind. "And we will help you through it." He glanced around him. "It's dark as a cave in here. I need more light."

"I'll bring in more lamps," Millicent responded quickly.

"I'm not sure it will be adequate. There are no windows in this room. It's dawn; it's turning light outside. We should move her into a room with windows."

Millicent stared at him. "But where? The bedrooms are all upstairs. She couldn't manage to move up the stairs."

The doctor frowned. Quickly Alan stuck in, "We can move Opal to my room. It's probably the lightest room in the house; the windows face east. And there's a bed for her."

Millicent looked doubtful, but the doctor said, "Excellent! Now, is there someone who can carry the young woman to the other room?"

"I—no," Millicent replied. Johnny won't get here for a while yet. I could support her if she can walk." It was obvious that the doctor, graying and portly, would not be up to carrying even someone small like Opal.

"I guess we'll have to," the doctor agreed and bent over Opal, curled up on her side. "If you can walk, ma'am, Miss Millicent and I will support you on either side."

Opal nodded and sat up slowly, pushing herself up with her hands. She looked so frail that Alan's throat swelled with emotion.

"No, wait!" he said quickly, wheeling his chair back to her bed. "I'll carry her."

Dr. Morton's eyebrows rose expressively, and Alan saw the same doubt registered on his sister's face.

"I will," Alan assured them. He reached over and curled an arm around Opal's shoulders, another under her legs. "Come on. I'll try my best not to hurt you."

The muscles in his arms flexed as he pulled Opal out of her bed and across into his lap. Her weight was far less than what he pulled out of bed every day. What concerned him was the additional pain it might bring her to be moved.

Opal gave a muffled grunt, but she helped push herself out of bed, and once she was in the chair with Alan, she curled up trustingly upon his lap, leaning her head against his shoulder. Alan's chest filled with warmth; he felt as if his heart were swelling within him, choking him with emotion. Carefully he turned the chair and pushed it across the room.

He rolled out into the hallway and down to his bedroom, with Millicent and the doctor following. When he reached his bed, Millicent hurried to help him lift Opal onto it. Alan was grateful for its lower height.

A little reluctantly, he slid back out of the way. His arms felt very empty now.

"All right, Millicent, open those curtains," Dr. Morton ordered, shrugging out of his coat and tossing it across a chair. "We have some work to do here." He swung his head toward Alan. "Thank you for your help, but I believe it's time for you to go now."

"Oh! Yes, of course."

"No!" Opal gasped and stretched out one hand toward Alan. "Please," she said, panting, "don't leave me."

"Nonsense," Dr. Morton said inflexibly. "The childbed is no place for a man, at least a nonmedical one. Miss Millicent will help me, and we'll be adequate to the task, I assure you."

"Me!" Millicent squeaked, gaping at the doctor. Her hands dropped away from the heavy drape she had just opened. "But, Doctor, I've never—I mean, I'm completely without experience in—in such things. I'm a single lady," she finished in a whisper.

"Well, you'll get experience this morning. I need another pair of hands, and we haven't time for you to run off to find some suitable female relative. There's a baby about to be born here. You must fetch some extra sheets and towels to put under her.

Millicent turned white, and her eyes flew to Alan. They were filled with terror. Alan looked back at her. He knew how she felt; his stomach was a knot, too, and he wasn't sure how he could stand to go into the parlor and wait. But it would be even worse to have to help the doctor, knowing that you knew nothing about what you were doing and that you might at any moment make a horrible mistake.

"Please, Millie," he told her quietly. "You have to help her."

Millicent straightened, drawing in a breath, and smoothed her face into a calm mask. "Of course."

She hurried out of the room to get the things the

doctor had requested. Alan rolled his chair out of the room after her, softly closing the door.

Alan didn't know how long he waited in the parlor; it seemed like an eternity. Through the connecting wall, with its sliding pocket doors, he could hear Opal's moans and cries. He curled his fingers more tightly into his palms with each fresh sound of Opal's pain, until his own nails had inflicted even more damage to his hands than Opal's had. He thought he would go crazy. *Why couldn't he do something!* It was the most awful thing in the world to sit waiting helplessly while Opal's very life was in jeopardy a few feet away from him.

Dr. Morton was a good doctor, Alan knew that. And Millicent, inexperienced though she might be, would be an efficient, calm helper. Opal couldn't be in better hands, really. But, much as he tried to reassure himself, he couldn't help but think of all the women he had heard of who had died in childbirth or soon thereafter. Opal had been right. There was nothing a doctor could do if the baby came out wrong.

At last he heard the doctor's and Millicent's voices, rising in excitement, and a hoarse cry from Opal, and then, like a miracle, came the thin wail of an infant.

Alan's heart skipped a beat. He raised his head and stared intently at the double mahogany doors that separated the parlor from his bedroom, as though his gaze could somehow penetrate them if he looked hard enough. He heard Millicent laugh in a brief, triumphant way and more babble of voices. He wanted to shout to them to tell him what had happened.

Quickly he rolled over to the door into the hallway and opened it. Just then, the door to his bedroom was swung wide and Millicent stepped out. For an instant, before she closed the door behind her, Alan heard, incredibly, Opal laughing, punctuated with sobs.

"What happened? Is it over?"

Millicent beamed at him. Her hair, usually pinned up tidily, hung in a braid as it had last night when she'd jumped out of bed, and much of it had slipped free to hang messily around her face and down her back. Around the edges of her face, her hair was damp with sweat, the strands clinging to her skin. Her sleeves were unbuttoned and rolled up to her elbows; she was still drying off her hands with a towel as she came out. The buttons on the high collar were undone, and the skirt and blouse she had pulled on hastily in the night didn't go together. But it wasn't only her messy attire that made her look different. There was something about her face—a looseness to her mouth, a glow to her skin, a blazing light in her eyes—that changed her. She looked hot and tired and vibrantly alive.

"Alan! I was just coming to tell you. The baby's come. It's a boy."

"A boy," he repeated. He tried to imagine the reality of the baby and found it difficult. "But Opal—what about Opal? Is she all right?"

"Oh, my, yes." Millicent came closer and squatted down beside his chair. "She did wonderfully. I never would have thought that such a tiny thing could be so strong. She's tough as whip leather, you know."

"Yes, she is. But nothing went wrong? Opal's in no danger?"

"No. Dr. Morton says she'll be fine. You should have seen her when he handed her the baby. Oh!" Millicent drew in a long breath, and her eyes grew even brighter. "Alan, it was wonderful! I can't describe it. But such happiness, such love was in her face! It was beautiful." Tears welled in her eyes.

"Can I—I mean, when do you think I could, you know, go in and see her? And the baby. I mean, can I? Should I?"

"Of course you should! I know Opal will want you to see the baby. It's such a little thing, Alan! You won't believe it." She sighed happily, shaking her head. "Let's go sit on the porch. When the doctor comes out, I imagine he'll let you go in to look at the baby."

"All right." Reluctantly Alan rolled to the front door and out onto the porch.

Millicent followed him. She walked past Alan to the railing and placed her hands flat on it, leaning forward and gazing around the yard as if it were some wonderful place which she had never seen before. She reached up and untied the ribbon from her hair, then wove her fingers through the thick braid, undoing the remainder of it. It fell apart in thick strands, and she combed her fingers back through it to separate them, lifting her hair as she did so and letting the air touch her damp scalp.

Alan watched her in some wonderment. He couldn't remember when was the last time when he had seen his sister with her hair hanging down and free. It must have been when they were children.

Millicent leaned her head back a little and shook it, letting her hair fall as it would. She turned around to face Alan and sat down on the railing, leaning against a column of the porch and dangling her feet. "Isn't this the most beautiful day? What a perfect time for a baby to be born! Early in the morning on a summer day. That's when I'd want my baby to be born—if I had had one, of course."

He nodded. "It is a lovely time."

Millicent smiled. "I can hardly believe it. I don't remember when I ever felt like this. You know, when Dr. Morton asked me to help him, I was frightened. Extremely frightened."

"I know. I could see that."

"But, Alan . . . it was the most wonderful thing I've ever seen. It made me feel—I'm not sure what, exactly. As if I were young again, as if my whole life lay before me." She talked rapidly, her voice rising in excitement. "I can't explain it to you; I can't describe it. But I felt such hope, such life! Do you know what I'm talking about?"

"I think so." He wasn't sure he did, but he liked the light in his sister's eyes, the lilt in her voice. "I'm glad for you."

"I was a part of something, of a life beginning. I've never realized before how really, really miraculous a child is. Or how beautiful life can be. Everything looks so different to me this morning, every color so vivid, each detail perfectly wrought. It's as if I can see each individual leaf, each blade of grass." She stopped and chuckled. "Oh, my, I'm really babbling on, aren't I?"

"I enjoy seeing you so happy."

"Thank you. I enjoy feeling it." She looked away, and Alan noticed that her gaze strayed over to the Lawrence house next door. "When you think of how precious life is, it seems foolish to waste it. It's mad to have everything right there in front of you and ignore it." She turned back to Alan, flashing him a sunny grin. "What a philosopher I am this morning! You must think I've lost my mind."

"No, not at all. I just think you're gloriously happy."

"I am. And you will be, too, when you see that baby. I held him, all wrapped up in towels. He was so small and moving constantly, his tiny hands and feet flying. You should have seen him!" She laughed again at the memory.

The door opened and the doctor stepped out onto the porch, adjusting his suit coat. "Well, it's getting late in the morning out here, isn't it?" he commented. "I guess I've missed church."

"Oh, my goodness! Church! I completely forgot that this is Sunday. I missed it, too." She looked guilty.

"I wouldn't worry about it, Miss Millicent," Dr. Morton said. "I have found that I'm closer to God at a birth than I am in any church."

Millicent's eyes widened a little at such heresy, but then she smiled. "You know, Dr. Morton, I believe you're right."

The doctor smiled at them both. He clapped his hand to Alan's shoulder. "Good to see you looking so well, Alan."

"Thank you, Dr. Morton."

"Good-bye." He tipped his hat toward them, and Alan and Millicent chorused an answering good-bye. He started down the steps and paused, looking around him and taking in a long breath. "Beautiful morning, isn't it?"

After the doctor left, Millicent went in to Alan's room, and he waited impatiently in the hall. He could not quite believe that Opal was all right until he saw her for himself. Moments later Millicent came tiptoeing back out.

"Opal would love for you to come in, but shh. . . . The baby's asleep."

Alan nodded in understanding and wheeled into the bedroom, moving as softly as he could. Opal lay in his bed, propped up against the pillows, smiling at him. She looked weary, her skin sallow and dark stains under her eyes. But she was smiling, and there was such peace and joy on her face that it made Alan's chest knot up with the urge to cry.

"Opal . . . " He whispered her name as he moved toward her. It was odd to see her there in his bed, yet it felt very good, too.

"Alan." Opal's voice was low but steady, and she stretched out her free hand toward him. The bundle that was the baby rested in the other arm, snuggled against her heart.

"How are you?" Alan asked, taking her hand in his, inordinately pleased that she had reached out to him.

"Wonderful," she breathed. "Absolutely wonderful."

He chuckled softly. "You had me scared."

"I know. Thank you for staying with me. I don't think I could have made it without you. You were awfully kind."

"Not kind. I couldn't possibly have left you." Alan clamped his lips together. There was no telling what might come tumbling out of his mouth if he wasn't careful—crazy things Opal wouldn't want to hear, things he would regret.

Opal smiled. "Well, thank you anyway." She turned her head down to gaze at the baby beside her. "It was worth it. Look at him. Isn't he beautiful?"

Alan leaned forward to peer down at the infant. He was wrapped up in a soft little blanket, and all Alan could see was his little head. His face was red and wrinkled, his eyes squeezed shut, and he was almost completely bald, except for a fine down of white-blond hair around the back and sides. He was, all in all, Alan thought, rather ugly. And yet there was something beautiful about him, as well. Alan didn't understand it, but when he looked at the little thing, his heart grew heavy and warm.

"Yes," he said, reaching out to touch the baby, then jerking his hand back guiltily. He glanced at Opal.

"Go ahead." She smiled. "You can touch him. It won't hurt him."

Alan gingerly stroked his forefinger down the baby's cheek. It was softer than anything he'd ever felt.

Opal pulled aside the blanket so that he could see all of him. "Look at him. Isn't he incredible? See those tiny fingers and toes?"

Alan had never seen so young a baby; they were always plump and porcelain white by the time he met them. But this one was red all over, just like his face, and it seemed to Alan that his arms and legs were unusually thin. He was curled up tightly, his legs up against his body, but when Opal removed the blanket, he jerked, and his arms and legs began to wave around spasmodically. His eyes opened, and so did his mouth. He began to cry, and his whole face screwed up until he looked like a prune. He was even uglier than he had looked a minute ago, but Alan stared at him in wonderment.

It seemed impossible that anything could be this small and perfectly formed. "His fingernails!" he breathed, reaching out to touch one of the flying little hands. He put his finger against the baby's palm, holding it so he could look at the incredibly small fingernails, exactly like his own, yet in miniature. The tiny fingers curled automatically around his.

"Look at that!" Alan exclaimed softly. "He's holding on to my finger!" He didn't understand it, but he wanted to cry. How could anything be this small? This marvelous?

Alan looked up at Opal. She was gazing at him, her face glowing. In that moment he was certain that he loved Opal with all his heart. She was beautiful, and her baby was a gift from God. He was filled with joy to see them lying there in his bed, to know that the miracle of the baby's birth had happened there. It made them somehow belong to him, and he reveled in that feeling. He wanted to blurt out that he loved her, though he was not foolish enough to do that.

Instead, he reached out and took her hand. For a long time Alan sat gazing at Opal, the baby's hand curled around his finger and Opal's hand trustingly in his other hand. No other moment in his life, he thought, would ever equal this one.

Eighteen

Pebbles rattled against the side of the house, waking Millicent. Frowning with puzzlement, she left her bed and went to the window. It was dark outside, with only the first pinkish-yellow tinge of light on the eastern horizon. Millicent heard a sibilant "pssst" below her, and she looked down. Jonathan and his daughter Betsy stood in the yard below, looking up at her and grinning. Betsy waved exuberantly. Millicent gazed at them in bewilderment. It wasn't even dawn yet. What were they doing up? Stranger than that, what were they doing here?

But she couldn't help but smile back at them; the Lawrences seemed to have that effect on her. She crossed her forearms, resting them on the windowsill and leaned out of the open window. "What are y'all doing?" she called down softly. "It's the crack of dawn."

Jonathan motioned to her. "Come down." His voice was buoyant. "We have a special treat for you."

"At this hour?" Millicent's voice was skeptical, but she pulled back inside and went to get her clothes.

Standing well back from the window so that she

would not be seen from outside, she dressed hastily. She left her hair hanging in its slightly disheveled braid, and, tying the sash of her wrapper as she went, she tiptoed down the back stairs, not wanting to wake either Alan or Opal—and especially not the baby, who, she had discovered, awoke crying with distressing frequency.

"What in the world are you doing?" she asked in a loud whisper as she slipped out the back door and found Jonathan and his daughter waiting for her at the foot of the porch steps.

"We wanted to show you something," Jonathan told her, still grinning, and reached up to take her arm as she came down the steps. She didn't need the help, but she didn't object to his hand on her arm.

"What?"

He shook his head. "You can't see it here. You have to come with us. Betsy and I discovered it about a month ago, and this morning Betsy suggested that we share it with you. I thought you would have a proper appreciation of it."

"This sounds most suspicious," Millicent said skeptically, but she was intrigued and amused, and she went along easily with them. The truth was, she would have gone with them just about anywhere, but she saw no reason to let Jonathan know that.

Jonathan's hand slid down her arm and clasped her hand naturally. Betsy bounced around and took her other hand, and the three of them set out across Millicent's back yard and into the side street. They strolled along the street until it ended in a small earthen track and then disappeared almost entirely. It was the way to the pond, and Millicent had walked it countless times when she was a child. But in the hush of dawn, it had a different quality, dim and faintly mysterious. The air was redolent with the smell of recently cut hay, and the birds were beginning to chatter.

Millicent wondered why they were going to the pond, but she didn't ask. It was too pleasant to walk like this, Jonathan's hand around hers. When they reached the pond, they circled around to the west side. There were two fishing poles lying on the ground.

"You're going fishing!" she exclaimed. "But why did you bring me?"

Betsy giggled and jumped around in the sheer exuberance of youth. "Because we wanted you with us!" she cried, with the air of one stating the obvious.

"I see." Her words warmed Millicent. "But I'm afraid I'm not much of one for fishing."

"Ah, but have you ever fished at dawn?"

"No," Millicent replied honestly. "Actually, I've never fished—well, except for once or twice when I'd hold Alan's fishing pole for him for a while."

Betsy gaped at her. "Never? Truly?"

"Truly." Millicent shrugged. "I never had a pole. I never—well, I never thought about it." She didn't add that fishing was a boy's entertainment; she knew that Jonathan had rather strong opinions on the subject of his daughter being confined to ladylike activities. And now that she thought about it, though she had never questioned it before, she could not understand why fishing should be an exclusively male territory.

"Then you must try it now, by all means," Jonathan

insisted and thrust one of the poles into her hand. "Betsy, let's show her how."

So, while the sun crept over the horizon, Millicent sat with a simple fishing pole in her hands and her feet curled up under her, dangling a line in the small pond.

"Have you ever caught anything here?" she asked.

Betsy wrinkled her nose, thinking. "Let's see . . . once I got an old glove."

Millicent laughed. "Actually, I meant fish."

"Nope." Betsy shook her head. "But there are some in there; I've seen them. Papa and I go swimming in it, and sometimes the fish'll touch you." She gave a shiver of combined delight and apprehension.

Millicent smiled. "I remember. I used to swim here, too, when I was a child."

"Did you?" Jonathan looked at her quizzically. "I'm surprised your parents allowed you."

"Oh, they didn't," Millicent retorted.

"Why, Miss Hayes," he teased. "Do you mean to say that you disobeyed your parents?"

Millicent cast an uncertain glance toward Betsy. This didn't seem a proper topic to discuss in front of a child. "Well, I . . . I didn't disobey them, exactly."

"I see. Just neglected to tell them." His eyes were dancing. He turned toward his daughter. "Pretend you didn't hear that, Betsy. Miss Hayes fears it will lead you astray."

Betsy gazed at him, puzzled. "What do you mean?"

"That you will follow her wicked example and not tell me what you do."

"Why wouldn't I tell you what I do?"

"I might have known," Millicent said crisply. "The child has no fear of telling you anything."

"Is that so wrong?" He looked serious now.

Millicent sighed with exasperation. "The reason is because she knows nothing will upset you; you have no standard of conduct."

"No standard of conduct!" His eyebrows rose. "Why, I've taught Betsy about truth and integrity and honesty, haven't I?"

"I'm not talking about the grand subjects. I'm speaking of the daily details of conduct. That's where you have provided an inadequate education."

Betsy was watching them with interest, and she asked now, "Are you-all fighting?"

"Yes," Millicent said.

"No," Jonathan replied at the same time.

They glared at each other in exasperation, then burst out laughing. Betsy grimaced and shook her head, as if to say she would never understand grown-ups, and turned back to her fishing.

Jonathan, his laughter subsiding, stretched out on his side beside Millicent, leaning on his elbow. "I'd like to have seen you when you were a little girl," he told her, his voice soft. "Were your braids always neatly woven, your pinafores starched and white?"

"They were when I began the day." Millicent gave him a disapproving look, but it was more lighthearted than real. "I also had a tied sash and untorn stockings and dresses that were long enough."

"Ouch." He winced comically. "You've made your point." He paused, then said soberly, "You have done a great deal for Betsy. I thank you for it." He raised his eyes to hers, and Millicent felt the full magnetism of his gaze.

She glanced away, unable to hold his gaze. "It's nothing."

"No. It's definitely not nothing. You have no obligation to her, but you have—well, you've been almost a mother to her. She needs one."

Millicent tightened. She didn't want to, but somehow she could not keep herself from saying, "You should marry so that she would have one."

Jonathan shrugged. "I couldn't." Sadness tinged his face for a moment, sitting oddly on his features. "No one could ever replace Betsy's mother. I—I didn't think it was right to marry a woman because I needed a mother for my child. And I never fell in love again."

"Your wife must have been a wonderful woman." Millicent's voice was stiff, her body rigid. The fishing pole lay unnoticed in her hands.

"She was." Jonathan stared out over the water. The sun was rising now, huge and golden, and its glow touched the surface of the pond in molten patches. But Jonathan did not see the beauty of the scene; his gaze was turned inward, looking at a picture that only he could see. "She was sweet and lovely, a little doll of a woman. I'd known her for years, since she was a girl. Her father was the editor I told you about, the one who took me under his wing. I never dreamed she'd have me; I thought I was the luckiest man in the world when she accepted my proposal."

Millicent's heart ached inside her. She hadn't

thought it possible to feel such physical pain from mere words, yet she did. Jonathan's love for his wife showed on his face. It was obvious that he had worshiped her, that he had never stopped loving her.

"She was a far better person than I. Gracious, kind, forgiving. A true lady in every sense of the word."

Millicent could picture the woman, a fragile beauty, blond, no doubt. Nothing like herself. She wouldn't have been argumentative or quick-tempered or bossy, as Millicent had been accused of being. He had called her a lady, but it was obvious that Jonathan had never found her rigid or too proper. No doubt he hadn't scowled at her or told her to mind her own business. Millicent knew that she could never hope to compare to her.

She understood now why Jonathan was interested in her, why he had asked to come calling on her. He wanted a companion, an adult with whom he could talk and laugh, but not a love. His love had been his wife. Millicent saw that she was safe, no threat to the beloved memory of Elizabeth and it hurt.

"What's the matter?" Jonathan asked.

Millicent turned to look at him, startled. "What? What do you mean?"

"You looked—I don't know, sad or something."

She wasn't about to let him know that she was jealous of a dead woman. She shrugged. "You were talking about something sad."

He didn't look entirely satisfied with her answer, but he let it pass. He nodded and said, "Yes. But it's been years now. The pain's faded away. At first I thought it never would, that I'd hurt like that forever. But I guess eventually you get over anything."

"Not entirely."

"What do you mean?"

"Well, you've never remarried. You don't have a—a particular lady friend."

"I don't?" He smiled engagingly. "Why, that is what I thought you are. My 'particular lady friend.'"

Millicent glanced away, unable to meet his gaze, afraid that his sharp eyes would see the quickening hope in her eyes.

"Am I?"

"Of course."

Millicent could feel his gaze upon her, studying her, but she couldn't meet his eyes.

"Who else would I take fishing at sunrise?" he continued jokingly.

Millicent couldn't hold back the burble of laughter that rose to her lips. "Is that what one does with a 'particular lady friend'?"

She glanced up at him as she said it and was caught by his gaze, serious and warm.

"I think so," he said, unsmiling. "Sharing a sunrise over the pond is something you can do only with someone you care about."

Her heart began to beat in double time. She didn't know what to say. She wanted to ask him if he cared about her, but she couldn't; she hadn't the nerve.

Jonathan leaned toward her. Millicent sat unmoving, her heart speeding up even faster. Gently he brushed his lips against hers. It was a touch as light as a butterfly's wings, yet it sent shivers all through her. Millicent had a decidedly unladylike urge to throw herself into his arms. Her fingers curled up into her palms and dug in.

"Thank you for coming out with us this morning," he told her softly.

Millicent smiled a little shyly. "Thank you for asking me."

They sat together in close, sweet silence, not looking at each other, not even touching, but bound in a fragile web of feeling, as they watched Betsy fish and the sun color the day. Finally, reluctantly, Jonathan stirred. "It's getting late."

They rose, brushing the grass from their clothes and calling to Betsy to abandon her fishing. It took some doing to persuade her to come, but finally the three of them turned toward home, strolling along with their hands linked. Millicent knew it would cause quite a scandal if anyone saw her returning to the house dressed as hastily as she was at eight o'clock in the morning. But she couldn't bring herself to worry about it. She felt too good.

They cut across the backyard as they had done earlier and walked up to the back door. Millicent turned to Jonathan, reluctant to end the moment. "Would you like a cup of coffee before you go to work?"

Jonathan smiled lazily. "I could probably be persuaded.

"Yes!" Betsy added excitedly, tossing down her fishing pole onto the porch. "Maybe we could see the baby! He's been asleep every time I've come over."

"That's true. This is a good time to catch the little

fellow awake," Millicent agreed. She looked up at Jonathan. He gazed back at her; his eyes said nothing about babies and nap schedules or cups of coffee.

"I'd love to," he told her.

Millicent swallowed. She didn't understand how just hearing him speak could make her feel the way it did.

They stepped into the kitchen. Ida was bustling about, making breakfast and Alan sat in his invalid chair, holding the baby in his hands.

"Can you talk?" Alan was cooing nonsensically down at the baby as they came in, and the baby was staring up at him, feet and hands moving, frowning in the comically serious way he had. Alan bent lower and rubbed his nose against the baby's. "Hmmm? Do you want to say something?"

"What you talking about, Mr. Alan?" Ida asked in amusement. "That baby cain't say nothing."

"I know. But doesn't it look as if he'd like to?" Alan glanced up at Millicent and Jonathan and smiled. Usually he was rather constrained around Jonathan, but this morning, playing with the baby, he was much more at ease and friendly. "Mill, come look at him. Doesn't he look as sober as a judge? I think he'd like to hand down a sentence."

Millicent smiled. Alan was as silly as could be about Opal's baby. "Yes, he does," she agreed.

Jonathan and Betsy stayed with them for a brief time, making the appropriate "ooh's" and "ahh's" over the baby. After they left, Millicent went upstairs and put up her hair and tidied her dress. Impulsively she decided to visit her cousin Susan. It had been a long time since she'd had a chance to chat with her. Since Susan's lying-in, Millicent had seen her only briefly once or twice and then always with several other women around. Susan had looked so pale and worn that Millicent hadn't gone back to call on her, feeling it would be a burden. With Polly so far away, Millicent had been utterly bereft of confidantes during the past few weeks, and she needed badly to talk with a friend.

Susan greeted her with delight and led her back into the informal parlor. "I'm so glad you came. We're in luck. I just put Amanda down for a nap and the boys are outside. We can have a nice long chat."

They sat down side by side on the sofa, and Susan turned toward Millicent, her eyes shining with interest. "Now tell me. What is all this I hear about you and Jonathan Lawrence?"

"There's not much to tell, really. Everyone's making more out of it than's there. You know how Emmetsville loves to gossip."

"Of course. But where's there's smoke, and all that . . ." She pushed Millicent's shoulder playfully. "Mama told me how you danced with him at the Miller's barn dance and how livid Aunt Oradelle was." Susan giggled. "I wish I'd been there to see it!"

Millicent smiled. "That's true. I did dance with him, and I—oh, Susan, I'm having so much fun!" Millicent's face lit up. "I haven't felt like this in years. He's such a—oh, I don't know how to describe him. Nice and good are completely inadequate, and yet it's not that he isn't nice or good. He is. But he's such fun, as well. He's . . . exciting."

"And handsome."

"Yes. And handsome. He makes me laugh, and we do all sorts of things that I can't believe I'm doing. I feel like a girl again."

"You are a girl."

"No. I'm a grown woman." Millicent frowned a little. "But I have a hard time remembering it when I'm around Jonathan. He's utterly maddening, and we have tremendous arguments, but it's all right somehow."

"And you're in love with him," Susan guessed shrewdly.

"No!" Millicent drew back sharply. "Of course not. It's just fun, I told you. Nothing serious."

Susan raised a skeptical eyebrow. "Millicent, I don't know who you think you're fooling, but it isn't me. I know a woman in love when I see one. And from what I hear, there will be an engagement announcement any day now."

"No. Susan, really, you're fair and far off. We aren't about to get engaged. I told you; everyone in this town is making too much out of it. Jonathan and I simply enjoy each other's company. I have no intentions of marrying anyone; I couldn't. After all, there's Alan. And Jonathan is no more interested in marriage than I am. He's still in love with his dead wife. All you have to do is listen to him talk about her and you can tell. He wants companionship, that's all. That's why he chose an old maid to court."

Susan made an unladylike grunt. "He didn't choose an 'old maid.' He chose a lovely, intelligent woman because he's obviously a man of taste. I don't care how much he loved this wife of his, she's gone and he's here and you have caught his eye. More than that, I think you've captured his heart."

"Don't be silly."

"*I'm* not," she replied pointedly. She leaned forward, taking Millicent's hands in hers, and said earnestly, "Sweetheart, don't cut yourself off from this chance. You deserve to be happy."

"I am happy."

"I know; that's obvious. But I'm talking about the future. I don't want you to think that this is the only kind of happiness that you can have. There are other things, wonderful things, that you can feel only . . ."

She hesitated, color rising in her face, then continued, "only with a man. When you get married, well, it's different from anything you've ever known. It's deeper and grander and, oh, Millie, I can't describe it! I'm no good at this."

Millicent looked down at their linked hands, too embarrassed to meet her cousin's eyes. This was what occupied her mind the most, yet it was the one thing that she could not talk to anyone else about, not even another woman, not even her closest cousin and friend. Everything she had told Susan was true; she did have fun with Jonathan, and it was wonderful to talk and dance and do things with him. But there was far more. There was the wild, delightful tumult that arose inside her whenever he was near. There was the heat that ran through her when he took her hand or when his arms went around her for a waltz. There were the pounding of her heart and the racing of her blood, the fiery tendrils of desire that twisted deep in her loins when he kissed her. She felt things, wanted things, that she had never even dreamed of before. She was sure they were utterly improper, and she felt guilty for thinking of them, but she wanted them nevertheless, wanted them with a deep, insistent hunger that amazed her.

Jonathan had acted like a perfect gentleman. He had done no more than kiss her a few times when they were alone. He had not pressed her to do anything more.

The awful thing, Millicent knew, was that she wanted him to. It was no doubt brazen and sinful, but she yearned for him to take her beyond herself into that realm of heated, drumming desire. The other night, when he had said good-bye and started out of the door, he had come back and taken her in his arms and kissed her, his mouth hot and hard and digging into hers, heedless of who might have come into the parlor and seen them. And when he tore himself away from her and left, Millicent had been aching to feel his body against hers again, to taste his mouth. Every nerve in her body had been alive, and it had taken her hours afterward to fall asleep. It was his body that she hungered for, the act of the marriage bed.

"Is it really, Susie?" Millicent asked softly, still avoiding her cousin's gaze. Was it as fiery and grand, as painfully sweet, as Jonathan's kisses promised it would be?

"Oh, yes." Susan squeezed her hand. "Yes, it is—at

least when you love a man, it is. I promise you. And I want that for you."

That was what she wanted for herself, too, Millicent knew. She loved Jonathan.

Nineteen

Opal paused at the doorway to Alan's room. He was lying on the bed, playing with the baby, and he hadn't heard her approach. Opal stood and watched for a moment, entranced by the picture they made. Robert was over two months old now, a healthy, chubby boy, as bright as a button, and he lay, arms and legs kicking with more volition now, watching Alan intently. Alan hung over him, raised up on one elbow, chuckling and talking softly to him, letting Robert grasp his finger and tug it around.

"My, what a strong one you are," he teased softly, bending down to rub noses with the baby. "That's right. You're going to tear that finger right off if I don't watch it. Aren't you?" The baby gurgled back, and Alan laughed. "Is that right? Talking back to me already, are you? I can see you now when you're twelve. You'll be a worse hellion than I was. But you better not give your mama too much trouble. You hear me?"

Robert smiled toothlessly, and Alan brushed his lips against the baby's forehead.

Opal leaned against the doorjamb, a lump in her

throat. Alan loved Robert, he had from the first. One would have thought he was the baby's proud father, the way he acted. Opal wished fiercely that he was. No one could have asked for a better father, a better husband.

She closed her eyes at the thought. It was a dangerous idea, one that would only lead ultimately to her unhappiness, but more and more these days it was one that she had trouble getting out of her head. Alan was so handsome, so kind, so gentle. Yet there was strength in him, too. Not simply the physical strength he'd built up in his arms and chest the last few months—though, Lord knows, that had its own appeal—but strong inside, where it counted. He had overcome the adversity of his crippled state; he had become practically independent of Johnny. And he had done it all himself. Opal didn't think that they came any better than Alan Hayes.

Opal would have been mortified if anyone had learned how she felt about Alan. She didn't expect anything to come of her daydreams, and she was careful to hide her feelings from everyone, especially Alan. He was so kind that she was sure that he would feel uncomfortable around her if he knew she loved him. It would spoil the nice, easy friendship that lay between them now, and that was the last thing Opal wanted.

So she pushed down the warmth and pleasure that filled her at watching him with her son and fixed a carefully neutral expression on her face as she left the doorway and walked into Alan's room.

He glanced up at the sound of her footsteps on the wooden floor and smiled. "Opal."

Opal's stomach flip-flopped at his smile. It lit up his

features and was so sweet and pleased that she could easily have mistaken it for an expression of loving happiness at seeing her.

"Hello, Alan." She loved the way his soft, dark hair fell across his forehead. His hair was getting too long, beginning to curl up a little in back and to fall shaggily over his ears. Opal found it endearing; she found most things about Alan that way these days. "How are you?"

"Fine. And you?" He brushed back his hair impatiently. "Damn this hair anyway. I need to get it cut."

Opal smiled indulgently. "Do you want me to call Johnny?"

"No. He butchered it last time he cut it; I don't know what I'm going to do. Cherry always cut my hair, and now she's gone." He grinned. "I may have to let it grow."

"How long?"

"I don't know. Maybe down to my ankles."

Opal chuckled. "Now that would be a sight, I'm sure." She went closer to the bed. "I could try cutting it for you, if you'd like."

"You?" He went still. "Really?"

Opal nodded. "I've done it before. I did it some at the orphanage, and I used to cut all Mrs. Reilly's children's hair when I lived with them." She grinned. "And they were squirming, too."

"At least I don't squirm. All right, I'm game. Let's try it."

Opal smiled and went over to pick up the baby. "I'll put Robert down for a nap. He ought to be getting tired." She paused. It was almost time for the baby to nurse, and her breasts were swollen and sore as they always were about that time. "Uh, would you mind if I, uh, went ahead and fed him?"

"No. That's fine." His voice sounded odd, even hoarse, and he cleared his throat and continued, "I'll get out of bed in the meantime."

Opal nodded without looking him in the face and left the room with the baby. She hurried upstairs to her bedroom and closed the door. She laid Robert down on the bed, unbuttoned her dress to the waist, and pulled it down. Her breasts were already beginning to leak, dampening the chemise as well as the pads she'd stuck in it. She pulled down the chemise as well and tossed the folded squares of cotton onto the bed.

She was sure that Alan had understood what she meant when she said she would feed Robert. It had been embarrassing, both of them knowing that the baby would suckle at her breast. She wondered if Alan had thought about her breasts when she said it. She wondered if he ever thought about her breasts. In her limited experience, that seemed to be a topic that was often on men's minds. Alan was such a gentleman that it seemed unlikely, but he was a man and he had appetites like other men. Or had the accident in his youth taken that away from him as well?

Opal glanced at herself in the mirror above the dresser. Her breasts were heavier than normal these days, swollen with milk. She had never before had a particularly big bosom; she had been slender all over. But her breasts were so large now that all of her dresses were too tight across the bust. Unconsciously she cupped her breasts. Her eyes fluttered closed, imagining Alan's touch. His fingers would be light and gentle, moving sweetly across her flesh.

She moved her fingers lightly over her skin, imagining Alan's hands on her. Warmth flooded her abdomen, and a tiny groan escaped her. Lately she had awakened at night feeling this way; every time she had been dreaming about Alan. Opal squeezed her legs together, enjoying the secret pleasure. She couldn't remember ever feeling this way.

But it was stupid to want Alan, she knew. He was as far away from her as the earth was from the sun.

The baby let out a disgruntled cry, tired of waiting for his feeding, and the sound brought Opal back to the present. With a sigh, she went to pick up the baby.

Alan pulled himself out of bed and into his invalid chair. He kept thinking about her upstairs, feeding the baby. From the time she'd said that she needed to feed him, Alan had been unable to think of anything else. He could see Opal in his mind's eyes, peeling down her dress and undergarments, exposing her naked breast, putting the baby up to it. He tried to imagine her breasts, remembering their shape and weight from that night when she had awakened him from his nightmare and he had caught a glimpse of them, unbound beneath her thin nightgown. Her nipples had been large, darker circles, with hard, fleshy centers.

He released a long, slow sigh. Just thinking about her naked breasts was making him hard. Opal would be back in a few minutes and he couldn't let her see that, couldn't let her guess what he'd been thinking of while she was gone. She would be appalled, he was sure, repulsed at his being aroused by the thought of a babe suckling at his mother's breast.

He leaned his head back against his chair and tried to think of other things. He had almost managed to empty both desire and Opal from his mind by the time she returned to the room. But the minute she stepped inside, all his good work went for nothing. Just at the sight of her, fully clothed and smiling shyly, he wanted her all over again.

Alan tried to smile at her. "Hello." He couldn't think of anything to say without touching on the subject of the baby nursing.

"Hello."

"How's Robert?"

"Full as a tick and fast asleep," she said before she thought. It was indelicate to even refer to a baby's nursing. Alan would think her a crude sort of woman for doing so. A blush rose in her cheeks. "I—uh—are you still willing to let me cut your hair?"

"Of course. Cut away."

"All right." She had brought in a towel and scissors, and she laid them down on the table as she went over to his chair. She frowned. "I can't do it in this, you know. The back's too high."

"Oh. Well, I can move to another chair." He gestured toward the smaller straight back chair on the other side of his work table.

"Yes. That would be wonderful."

Alan was glad that he'd been working on transferring

himself from his invalid chair to another chair or sofa or he would have had to go through the humiliation of calling Johnny to help him out of the invalid chair.

"But where'll we set it up?" Opal continued. "By the window? Or would you want your hair washed? It's easier to cut if it's wet."

"That's fine, if it would be easier for you."

"All right. Well, let's see. That chair'll do, but you need to lean back over something so we don't get everything wet."

"However you want. How did you wash the children's hair? We could do it that way."

"Well, uh, I did it when they were taking a bath." She glanced away, and color flamed in her cheeks.

Heat flashed through Alan at her words, and only a part of it was from embarrassment. He bit his lower lip, mentally cursing himself.

Opal looked around the room. "That'll do." Her face brightened, and she picked up the low chair beside the table and moved it over in front of the washstand. "If you sit here, you can lean back over the stand, and I can put the washbowl right beneath your head to catch the water."

Alan nodded and wheeled over to the washstand. It took all his concentration and strength to transfer his body from the wheeled chair into the lower, smaller chair in front of the washstand. It didn't help any to know that Opal was standing there watching each ungainly motion he made, each mistake. He almost went tumbling to the floor as he made the swing over to the chair, but he managed to catch himself and bring most of his body onto the chair, if somewhat awkwardly. He straightened up, pushing back until he touched the back of the chair. He kept his face turned down.

"You'll have to lean back," Opal said softly, coming up beside him.

The thought of her doing so personal a task for him as washing his hair swept Alan with heat again. He wanted more than anything for her to do it, but he felt he should absolve her from the duty. "I—I can wash it."

Opal screwed up her mouth in that little worried way she had. "Well, if you'd rather. But it'd be easier for me to do it."

"All right." He clasped his hands together to hide their trembling. He couldn't wait to feel her hands in his hair, on his scalp.

Alan tilted his head back, and Opal reached out to take the weight of his head in her hands and guide him to the bowl. Alan closed his eyes at the touch of her hands. She let his head rest against the cool rim of the china washbowl and started to pour water over his hair. She stopped.

"You know what? I'm afraid this'll get your shirt wet," she told him. "Maybe we better take it off." She reached down to the first button of his shirt and began to undo it.

Alan jackknifed back up to a sitting position. "I'll do it," he told her gruffly. Her movement had sent desire lancing through him. There was no way he could sit through her unbuttoning his shirt without his passion pouring out of him.

With nervous fingers, he unbuttoned the shirt and

tossed it aside. He was very aware of his naked chest. Opal was watching him. He couldn't imagine what she was thinking. It both scared and excited him. She put her fingertips against his bare skin and pushed him back gently. He felt her skin upon his, texture against texture, heat blending with heat. He didn't know how he could stand to sit there naked from the waist up, with her right beside him, her hands in his hair. It was a diabolical combination of pleasure and agony.

Opal carefully ran water from the pitcher over Alan's head. It sluiced down through his hair, and Opal pushed his hair back, her fingers brushing his face and neck. Everywhere she grazed his skin, it burned like a brand.

When his hair was thoroughly wet, she picked up the soap that lay on the washstand and worked up a lather in her hands. Then she plunged her fingers into his hair and rubbed the soap into it, working her way from his scalp to the tips of his hair. With her fingertips she massaged his scalp, moving slowly over his head. It melted him. It turned him to fire. Alan couldn't quite stifle a low groan.

Opal smiled, misinterpreting the noise of pleasure. "Feels good, doesn't it? There's nothing relaxes you like rubbing your head. I always love to wash my hair."

"You have a gentle touch." His words were spoken so low she could barely hear them. He closed his eyes to hide the intense pleasure he was sure must shine in them. Her hands were magical.

"Thank you." She smoothed his hair back from his face. "I'm going to rinse it now. Don't open your eyes."

He heard her picking up the pitcher, felt the first cool trickle of water on his hair. The sensual caress of the water was delicious, the pleasure heightened by Opal's combing his hair with her fingers as she rinsed it. She bent over him, reaching around under his head, and her position placed her breasts only inches from his face. He could see their roundness, their fullness straining against her dress. If he raised his head, he could bury his face in their pillowy softness. He thought of reaching out and seizing her with his hands, holding her still, and pressing his mouth against her breasts.

He was growing hard as a rock, thinking about it. A flush stained Alan's cheeks. Opal would be bound to see it, to notice the eager flesh pressing against the cloth. He had nothing to throw across his lap to hide it. There was nothing he could do except to wait it out and hope that she didn't look down, didn't see.

She lifted his head, wrapping a towel around it, and he sat up. Opal dried his hair vigorously, then combed it and began to clip away with the scissors. Alan sneaked a glance at her. She was intent upon her job, looking only at his hair as she snipped. She glanced down, and her hand stilled for an instant. Then she began to cut again without saying a word.

It was a relief at last when she finished trimming his hair and left the room. He brushed the stray hairs from where they had clung to his naked skin and pulled back on his shirt, buttoning it up to the neck. He didn't know how he would ever look Opal in the eye again. He had made a fool out of himself. Worse than that, he'd revealed his hunger for her.

* * *

Cousin Tilda's wedding was late in November, a time that Millicent privately thought was rather dreary for a wedding. But Tilda's husband-to-be, Mac Gaskins, was a farmer, and he had been emphatic that the ceremony had to take place after the fall harvest and before the next spring's planting. Millicent supposed that it was better to have it in November than in the chill of January or overshadowed by Christmas.

It was, as all Hayes weddings were, a large gathering. By the time one had invited all the near and distant relatives as well as the various friends and families of friends who could not be left out, it seemed as if most of the town of Emmetsville and its environs were there. The church was filled to bursting, and the reception afterward filled Aunt Oradelle's house and overflowed out onto the porches and lawns. It was fortunate that the weather was unseasonably mild.

For the first time, Millicent took Jonathan and his daughter to one of her family's occasions. It scared her, but for some reason she hadn't been unable to resist the impulse. There was something warm and wonderful about walking into the church on Jonathan's arm, even if it did mean that almost everyone craned around to get a look at them and whispers flew left and right.

As soon as they stepped into the Holloway house after the wedding, one of Millicent's aunts-in-law neatly separated her from Jonathan and Betsy and whisked her away to the kitchen to help.

"But, Aunt Lenore," she protested in vain, glancing

back toward Jonathan and his daughter, "I have guests."

Aunt Lenore raised an eyebrow, retaining a firm grip on Millicent's arm as she led her into the kitchen. "They'll have plenty of people to talk to. And you know we need your help."

It was taken for granted that Millicent would help, she knew. She had long since fallen into that role at most functions, going with the married women and other old maids into the kitchen to cook or fetch and carry or scrub up afterwards, leaving the men, children, and young courting people to separate into their natural divisions also.

But today the kitchen was the last place Millicent wanted to be. She needed to guide Jonathan through the treacherous waters of her family. Betsy would do all right. Millicent had introduced her to Cousin Bertie's daughter, Annabeth, several weeks ago and they had become fast friends, so she would doubtless run off to play with Annie. But Jonathan—well, who knew what someone might say to him or what questions they might ask if she wasn't there to thwart them or dodge the worst offenders? Besides, she simply wanted to be with him. Nothing was ever half so enjoyable as it was with Jonathan beside her.

However, Millicent couldn't come up with an adequate reason to avoid doing her usual work, so she grudgingly donned an apron and began to carry platters and cake plates to the quickly emptying refreshment tables. She would do a bit of work, she reasoned, enough to satisfy politeness: then she would sneak away from the bustle of the kitchen and find Jonathan.

Jonathan and Betsy, meanwhile, marooned at the front door, glanced around the chattering, shifting crowd with a kind of horrified awe.

"Do you suppose that all these people are Miss Millicent's family?" Betsy breathed.

"I sincerely hope not," Jonathan replied.

Within moments after they had stepped in the door, Millicent had pointed out to him at least three cousins, each qualifying for the title through different aunts and uncles, a second cousin, two uncles, a great-aunt, and one double cousin. Jonathan had never been around such numbers of people claiming often tangled kinship to each other. An orphan, he, of course, had had no relatives, near or distant, and Elizabeth was the only child of a couple who had moved to Texas, leaving behind both groups of families in Alabama. Family occasions, consequently, had been very small.

"Annie says that when you and Millicent get married, they'll be my family, too. Is that true?" Betsy seemed somewhat daunted at the prospect.

"What?" Jonathan, who had been surveying the crowd, only half paying attention to his daughter's words, now snapped his head back toward her. "What did you say?"

"I said, when you and Millicent get married, will all of them be my family, too?"

He stared at her for a moment. "What makes you think Millicent and I are going to be married?"

Betsy shrugged. "That's what Mrs. Rafferty said. She

said that pretty soon Miss Hayes would probably be my new mama. Only I don't see how she could be because I already have a mother, and she's dead. But Annabeth said that Mrs. Rafferty just meant that Miss Millicent and you are going to get married. Annie said everybody's talking about it. Her mama, Miss Millicent's cousin, said that lots of people in her family think you-all will get married, too, and they're arguing about it."

"Arguing about it?"

"Yes. On account of some of them don't want her to marry you. And some of them don't want her to marry anybody. But then others of them, like Aunt Sophie and Cousin Susan and their family—they're real happy about it."

"Are they?" He responded wryly. "It's nice to hear that everyone has my future mapped out for me."

"Well, aren't you?" Betsy's face clouded up. "Aren't you and Miss Millicent going to get married?"

"I haven't really thought about it. We certainly haven't discussed it—unlike everyone else, apparently." Jonathan was slightly stunned by his daughter's remarks. Marry Millicent? She fascinated him; she excited him. Sometimes he thought he'd explode from wanting her. He had fantasized often enough about making love to her, but that wasn't the same as thinking about marrying her.

"Why not?" Betsy looked at him with her usual frank curiosity. "Mrs. Rafferty says you've been courting her."

"Mrs. Rafferty talks entirely too much."

Betsy ignored his complaint. "Are you courting her?"

He shrugged. "Yes, I suppose I am."

"Then doesn't that mean you want to marry her?"

"With Millicent, I'm not sure exactly what it means. She's a very maddening woman." He sighed and shook his head. "I don't know what to say, Bets. I always try to be truthful to you, but this time I'm not even sure what the truth is. I'm usually in a state of confusion where Millicent Hayes is concerned."

"I like her," Betsy offered. "I think I'd like to have her as my new ma."

"Would you?"

Betsy nodded. "She teaches me lots of stuff, and she's nice—once you get used to her, that is. At first, I thought she was kind of prickly, you know, and stuck-up, but she laughs a lot more now. She's pretty, too."

"Yes, she is." His eyes strayed to the double doorway into the dining room, where he could see Millicent setting down a cake and returning to the kitchen. He often found himself looking for her these days, wherever he was—checking to see if she happened to be in her yard or on the porch when he left or returned to his own house, even scanning the streets when he stepped out of the newspaper office on the chance that she might have happened to walk downtown on an errand. It added a fillip of pleasure to his day when he ran into her unexpectedly in the post office or at Hunter's Mercantile or on the street.

"I like her. I more than like her. I think she's my favorite person besides you." Betsy glanced up at her father.

He smiled at her. "Yeah. Me, too."

Betsy grinned with the air of one who had won her case. "Does that mean you're going to marry her?"

"I don't know, sweetheart. Don't you think Millicent might have some say in the matter?"

"Oh, she'll say yes," Betsy replied confidently. "She loves you."

Something fluttered in his chest at her words. "You think so?"

"Sure. I can tell, the way she looks at you." Betsy cocked her head to one side, thinking. "You know what? You look at her the same way sometimes."

"Do I?" His lips curved up in a contemplative, almost secretive smile.

"Betsy!" A dark-haired, rosy-cheeked girl bounced up to them, smiling. She was far more soft-spoken than Betsy, and her dress was all ribbons and lace, her hair in long curls, but there was a sparkle of mischief in her eyes that reflected Betsy's.

"Annie!" Betsy turned, delighted to see her friend, her mind immediately going to new and more interesting pursuits.

"We'll be out in the back yard playing."

Betsy flashed her father a smile and a quick good-bye, then took Annabeth's hand and hurried off with her, already deep in conversation.

Jonathan glanced around the room. A determined-looking matron was bearing down on him, and a quick glance into the front parlor told him that it was no use ducking into there to get away from her. He slipped out the front door, pulling a slender cigar from his inside pocket for an excuse, and strolled across the lawn to the low wrought-iron fence. He lit the cigar and stood smoking it, arms crossed, staring out across the street in apparent fascination with the view of the mayor's house.

Jonathan couldn't have said what his eyes were fixed on, however. His head was too filled with his conversation with his daughter. Marry Millicent. He hadn't considered it; he supposed, actually, that he had avoided thinking about it. When Elizabeth died, he had vowed that he would never marry again. Torn and bitter with grief, he had been sure that he could never love another woman as he had loved Elizabeth.

And he didn't love Millicent in the same way. It was far, far different. She wasn't sweet and gentle, wasn't mild and forgiving. No, she was a difficult, complex woman. She exasperated and intrigued him; she turned his blood as searing as bourbon sliding down his throat. Lord, but he wanted her. There were times when he couldn't sleep for thinking about her and what it would be like to make love to her. Passion, he'd thought, not love. But was that the truth? Did he want to marry her? To give her his name, to have her in his house, his bed, for the rest of his life?

The thought sent a quiver of longing through him. Suddenly he felt unbearably lonely, incredibly bereft. And he realized that there was no other way he could spend his life except with Millicent Hayes.

Twenty

"I like your young gentleman, Millie," Aunt Virginia confided, slipping into the seat beside Millicent at the long wooden worktable in the Holloway kitchen.

Millicent smiled faintly. It was funny to hear Jonathan described as her young gentleman. It made him sound like a boy, aimless and just out of school, not the purposeful, strong man that he was. "Thank you. Though I don't know that I'd call him *my* 'young gentleman.'"

"And who else's would he be, I'd like to know?" Aunt Sophie asked from across the table. They were seated in Aunt Oradelle's kitchen, the reception over, having helped clean the dishes and now enjoying a cup of coffee after their labors.

"I don't know. His own, I guess." Millicent glanced out the kitchen window into the back yard, where Jonathan was laughing, talking, and playing horseshoes with Susan's husband Fannin, Uncle Chub, and two of Aunt Oradelle's sons. Millicent had been surprised to find that the reception had not been as difficult as she had thought it would be. Jonathan had fit in more easily with her family than she had dreamed, and though one of her great-uncles had taken him to task over something written in his newspaper, he hadn't gotten into an argument over it, only a mild and rather interesting discussion. When the reception had wound to a close and Millicent had been commandeered back into the kitchen, Jonathan had helped the men of the family dismantle the long trestle tables and store them away in the carriage house. Then Uncle Chub had suggested pitching horseshoes as a reward for their work, and he had joined in with them readily.

Jonathan's suit coat was off, lying across the back of a chair in the dining room, and his shirt was rolled up at the sleeves almost to his elbow and unbuttoned at the neck. His blond hair glinted in the pale November sun, and he laughed as he listened to Fannin, his teeth flashing white and strong in his face. He looked healthy and vital, handsome in a way that sent shivers through Millicent.

"Well, it's you he's been tagging around after the past few months," Aunt Sophie pointed out. "I'd say that gives you some claim over him."

Millicent grinned, amused at the thought. "I'm not sure anyone can really have a 'claim' on Jonathan."

"Don't ever let him hear you say that," Aunt Virginia warned, looking serious. She was in actuality not an aunt but a cousin of Millicent's father. It was said that she had been quite a belle in her day, and there were traces of it still, in her smile and manner more than in her looks. "You mustn't let a man know you think you don't have any control over him. It's the surest way to lose your advantage."

"Must I have an advantage over him?" Millicent cast a glance toward Susan, who smiled and rolled her eyes.

"Oh, yes. My goodness." Aunt Virginia chuckled at Millicent's naivete. "Otherwise you'll be under his thumb all your life."

"You make marriage sound like a battle, Aunt Virginia," Susan commented.

The older woman pursed her mouth, considering. "Well, so it is, dear, in a way. And if we hadn't been waging it all these years, we'd still be living in huts and walking ten paces behind our menfolk."

"I wouldn't say that, Virginia," Aunt Sophie protested slyly. "Our men couldn't bear having us that far behind them—they'd have to turn around and shout to complain to us."

The other women laughed and exchanged knowing looks that were wry, resigned, and fond, all at once. For a moment Millicent felt the old familiar chill of exclusion. She alone was not married. She alone did not know the pleasures and aggravations of living with a husband.

The laughter seemed to signal that it was time to break up the group and leave. The work was done, the cups were drained of coffee, and even the socializing had slowed down. Millicent's aunts and cousins got up and started picking up their belongings. Millicent, too, rolled down her sleeves, which she had turned up while washing dishes, and buttoned the cuffs, looking around for the cake plate which she had brought over for the reception.

As everyone was chattering their good-byes, admonishing one another to come visit, Aunt Oradelle came up beside Millicent and laid a staying hand on her arm. "Millicent, wait a minute. I need to talk to you."

Her expression was serious. Millicent's heart sank. This looked like a long conversation—and one in which Millicent suspected that she didn't want to participate. She glanced out the window at Jonathan again. "I need to leave. Could I come back tomorrow?"

"The boys'll keep Mr. Lawrence occupied with those silly horseshoes as long as you want." Aunt Oradelle waved toward the group of men dismissively.

"Well, all right . . . ." Millicent couldn't think of another excuse to put off the talk. She sat back down in the chair she had just vacated, inwardly sighing, and waited for her aunt to return from her farewells and thank-yous with the others.

Aunt Oradelle made quick work of sending everyone off, and it wasn't long before she was back in the now-empty kitchen. "There, that's done with."

"It was a lovely reception." Even though her aunt was not the bride's mother, Oradelle was generous in providing her house (and not inconsiderable expense and efforts) for such family events, since her home was larger than anyone else's in the family. As a consequence, Aunt Oradelle took a proprietary interest in the whole family's weddings and receptions.

"Yes, it did come off rather well, I thought," Aunt Oradelle agreed complacently as she sat down beside

Millicent. "At least nobody made a fool of himself, and Tilda didn't giggle herself silly. But, needless to say, that's not what I wanted to talk to you about. Well, not directly, anyway, though weddings have some bearing on it." She laid a hand on Millicent's arm and leaned closer earnestly. "Millicent, dear, I feel that I am in the position of a parent to you, now that both your dear mother and father are dead. And I must speak to you."

Oh, dear, Millicent thought. This looked worse and worse by the moment.

"I'm worried about poor dear Alan."

"Alan?" The seeming switch of topic surprised Millicent. "Why? He's in very good health, you know, better than I've ever seen him, in fact."

"Of course, dear, and it's entirely due to your excellent care of him, I'm sure." Aunt Oradelle smiled approvingly. "You've been a model sister these past few years. I'm sure your dear father would have been very proud of you. Well, he was proud of you, even before you had to take on the sole responsibility for Alan. He told me so himself."

"Really?" Millicent brightened.

"My, yes, he told me so himself. Several times. He said, 'Ora, that girl's turned out to be steady as a rock. She's all a man could ask for in a daughter.' "

Millicent's cheeks turned pink with pleasure. Her father's praise had always been given sparingly, only for something well deserved, and, though she had striven hard for it, she had often been uncertain whether her efforts had been enough for her father. It was warming to hear that he had told his sister how pleased he was with Millicent.

"I'm glad," Millicent murmured.

"Of course. Poor Benjamin." Oradelle shook her head sadly. "He would have worried himself sick about Alan if he hadn't known how well you took it on yourself to care for him." She paused. "That's why I felt it was incumbent upon me to talk to you about the situation. In the place of your father."

"What situation?" Millicent wondered if Aunt Oradelle was going to go into another diatribe on the evils of having Opal Wilkins in the same house with Alan.

"This one with you and that newspaperman."

"Jonathan?" Millicent's eyebrows went up, and her stomach clenched. This was worse than some silly fear of her aunt's about Opal's bad influence. "What do you mean?"

"I mean: What's going to happen to Alan?"

"What's going to happen to him? Why, nothing."

Aunt Oradelle cocked an eyebrow in polite disbelief. "It's clear that you and that Lawrence fellow are getting mighty serious. Everybody's whispering that it won't be long now until the two of you announce your engagement."

Millicent colored. "Oh, Aunt Oradelle . . . Jonathan and I aren't about to become engaged."

"Don't deny that you'd like to."

"Well, I . . ."

"He's a grown man with a daughter to take care of, not some flirtatious boy. When a man like that takes an interest in you, it's serious."

"I think Jonathan is different. He—I—well, he was very much in love with his wife, and since she died, he hasn't wanted to marry again."

"Nonsense. Widowers always want to marry again, even if they deny it. Especially widowers with children—and a girl, no less. It's clear from looking at the two of you that you're not this far away from getting married." Aunt Oradelle indicated a tiny distance with her thumb and forefinger.

Millicent felt flustered and gratified and nervous all at once. Why did Aunt Oradelle have to bring this up?

"There's no one who wants more than I do to see you happy, Millicent. You're a good woman, a fine daughter and sister. A credit to your family." Aunt Oradelle delivered her highest encomium. "And I wish there was some way you could marry this Lawrence fellow, if that's what would make you happy. There've even been times when I've thought it would have been better all around if Alan had just died that night."

"No! Aunt Oradelle, how can you say that!"

"At least you would have been able to get on with your life, to have a family and some happiness."

"I *am* happy."

"Right now," Oradelle corrected darkly. "That's 'cause you're floating along, enjoying what's happening without thinking about the future. But pretty soon you'll have to make a decision. Are you going to continue to take care of your brother? Or are you going to marry Jonathan Lawrence?"

"Jonathan Lawrence hasn't asked me to marry him. It's probably not even likely."

"Don't fool yourself. Things don't stand still. You have to go forward or back. The longer you wait to make up your mind, the more likely you are to get your heart broken. That's the truth, Millicent; I'm not just saying it to hear myself talk. If you wait until he asks you and then have to admit you can't marry him, you're going to hurt yourself and him and that little girl, too. You have to look ahead; you have to face the truth. You can't keep on, hoping that you'll never have to make a choice. And the longer you wait, the harder it's going to be to say no. Then what'll happen to Alan? What's he going to do if you get married and go off? How's he going to live?"

"He'll be right next door," Millicent pointed out desperately.

"It isn't the same, and you know it."

"Well, sometimes I've thought, perhaps Alan could live with us," Millicent suggested, a little shy at even admitting that she had thought this much about marrying Jonathan.

"Live with you! What an idea! Alan, set in his ways as he is? You know how much he dislikes company. And, pray tell, what man wants to be saddled with a brother-in-law in his house first thing after he marries? There's no better way than that to ruin a marriage. Just look at the Howells."

Aunt Oradelle fixed her with a stern look. "Your father relied on you, Millicent, and so did your mother. They trusted you to stay and take care of Alan the rest of his life, to not let anything happen to him."

"I know." Millicent looked down at her hands. Her voice was low and fraught with emotion. "And I will take care of him. I will."

"I know it's hard and unfair. But life's like that. You can't always have things nice and sweet; sometimes you have to make sacrifices. You know, Alan didn't ask for that to happen to him. He doesn't have much of a life, and that's not fair, either. But what can he do? What can any of us do, except to keep on and try our best to do what's right?" Aunt Oradelle paused and looked at Millicent intently. "You can't abandon Alan."

"I won't! I wouldn't think of it."

"I know you wouldn't want to. You'd hate yourself for doing it. But when we let ourselves get too deep into a situation, we can't always find a way out. Sometimes we do what's easiest or most pleasant. It's only afterward that we think about what we've done—and regret it. I don't want you regretting it, Millicent. I don't want you casting aside everything in the heat of the moment and marrying Mr. Lawrence, then watching Alan wither away without your love and care. 'Cause you'd regret it for the rest of your life; you know you would."

"I wouldn't do that!" Millicent protested, her throat clogged with tears at the thought of Alan alone in their house, growing smaller and sicker, dying by degrees in his loneliness and lack of care.

"Of course you wouldn't." Aunt Oradelle reached over and patted Millicent's hand, her point made. "I know how much you love Alan. And how you promised your parents. But it's hard to see clearly when you're in the midst of something. I don't want you to make a mistake."

"I won't. I wouldn't abandon Alan. Ever."

All the way home, Millicent was quiet, thinking about her aunt's words. Was Aunt Oradelle right? Was she ignoring what was happening because she couldn't bear to face the truth? Had she made herself believe that it wouldn't hurt to spend so much time with Jonathan just because it was what she wanted to do? Was she hoping that somehow Alan would release her from her obligation and she would be able to marry Jonathan if he asked her? She wasn't nearly as certain as her aunt that Jonathan would want to marry her. But she had to admit that their courtship appeared headed in that direction. Given how often she and Jonathan were together and how much emotion and frustrated desire she felt around him, something was bound to happen. Their relationship had to go forward in some way. Aunt Oradelle was right; things didn't stay the same.

It was dusk by the time they reached her house, and in the growing dimness Jonathan took her hand as they walked around the house to the back door. Even though it was growing chillier by the moment, they sat down on the porch steps, reluctant to part. Millicent looked down at the hand Jonathan held, his fingers threaded through hers, browner than her own skin, rougher, masculine. It always made her breath come a little differently to look at his hands, competent and strong and male; she couldn't help but remember the way they felt on her.

She glanced up at him and found that Jonathan was studying her face as intently as she had been looking at their linked hands. He reached up and caressed her cheek with his free hand.

"You're beautiful," he murmured, his light brown eyes staring deeply into her own. He bent and kissed her, and the sudden passion of his kiss took her breath away. Millicent felt his skin flare into heat against her hand, and his arms went around her, holding her, bracing to take their weight. He pressed into her, bearing her back against the steps. He surrounded her with heat; it was like stepping into the depths of a fire. She was aware of an urge to go in even more deeply, to surrender herself to the flames.

Millicent threw her arms around his neck and pushed up into him, kissing him back fervently. He trembled, and for an instant, it felt as if they were about to explode into something wild and reckless and unknown. His lips moved over her face and down her neck. He mumbled something, his voice muffled by her flesh, and his hand made a long, slow journey down her body, gliding over the curves of her breast, waist, and hip. Millicent had never been touched so intimately, and it was shocking, thrilling. Heat flooded her abdomen. It was even more shocking how much she wanted him to continue touching her; she wanted to feel his hand on her bare skin.

Jonathan pulled back, gasping for breath, and shoved his hand back into his hair, closing his eyes as if in pain. "God, Millicent!" His voice was ragged. "I want you so much."

She wanted to pull him back to her, to tell him that she wanted him equally as much. It was only years of training that enabled her to say weakly, "We mustn't."

He nodded, turning away from her slightly and rubbing his hands over his face. He sighed, and a little of the tension eased out of him. After a moment, Jonathan turned and looked at her. "Millicent . . . I . . . " He stopped and shook his head.

"What?"

"Never mind. I'll talk to you another time. Right now I'd better be by myself for a while." His grin was rueful. "Sometimes I find it a trifle difficult to think around you."

Millicent smiled a little. She found it rather hard to think herself when her body was on fire from his caress. "All right."

"I'd better go." Jonathan picked up her hand and pressed a brief, firm kiss into her palm.

Millicent nodded. She wanted to wrap her fingers around his and hold on, to entreat him to stay with her. She didn't want to have to think about what her aunt had said.

But she made herself let him go. She watched him cross the back yard until he disappeared in the deepening shadows. Then she stood and walked into the house. Much as she didn't want to find out, she knew that she had to talk to Alan. Perhaps she would find out that she was worrying for nothing, that Aunt Oradelle was wrong. Perhaps Alan would say—what? That he was able to take care of himself? That he wouldn't mind her leaving him? No. That was foolish. She couldn't expect that of him. She was hoping for an easy way out, a way to salve her conscience and still follow her heart.

Millicent paused in the hallway and smoothed back her hair in front of the small mirror that hung there. She shook out the folds of her skirts and straightened the front of her blouse, fractionally askew. Her eyes were too large and velvety, her lips still showing the faintly bruised look of having been kissed. She closed her eyes and turned away, mentally trying to pull herself back into the same neat order as her clothes. She wet her lips. She drew in a long breath and released it slowly. She glanced at herself again.

A little better, she supposed. She couldn't hang around in the hall, waiting until she was entirely free of the humming passion within her. It seemed as if she always carried it somewhere in her these days. Well, perhaps Alan wouldn't notice it. She turned and went into his room.

He wasn't reading or occupied with any of his many hobbies. He lay on his side in bed, staring moodily in front of him at nothing. Millicent hesitated. It didn't appear to be a good time to talk to him. But before she could back quietly out the door, Alan glanced up and saw her.

"Hello, Millie."

"Hello, dear." She fixed a smile on her face and advanced into the room. "How are you?"

He shrugged in answer. He could hardly tell her that he'd been lying there thinking about Opal and how hopeless his passion for her was. "All right, I guess. How was the wedding?"

"Oh, it came off just fine, as did the reception. You know how it is when Aunt Oradelle's in charge."

"Yes. Nothing would dare to go wrong."

Millicent chuckled. "You're right." She glanced around the room. "So, what have you been doing while I was gone?"

"Not much." He pulled himself up in bed. "A little reading. I played with Robert some." His face brightened at the memory.

"He's sweet, isn't he?" Millicent strolled around to his table and looked at the collection of coins laid out there, which Alan was in the midst of labeling. She didn't know exactly how to bring up the subject she wanted to talk to him about.

"I'll enjoy watching him grow up," she went on while her mind scrabbled to find the right words to say.

Alan looked at her oddly. "Do you think he'll always live here?"

Millicent glanced at him. "I don't know. I hadn't really thought about it. Opal seems happy here. Isn't she?"

"I suppose she is right now. But surely someday she will want to leave. She'll find someone, fall in love. Marry."

His face looked bleak for a moment, and Millicent's chest contracted. *Oh, Lord, had she made a mistake bringing Opal into the house? What if Aunt Oradelle had been right and Alan had come to care for her? What if she had broken his heart?*

"I—I suppose so. Has she said anything like that?"

"No. But that's what most people do, isn't it?"

"Yes." There was nothing odd in his expression now, and Millicent wondered if she had imagined the earlier bleakness. "I guess so. Alan . . . do you, that is, well, do you have any special feeling for Opal?"

His head snapped toward her, and he looked alarmed. "What do you mean?"

"I'm not sure." She frowned with concern. His reaction to her question made her wonder even more if he cared for Opal.

"It'd be silly, wouldn't it?" he said shortly. "Someone like me falling in love."

"Not silly, Alan. Never that."

"But hopeless, right?" He gave her a lopsided grin that almost broke her heart. "I'm not a fool, Millie. I know no woman wants a cripple."

"You're a wonderful man!" Millicent protested staunchly.

"And you're my sister. Loyal to the bitter end." He reached out and took her hand and squeezed it, and he smiled at her fondly. "You're the best. Don't think I don't know it. You're always there. You always have been. I know I can count on you."

"I love you, Alan. You know that."

"I know. But I also know how much I can test that love. I'm not an easy man to live with. I'm always wanting to be left alone, putting all the social burdens on you. Not many people would put up with me the way you do."

Millicent's heart sank. He was as much as saying that Aunt Oradelle was right. Alan wouldn't want to live with Jonathan and Betsy and her; it would be torture for him.

Alan went on, "I never told you how much I appreciate what you've done for me all these years."

"No, you don't have to—"

"I know I don't have to. I want to. I'm not very good at saying something like this. But sometimes I think I'm an awfully selfish person to take what you've given me and never even express my gratitude. As if it were my right. But it's not. I know that. There are lots of women who wouldn't have done what you have."

Millicent looked at him, her eyes glittering with tears. Each loving word he spoke was an arrow in her heart. She shook her head helplessly.

"No, don't deny it. Few sisters are that loving, that loyal. You've done more than anyone could expect. I only wish there was some way that I could repay you, that I could do as much for you."

"No. You don't need to repay me. I love you; I never regretted a moment of the time I've spent with you. I never wanted to leave you."

"I used to be so scared that you would." He shook his head, his smile full of remembered pain. "I knew you; I knew you wouldn't go. But deep inside, I was scared you would. I was afraid that if I died, it would be a—" His voice cracked with emotion, and he paused, bringing it under control again. "I was afraid it would be a relief to you, that secretly you'd be glad because you'd be free of the burden at last."

"You are not a burden to me!" Millicent told him fiercely, sitting down beside him on the bed and clutching his hand. She was swamped with an aching, bittersweet love for him. "You are my brother, and I love you. Everything I did, I did freely."

"Honestly?"

"I swear it. I didn't turn anyone down that I wanted to marry. I *chose* to stay with you. It was what I wanted."

It was true, she knew, but her use of the past tense echoed in her mind. How she felt now was an entirely different matter. But Aunt Oradelle was right. Having heard what Alan had just said, how could she leave him now?

Millicent leaned forward and embraced her brother, pressing her cheek against his. "Don't worry. Don't even think about things like that. I won't leave you. I'll always stay with you."

Twenty-One

Millicent left her brother's room and walked slowly upstairs. Weary from the emotional storm that had raged inside her the past hours, she undressed, tossing her clothes aside, and washed, then pulled a nightgown over her head. She sat down in the chair by the window and took down her hair, brushing it out with long strokes.

It was painful, but she knew that she had to give up Jonathan. She had to give up the romance that had been so sweet and yet so fiery, so full of laughter and passion. It was time to face reality. She couldn't keep on dancing through the fog, happily pretending that there wasn't a cliff somewhere before her.

She stood up and looked out the window at the night. She leaned her head against the window frame, closing her eyes. Deep within her the passion Jonathan had aroused in her tonight still burned, a ceaseless flame, tormenting her with visions of what she might have—if she were heartless enough to leave her brother to fend for himself. But she knew that she could not, would not, do that.

She would remain forever barren. Forever untouched. She would not know the pleasure of Jonathan's hands, his mouth. She gripped her nightgown tightly in her fists, suddenly awash with desire and despair.

It wasn't fair! Her heart was breaking, knowing that she would have to give up her dreams of marrying Jonathan, the hope of loving him and being loved in return. She would never know how it felt to lie in Jonathan's arms, pressed against his chest, the rhythm of his heart under her head. The hunger inside her now would never be satisfied; she would not have the joy that Susan had talked about with that soft, secret smile on her face. She would grow old forever wondering what it might have been like, forever envying her cousins and friends. It seemed too harsh. Must she give up everything? The one man who brought every feeling in her to life?

"No!" She whirled away from the window, her eyes flying open, surprised to realize that she had said the word out loud.

She would not give up everything. She refused to do it. She could at least have this one moment for herself. She could be with Jonathan, could experience what it was to be loved by him, and she would have that memory to warm her for the rest of her life.

Without giving herself time to think, Millicent grabbed her shawl from its drawer, shoved her feet into her soft slippers, and hurried out of the room. She fled down the back stairs and out into the night, throwing her knitted shawl around her shoulders against the chill of the evening. She crossed the yards and went to the

Lawrences' back door. She hesitated for a moment, then tapped at the door.

Betsy would not be there, she knew. She was spending the night with Bertie's daughter. Jonathan would be home alone. She would not think about whether he would take her up on her offer. That was another thing that was too frightening to contemplate.

There were footsteps on the kitchen floor inside, and the door opened. Jonathan stood in the doorway, holding a kerosene lamp; its glow highlighted his face. "Millicent?" His voice rose in surprise and he held the lamp out slightly to see her better. "What are you doing here?"

"I—I came to see you," Millicent replied breathlessly. Now that she was here, she didn't know what to say. What if he refused? What if he didn't want her?

Jonathan looked puzzled, but he stepped back, holding the door open for her to follow. "Come in. Is something the matter?"

"No." She went inside, and he closed the door. They looked at each other for a moment in silence. Millicent dropped her gaze. Heat rose in her cheeks. She felt foolish and more than a little uneasy, but she could not stop now; she was determined to go through with it.

Jonathan's eyes ran down her body, taking in the nightgown, the shawl thrown over it, her hair, unbraided and recently brushed into a smooth, burnished fall over her shoulders. "Would you . . . like to come into the parlor?"

Millicent shook her head, unable to speak. She didn't want to go into the formal parlor, where she would be even more out of place. She wished there were an easy way to do this, some way she could let Jonathan know what she wanted without having to say it. But she could see no possibility of that.

She straightened her shoulders and raised her head, looking him straight in the eye. "I came to ask if you—"

"If I what?" he asked gently, his brow wrinkling in concern.

"Would you—" she closed her eyes and finished in a rush "—take me to bed?"

"What!?" His jaw dropped. He set the lamp down with a thud on the counter beside him. "Millicent, what the devil are you talking about?"

Millicent's jaw came up in an instinctively defensive gesture. "Don't you know? I'm asking you to—" She couldn't think of any way to phrase it. No lady ever talked about it, and the euphemisms she had heard used sounded stupid, especially in this context. She could hardly ask him to "have his way with" her or to "take advantage" of her. Was there nothing that indicated that she came to him of her own free will?

"Make love to you?" he supplied, his voice low and, she thought, a little tight.

"Yes."

"You want to make love with me now?" His hands curled up into balls at his sides. He crossed his arms and clamped his hands against his sides, firmly under his arms. "I don't understand. Are you serious?"

"Of course I am!" Millicent snapped, irritated by his apparent lack of interest. "Do you think I'd make a fool of myself like this for fun?" She whirled and started to walk away.

"No, wait!" He grabbed her arm, holding her in place. "Dammit, you can't walk out now, after that little bombshell."

"I didn't mean to place you in an awkward situation," Millicent went on stiffly, not looking at him. "It's perfectly all right if you don't wish to—"

Jonathan bit back an oath. "My God, Millie, of course I want to. I—but you've stunned me, that's all. I don't understand why you're asking me this. Why you're—surely it must be against everything you've been taught, everything you believe in."

"Because I want you!" Millicent replied fiercely, fixing her clear, steady gaze on him. "I want to have something for myself."

"Millicent . . . " Involuntarily his eyes traveled down her again.

The heat in his gaze emboldened Millicent, and she let her shawl drop off her arms and onto the floor. In the glow of the lamp, the shape of her body was clear. He could see the suggestion of the darker circle of her nipples beneath the cotton nightgown, the centers hardening as he watched and pressing out against the cloth.

"Millicent . . . " he repeated, and he came toward her a step, his eyes still on her breasts. "You're beautiful. I can't help but want you. But—are you sure?"

"Very." Millicent's voice shook, but less from uncertainty this time than from the effect his hungry eyes had on her.

Jonathan took one of her hands in his and raised it to his mouth, pressing his lips softly to her skin. The touch of his lips sent shivers up her. Millicent could feel her loins turning heavy and warm, loosening, and her breasts were suddenly so sensitive she could feel the scratch of the cloth against them and their responsive tightening.

Jonathan closed his eyes almost as if in pain, and he turned her hand over, kissing her palm in the same slow, heated way. "If I were a gentleman," he murmured against her skin, and his teeth nipped gently at the fleshy pad below her thumb, "I would not agree to this."

Millicent's knees went weak and she swayed toward him.

"I would remind you that it isn't moral," he went on, "and that you would regret it tomorrow morning." His mouth traveled to the soft, thin skin of her wrist. "But you know I'm not a gentleman."

"I know." Her voice was little more than a sigh. His mouth did strange things to her senses. "I'm glad."

Jonathan chuckled, and his breath on her flesh sent more shivers through her. "Ah, Millicent, your honesty will get you in trouble someday. Thank God for it."

Jonathan lifted his head, and his hand went to the nape of her neck, holding her still beneath his gaze. He looked down into her face for a long moment. He bent and pressed his lips to hers, at first gently, then with ever-increasing hunger. Millicent trembled at the force of her feelings, and her hands went to his shoulders to steady herself. He wrapped his arms around her and pulled her up into him, pressing her hard into his body, and his mouth devoured hers. His tongue seduced her, as soft and slow and inviting as his lips were hard and demanding. A moan escaped Millicent. She felt wild and out of control. It was almost frightening, and yet she wanted it, wanted more.

When he pulled back, Jonathan was panting as though he had been running, and his face was flushed, his eyes glittering. "Tell me to stop now," he said hoarsely, "or I can't turn back."

"Make love to me," she whispered.

His nostrils flared, and his arms tightened around her. For an instant, Millicent thought he would pull her down to the floor and take her right there, but he released her and, taking her hand, grabbed the oil lamp and led her out into the hall and up the stairs to his room.

It was odd to be upstairs in this house. She had been inside his home only a few times, and never upstairs where the sleeping quarters lay. It was a private place, foreign, a man's domain. The lamp cast a small circle of yellow light in the long darkness of the hallway, leaving the majority of it in shadows, which made the hall seem even stranger. Millicent felt guilty as she walked along the hall, almost tiptoeing, as if her intrusion into this forbidden area was the real sin.

Jonathan paused at the doorway to his room and stepped back to let her enter before him. Millicent went inside and stopped. This was Jonathan's bedroom. She felt out of place and faintly scared, yet eager and excited, too.

She had never been inside a man's bedroom, except

for her father's and her brother's. Being here held an intimacy, a familiarity that she had never experienced with anyone. Even though she had just kissed Jonathan passionately, had had her body pressed against his so tightly that she could scarcely breathe, standing here seemed somehow an invasion into his inner self, into a place where she should not reach.

Tonight she would know him as she had never known anyone—and he would know her.

Millicent turned and looked at Jonathan. As if sensing her confusion and the panic that just stabbed her, he reached out and curved his hand over her cheek, caressing her softly, reassuringly. He smiled a little. "Frightened?"

Millicent nodded. "A little." She was breathless, her heart racing, and she could no longer separate her fear from excitement and anticipation.

"Don't worry." He took her loosely in his arms, rubbing his cheek against her hair. "I won't hurry. I'll do my best not to hurt you."

She wasn't really worried about physical pain, though she had gleaned over the years from overheard bits of conversation that there was pain involved, at least the first time. Her fear, she knew, was more of the unknown, of giving herself to someone, uncertain of what she would lose of herself, of how much he would take from her. After tonight she would no longer be the same Millicent Hayes, and she wasn't sure who the new one would be or whether she really wanted to be that woman.

She turned her face up to his, her eyes shining. Jonathan drew a quick breath, stunned by the desire and love he saw in her luminous eyes, and he bent to kiss her. He kissed her again and again—on her mouth, her cheeks, her ears, her neck—softly, then passionately; lingering, then fast and demanding. Millicent melted against him, giving herself up to his mouth, all fear and nervousness fleeing before the upwelling of desire in her. She moaned unconsciously, moving her hands over him. He trembled, and his fingers dug into her.

His hands slid down her back and slowly over the curve of her hips to her legs, then came back up her sides, gliding over her ribs and up to the soft swell of her breasts. He cupped her breasts through the cloth of her nightgown, gently rubbing his thumbs over the hard points of her nipples. Millicent gasped, stunned by the sensations that flooded her at his touch. She had never dreamed that it would be like this. She was hungry to feel his hands all over her, to know the friction of his bare skin on hers.

Jonathan moved back, reluctantly releasing her, and began to unbutton his shirt with fingers that shook a little. Millicent watched, unable to look away, as he undid his shirt and pulled it off, exposing the bare breadth of his chest. His skin was smooth and leanly ridged with muscle, dotted with light reddish-brown hair that grew downward in a **V** to his navel. He kicked off his shoes and pulled off the rest of his clothes, revealing the long, smooth line of his legs and hips.

Red flooded Millicent's face as she looked at him naked, embarrassed by her own flagrant curiosity, yet too fascinated and aroused to turn away. She had not expected him to undress like this, with the light still on, but she had to confess that she was glad he did. The mere sight of his masculine body stirred her, bringing up hot, hungry longings that shocked her with their intensity.

Jonathan came back to her and reached out to grasp her nightgown. Bunching it up in his hands, he pulled it up her legs and torso and off over her head. His eyes went to her breasts, rounded and pink-tipped, the nipples pebbling at the touch of air upon them. They tightened even more at his gaze, and Millicent felt as if her breasts were swelling, suddenly extremely sensitive. A throbbing started between her legs, heated and urgent. She realized that she loved having Jonathan's eyes on her, that she thrilled to the heat in his gaze and gloried in the eagerness with which his eyes ran over her body.

"You are beautiful," he told her hoarsely.

His hands returned to her breasts, his fingers curving over them as if he touched something priceless and fragile. His fingertips brushed down her body, exploring every inch of her pale skin. He grazed the satiny skin stretched across her pelvis and caressed the fleshy curve of her buttocks. He storked her legs and back and torso, introducing her to every delightful shimmer of sensation in her body. Millicent forgot the embarrassment of their nakedness and his intimate touch, forgot everything except the quivering heat within her and the pleasure of his hands.

She groaned, and her hands went out to his shoulders. She had to touch him. At first her hands were tentative on him, but when she saw the fierce glitter of pleasure in his eyes, she let her fingers roam further. They slid down over the muscles of his shoulders and chest, exploring the masculine textures of him—the wiriness of curling hairs, the firmness of muscle overlaid by smooth, warm skin, the hard shape of bone, the flat nipples that tightened into little buds at her touch. It was all so different from herself, so exciting and forbidden, and she felt strange, compelling urges; ideas that made her blush to even think them filled her head.

Jonathan guided her back to the bed, and they stretched out on it, continuing to stroke and caress each other, but now, as his hand moved over her, he began again to kiss her, intensifying her pleasure until she thought she might explode. Just as she thought there could be no higher plane of passion, his mouth traveled down her throat and across her chest onto the quivering flesh of her breasts. Millicent tensed at the intimate touch, but she did not move away. Unexpected as it was, it was too delightful to end it. His lips trailed across her breast, and his hand came up to cup it, seemingly holding it for the delectation of his mouth. When his lips reached her nipple, he kissed the delicate bud and then, startling her even more, his tongue traced it. Millicent gasped, and her fingertips dug into his arms.

He went still for a moment, then his tongue went back to work upon the button of flesh. He took the nipple into the warm wet cave of his mouth, his tongue lashing and stroking. Moisture flooded between her legs, increasing with each new pull and caress of his mouth. Millicent's breath came raggedly in her throat. She was awash in a wild, heated haze of sensations. Her body was something new and strange to her, an animalistic thing of vast and primitive feelings.

Jonathan moved to her other breast, reawakening all over again the new sensual pleasures. His hand slid down her body to tangle in the hair between her legs, and Millicent jerked in surprise. He could not touch her there!

But he did. And she wanted to feel it, wanted it despite the embarrassment. She hated for him to feel the wetness there, sure that he would be repulsed, but there was no revulsion in him when he slid across the slick, satiny flesh. Millicent trembled, digging in her heels and rising up off the bed, driven by the tremendous pleasure and the almost unbearable tension he was creating in her. Her hips moved involuntarily. There was a deep, primal need in her; she wanted something, though she wasn't sure exactly what. She had to have it. Had to have him.

"Jonathan . . . " She groaned his name, and his skin flamed even hotter beneath her hands.

Then he moved over her and entered inside her. It hurt, and yet it was what she wanted. Her teeth dug into her lower lip. He filled her, satisfying her in a primitive way, fulfilling the strange new need she had felt. Then he began to move, and she realized that it hadn't fulfilled her after all because this was even more and better, taking her into a realm of pleasure she'd never dreamed of. She gasped and moaned, and the raw sounds of his own hunger heightened her desire. He was driving into her, and she met each thrust, something wild and aching building in her, spiralling ever upward, until she felt as if she were chasing it, afraid she would not catch it.

It exploded within her, a fierce, stunning burst of pleasure, so intense it forced a cry from her. Jonathan's response was immediate and deep, and he shuddered against her, his passion flooding out. Millicent took it from him gladly, wrapping her arms and legs tightly around him and holding him through the storm.

Slowly they relaxed, and rationality began to return. Millicent felt limp, mindless and will-less, her entire body weak with the aftermath of the greatest pleasure she had ever known.

"I love you," she whispered. Tears clogged her throat. "I love you."

For a while they lay awake, murmuring soft, rambling words of love, his arms wrapped around her, and gradually they drifted to sleep. Jonathan slept heavily, but Millicent awoke after a time. She lay for a moment, still drained and hazy with contentment. But she knew that she had to leave; she couldn't stay here through the night. Reluctantly she slipped from the bed, not disturbing Jonathan, and pulled back on her nightgown. She took one last long look at his sleeping form on the bed, and her heart clenched within her. Pain mingled with the pleasure and satiety within her. How could she bear to leave him? How could she bear never to see him again? Millicent began to fear that she'd made a terrible mistake. It might be worse, far worse, to spend the rest of her life without Jonathan now.

Closing her mind to the thought, she left the room and hurried back home.

But she could not escape the heavy fear; it was there the next morning when she awoke. She blinked, looking around her. It was her old, familiar room; but she had changed. She got up, aware of the soreness inside her. Her hand drifted down across her front, and her nerves, newly awakened to life last night, tingled. Oh, Lord, what was she to do?

But she knew the answer to that, of course. She would do what she had to do, what she had decided last night. She had had her moment of pleasure with Jonathan, just as she had wanted, and now she would have to live out the rest of her life as she had planned. It seemed a bleak prospect.

She washed and dressed and dragged herself downstairs. She couldn't face going to church. She would simply have to plead sick. It wasn't much of a falsehood, really. While part of her still felt the satisfaction and pleasure of the night before, another part of her was lost and drowned in gloom.

Jonathan came calling on her before noon. He looked bright and fresh and overwhelmingly exuberant. It hurt her to look at him. Millicent realized that she hadn't thought ahead to this moment last night when she had made her decision. She had to tell him now that she could no longer see him. She also realized that she had not thought at all about Jonathan when she had decided to seek him out; she had thought selfishly, only of herself and what she wanted.

"Millicent." His smile was slow and incendiary. Millicent's breasts tingled with anticipation. "How are you?" The question was ordinary, his eyes warm and intimate.

"F—fine," she stammered, stepping back to let him in. She linked her hands behind her back to keep them from going out to him. She could tell from the expression on his face that he wanted to kiss her, hold her. She wanted it, too.

She wanted to cry. This final meeting would be torture.

"I wanted to talk to you," he began, his voice still in that low, intimate tone.

"All right." Millicent struggled to maintain a formality between them. She led him to the parlor and closed the door behind them. It might be improper, but she was long past worrying about that now. "I—I must talk to you, also."

Jonathan smiled. "It's impolite, but I want to speak first."

Millicent linked her hands together, her stomach twisting. What was he going to say?

"Will you marry me?"

Millicent stared at him. She felt as if all the air had been knocked out of her. She opened her mouth, but nothing came out. Finally she whispered, "What?"

"I said, will you marry me?"

"Oh, Jonathan!" Millicent's knees gave way, and she sat down heavily in her chair. He frowned uneasily.

"Millicent?"

"I never thought—I didn't dream that you would ask me to marry you." She looked up at him. "I didn't come to you last night to force you into marriage."

"I know that." He smiled. "You think I don't know you better than that? I didn't ask you to marry me because I *have* to. I want to marry you. I love you. I knew it yesterday before you even came to my house. Last night only confirmed it. I want you in my life every day for all the rest of it."

Millicent stared at him for a moment, stunned. Then she looked away, raising a shaky hand to her forehead. "I—I didn't know. I didn't realize."

"You didn't realize that I love you?" Jonathan looked astonished, and the careless happiness with which he'd entered the room began to slip into irritation. "Did you think that I was that callous, that I would take you and then discard you? That I would bed a virgin without loving her, without any intention of marrying her?"

"No, I don't think you're callous! I—I knew that you cared for me. But I thought, well, men don't seem to require love, and I thought you had no intention of marrying. I—you—Elizabeth—" she stumbled to a halt, unable to fashion her boomeranging thoughts into a coherent sentence.

"Elizabeth!" Anger rose in his voice. "What the devil does she have to do with this?"

"You're still in love with her! You said you'd never found anyone that you could love as much and you didn't want to marry for anything less."

"My God . . . do you mean that you think I took you last night without loving you? Millicent! I love you; I want to marry you!"

Millicent clutched her skirt with both hands, digging in her fingers. Tears sprang into her eyes. "I—oh, Jonathan, I've made a terrible mess of everything! What have I done? I didn't mean to hurt you!"

He went to her and took her hands in his, pulling them away from their frantic clutching of her skirt. "I thought that you loved me."

"I do love you. I want to marry you. But I can't. It's impossible."

"Impossible? Why? I don't understand. Were you— no, you couldn't have been married already." He stared at her in confusion.

"No, of course not. I'm not married or anything like that. It's not a legal impossibility. It's just that I can't. I told you a long time ago that I could never marry. I must stay with Alan. That's where my duty lies."

Jonathan's hands slid from hers and he stepped back heavily. "Because of Alan? You refuse to marry me because you are going to stay here and take care of your brother? That's your duty? Your responsibility? To sacrifice your life for your brother?"

"Yes, if I have to." Her voice was barely above a whisper, and she could not bring herself to look into his eyes.

"There are other choices."

"None that are acceptable. I can't leave him alone. He'd wither away and die."

"You don't give your brother much credit, do you? I believe you'd find he's stronger than you think. Why don't you talk to him? Ask him?"

"I have!" Millicent flared. "That's why I came to you last night. I knew after I talked to him that I could never leave him, that I'd be killing him if I did. That's why I threw myself at you that way; I wanted at least that one night of happiness with you. I wanted to know what it was like to lie in your arms, to be loved by you."

"And that's all you need?" His voice was bitter. "One night is enough for you. You tested it and found out what it was like, and now you can live without me quite well, thank you? Is that it?"

"No!" The cry was torn from her, a deep and primitive thing. "I don't know how I can live without you! It would have been better not to know. Now I'll always think about you, always miss you."

"That's all you can say, that you will always miss me? It could have been a wonderful life, but now I'll never know, and good-bye?"

"You make it sound so easy, but it's not! You think I enjoy doing this? You think I want to give you up? And Betsy! A family!"

"I don't know. You seem to be doing it willingly enough."

"I have to!"

"You don't *have* to."

"No, but how can I live with myself if I desert him? How can I face myself every day for the rest of my life, knowing I abandoned Alan? Knowing I broke my promises to my mother and father and ignored my duty!"

"What about your duty to yourself! Do you owe yourself nothing?"

"Sometimes you have to put others before yourself."

He whirled away, slamming one fist into the other hand in frustration. "This is insane!" He turned back toward her. "Why can't you compromise? We'd live right next door to him; you could come over to see him whenever you wanted. Hell, he could live with us. Or Betsy and I could even move in here, if it's too difficult for you and him to leave."

"Alan wouldn't be happy living with us. He'd feel like a fifth wheel. And Betsy shouldn't have to refashion her life around an invalid."

"Alan! Betsy! Damnation, what about us? Doesn't it matter that you are in pain? That I am? Do we count for nothing? Why is it always Alan, Alan, Alan? Why is he the only one who's important?"

"I promised my parents that I'd look after him. When he was injured, it devastated my mother. She was never a strong person, and those long months of his illness, watching over him, caring for him . . . It killed her. She died less than a year after his accident. All she asked of me, as she lay dying, was that I take care of Alan."

Millicent's eyes filled with tears, and her voice trembled. She closed her eyes, seeing again, feeling again those long, horrible nights when Alan was first hurt, when she and her mother had sat by his bedside, watching his shallow breathing, hearing the small, pain-filled sounds he made, the little gasps that made them jump to their feet, sure that this was his final breath. Millicent had prayed frantically then, offering God everything she could think of in return for her brother's life, all the while torn apart inside, knowing that she was to blame.

"I swore to God that I would give up my life for him. I prayed that if He'd only give me another chance, give me Alan back, I'd take care of him always."

"Millicent . . . everyone makes that kind of promise when they're in the midst of a crisis. I can't begin to tell you the things I promised if only Elizabeth could live. No one expects you to follow promises made in such fear and sorrow. Is that really what your God asks of you, to give up your life in return for His help? Is that mercy?"

"You don't understand."

"I understand that you're tearing yourself apart needlessly. I understand that you've condemned yourself to unhappiness on the basis of some foolish promise that no one, especially a tender and merciful God, would expect you to follow."

"I promised my mother on her deathbed. I promised myself! It was my responsibility. I have to live up to it. It isn't something I can toss aside."

"Why? Why are you so goddamn responsible for your brother? You are responsible to yourself. And Alan is responsible for himself, not you."

"Yes, I am!" she cried, her whole body rigid from the conflict that raged inside her.

"Why? Dammit, Millie, tell me why!"

"Because it was my fault!" she shrieked. Silence dropped between them, thick and impenetrable as a wall. Jonathan stared at her.

Finally he said, "Your fault? How could it be your fault?"

"I did it! I as good as pushed him off that wagon!" The words burst out of her like blasts from a gun, released from a years-long prison of silence. She had never before said them, hardly even formed them into thoughts; she had only felt them deep within her, fierce and inchoate, a seething mass of guilt and recrimination. Her breath came out in little pants, and her voice shook as she went on, unable to stop the rush of words now. "I did it. They told me to take care of him. I'd always taken care of him. Looked after him. Ever since I can remember. I was his big sister. He loved me; he looked up to me; he wanted to go wherever I went. Sometimes I hated having to take him along." She slammed her fist into her other palm with each word. *"I hated looking after him!"*

Jonathan said nothing and carefully refrained from touching her. She looked so taut that it seemed she might shatter at the slightest touch. He waited, watching, his face drawn into sympathetic lines of pain.

"I didn't want to watch him. They told me, 'Look out for Alan, now, dear. You know how boys are.' Why couldn't he look out for himself?" The ancient resentment tinged her voice again, as though she felt once more what she had felt that day, and her eyes had the blankness of someone stepping into the past. "I wanted to laugh and have fun. Jimmy was going to be at the hayride and most of the other boys I liked. I didn't want to be saddled with Alan. Besides, he was too old to need looking after. He could take care of himself. He kept bothering me, making a fool of himself in front of everyone, clowning around with the other boys. He wanted me to look at him. All evening, he kept hollering, 'Look at me, Millie! Look at me!' I was sick and tired of looking at him. I was talking to three boys; they were flirting with me, and it was so funny because Rebecca Ordway kept shooting horrid looks at me. I was full of pride. Full of conceit."

Her face began to crumple, and Millicent raised her hands to her face, as if to hide her melting composure— or perhaps to hide the past from herself. Her hands trembled, and tears began to leak from her eyes. Her mouth contorted, and her words came out in desperate, desolate gulps. "He kept wanting me to look, and I wouldn't. I refused to turn my head toward him. I hoped that he would somehow disappear. Just go away. 'Look at me, Millie! Look at me!' But I wouldn't. Then he climbed up higher to balance on the edge of the wagon. To make me look at him." She burst into sobs, unable to hold back.

"And he fell," Jonathan supplied the ending to her story, and Millicent nodded, unable to speak for the storm of sobs that racked her body. "Ah, Millicent . . . sweetheart."

He moved forward and reached out his hands to take her by the shoulders. She stiffened at his touch for a moment, then crumpled, and he pulled her against him, wrapping his arms around her and cradling her to his chest. She wept in great, shuddering sobs, years of pent-up anguish pouring out of her. Jonathan smoothed his hand over her hair and down her back, murmuring meaningless noises of comfort and compassion.

When at last Millicent's sobs stopped, she stayed quiescently in his arms, her head resting on his chest. Jonathan kissed the top of her head.

"I know," he began in a low voice, "that right now you can't take it in or believe it, but I have to say this anyway. It wasn't your fault that Alan was crippled, Millicent. You couldn't have prevented it. If you had been watching him, you couldn't have reached him in time, and even if you had, you probably hadn't the strength to pull him back. Alan wasn't a child who needed to be watched constantly; he was almost grown. There was nothing wrong with your resentment at your parents' giving you that task. After all, Alan wasn't your responsibility; he was theirs. If he was that immature and incapable of handling himself, they shouldn't have let him go on the hayride. When did a fourteen-year-old boy ever listen to his sister, anyway? You don't deserve the blame. You don't need to punish yourself for the rest of your life because you think you made a mistake. It's not fair. Neither to you nor to Alan. Give Alan a chance to grow up. Let him accept the responsibility for what he did. You didn't make him climb up there. You didn't make him lose his balance. Those are things that he did. If he was acting foolishly because he wanted your attention, that's sad, but it still is his action. His responsibility."

"He was only a boy. He didn't realize how dangerous it was."

"Neither did you, or you wouldn't have not looked at him when he called to you. Remember, Millicent, you were just a girl, too. What, eighteen? Nineteen?" Millicent nodded. "That's not full grown, even though physically you might have appeared to be. You were young, and you were flattered by the attention of your admirers. What young lady wouldn't have been? It doesn't make you wicked. And it doesn't make you guilty of maiming your brother. It was an accident."

"It wasn't fair. It wasn't his fault."

"Does it have to be somebody's fault?"

Millicent shook her head wearily. "No, but . . . " She sighed and stepped back from Jonathan, wiping the tears from her face. "I must look a mess."

"You look fine."

"You understand now, don't you?" she asked, looking up at him with tear-reddened eyes.

Jonathan hesitated, then said slowly, "I understand why you feel the way you do. Why you think it's your obligation to take care of Alan, no matter what. But it isn't right, and I won't agree with you. I won't approve of it. Millicent, it's your life, and you have to break free of all that . . . that deadweight. Sweetheart," he reached out and brushed his fingertips down her cheek, "I love you. I want to marry you. I want us to have a life together, children, a home. Everything. Don't you want that enough to break out of your prison?"

She didn't speak. She couldn't look at him. Jonathan paused for a moment. Then she heard him slowly walking away.

Twenty-Two

$\mathcal{M}$illicent was miserable. She dragged through the rest of November and December lost in her sorrow. With each day she realized more how much she had given up. Her life was the same as it had been before Jonathan arrived. She got up; she ate; she worked in the house; she visited with her brother; she went to club meetings and family gatherings. But she hadn't known how empty that life was. Now, without Jonathan and Betsy, she knew.

The pecans rattled down on the roof, announcing the coming of the Christmas season. Since she had been a child, pecan gathering had been a major, joyous event; this fall it was a chore. So were the thousand-and-one other tasks that preceded Christmas: shelling pecans and picking out the meats, cutting up candied orange peel, citron, and dates, making the fruit cakes and putting them aside in a warm dark closet to set, hanging the swags of evergreen on the mantels and stair railings, making strings of popcorn and cranberries to hang on the tree, carrying gift baskets of food to the poor of the town. With every task, she thought of how different it would be if she were celebrating the season with Jonathan. When she took the baskets of food to the riverfront houses, she thought of his newspaper articles about the section and its iniquities. As she pondered over a present for Alan, she thought about what she would have given Jonathan and wondered what he would have given her.

She tried to keep herself busy. She began a campaign within the church to imrpove the riverfront property, buttonholing every deacon and leading member of the congregation, as well as the minister himself. Through persistence, craftiness, and sheer determination, she eventually won out, and the church fixed up its holdings. But it was a hollow victory; Millicent could feel no satisfaction, for she had little joy in anything. When Jonathan came to her door to thank her for her efforts she wanted to burst into tears; she wanted to throw her arms around him and kiss him forever; she wanted to turn and run from him as hard as she could. It took every bit of willpower she had to stand and accept his thanks politely, and after he left, she fled to her room and cried for an hour.

Millicent had thought that eventually it would get better, but weeks passed, and still she was as lonely and unhappy, even more so. It seemed horribly unfair: She was doing what was right, so why was it so hard? She would have thought that there would have been at least an easing of her pain. She would have thought that she wouldn't continue to ache with missing Jonathan.

Christmas came and passed. Betsy came over on Christmas afternoon to give Millicent her present, a potholder which Betsy had made for her herself. Millicent took the gift and unwrapped it, then stood looking at the crudely woven object, and her eyes filled with tears.

"I—I'm sorry." Betsy's eyes were huge and sad. "Don't you like it? Papa said he thought you would."

"Oh, yes! Yes, I love it." Millicent threw her arms around the girl and hugged her to her tightly. "It's the most beautiful present I've ever gotten. I'll treasure it forever." She released her reluctantly and stepped back, wiping the tears from her face. "I have something for you."

Millicent handed Betsy a box and watched as she unwrapped it to reveal a doll with painted porcelain head, hands, and feet, dressed in a blue frilled dress. "It's beautiful," Betsy breathed, touching the lacy ruffles with an admiring finger.

Betsy cradled it carefully in her arms, and Millicent watched her, taking in and savoring every little detail about her. Betsy didn't come to see her as often anymore. Since school had started she had spent more time with her friends and less with Millicent. Millicent also thought that Betsy suspected the tension between her father and Millicent and felt somewhat uneasy about coming to visit her.

"Miss Millie," Betsy said slowly, keeping her gaze fastened on the doll. "Don't you like us any more?"

"Oh, Betsy, no! Of course I still like you. I love you. You're my favorite little girl."

Betsy smiled. "That's what Papa said, too. He said it

was just him. But I don't understand. Why are you mad at him? It—it makes it hard."

Millicent swallowed. How could she explain this to a child? "It's not an easy situation." She stopped for a moment, then went on, "I don't hate your father. I like him very much, but nothing can happen with us."

Betsy frowned. "I don't understand."

"I know you don't. But, believe me, I do love you. I still love to see you. But with your papa and me—it just can't be helped."

Betsy grimaced. "I don't understand grown-ups."

Millicent smiled tremulously. "Sometimes we are a little odd."

"Will I be like that, too, when I get bigger?" Betsy looked dismayed by the prospect, and Millicent chuckled, her heart aching. Betsy was so dear to her. There had been times when she had imagined that she and Jonathan might have a child like her. But it was better not to think about things like that.

"I don't know, dear. But it won't seem as odd to you then."

Betsy nodded, unconvinced, and turned to go. At the door, she swiveled back. "Miss Millicent . . . "

"Yes, dear?"

"Papa misses you. I can tell. He looks sad a lot nowadays. He doesn't laugh as much." Having said her piece, Betsy turned and left the house.

Millicent stood looking after her, her hand pressed to her mouth and tears standing in her eyes. Betsy's words were a physical pain to Millicent. She hadn't meant to hurt Jonathan. It made her own pain ten times worse, knowing that she had hurt him. Jonathan probably hated her now for the pain she had caused him. She had been selfish and unthinking; she should not have let him come courting at all. Certainly she shouldn't have gone to him that night and asked him to make love to him. It had been wrong, and she had only ended up hurting both of them even more.

She had wanted a memory. She hadn't realized how the memory would haunt her.

Alan wheeled his chair into the library and maneuvered it to a shelf of casebooks. He picked up the large tome in his lap and fitted it back into the empty slot on the shelf, then ran his index finger along the leather-bound books until he found one on evidence. He pulled it out and set it in his lap. He started to move back to his room, but then he stopped and glanced around the library. It would be easier to read the book in here instead of carting it back and forth. He hadn't thought about using the library before because it remained his father's sanctuary in Alan's mind. Mr. Hayes had discouraged his rambunctious young son from entering the room and disturbing him.

It was silly now. The library was as much his as any place in the house. Alan moved his chair over to the set of windows on the west wall and pushed back the heavy green velvet curtains to let in the sunlight. He angled his chair so that the light fell on the pages of the book and settled down to read.

He had been browsing among his father's legal books for several weeks now. It had started before Christmas when Opal had asked him a question about the law. He had had no idea what the answer was, but he hated to disappoint her, so he had gone to his father's law library and looked up the point. He had found the matter rather interesting; even the search for the right book and answer had been something like a treasure hunt. He had continued to dabble in the books, moving from one subject to the next as his interest dictated.

There was a woman's light step in the hallway, and he heard Opal humming. Alan smiled, raising his head to see her. She passed by the door, rags and a bucket in her hand, glancing into the library as she did. She stopped abruptly and looked in again.

"Alan?" She came a step into the room. "Oh, I'm sorry to disturb you. But it surprised me to see you in here, usually this room's closed."

"Yes, I know. I was borrowing one of Father's books, so I thought I might as well read it in here. At least it's a change of scenery."

"That's good." Opal nodded in approval. "You could use a change. You know what I was thinking?"

"What?"

"You ought to get outside more. 'Course, the weather's not too nice right now, but in the spring and fall, it's beautiful outside. It'd do you good to take a walk."

"A walk?" he repeated ironically.

Opal blushed. "I'm sorry. Well, you know what I mean."

"Yes. I know." He shrugged. "I'm afraid I don't get out much."

"Why not? You can move around practically as good as anybody. I figured you'd like to see some other things."

"I would, I suppose. It's the people I hide from."

"Hide from?" Opal looked at him, startled. "Are you scared of people? I didn't figure you were scared of much of anything. I mean, all that pain and everything you went through, well, it's a lot more than most people bear in a lifetime. Since you pulled through that, I'd think you could get through almost anything."

"I don't know that that was bravery. Only survival."

"Survival can take a lot of courage."

Alan smiled. "I'm afraid you have me mistaken for someone like you."

"Me? Oh, no, I'm not brave." Opal looked sheepish. "I don't much like to go out myself. You know, walking the baby or something. I know people talk about me."

"They aren't worth worrying about," Alan assured her. "No one who knew you could dislike you or say anything bad about you."

"The same's true for you, so why do you hide from folks?"

He gazed at her assessingly for a moment. A smile stole across his mouth. "You don't give an inch, do you?"

"What do you mean?"

"Most people allow me my excuses and my quirks. They forgive my bad traits because I'm crippled. Even Millicent doesn't pull me up short."

Opal suddenly looked anxious. "I didn't mean to act

like I was correcting you. I'm in no position to tell you something's right or wrong."

"Don't apologize. You're right. I think I've been too spoiled over the years. Everyone in my family pitied me; they wanted to make up to me for my accident, especially Millicent." He shrugged. "I don't know why, exactly. I guess she felt bad because she was still young and full of strength, able to do the things we'd done in the past, whereas I was not."

"Millicent loves you."

"I know." He sighed. "That's why it's hard to see her feeling this way and not know what to do to help her."

"I know." Opal nodded. "She's been awfully sad lately. Mr. Lawrence hasn't been around at all. Even Betsy's not here as much."

"It's bound to be something to do with Jonathan. They must have had a falling out. But what can you do to help a person with something like that?" Alan understood the pain of loving and not receiving love in return; he'd felt it often enough about Opal. But as far as he'd been able to discover, there was no comfort for that kind of hurt.

Alan didn't like to think about the subject, and he cast about in his mind for something that would get them off the topic of wounded hearts. "Tell you what— I'll make a pact with you."

"A what?"

"An agreement. A deal."

"All right," Opal agreed slowly.

He chuckled. "Don't look so suspicious. Here's what I propose: I will go out for a walk tomorrow afternoon, provided the weather cooperates, of course, but only on one condition."

"What's that?"

"That you go with me."

"Me! But why?"

"You told me you're scared to go out there, too. If I'm going to risk the ridicule of the world, I'm certainly not doing it alone. You need to get out as much as I do, if not more."

"But it'll help you," Opal pointed out.

"It will help you," he countered. "You stay as holed up in this house as I do—and you're able to walk, which makes it even worse."

Opal hesitated. "I don't know. . . ."

He waited, not saying anything, just crossing his arms and looking at her.

"All right." She looked almost panicky. "But you'll be there with me?"

"Yes. Right beside you." Without thinking about the gesture, he held out his hand reassuringly, and Opal slipped hers into it.

"Maybe I can do it, then . . . if you're with me."

The following day they took their walk and found, to their surprise, that it was less of an ordeal than they had expected. There was, in fact, a tremendous feeling of freedom and release in managing to get along outside the sanctuary of the house. By the end of January, Alan was ready to go on.

"I have another pact for you," he told Opal one evening as they sat in the parlor. He was bouncing

Robert in his lap, making him squeal with delight, while Opal stitched away at a new gown for the baby.

Opal looked up, half alarmed, half interested. "What?"

"I've been thinking about going to Sunday dinner at Aunt Maude's this week."

Opal stared. "Really? You mean, with Millicent? Why, that's wonderful!"

He shrugged. "I don't know if it's wonderful, but, I've been thinking that it's something I should do. I mean, what are they going to do, eat me? It might be interesting. A change."

Opal smiled. "I'm glad." She paused, her smile turning to a puzzled frown. "But what do you mean about our making a pact? What does it have to do with me?"

"I want you and Robert to come with me."

"What?" Horror washed over her face. "Oh, no! We couldn't. Robert and me—I mean, Robert and I don't belong there. That's your family. They'd think I was terrible!"

"Nonsense. I promise you, none of them would say a thing untoward to you."

"They might not say it because of you and Millicent, but they'd think it. They'd all wonder why you were bringing a servant to a family dinner. It wouldn't be right."

"You're not just a servant!" Alan hated to think of Opal as a servant. He hated for her to think of herself that way. "You're our friend. They'll like you; all the family will. And they'd love to see Robert. My entire family is silly over babies."

Opal continued to look scared and uncertain. "Please . . . no. I couldn't go. I'd be too embarrassed. They'd know about me and—and how I came here. The baby. Everything. I couldn't bear it."

"They'll have forgotten all that by now," Alan assured rashly and untruthfully. He knew that where gossip was concerned, his family, and indeed, most of Emmetsville, had a memory like an elephant. But he also knew that the best way to wear away at that gossip was for people to meet Opal and see for themselves what she was really like. Then a great deal of the speculation would falter and die. Going to a family get-together under Millicent's and his aegis was the best way to present her; no one would snub her or let her hear anything hurtful about herself. "Besides," he added with a great deal more veracity, "if I'm there, they'll be so busy jawing about me that they won't have time to pay attention to you. I chose the easier side of our family. The Connallys aren't nearly as inquisitive as the Hayeses—and they have no Aunt Oradelle."

A giggle escaped Opal. "I've heard Millicent talk about her."

"Complain is probably closer to the truth. Aunt Oradelle could drive a saint to murder." He looked deep into her eyes. "Say you'll come with me, Opal. I won't go without you. You give me strength."

"All right."

Opal had given in to Alan because she was unable to refuse him anything, especially when he asked her in the way he had, contending that she helped him. But by the time Sunday came around, she was regretting her decision. She hated the prospect of facing Alan's large and well-bred clan, certain that they would look down their noses at her. Alan was a dear man and he thought that everyone else was as kind and tolerant as he, but Opal knew that that wasn't true. Perhaps her being with Alan and Millicent would keep anyone from saying anything hurtful to her, but she knew what they would be thinking. Why, the fact that Alan was showing up with her might make them decide that he was interested in her as something more than an employee, and then they would blame her for trying to entrap him, playing on his crippled state.

There had been a time when Opal herself had thought that Alan might be interested in her as something more than a friend. The day that she had cut his hair, she would have sworn that he had responded to her on a deep male level; after all, there was some physical evidence that a man couldn't hide. She had hoped that she was right, and she had waited for Alan to give her some further indication of how he felt, but in the months in between, he had not made any advances toward her in any way. She had had to accept that what he had felt for her, if anything, had been merely a stray desire and, since he felt nothing more for her, he had been too much of a gentleman to act upon it.

For the first time, Opal resented Alan's gentility and morality. She knew that she was not his equal, and she would never expect marriage, or even love, from him. But she would have liked to have what she could with him. She would have gladly gone to his bed. Her heart might not have been satisfied but at least the passion that had flared to life inside her would.

The desire had come as a surprise to her. With the way she felt about him, she would have slept with Alan if he wanted simply because she would have given him anything she had in her power to give him. She would have been proud and happy to please him. But she had not expected the passion that flared up in her, the hot and sizzling eagerness she had felt when she touched him, the yearning to taste his kiss. After what Johnston had done to her, she had expected never to want a man to touch her again. But Alan was different; he was not grasping or frightening. He was a good man, and in the security and comfort of his house, her natural instincts had come to life.

She wished that Alan did want her, even if it was only for a brief time. She wanted to be held in his arms and feel his kisses, his heat; she wanted to take him into her, to be filled with his passion. But Opal had neither the confidence nor the selfishness to try to lure him into an affair, to seduce him with sidelong glances and "accidental" brushings of her body against his. She could only wish and hope and suffer through the nights without him.

The afternoon at his relatives' house turned out to be easier than she had expected. Though there were some odd looks cast her way, no one said anything about her presence, and several of the women even made much of Robert. A large part of the reason she was able to slip into the background was because of the tremendous stir that Alan's arrival created. Everyone was far too amazed over his coming to a family gathering to even bother wondering about her. They surrounded him immediately, exclaiming how marvelous it was to see him and commenting on the good state of his health. He was quickly separated from Opal and Millicent and pulled this way and that to talk to various members of the family.

Without his presence, Opal felt frightened and insecure, and she stuck by Millicent's side. Fortunately Millicent went into the kitchen to help, where Opal was more comfortable, and Opal was able to spend most of the afternoon there helping in one way or another. It was the only way she knew to blend in with this group of people, who seemed to her to be smarter, prettier, and better dressed than anyone she'd ever been around before. She was acutely aware of the fact that she didn't belong with them.

The meal was the worst time, for she was certain that the family would not approve of her sitting down to eat with them, yet it would have been odd for her to be the only person eating in the kitchen. She didn't know where to go or what to do, and she was relieved when Millicent took her hand and firmly led her to a seat between Alan's and her own chair at the end of the table.

Alan smiled at her. "Where have you been? I haven't seen you since we got here." He seemed lighthearted, even jovial.

"You've been enjoying being with your family," Opal told him. "I'm glad."

"It has been nicer than I expected," he admitted. "But you could have been there, too."

"No," she demurred, smiling and shaking her head. "I didn't belong there. They wanted to be with you. I would have been in the way."

"She's been helping in the kitchen with me," Millicent stuck in.

"You mustn't let them put you to work. This family will work a person into the ground, won't they, Millie?"

"They have been known to." Millicent gave Opal a shrewd glance. "But I think Opal didn't mind helping."

"No, not at all! I was glad to."

"Good. But don't you dare go back there and slave over dirty dishes all afternoon. I'll take you around and introduce you to everyone."

Opal looked horrified at the thought, but Alan, usually so sensitive, paid no attention to it. After the meal was over, he insisted that she come with him to meet some of his cousins, and she spent the next hour or so uncomfortably trying to make conversation. One of his cousins, a young man named Harry, was nice enough to talk to her for several minutes, and Opal relaxed a little with him, grateful for his easy way and nonstop flow of conversation. Still, it was a relief when she was able to slip back to the kitchen and even more of a relief when the time came for them to leave the house altogether. She knew she didn't belong with the Hayes and Connally families, no matter how nice Alan and Millicent were about it.

* * *

Thunder cracked through the night, and Alan came awake with a start, his heart pounding. It took him a moment to realize what had awakened him. Then the heavy boom sounded again, confirming the thunder.

It was odd. Thunder was rare in the winter, much more a product of the spring and summer storms. He couldn't remember the last time he had heard it. There was an eerie, ominous quality to it.

It came again, and upstairs he heard the thin cry of a baby. The thunder had awakened Robert.

Alan scooted across the bed and lowered himself into his chair. Over the past few months he had become quite expert at it, and he no longer even thought about it. Releasing the stop, he rolled across the floor to the window and pulled aside the heavy curtain to look out. The sky was oddly pale for this time of night, reminding him of the yellowish-tinged clouds in summer that carried hail with them. Lightning flickered somewhere behind the heavy curtain of clouds, lighting up the sky for an instant, and thunder rolled once more.

He heard the baby cry again, and a few moments later there were light steps on the stairs. Alan wheeled into the hallway just as Opal stepped down from the last stair. She jumped when she saw him, then relaxed.

"Alan! You startled me!"

"I'm sorry. I didn't mean to."

"Did the baby wake you up?" she asked, coming closer. She carried Robert on her shoulder, jiggling him gently to stop the cries. Robert was twisting his face sleepily against her. "I'm sorry."

"No, it wasn't the baby. It was the thunder that woke

me. Then I heard Robert cry. Did the thunder scare him?"

"It certainly woke him up." She continued to pat him and bounce a little, but it was clear that he was not about to go back to sleep easily. He was disturbed and fretful. "But I'm afraid that now he's hungry. I could feed him, but he's getting to where it's not enough. That's one reason the noise woke him up; his stomach's not full. He fell asleep tonight before I could give him his cereal."

Robert was a chubby, fast-growing boy, and Opal had already started giving him a little bit of hot cereal in the morning and evening.

"Why don't you make him some now? That way maybe he'll stay asleep when he goes back to bed. Here, I'll hold him if you want to go cook it."

"Would you?" Opal smiled gratefully. "It makes it twice as hard to do anything, holding him. But I'd hate to keep you up any later."

"It's no problem." Alan reached up for the baby, and Opal handed him to him. Robert wailed briefly at the separation, but settled down against Alan's chest, soothed by the familiarity.

Alan followed Opal into the kitchen, where she quickly lit a lamp and started a fire in the stove for a pot of water. It was cold, and she shivered a little. She had not thrown anything on over her nightgown before she had come downstairs, only put on soft slippers.

Alan could see the outline of her figure in the light from the lamp, and when she turned he could see her nipples puckering in the coolness, pushing out against the soft flannel of her gown. Desire flooded him. He watched Opal as she moved about the room, filling the small pot with water and putting it on the stove, pulling out the jar of finely ground cereal. Her movements were quick and economical, but fluid; there was always something graceful about Opal, whatever she was doing. Her breasts, heavy and uncontained beneath the soft gown, jiggled a little with her movements. Alan's mouth grew dry and he felt warm despite the cold air of the kitchen.

He felt guilty, watching her with hunger. He often watched her as she worked, and it never failed to stir him, yet he was sure that there must be something perverse about doing so. Surely it must be wrong for him to watch her with lust in his heart.

Alan turned around abruptly and wheeled out of the room. He went into his bedroom and grabbed an afghan from atop the trunk at the foot of his bed, then returned to the kitchen. "Here," he said gruffly, "put this on. You must be cold."

Opal glanced up from her work, surprised. Her face softened. "Why, thank you." She came over and took the afghan from him, draping it around her shoulders and letting it fall down her back. "I was a little cold, but I hated to run back upstairs for a shawl." She smiled at him. "You're an awfully nice man."

He shrugged off her thanks. He doubted she'd feel that way if she knew the thoughts that had been running through his mind as he watched her. Backing the chair away to a safer distance, he patted Robert and waited for her to finish. He couldn't keep his eyes off her breasts, bobbing as she stirred vigorously. He couldn't keep his mind off the thought of running his hand over the sweet curve of her buttocks and down her leg, slipping it between her legs to stroke up and down.

He sank his teeth into his lower lip, suppressing a groan. Why did he torture himself this way, thinking about things that were forbidden to him? It seemed wicked to dream this way about Opal, who was so delicate, so sweet and good to him; she didn't deserve his secretive, lascivious thoughts. No doubt she would be appalled if she knew what he was imagining about her. But he couldn't control his thoughts; it was difficult enough to control what he said and did with her.

"Here we go," Opal said brightly, jerking him back from the dark realm of his thoughts. She came briskly to the table, stirring a small bowl of cereal. "Come here, sweetheart," she crooned, setting down the bowl on the table and reaching out to take Robert. "Let's get something in that tummy."

She settled down in the chair, tucking Robert into the crook of her arm, and began to spoon the warm mush into his mouth. Alan watched her as she first blew on the spoonful of cereal to cool it, her lips pursing prettily, then bent her head and eased the spoon into the baby's mouth, cooing and talking to him. She was so lovely it made his entire chest ache.

He stayed with her as she fed the baby, talking desultorily about the weather and whether the winter thunder signified a chance for snow or was merely freakish, then going on to discuss the Sunday dinner at Aunt Maude's a few days ago, and finally wandering off to Alan's recent reading in his father's library.

"It's interesting," he told her, trying to keep his mind off the heat in his abdomen and the sight of her breast pillowing the baby's head. "I never wanted to read for the law; I suppose I didn't want it precisely because Father did want it so much. But now, you know, there's a certain fascination to it. I can see why Father was committed to it."

"I knew you were smart enough to be a lawyer or something."

Alan looked at her. "I've been thinking about that. Do you think it's possible that I could do it? Become a lawyer, I mean?"

"Of course you could," Opal replied staunchly. "Why, you could do anything you wanted."

"There are lots of obstacles. Why, I never even finished school, let alone college. But I don't think that means I couldn't read for the law. I could study with an attorney. I think my father's old partner would let me work with him. I could learn what I need to know clerking with him and studying. If I could do that, there's no reason why I couldn't practice law. I mean, you don't have to be able to walk to write a contract or a will or even to argue in court." He paused. "Do you think it's foolish? Would everyone think I'm crazy?"

"I don't know. Maybe some people would. But they're the kind who'd think anything different was crazy."

Alan smiled. "You're probably right about that. Maybe I ought to talk to Mr. Carter, Father's partner, and see what he thinks."

"That sounds smart." Opal teased the spoon at Robert's mouth, but he refused to open. His eyes blinked sleepily. "I think this little fellow's about done." She wiped off his mouth and put him up to her shoulder. "I'll take him upstairs and put him to bed. Then I'll come back and clean up the mess." She waved a hand toward the dirty bowl and pan.

"You needn't bother about that. Go on to bed. Ida will see to it in the morning."

"No, I hate to leave a messy kitchen. And I've gone past the point of being sleepy, anyway."

"Me, too."

She left the kitchen, carrying Robert, and Alan heard her climbing the stairs. He remained in the kitchen, waiting for her. He should go back to bed, he knew. There was no reason to stay up and nothing that would keep him awake any longer. The thunder had receded, and with it gone, there would be no disturbance from Robert, either. Opal would probably think it odd that he stayed there instead of going to sleep.

But he knew there was no possibility of his going to sleep, not now, when his blood was still on fire and his mind occupied with thoughts of Opal. He wanted to be with her alone; it was something he yearned for, and during the day, with the baby, Millicent, Ida, and often Johnny around, it was difficult to be alone with her without fear of interruption.

It was some time before she came back down. Alan thought she was probably nursing the baby before she put him down to sleep. As always the thought stirred him in a mixed, peculiar way—warm and loving, yet fraught with sexual hunger, too. But, then, was there anything concerned with Opal that didn't carry that underlying passion? He wanted her, and it tinged his every thought, every emotion.

He turned at the soft shuffle of slippers in the hall, and Opal came into the kitchen, the afghan still wrapped around her shoulders like a shawl, a splash of color against her pure white gown. "You stayed up," she said in a pleased, surprised tone.

"Yes. I don't think I can go back to sleep for a while."

"I'm like that." Opal picked up the bowl and carried it to the washpan. She dipped out water from the tank of the stove, warmed from the fire, and added water from a pitcher on the counter. She washed the bowl, spoons, and pan and dried them, and they chatted as she worked.

When she was through, she turned. "I hate to throw out the water; I've used it so little. Perhaps I'll leave it. Ida can use it for the dishes tomorrow."

Alan nodded. He couldn't speak. Water had splashed on her while she was washing, wetting her nightgown in several places. One spot clung damply to her breast, revealing the edge of a dark nipple; another was plastered against her stomach.

Alan couldn't keep his eyes from the spots. His breath came raggedly. Opal went silent and glanced down, following the path of his eyes. Color stained her cheeks, and one hand went automatically to the damp spot on her stomach. Slowly she raised her eyes, and her gaze locked with Alan's. Unmistakable passion blazed brightly in his eyes. Her breath caught in her throat.

She walked toward him as if pulled by the elemental force of his gaze. She stopped only inches from his chair. He raised his head, his eyes moving up her body to her face. He stared into her eyes for a moment. He was silent, his body taut, his lips heavy with sensuality. His desire sizzled between them, igniting Opal, as well.

"Alan," she breathed, his name an invitation.

He reached up and took her arms, pulling her gently down. He could not stop himself. Opal bent to him, her eyes fluttering closed. Their lips met, and passion jolted through him like the lightning that had flashed outside earlier. His fingers dug into her arms. His mouth pressed against hers urgently, and he pulled her down into his lap.

Twenty-Three

*H*e didn't know how to kiss. He had never kissed a woman other than Millicent or his mother, and that had been a far cry from what he sought now. But instinctively he pressed his lips hard against Opal's, moving his mouth a little. Her lips opened beneath his, and he knew that this was what he had wanted without even realizing it. His tongue slid along the parting of her lips, and the tip of her own tongue stole out to touch it. It startled Alan, sending explosive shivers through him. His tongue chased hers back into her mouth. He trembled, drawing in a ragged breath. The smell and taste and feel of her was all around him; he was drowning in her, yet he couldn't get enough. He wanted her so much he felt as if he might simply fly apart.

Alan pulled back, looking into Opal's face. His breath rasped in and out of his throat, and his face was flushed. His hands itched to touch her. He felt like a fool; he was ashamed and guilty; he was frightened. But overpowering all other feelings was a rushing, pounding desire. He had to have her. He couldn't wait, couldn't let her go.

Opal curled up in his lap, gazing up at him. Her eyes were like stars, and the expression in them enflamed his desire. She looked as if she wanted him; no, more than that—as if she gladly placed herself, body and soul, in his hands. It was a heady sensation. She put her hand up to his cheek, and his skin burned where she touched him. Alan closed his eyes at the rush of pleasure, his fingers knotting into fists. The ache in his loins was fierce and demanding, driving him onward.

He touched her face lightly, letting his fingertips drift downward to her neck. "I don't want to hurt you," he whispered hoarsely.

Opal smiled, her face glowing. "You won't hurt me."

He wished he were as sure of that as she appeared to be. He hardly knew himself; he was certain that he teetered on the edge of utterly losing control. His fingertips trembled against her skin. Her throat was like satin. He wanted wildly, insanely, to hook his hand into the neck of her gown and rip the gown apart, exposing her to his eyes.

Alan whipped the chair around, expending some of his energy on shooting across the kitchen floor and out the door. Opal cuddled up trustingly against him, her face buried in his shoulder, and the feel of her only increased his desire. When he reached his room, he closed the door behind them, locking it, and rolled over beside the bed. He stopped, and Opal slipped out of his lap to stand before him. Without a word, her eyes gazing into his, she reached down, grasped her nightgown, and pulled it up over her head. She stood before him completely naked in the dim light.

Alan gripped the arms of his chair. He could hardly breathe. She was lovely, surely too fragile and small to take a man and yet so womanly and desirable with her rounded hips and high, pointing breasts that it was all he could do not to reach out and touch her. His hand curved over the rounded point of her shoulder and down her arm, then back up. Gently his fingertips grazed across her chest, touching the rows of ribs and moving down onto the soft mounds of her breast. The exquisitely soft flesh trembled beneath his touch.

Alan swallowed hard. Sweat broke out across his forehead. He brought up his other hand and tenderly circled both her breasts, cupping them from beneath. Her breasts were plumped up in his hands, the nipples thrusting saucily toward him. Tentatively he touched one with his forefinger, and it prickled beneath his touch, growing harder and more pointed. He drew in his breath, heat flooding him.

He felt as hard as a rock, as if he would burst, but he had to have more. He had to explore the sweet beauty of her body, had to learn every inch of her. A little clumsily his hands moved down her body, covering the flat plane of her stomach and slipping around to follow the shape of her lips. With every movement passion surged and pounded in him more.

Unsure what to do, he followed where instinct led him. One hand slid down her thigh and back up the inside, fingers trailing along the incredibly soft skin. He neared the nest of curling pale hair, feeling her intense heat. Opal whimpered, and he glanced up quickly, afraid that he had hurt her. Her face was taut, but not with pain, and her mouth was slightly open, panting. As he hesitated, she moved down, bringing herself against his hand. She was hot and wet, tantalizingly slick to his touch. The moisture excited him almost past bearing, and he moved his fingertips over her flesh, rubbing gently. Opal moaned, her head falling back, and her hips circled. She whispered his name.

He put his arms around her and pulled her up hard against him, burying his face in the satiny skin of her stomach. He kissed her, his mouth trailing across her, nuzzling into her, frantic to have her and yet equally desperate to experience each joy of her body. Her scent drove him wild. He felt unbelievably powerful, incredibly alive.

He released her and fumbled at his nightshirt, yanking it off over his head. Opal moved back and sank down onto his bed, lying back and holding out her arms to him. He grasped the bar and swung onto the bed. He rolled onto her, and she opened her legs to him. He supported himself on his arms and thrust deeply into her. He moved within her in a natural rhythm, his arms holding him up, then back. Opal arched up against the bed, her hips moving with him. She was hot and tight around him, and the reality of being deep inside her aroused Alan past anything he had ever imagined. The pleasure he felt was so intense it was almost pain, and each intimate stroking pushed him farther and farther into the maelstrom of desire. At last the explosion came, shaking him to the depths. He groaned, shuddering, and his seed poured into her in a release so vivid and strong he felt as if for an instant he moved completely outside himself, and there was nothing in him but the hot, black, spinning passion.

He collapsed, dragging in gasps of air. He rolled to his side, wrapping his arms around Opal and holding her tightly to him. For the first time in his life, he felt the blissful exhaustion of complete satisfaction, and, smiling a little, he drifted into sleep.

Alan's arm was numb, and at last the pain of it woke him up. He blinked in the pale light of dawn, trying to orient himself and identify the pain that plagued him. He realized it was his arm and he looked down. Opal's head lay upon his upper arm, heavy in sleep. Her hair tumbled, silky and golden, over his arm and across the sheets. He remembered what had happened, feeling again a stab of the awe that had seized him the night before. Quickly on the heels of that thought followed a rush of guilt. *Oh, God, what had he done?*

He pulled his numbed arm out from under Opal's head and sat up, rubbing his arm absently as his thoughts raced. He had taken his pleasure with a woman—little more than a girl, really—who was under his protection. She had lived in his house feeling safe from the things that had harmed her before, and now he had destroyed that safety, that trust.

Without thinking, Alan let out a groan. Opal stirred and woke up. She looked around groggily, and her eyes fell on Alan. She started to smile, then stopped abruptly and sat straight up in bed. "Oh, my! What time is it?"

She turned toward the window. "Oh, no, the sun's up! What if everyone's up already? What if they see me coming out of your room?"

With an expression of horror on her face, she jumped out of bed with complete disregard for her naked state and ran to pick her nightgown up off the floor. She whisked it back on and hurried to the door. She paused with her hand on the knob and turned to look back at Alan, then hastened out the door. Alan watched her go, his heart twisting in his chest. He needed no better proof of what harm he had done Opal than this: She was humiliated by what had happened, terrified that someone would find out, that Millicent would begin to think of her in the same way that others had after Johnston had done what he did to her.

Alan groaned at the thought of her former employer. Was he any better than Johnston? He hadn't raped her. He knew that; he might be inexperienced, but he was not a fool. Opal had come willingly to his bed. Physically he hadn't forced himself upon her, but when he began making advances toward her, she must have felt as if he were giving her an ultimatum to accept his lovemaking or risk losing her livelihood and the roof over her child's head.

Even if she hadn't been afraid of losing her job and home, he suspected that Opal would have felt obligated to let him make love to her. She had always felt disproportionate gratitude toward him for their taking her in, and she seemed to hold him in some sort of awe. He had taken advantage of her gratitude and generosity, of her fear, and her need to provide for her child. Just by pulling her down and kissing her, he had put her in a situation where she couldn't refuse him. She probably thought that she *owed* it to him to let him take her.

Alan sighed and threw his arm across his eyes. He had ruined everything now, and all because he couldn't control himself. He wished he could bring back the moment, change what he had done, but of course that wasn't possible. There was nothing that could be done except to try to make it as right as possible. He would have to apologize, have to make it clear to Opal that she was under no obligation to come to his bed, that he would never ask her to do so again. But that, he knew, would be the hardest thing he had ever done, for now that he had made love to Opal, he didn't know how he could live without doing so over and over.

The day passed miserably slowly. Alan couldn't concentrate on anything, either his law books or hobbies. He alternated between condemning himself for his loss of control last night and daydreaming about how wonderful it had been. He couldn't stop thinking about Opal's beautiful white body or imagining how he wanted to kiss and caress it tonight, until he was stiff and aching for release, but then he hated himself for being willing to sacrifice Opal's happiness for the satisfaction of his own lust.

He saw Opal only once during the day. It seemed to him that she was avoiding him. The one time he chanced into a room where she was cleaning, she jumped, startled, and cast a nervous glance at him, her cheeks flushing with color. She looked from him to Millicent, sitting by the window in the same room, listlessly sewing, then she mumbled an excuse and fled from the room. Alan was cold and sick and more certain than ever that he had been accurate in his assessment of the situation.

That night he lay awake long after he had gone to bed, wondering how he would even get the chance to apologize to Opal and release her from the dilemma in which he had placed her. Just as he was finally drifting off to sleep, he heard a timid knock at his door. It opened a fraction and Opal slid in, closing the door behind her.

Alan sat up in amazement, his throat suddenly closing. Opal walked around to the side of his bed. Her back was to the windows, and the pale light that shone around the edge of the curtain backlit her so that her every curve was plainly visible through the cloth of her nightgown. Alan swallowed, embarrassed by the desire that swelled in him.

"Opal?" The word came out sounding strained.

"Alan." Her voice shook a little. He could not see her face, standing as she was. She came closer to the bed and stopped beside him, turning just a little, so that now he could see her face in the dim light. It was etched with nervousness. His heart sank even lower. She was scared of him.

"Wait. Stop. You needn't do this."

"What?" She halted and turned her face so that it was in the shadows again and he could no longer read her expression.

"I—I've been meaning to talk to you all day, but I haven't been able to find you alone."

"I'm sorry." She twisted her hands together in front of her. Her voice was low and, he thought, thick with tears. It wrenched his heart to think that he had made Opal cry. "I was a little—I didn't know how to act when you were around. I was afraid Millicent might see. Might guess."

"I know. I understood. But I wanted to tell you something, and I'm sorry that I couldn't earlier; it would have alleviated some of your fears, I hope."

"What?"

"I wanted to apologize for what I did last night."

"Apologize?" She sounded stunned. Did she think him so arrogant and unfeeling that she was amazed that he would admit that he had been wrong?

"Yes. It was wrong. I shouldn't have put you in that position. I shouldn't have done what I did."

"Oh." She seemed to shrink. He winced to see it, knowing how humiliated she must feel. "I'm sorry."

"No, please don't apologize. It is I who was wrong. You mustn't feel to blame in any way. It was entirely my fault. I can't tell you how sorry I am, how much I regret it. And I promise you that it won't happen again."

"No. No, of course not. I understand." She retreated a step or two. "I won't—" Her voice broke, and she turned and fled from the room.

Opal pressed her hand against her mouth, stifling her sobs as she ran up the stairs to her room. How could she have been so foolish? Why had she thought that because of last night she could brazenly go into Alan's room tonight? She cursed herself for being an idiot, for letting her heart overpower her reason.

She should have known, she realized now, that just because Alan had made love to her in the heat of the moment last night didn't necessarily mean that he wanted it to happen again. Alan Hayes was not the kind of man who had cheap affairs with serving girls. He might slip and make a mistake when he was presented with a willing female dressed in the intimate way she had been last night, but he wouldn't continue to sleep with someone like her right there in his own house—especially not with his sister living in the house with them.

No doubt he had been shocked and surprised when she came into his room tonight. He must have thought that she was presuming on what had happened, that she was trying to live above her station in life. He had been as kind and gentlemanly about it as he was about everything, taking the blame upon himself and not repudiating her or rebuking her for assuming a claim upon him that didn't exist. But she knew how chagrined he must have felt despite his quiet, nonjudgmental manner when she had come barging into his room, obviously expecting to climb into bed with him.

Opal burned with humiliation. She had embarrassed both herself and Alan. No proper woman would have gone eagerly rushing to a man's bed that way. She was determined that she would not shame herself again. No matter how much it hurt to stay away from him, no matter how good she had felt last night in his arms and how much she longed to be there again, she would not go near him again.

* * *

Millicent was so wrapped up in gloom herself that it took her several days to realize that the rest of the household had descended into the same pit. Both Opal and Alan had turned glum and silent, and she noticed that the two of them avoided each other. She didn't understand it. It was obvious that something had happened between Opal and her brother, yet it didn't seem as though they were angry with each other. There were no resentful or angry remarks, even when they were alone with Millicent. On the contrary, they still spoke with affection and admiration if Millicent mentioned the other one, and they asked her searchingly how the other was doing. When they happened to be thrown together, they were quite polite, if somewhat constrained; Millicent could sense no animosity in the air. They seemed more than anything to be sorrowful, but since neither of them offered any explanation to her, Millicent had no idea why.

The sadness of the occupants of the house seemed to feed upon itself and each other, so that daily the atmosphere in the house grew darker. Betsy brought some ray of light into their gloom with her visits, but one week in early February, she stopped coming. Millicent wondered if their doleful natures had at last worn down even Betsy's cheerfulness. She could hardly blame her for staying away.

However, she found out the next day when Mrs. Rafferty came over to borrow some chocolate that it wasn't their gloom that kept Betsy away, but a cold.

"She's got it something fierce," the housekeeper

said, shaking her head. "I've never seen that young 'un stay still that long the whole time I've known her. Why, I haven't been able to get down to the grocery the past three days. She's been sick a week now. I thought I might make her some gingerbread; she's mighty partial to it, and she hasn't been eating too well. But then I saw that I was out of molasses."

"But . . . is she feeling better?" Millicent asked, her forehead knotting in concern. She felt cut off from Betsy, and it distressed her. Why hadn't it occurred to her that Betsy might be ill? She should have known that something was wrong. She had simply been too caught up in her own problems to worry about anything else, just as she hadn't noticed Opal's and Alan's problem for a long time.

Mrs. Rafferty hesitated. "Well, you know . . . I don't rightly think so. She still has that cough, though she doesn't seem quite as stuffed up. I made her a mustard poultice, but it hasn't done much good. Mr. Lawrence even had the doctor out to see her two or three days ago. He really worries about that child."

"Yes, I know he does. What did the doctor say?"

"Oh, he give us some stuff to rub on her chest, but I can't tell if it's changed her none."

"Why don't I go see her?" Millicent suggested. "I'd like to; I didn't realize she was sick. And it would give you time to get some things done."

"Would you? That'd be wonderful, Miss Hayes. I could get that gingerbread fixed up for her, and maybe I could even slip out to the store."

"Of course."

Millicent didn't bother to get her gloves or hat for the short trip next door; she was too anxious. She simply threw her cloak on and hurried after Mrs. Rafferty. Leaving her cloak in the kitchen, she tiptoed up the back stairs to the room where Mrs. Rafferty had told her Betsy slept. Being upstairs reminded her of the night she had gone up there with Jonathan, and her stomach quivered at the memory. But she pushed the thought out of her mind and plastered on a smile as she opened the door to Betsy's room and stepped inside.

Betsy was asleep, her thin face flushed against the white pillowcase. Millicent's heart sped up; it was frightening to see Betsy looking like this. Millicent was not used to sick children. She wondered if they always looked so ill with a cold.

Betsy's eyes opened, and when she saw Millicent, she smiled. "Miss Millie!"

"Hello, sweetheart." Millicent went to her side and bent over the bed to place a kiss on Betsy's forehead. "I just heard you were sick. How are you feeling?"

"Better, I think." Betsy coughed. "I'm glad you came. I've missed you."

"Me, too. I didn't guess that you were ill, or I would have come to visit sooner."

"Yes. I have to stay in bed." Betsy wrinkled her nose in distaste. "Will you stay here for a while?"

"Of course." It must be awful for her to be sick and stuck in bed, with only Mrs. Rafferty to keep her company. Millicent remembered how much she had wanted her mother when she had been sick as a child. A housekeeper simply wasn't the same. Millicent took Betsy's hand, and the girl curled her fingers around Millicent's tightly.

"Good," Betsy said simply. She closed her eyes and was asleep again almost immediately.

Millicent sat down on the edge of the bed, not wanting to take her hand away from Betsy's even long enough to pull a chair up to the bedside. She sat that way through most of the afternoon, not moving to a chair until Betsy's hand relaxed and slid naturally from hers.

Downstairs she could hear Mrs. Rafferty rattling around in the kitchen. Close to supper time, Mrs. Rafferty came upstairs, bearing a tray. "I made you some nice hot stew," she told Millicent. "Ah, it was such a relief to be able to get some of my work done. You're an angel to help."

"It was no problem, I was glad to. But you needn't have fixed me anything to eat."

"It wasn't any trouble. I had to make something for Mr. Lawrence anyway. And I reckoned you could use a little sustenance after being up here all afternoon. Was she much trouble?"

"No, not at all." Millicent's eyes opened a little in surprise. Why would Mrs. Rafferty think Betsy might be trouble? Then she remembered what she herself had once thought about Betsy, and she almost smiled. It was strange how one's perceptions changed. She loved Betsy now and wouldn't have changed her for the world. Funny to think how she had once been annoyed by her behavior.

"Mr. Lawrence isn't home yet. He's always late, that

man. But I told him specially that I had to get home this evening. My sister's down in her back, you see, and I need to take supper over to her house. She has a passel of boys and a husband, none of them a whit of good in the kitchen, and Mattie's worried that they won't get enough to eat." She shook her head. "As if those big lummoxes couldn't live without a meal or two. Anyway, if it wouldn't be too much trouble, I was wondering if you could stay with Betsy until her pa gets home."

"Of course." Millicent wanted to stay with Betsy; she hadn't liked the idea of leaving her, anyway. But staying meant that she would have to see Jonathan face-to-face, and her stomach did flip-flops at that idea. "I'll be happy to."

"Thank you. You're a good Christian lady, Miss Hayes, and I told Mr. Lawrence himself that."

"You did?"

"Yes'm, I did. One time about a month or so ago, when I come into the kitchen one morning, I found him standing looking out the window at your house. You were upstairs in your room, and the curtains were open, and there you were in nothing but your nightgown, looking out. 'Course it was early in the morning, but you really shouldn't leave your curtains open like that and you not dressed. Anyway, I told Mr. Lawrence it was downright indecent of him to be looking at you in that state, why, it's next to naked, now isn't it? And do you know what that man had the gall to say?"

Millicent shook her head. Warmth was stealing up in her face. "No. I can't imagine."

"Well, he said, 'Not as indecent as my thoughts, Mrs. Rafferty.' Now isn't that something to say?"

It sounded so much like Jonathan that it was all Millicent could do not to smile. But she felt sure that Mrs. Rafferty would not appreciate that response, so she kept her mouth pulled into a straight line. However, there was nothing she could do about the heat sneaking through her abdomen as she thought of Jonathan watching her dressed in nothing but her nightshift—and obviously thinking impure thoughts.

"That's when I told him that he was fair and far off if he thought anything wrong about you. 'Miss Hayes is a good Christian lady,' I said to him. 'Course he agreed that you were an excellent woman. Then he said something about you being sour and sweet, which seems a peculiar thing to me to say about a person. Sounds more like a pippin apple to me, don't you think? But he's an odd man. Nice as God makes them, but odd."

Millicent allowed herself to smile at that, hoping that it didn't look too fond.

"I best get moving. I can't stand here talking all day, or I'll never get that supper made." Mrs. Rafferty bustled out the door, calling back another thanks.

Millicent settled down in the chair beside Betsy's bed. The house was utterly quiet now with the housekeeper gone. Time passed slowly. It was growing dark, so Millicent rose to light the kerosene lamp on Betsy's dresser and close the curtains. She sat down again. She didn't want to eat. There was nothing to do but think. She thought about Jonathan climbing the stairs and coming into the room. She tried to imagine how he would look when he saw her and what he would say. She couldn't think of any graceful way for either of them to get out of the situation. Well, it couldn't be helped, she reminded herself. It wasn't as if she had planned to come here; it wasn't as if she wanted to be here when he came home. Betsy needed her; Mrs. Rafferty had asked her to stay. There was nothing untoward in that.

Betsy awoke a little while after that, and Millicent tried to persuade her to eat at least some of the stew broth, but Betsy fretfully refused to. Millicent thought that she looked even more flushed than she had earlier, and it worried her. She sat down beside Betsy and laid her hand across the child's forehead. She thought her fever was worse.

"Why don't you drink some water?" she suggested, pouring a glass from the small pitcher beside Betsy's bed.

"I don't want it," Betsy told her petulantly.

"Do it for me, then. Here, sit up a little and drink it." Millicent slid her hand beneath Betsy's neck and helped raised her head. Lord, but the child was burning up. Should she be this weak? She held the glass to Betsy's lips and persuaded her to drink a few sips, but then Betsy turned her head away, and Millicent could do nothing but let her lie back down.

She walked across to the window and back, chewing thoughtfully at a knuckle. She wished she had more experience with children. It seemed to her that Betsy was worse than she had been when Millicent arrived that afternoon. But fevers did tend to come and go, and she didn't know how Betsy had felt this morning or last night. Perhaps her rising fever was nothing to be alarmed about.

Still, she couldn't help being alarmed. She wished Jonathan would come home. He would know how Betsy usually felt and acted when she was sick. He would know how she had been doing earlier in this illness. And he would be able to go get the doctor if that was necessary, whereas she, all alone as she was, couldn't leave the house.

It was such a relief when she finally heard the door close and Jonathan's steps on the stairs that she forgot all about her earlier nerves at the thought of seeing him again. Instead she flew into the hall to meet him. "Oh, Jonathan, I'm so glad you're home!"

He came to an abrupt halt, startled. "Millicent!" He smiled and started toward her. "What are you doing here?"

"I was sitting with Betsy; Mrs. Rafferty had to leave."

"Damn! That's right, I'd forgotten. Something about her sister." His smile disappeared. "Well, thank you for staying with Betsy. I—"

Millicent impatiently waved aside his words. "Never mind that. I want you to come look at Betsy. I'm worried."

"Why?" Alarm spread over his face, and he hurried past her into Betsy's room. "What's the matter?" As soon as he saw his daughter asleep on her pillow, he frowned. "Has her fever gotten worse?"

"I think so. I wasn't sure. But it seemed to me that she is much hotter than she was when I came this afternoon. She hardly said anything when she woke up a while ago, and she fell right back to sleep. Is she all right?"

Jonathan laid his hand on his daughter's forehead. His face looked older and tired. "She's too hot. Damn! I wish I knew something about this. Betsy's never sick." He smoothed his hand down her cheek, and she stirred restlessly, mumbling something.

Betsy's eyes opened and she gazed up at Jonathan blankly. "I don't think the Fairy Queen is happy, Papa."

"What?" He stared at her.

"Jimmy told me so."

"Jimmy!"

"What's she talking about, Jonathan?" Millicent asked uneasily. Betsy's words sounded crazy.

"I don't know. Jimmy was a little boy who used to live down the street from us back in Dallas. She hasn't seen him in months."

Betsy wet her lips. "I'm thirsty," she said plaintively. "It's too hot here. The Fairy Queen's hot, too. She doesn't like to come out in the day, you know."

"Jonathan, she's delirious. I've seen it before with Alan, after his accident. He'd talk crazy like that."

Jonathan turned toward Millicent. "Her fever must have gotten so high that—" He broke off and started toward the door. "Stay here. I'm going to get the doctor. This can't be just a cold anymore."

Millicent nodded. Her stomach was tight with fear. She walked over to Betsy's bedside. In the distance she heard the front door slam as Jonathan ran out of the house. She looked down at Betsy's flushed face; her eyes were bright with fever. Millicent remembered the long nights she'd spent hanging over her brother's bed, taut with terror, afraid that this night they would lose him. She reminded herself that simply because Betsy was out of her head with fever didn't necessarily mean she was as sick as Alan had been. It didn't mean she was hovering on the edge of death.

Millicent wet a cloth and wrung it out, then bathed Betsy's face with it, forcing herself to be calm and competent, as she always was. It never helped a patient for you to get hysterical. She had to help Betsy.

Betsy's eyes fluttered open and she smiled. "Hello," she croaked. "I feel hot, Miss Millie."

"I know, dear. I'm trying to cool you off."

"Thank you." Her sweet politeness tore at Millicent's heart. It was such a contrast to her hot, sick face. At least her mind seemed to have stopped wandering.

However, Betsy soon started talking nonsense again, and when Jonathan returned with the doctor, she was still slipping in and out of a delirious fog. Dr. Morton examined her, and Jonathan and Millicent waited together at the other end of the room. Jonathan's face was so creased with worry that Millicent reached out instinctively to take his hand. He squeezed it gratefully.

"Thank God you were here," he whispered.

Millicent nodded. What had happened between them, her decision to stay with Alan—none of that mattered now. Jonathan needed her. She would do whatever it took to help him.

Dr. Morton turned around and walked ponderously over to them. "Betsy's gotten sicker," he told them in a lowered voice. "It's been a bad winter. A lot of sickness, unfortunately." He sighed and looked at Jonathan. "I'm afraid that Betsy has developed pneumonia."

"Pneumonia," Jonathan repeated dully.

The doctor continued to talk, telling them what to do, but Jonathan cut in, "Wait a minute, doc, what are you saying? Is Betsy in danger? Is she going to—" He stopped, unable to voice the words.

"Pneumonia is serious, Mr. Lawrence, I won't pretend that it's not. However, it doesn't mean that Betsy is going to die. She's young and healthy. She has a good chance. Tonight and these next few days will be critical, however. You will need to watch over her carefully." He turned toward Millicent. "You know a lot of what to do. Keep her warm. She needs to drink as much as you can get down her; the fever'll dry her out. She'll have difficulty breathing. Prop her up on pillows instead of lying flat in bed. Steam will help keep the air passages open." He explained how to set up a steam tent.

Millicent nodded. She was almost paralyzed by fear and she could tell by looking at Jonathan that he felt much the same way.

After the doctor left, Millicent went downstairs and heated up water while Jonathan attached a sheet to the headboard of her bed and draped it down to form a kind of tent. He pulled Betsy up higher in the bed, stuffing pillows behind her, and tugged her blankets up to her chin. When the water was boiling, they brought it up and set it in pans beside Betsy under the tent, putting boards beneath the pans to keep them level. The steam rose and filled the little area.

They stepped back and looked at each other. There was nothing more they could do except wait. Millicent turned and started toward the stairs.

"No, wait." Jonathan grasped her wrist, pulling her to a stop.

Millicent turned inquiringly.

"Don't go," he said hoarsely. Pain was stark on his face. "Stay with me . . . for a while. I need you right now."

Millicent stared at him blankly for a moment. "What are you talking about? Where do you think I'm going?"

"Home."

"Jonathan Lawrence! You actually think I'd walk away at a time like this? Go blithely home and leave you and Betsy here?"

"I don't know. You have no ties to us."

"Except my heart," she answered rashly.

His face moved with emotion, and he jerked her to him, bending over her and holding her tightly. "Oh, God, Millicent, I love you. I need you so much. What am I going to do? What if—what if I lose her, like I did Elizabeth? I'd have nothing."

"You have me."

"Do I?"

Millicent realized how foolish her words were. Jonathan didn't have her; she had turned away from him weeks ago. She shouldn't have been surprised that he thought she was going home. She had left him before. It hit her how very much she must have hurt him, how much she had sacrificed of his life as well as hers.

"I'm sorry." Tears clogged her voice. "I'm so sorry.

I never meant to hurt you." She looked up at him. "I won't leave until Betsy's better. I promise. I'll be right here with you."

"Thank you." He bent and kissed the top of her head, holding her.

"I wasn't leaving, you know," Millicent said softly after a while. "I was going down to boil more water for the steam and to make us coffee. I'm afraid it will be a long night."

"You're right." Jonathan stepped back, releasing her. "Go ahead."

She started out the door, then turned to look back at Jonathan. He was standing at the foot of the bed, gazing disconsolately at Betsy beneath the veil of the tent.

"She's going to be all right," Millicent said fiercely, and Jonathan glanced around at her. "Really. She'll pull through this. I know she will."

Jonathan smiled faintly. "With you on her side, I don't know how she could not."

Millicent went down and set more water on to boil in the stove well, then started a pot of coffee. When it was done, she took them each a cup of coffee. Through the night they maintained their vigil, one or the other or both of them constantly by Betsy's side. Millicent kept water hot on the stove and brought up kettle after kettle of it to keep the pans steaming beneath the make-shift tent. When it became too hot beneath the tent and the sheet was heavily damp from the steam, they took the pans away and removed the sheet. Later, when Betsy's breathing became more labored again, they

up a new sheet and replaced the cooling pans of
er with steaming ones. Off and on they continued
the process through the night.

Millicent worked at bringing down Betsy's fever,
bathing the girl's face and wrists in cool water. She
replaced the sheets and pillowcases, soaked with Betsy's
sweat and the steam, with dry ones. Every once in a
while Betsy awoke and talked, usually incoherently, but
sometimes as lucidly as ever. Millicent and Jonathan
worked side by side, and when there was nothing to do
but sit and watch and wait, they did that together, too.
Now and then one of them fell asleep for a few minutes,
too exhausted to hold their eyes open any longer, but
the other one stayed awake for both of them, keeping
watch.

The night stretched on endlessly. Betsy's fever and
coughing continued. Finally morning came, and even
though Betsy seemed no better, it was a relief simply to
have light in the room, so that the darkness no longer
seemed to be pressing in on them.

Mrs. Rafferty arrived for work and was surprised to
find Millicent still there, both of them obviously exhausted from spending the night by Betsy's bedside.
The housekeeper exclaimed over Betsy and her illness
and bustled about, fixing breakfast. Neither Jonathan
nor Millicent were really hungry, but they readily drank
more coffee as they sat beside Betsy's bed and waited.
They had talked on and off throughout the night, more
to keep their mind off Betsy's danger than anything else.
They had discussed all kinds of things: their childhood,
foods, games, holidays, anything and everything except

the painful issues that lay between them. But when daylight came, their conversation dragged. They were too weary to want to talk, and the presence of light stole away the intimacy that the darkness had given their conversation.

They fell silent. Millicent, sitting in a chair beside the bed, leaned forward, crossing her arms on the bed, and laid her head upon her crossed forearms. She was soon asleep.

"Millicent! Millicent, wake up!"

Groggily she opened her eyes. "What?" She looked around vaguely, trying to orient herself. It took her a moment to realize where she was and why she was there. And why Jonathan Lawrence was with her. She straightened up as she remembered and looked up at the head of the bed. Betsy was still asleep against the fluffed-up pillows, without the steam tent over her.

"Millie," Jonathan said excitedly, pulling Millicent up out of her chair, "come listen to her."

His exclamation jerked Millicent out of her mental haze, and she went with him to the head of the bed and bent over, listening to Betsy's breathing. Millicent turned wide, hope-filled eyes on Jonathan. "Is it better?"

"Does it seem so to you, too?" Jonathan beamed, his eyes filling with tears. His face was lined, one cheek red from where it had lain pressed against his hand, and there was a stubble across his jaw, but the joy in his expression made him the most beautiful thing Millicent had seen in a long time.

"Yes. Yes, I think it is."

Millicent looked at Betsy's face; it seemed less flushed

to her. Shakily she reached out and laid her hand on Betsy's forehead. It was damp, but no longer burning hot; in fact, it was almost cool. "Her fever's broken!"

Jonathan reached past Millicent to touch Betsy's face himself, and when he felt its coolness, he let out a muffled whoop. Grabbing Millicent, he lifted her into the air and swung her around, holding her tightly. "She's going to be all right! She's going to be all right!"

They laughed and babbled. They squeezed each other hard, and Millicent kissed Jonathan's cheek. She was so happy she thought she could fly, and she could feel Jonathan's happiness as clearly as if it were her own. Jonathan buried his face in Millicent's neck, and she felt the dampness of his tears upon her skin, the shuddering of his body against hers. Millicent wrapped her arms around him tightly and hung on to him, letting him cry out his fear and joy. She had never in her life felt as warm or as close to anyone, as much a part of another person as she was right then with Jonathan.

"I love you," she whispered. "I love you."

Twenty-Four

$\mathcal{B}$etsy's fever went back up later, but she was no longer delirious. As the day passed, it became more and more obvious that the worst of her illness was over. Millicent, exhausted, went home to sleep. When she woke up, she felt warm and happy. Betsy was going to be all right. And she and Jonathan—

The warmth vanished. She sat up in bed, letting out a groan. The closeness she and Jonathan had felt as they sat by Betsy's side had been sweet despite their worry. And that moment when they had realized that Betsy's fever had broken and they had held each other in joy, she had felt utter peace and oneness with him. Nothing had ever been as wonderful. But now, she knew, life would return to the way it had been, and the closeness would be gone. It couldn't last if she was not going to marry him. Millicent felt as if she were being ripped away from Jonathan all over again.

She returned to the Lawrence house that evening to sit with Betsy. Jonathan opened the door at her knock and smiled to see her.

"Millicent." He reached out to take her in his arms.

Millicent stepped hastily back. Jonathan stopped, and the light vanished from his face. The weary lines returned. "Oh," he said. "I suppose you've come to see Betsy."

"Yes. How is she?"

"Better all the time. She's asleep now, but she's been awake and talking to me."

"Have you had a chance to sleep any?"

"A little—mostly in the chair," he admitted ruefully. An awkward silence followed. "Well," he said finally, looking away from her, "come in. If you're going to sit with her for a while, perhaps I'll take this opportunity to sleep."

Millicent nodded. She felt like crying.

Over the next few days Betsy recovered rapidly in the way that children had. Millicent came over several times during the days to sit with her and read or play a game to keep Betsy, who was getting more and more fretful at having to stay in bed, occupied. She didn't see Jonathan often, as she usually left before he returned from work, but when they were together, they fell into the same uneasy formality that had been between them ever since Millicent refused his proposal of marriage.

Lonely and confused, she dragged through the days. There was plenty of work to keep her occupied, for Ida and her family came down sick, and only a few days after that, Opal did, too. Opal tried to stay on her feet working, but Millicent insisted that she go to bed and rest, pointing out that she'd be sick twice as long if she didn't take care of herself. Opal was an undemanding patient, but there was of necessity the extra work involved in bringing up soup and hot tea for her and checking on her every once in awhile. In addition, all the housework was now on Millicent's shoulders. She was glad that Alan was able and willing to do most of the caretaking of the baby. Betsy, who had bounced back rapidly from her illness, wanted to come over and help, but Millicent refused, afraid that she might catch the virulent illness all over again.

As if she didn't have enough to do, her grandmother grabbed her arm in the vestibule of the church Sunday morning as she was walking in and reminded her that she hadn't been to visit Cousin Agnes yet.

Millicent groaned inwardly. She had no interest in visiting Cousin Agnes. She was not close to the woman; Cousin Agnes was one of those relatives to whom she had been dragged with her mother two or three times each year when her mother had done *her* familial duty of visiting her. After her mother died, Millicent had inherited the obligation, and she had gone by at least once or twice a year to see her. Cousin Agnes was of her mother's generation, a war widow who had never married again, and she lived in a tiny house crammed full of things. Visits to her were invariably boring, and Millicent disliked the dark, cramped atmosphere of the front parlor of her house.

"Well, everyone's been sick the past few weeks," Millicent excused herself.

Grandmother Connally was not about to be fooled by that weak statement. She turned her faded blue eyes upon Millicent with a sorrowful expression; she didn't have to add that she had asked Millicent to go over three months earlier.

Millicent dropped her gaze. "You're right. I'm sorry. I should have gone long ago. Why don't I visit her this afternoon?"

It would be as good a time as any. Opal was still sick enough to stay in bed a good deal of the time, but she didn't need any real care, and Millicent hadn't planned to do housework this afternoon anyway, except perhaps for some sewing. She would have to sacrifice only the leisurely afternoon she had envisioned for herself today.

"That would be perfect." Mrs. Connally smiled at her. "Why don't you take her a little something to eat? I hear she's been feeling poorly."

"Of course." She could dish up some of the soup she'd been giving Opal and take that.

Grandmother Connally took her arm and walked with her down the aisle of the church. Millicent left her with Grandpa Connally and continued down the aisle to where Susan and her husband sat with their children. She slid in beside them, smiling and greeting them.

The choir filed in and sat down at the front of the church, facing the congregation. In another moment the minister would walk out and everyone would rise for the first hymn. But just then a ripple of conversation ran through the church. Millicent glanced behind her to see what had created the stir. Jonathan and Betsy were walking down the aisle!

She stared, stunned, as they sat down a few rows behind her. Jonathan smiled at her, and Betsy gave her a little wave. Millicent turned back around and faced the front. Jonathan Lawrence in church! Whatever had happened to the man?

She couldn't get her mind off it all through the service, and afterwards she couldn't remember a thing the minister had said. When the service was over, she strolled up the aisle with Susan. Her cousin glanced at her and commented, "That's the first time I've seen Jonathan Lawrence in church. My, my, Millie, you must have had a profound effect on him."

"What nonsense. He's not here because of me." Her gaze flickered around the vestibule, searching for him.

Fannin opened the door for them, and they stepped outside. "Oh, no?" Susan asked, her eyes dancing with amusement. "Then why is he waiting for you?"

Millicent looked at the bottom of the church steps, where Susan nodded. Jonathan and Betsy were standing there, watching the rest of the crowd come out. Millicent's heart speeded up, but she managed to keep a calm expression on her face as she went down the steps toward them.

"Miss Hayes," Jonathan greeted her formally. "Would you care to walk home with us?"

"Yes, thank you." Millicent ignored her cousin's meaningful looks and turned in the direction of her house. Betsy took her hand on one side, and Jonathan put his hand beneath her elbow on the other. Millicent felt warmed all through, despite the chilly weather. This is what she wanted, she knew—to walk home from church with Jonathan and Betsy, *her family,* every Sunday for the rest of her life.

They walked for a while, then Millicent said, "I was surprised to see you at church."

Jonathan chuckled. "I figured you were. So was everyone else."

"What made you come?"

"Oh . . . a certain pillar of the community convinced me that I was wrong."

Millicent stared, barely able to keep her mouth from dropping open. "What?"

"Don't look so astounded. I admit my mistakes." Jonathan's grin broadened, and a mischievous light came into his eyes. "On the rare occasion that I make one, of course."

"Of course." Millicent wasn't about to push the issue; she was simply glad that he had decided to come.

But, to her surprise, he went on without any prodding, "When Betsy was ill, I found myself praying that she'd get better. I thought about what a hypocrite I was, claiming I don't believe. I thought about it a lot the last week or two. And I realized that the bitterness I've felt all these years wasn't there anymore."

He turned his head toward her and looked at her intently. "I think that after Elizabeth died, I took on that bitterness as a . . . a kind of armor to protect me from the hurt and the loss. But you managed to pierce my armor anyway. It disappeared. And I thought about how armor, of any kind, can be as much a prison as a shield. It keeps you locked in with the grief. It doesn't really matter whether you've armed yourself with bitterness or duty or something else altogether. It's the same effect."

He was talking about her now, she knew. Millicent turned her face away.

"I don't want that for myself. Not anymore," he continued softly. "I don't want it for you, either. There's nothing to be gained by locking yourself away in the past."

His words came back to her in full force an hour later when she went to visit Cousin Agnes. Cousin Agnes, a faded ghost of a woman, spent the entire time talking about her long-dead husband. He had been killed in the war almost thirty-three years earlier, and Cousin Agnes had made a vocation of mourning him ever since.

His death had always been her prime topic of conversation, and the house was full of mementos of him, including his Confederate uniform, which Agnes was happy to show anyone who showed even the faintest interest, but Millicent had in the past regarded her obsession as merely boring and a trifle ghoulish. Now, with horror, Millicent realized how the woman had rooted herself in the past, tying herself to a man long dead. Cousin Agnes had been with her husband for only four years, but her life had ended there, when she was twenty-two. Now she was almost fifty-six, and for over half of her life she had done nothing, been nothing but the keeper of a memory. She simply couldn't let go, even though her clinging to her husband had made a desert out of the rest of her life.

Was that what she herself had done, Millicent wondered bleakly. Had she tied herself to an incident in the past, Alan's accident, and let the rest of her life go to waste? Would she, when she was fifty-five, look back on her life and see that, like Cousin Agnes, she had grown faded and reclusive, a sorrowful relation whom Susan's and Hannah's and Bertie's children would be forced to visit as a family obligation? Would they sigh and be bored and think how little she had made of her life? And would they be right?

She walked home slowly, too occupied with her thoughts to even notice the cold that seeped through her wool cloak. But, at last, when she was only a couple of blocks from home, a clanging penetrated her thoughts. She looked up and glanced around, puzzled by what had pulled her back to awareness, and even as she did so, she realized that it was the insistent ringing of the fire wagon. There must be a fire somewhere nearby. Above the treetops she caught sight of a spiral of smoke going upwards.

She stopped, suddenly rooted to the ground. The smoke was rising from precisely the area where she was headed. Where her home was—and where Jonathan and Betsy were!

Alan looked up from his book and frowned. He smelled something odd. What was it? He sat for a moment. It smelled like . . . like . . . something burning. That was it. Millicent must have burned something when she was cooking dinner earlier. He went back to his book, but he couldn't concentrate. He normally had difficulty keeping his mind on anything these days; it kept straying back to Opal and the awful emptiness he felt. But this was something different, some niggling little thought that nagged at the back of his mind.

His head came up sharply. Millicent hadn't cooked dinner today. She had merely reheated some stew for the two of them because she had to visit Cousin Agnes and hadn't had time for anything more. They had eaten it together in the kitchen, and she had put the empty pot in the washpan. There had been nothing burned. There had been no food left cooking on the stove which could have burned while she was gone, either.

His heart began to pound, and he wheeled out from behind the desk and across the library into the hall. The smell was stronger here.

Alan hurried down the hall and into the dining room, then through the butler's pantry to the kitchen, the most likely spot for something to have caught on fire. But there was nothing burning there, and he realized that the smell of smoke was less than it had been in the main part of the house. Quickly he wheeled the chair around and pushed back through the set of doors into the dining room. The smell was worse now, and it continued to grow as he rolled into the wide hallway.

"Opal?" he called, tilting back his head and looking up the back staircase. "Opal? What's that smell?"

He saw wisps of smoke drifting down the staircase, pierced by the sunlight through the round window on the landing. His hands tightened on the arms of his chair. "Opal!"

There was no answer. Panic struck his heart. "Opal!" he roared, pushing his chair down the hall with all his might. "Opal! Where are you?"

He craned his neck back, staring up the wide, curving staircase in the front hallway. "Opal! Dammit, answer me!"

Alan could see smoke in the upper hallway, thick and dark, moving along the ceiling. "Opal!" The house was on fire, and it had obviously started somewhere upstairs.

Opal was upstairs. Millicent had told him that Opal planned to stay in bed again today with the baby, still tired and achy from her cold. She hadn't dressed and come down later, after Millicent left, or he would have known it. She would have come in to see him; she would have at least brought the baby for him to look at.

"Opal!" He screamed her name over and over. She did not answer. A chill pervaded his heart. She must have been asleep when the fire started and didn't notice it. She must have passed out from the smoke without ever waking. He had always heard that smoke could do that to people, rendering them unconscious so that they didn't flee the fire and so were burned to death. Oh, Opal! Was she even now lying up there, unable to awaken, both she and the baby helpless victims of the fire?

"Opal!" He grabbed a slender, straight-backed chair from its place against the wall and slammed it as hard as he could into the railing of the staircase. He banged it against the railing over and over, creating the greatest racket he could, until it splintered under the force. Still, Opal did not call back to him.

He could never wake her up this way. Someone had to carry her and the baby down from there, and quickly. Alan rolled to the front door and yelled outside. But that was no good, he knew. The Andersons across the street were old, and Jonathan Lawrence might not be at home. Besides, he only had a few minutes in which to act, or Opal might be dead. He couldn't wait for someone to come.

Alan rolled back to the foot of the stairs and stared up, rigid with frustration. There was no one to rescue Opal but himself, and he could not walk up the stairs to get her and pull her free from the fire. He had never felt as helpless and weak, as frustrated by his crippled legs. Opal would die, and the baby, too, because he couldn't walk!

With a wordless, animal cry of desperation, he reached out and grabbed the highest post of the stair rail that he could reach and pulled himself up and out of his chair. He fell heavily on his side on the stairs. There was a jab of pain in his side as the edge of a stair hit it, but he didn't notice it. He was concentrating too hard on reaching up and grasping the next narrow baluster above his hand. Slowly, hand over hand, he pulled himself up the staircase, using the bars of the railing, his legs bumping uselessly against the stairs.

He strained to move as fast as he could, but it seemed to take forever. He had to stop at the landing and roll to the other side, for above him on this side was only the blankness of wall, offering no purchase. On and on he climbed, the muscles of his arms straining sweat running down his face and chest.

When at last he reached the top of the stairs, he was able to crawl more quickly, dragging himself down the hall on his arms. He was below most of the smoke, but even so it stung his eyes and made him cough. The heat grew more intense with every move he made. He could see the flames at the end of the hallway, licking around the doorway of Millicent's sewing room and out into the hall. He felt as if his lungs were bursting as they pulled in the hot, acrid air.

Alan turned into the open doorway of the guest room, where Millicent had told him Opal slept, and dragged himself to the bed. He could see Opal's body above him on the bed. He knew he would never be able to climb up onto the high bed and lift her off. He paused, panting, beside the wide wooden steps leading up to the bed, then levered himself up with his elbows until his torso was braced against the heavy set of steps which concealed a cabinet for the commode. He dug his hands into the soft feather mattress on which Opal lay and jerked with all his strength. Again and again he pulled until at last he had pulled the mattress far enough off that the weight of Opal's body brought it all tumbling down on top of him.

He lay for a moment, panting, then edged out from beneath the mattress. Opal lay on top of it, the quilt over her, the baby in her arms. She looked pale and still and for an instant terror froze his heart. She looked dead to him.

But he saw the movement of her chest, rising and falling shallowly, and he let out a little sob of relief. He did not allow himself time to rejoice, however. The heat was growing more and more intense, the air thicker with smoke, even as low to the floor as they were. He had to get them out before he passed out from breathing in the smoke, too.

Alan pulled the quilt up over them all like a tent to protect them as much as he could from the smoke. He hooked one arm around Opal's waist over the baby and dragged her from the mattress to the door and out into the hall.

Afterwards he was never sure quite how he managed to get Opal and the baby to the stairs. It was a slow, agonizing process, a nightmare of heat and smoke that choked his lungs, of muscles that trembled beneath the strain, of awkward inch-by-inch movement. Sometimes he pulled himself along with one arm, the other hooked around Opal, pulling her. At other times he crawled forward a short distance and turned to drag her after him by the skirt of her nightgown.

But somehow he reached the staircase, coughing and panting, his strength almost spent. He laid his head down on his arm; he would have wept if he'd had the strength. *How could he ever get her down the stairs?* He could not drag her, yet he could not carry her. *God, he would kill them both trying to rescue them.*

Still, he had to do something, he knew. Otherwise they were all sure to die from the smoke if not the fire! He ripped the quilt off and spread it out as best he could on the floor, then rolled onto it. He lifted the baby out of Opal's arms and onto the other side of him, then awkwardly rolled and pulled Opal onto the quilt and on top of him. Then he rolled them all up in the quilt to provide what little protection he could against the fall, nestling the baby half on his chest and half in his arm.

Wriggling and squirming on his back, using his elbows to propel himself forward, he moved forward, sliding their feet and legs onto the stairs. He clutched Opal and the baby to him tightly with one hand as they slipped down the stairs, twisting and grabbing with his free hand at the banister as they went along. The edges of the stairs banged painfully into his back and sides and elbows as he worked his way down. As they went farther and farther down, the momentum of their combined weight broke his hold on the balusters and sent him sliding helplessly down the last few stairs to the landing, cracking his head hard against a step and dumping them in a heap on the landing.

He lay breathing heavily, pain crashing through his head and sending lights dancing behind his eyes. He gulped in air, struggling not to pass out. They still had the rest of the stairs to go. He couldn't give up now. Determinedly, he groped his way sideways to the stairs and twisted to bring his heavy, useless legs around and down onto the stairs. He was unaware of the raw scrapes and bruises on his arms or of the bump rising on his head, though he felt the blood trickling down from the cut above his eyebrow and into his eyes, obscuring his vision. It was annoying, but he couldn't take the time to wipe it away. His every thought, every muscle, every nerve ending was concentrated solely on moving down the stairs to the fresher air at the bottom.

Slowly he bumped down one step, then two and three and . . .

"My God!" He heard a man's voice below him. "Alan!"

Suddenly there were footsteps thudding up the stairs, and strong hands were lifting Opal from him, carrying her to safety.

"Damnation, Betsy, get out of here!" he heard the voice say and the high-pitched sound of a child responding, "I'll get Robert."

Then the baby's negligible weight was gone, too, and Alan finally let himself relax. They were safe. His lids closed; he was too exhausted to keep them open any longer, to fight any more. Darkness swirled in his brain, pain vibrating out from the spot where his skull had struck the stair. And then, finally, lying sprawled on the stairs, he let himself slide into unconsciousness.

Millicent ran down the street, heedless of who saw her. The closer she got, the more evident it became that the smoke was coming from somewhere very close to her house. She couldn't keep from thinking about how many people disliked Jonathan and the things he had said in his newspaper. She remembered the men who had beaten him up. Lately it had seemed as if things had calmed down, but perhaps they had merely been waiting to see if Jonathan heeded their warnings. What if they had decided to take more drastic measures? What if they had burned down his house to scare him out of town or teach him a lesson?

She thought of Betsy. Of Jonathan. Even of Admiral. Fear propelled her on ever faster, even though her stays were squeezing her lungs too tightly for running and her skirts impeded her. She paid no attention to such distractions. She could think of nothing but Jonathan and Betsy and the possibility that they might be hurt.

Millicent turned the corner onto her block and came to a sudden stop. She stared blankly down the street at the dramatic scene. It was not the Lawrence house that was on fire. It was her own house from which smoke bellowed!

Her first feeling was one of relief that Jonathan and Betsy were not in danger. Next she was swept with a sick guilt as she remembered her brother and Opal. She hadn't even thought of them or of her own house; she had thought only of Jonathan when she'd seen the smoke. She had been so afraid for him that it had blocked out everything else.

Her heart was pounding crazily and she could hardly breathe. Blackness swam in front of her eyes, and Millicent realized that she was about to faint. Hurriedly she dropped down onto the lawn beside her and drew in deep breaths. *Blast it, she was never going to wear stays again!*

It took her a moment to recover her breath. Then she stood and made her way shakily across the street. She was scared of what she might find when she reached her own yard. Had Alan and Opal made it out of the house safely? She couldn't get out of her mind the fact that the occupants of the house had been a crippled man, a sick woman, and a baby! It would be a miracle if they hadn't been killed, or at least injured. Her hands were like ice, and she felt sick to her stomach. Her steps grew slower and slower.

The scene in front of the Hayes home was chaotic.

The fire wagon had arrived, and the volunteers had pulled out the hose and were training a stream of water on the house. A line of people stretched from the Lawrence house next door, passing buckets of water to be thrown on the blaze. Elsewhere in the yard onlookers stood scattered around, watching the firefighting efforts. To Millicent, numb with fear, it seemed a jumble of people and noise, and she glanced around in a panicked way. Then, at last, her eyes focused on one particular figure standing across the yard. It was a man who had just carried a small desk out of the house and set it down in the yard. His face, hands, clothes, and bright hair were liberally smudged with soot.

"Jonathan!" Millicent cried out, heedless of the fact that so many people could witness her joy in seeing him. She ran across the yard, her arms reaching out to him.

He whirled around. "Millicent!" A huge white grin split his grimy face. He crossed the space between them in a few quick strides and pulled her into his arms, hugging her tightly against him. "Oh, Millicent!" he whispered, burying his face in her hair. "Sweetheart, I was so scared. I saw the smoke coming out of the house, and I was afraid you were in it."

"No. No, I'm fine. But what about Alan? And Opal? They were here. Are they all right?"

Jonathan squeezed her even more tightly. "Yes, they're fine. They're in our house next door, resting. All of them: Alan, Opal, and the baby. Alan saved them all."

"What?" Millicent pulled back slightly and looked up at him. "Alan saved them! What do you mean?"

"Apparently Opal and the baby were asleep upstairs when the fire started, and the smoke overcame them; they didn't even wake up."

"Oh, no!"

"Yes. But Alan was downstairs, reading, and he smelled the smoke. He called and when Opal didn't respond, he went upstairs and got her and the baby out."

Millicent gaped. "Got them out! But how? How could he possibly get upstairs?"

"He must have crawled. They were all lying on the steps when I came in and found them. Betsy and I got them the rest of the way out."

"He dragged himself upstairs and pulled them out? And got them downstairs!" Millicent shook her head in amazement. "I can't believe it. It seems impossible."

"Love can make a person capable of all kinds of feats, I suppose. And I suspect that your brother is capable of a great deal more than you or he realized. After all, look what he's accomplished the past few months. Betsy tells me he's even begun to read for the bar."

"Read for the bar!" And had Jonathan said something about love? Was he saying that Alan loved Opal? Were all these things going on, and she had been too blind to see them? She would never have dreamed that Alan would have been able to rescue someone from the second floor of the house, as he had done this afternoon. She was beginning to wonder how much she knew about her brother—and how much she had underrated his abilities. Was it possible that in her love, she had kept him always a child? That she hadn't seen what he could do, hadn't given him the chance to try? Her head whirled. "Oh, Jonathan," she whispered. "I don't know what to think."

"There's no need to think." He pulled her tightly to him again. "Everything's fine. Millie, I tell you, when I saw the smoke and thought you were in the house, it scared me to death."

"I saw the smoke, too, as I was walking home." Millicent, leaning against his chest, smiled. "I thought it might be *your* house, and I was afraid for you and Betsy." She wrapped her arms around him as though she would never let him go. It was so good, so right, to be in his arms. She felt as if she could stay there forever. "I've never been as frightened in my life. I thought I might have lost you forever, and I knew what a fool I'd been. I'd thrown away you and my happiness and I wasn't even sure why! I'm sorry. I'm so sorry. I know I've hurt you. Will you ever forgive me?"

She tilted back her head to look up at him, tears glimmering in her eyes. Jonathan smiled slowly, his eyes beginning to twinkle.

"Well, now, let me see." He pretended to muse on the subject. "I might be persuaded to forgive you— provided you'll promise me, right here, right now, that you'll marry me."

"Oh, yes!" Millicent responded without hesitation. "I will. Whenever you want. I realized it this afternoon—even before the fire, really. I don't want to waste my life. I don't want to spend it dwelling on the past or throw it away on other people's ideas of what my duty to my family is. This life is all I have, and I can't afford to waste it. I deserve to have a family and love and a wonderful life, and giving up all those things will never give Alan back the use of his legs. There's no way I can make it up to him. I love him; I'll still see him a lot. But I know now that I can't sacrifice my life for him."

For a long moment Jonathan stood gazing down into her face. Then he bent and kissed her. When he straightened up he grinned and glanced around him comically. "Well, you can't back out of this engagement, sweetheart. I have lots of witnesses that you said yes."

Millicent gasped and whirled around. She had forgotten that the yard was full of people, and the eyes of most of them were interestedly on them. She and Jonathan had been standing right there in the open kissing, and all these people had been watching! Millicent blushed red up to her hairline.

"Jonathan! You embarrassed me!"

Jonathan chuckled. "I'm sure it won't be the last time."

Millicent had to smile fondly. "No," she agreed. "I'm sure it won't be." She took his hand. "But I'll marry you anyway."

Twenty-Five

$\mathcal{A}$ Hayes family wedding was always a grand affair, and Millicent Hayes's was no exception. It was in March, which many people agreed was far too rushed. (It didn't look good, doing it that hurriedly.) But for once Millicent was oblivious to public opinion; both she and Jonathan were determined to have the wedding as soon as humanly possible. Aunt Oradelle's feelings were hurt because not only was Millicent going against her wishes in getting married, but Millicent also insisted upon organizing the reception herself and having it at her house instead of letting Aunt Oradelle run it.

The wedding itself was, as all the leading ladies of the town agreed, decidedly odd. The groom's daughter was the bride's flower girl, for one thing, and Millicent's sole attendant was Opal Wilkins, who, as everyone knew, was Millicent's *servant!* Her brother gave her away, which wasn't unusual in itself, since her father was dead, but Alan was crippled! He rolled down the aisle beside Millicent in his chair. It was a sight the people of Emmetsville, Texas, had never seen before. Sophie Hayes wiped tears from her eyes and declared that the ceremony was beautiful. Oradelle Holloway grimaced, convinced that her sister-in-law was as silly as the law allowed, and declared darkly that the union was doomed from the start. However, that opinion didn't keep her from hugging the bride tightly afterwards and even welcoming Jonathan Lawrence into the family. (For, after all, how could Oradelle ever hope to direct the two of them in the proper path if they were estranged from the family?)

Luck was with Millicent, for the weather was balmy for early March, and much of the reception crowd could overflow into the yards of the Hayes and Lawrence houses. Aunt Oradelle, though it wasn't her house, assumed her position of control in the kitchen, and the reception ran as smoothly as silk.

Millicent, however, hardly noticed. She was too excited and happy, drifting among the well-wishers as if she were on a cloud. Wherever she was, Jonathan was usually by her side, and if he was not, she would glance around until she caught sight of him. It wasn't that she felt unsafe or insecure without him. It was just that she felt the need to be connected with him in some way, if only by sight.

Millicent found her brother sitting on the side veranda in his invalid chair, watching the flow of people in the yards. He smiled at her as she approached, but there was a sadness in his eyes that tugged at Millicent's heart. She knew she had to leave Alan, but it hurt her to think that he would be unhappy. She bent and placed a kiss on his forehead, surprising him with the open display of affection, uncharacteristic of their family.

"What was that for?" he asked in amusement.

Millicent shrugged. "For being the best brother in the world, I guess."

"Is that what I am?" he asked in an ironic tone.

"Of course you are." She squatted down beside his chair and looked him solemnly in the eye. "You never said a word of complaint about my marrying Jonathan, and many men in your position would have. You've been kind and understanding; you haven't once tried to make me feel bad about it."

"What is there to feel bad about?" Alan asked reasonably. "You're doing what you should do, what I want you to do. I want you to be happy; that's all."

"And I want the same for you."

"Why are you looking at me in that meaningful way?"

"You know why. You and I talked about it right after I told you I had accepted Jonathan's proposal. You love Opal. Why won't you tell her? Why won't you ask her to marry you?"

His brows drew together in irritation. "Blast it, Millicent, you are the most persistent creature! You know good and well why I can't ask Opal that. She's too likely to agree out of her sense of obligation, her gratitude. I can live well enough by myself. You've seen how I've changed the last few months; I can do a decent job of taking care of myself, with Ida and Johnny helping me. I'll have work; I've talked to Everson Carter, and he's agreed to let me read law under him. And there are my hobbies; my life will be full."

"Busy, perhaps. But not necessarily full."

Alan shrugged. "I'll do well enough. Besides, with you and Betsy next door, you know I won't lack for company."

Millicent smiled. "That's true. I'll probably drive you mad popping over every few minutes."

Alan nodded. "I'm sure."

She paused, then went on. "It's still not the same."

"Millicent . . . we've been through this before. You know I refuse to be a millstone around Opal's neck."

"You could at least give her the choice."

"Millicent, honestly!"

"All right. All right." She held up her hands in mock surrender. "I won't badger you about it. I promise. But I can't help but want you to be happy, too."

"I know. And I will be. You needn't worry. Just enjoy your wedding. Enjoy your marriage. Your life. I want that for you, Millie. You've done more for me than I can ever repay. You deserve something in return."

Millicent smiled, and her eyes went instinctively to Jonathan, standing by the low fence between the front yards, engaged in earnest conversation with Elmer Holloway. "Uh-oh. I better rescue Jonathan from Uncle Elmer. Or perhaps it's the other way around. I'm not sure whether Uncle Elmer will bore Jonathan to distraction before Jonathan manages to offend him mortally."

Alan chuckled. "You're right. You better hurry."

A smile lingered on his lips as Alan watched her trot down the steps and march across the yard toward her new husband, her elegant dress rippling over the grass behind her.

"She's beautiful, isn't she?" a soft voice asked behind him.

Alan jumped, startled, and whipped around. "Opal! What are you doing there?"

"Just standing. Why?"

"How long have you been there?"

"I just this minute walked out the door. Why?" Hurt darkened her eyes.

"Nothing. No reason. I'm sorry." He reached out a hand apologetically, and Opal quickly slipped her hand into it. "I'm simply a bear today. I'm sorry you have to put up with me."

"It's all right. I understand. You'll miss her an awful lot, won't you?"

Alan sighed. "Yes. We've been far closer the last few years than most brothers and sisters. Her going rather leaves a hole in my life." His mouth twisted. "I'm selfish; I hate the thought of being alone."

"You won't be alone," Opal protested. "Ida and Johnny will be here. I'll be here. And Robert."

He gazed up at her, and there was pain in his eyes, but he said flatly, "You won't remain here forever, Opal. Surely you realize that. You'll meet someone; you'll want to get married, have a life of your own. A husband, more children."

"No, I won't!" Opal was shocked. "I wouldn't go off marrying somebody, however much I might like to have another baby. I couldn't go with another man, not after—"

"Not after what? After you've had two men you didn't love push their way into your bed? It won't be the same, Opal, not with a man you love. You'll meet a man that you can desire, that you'll want in your bed, and then it will be different."

Opal gaped at him. "What are you talking about? Two men! Are you lumping yourself with that devil Johnston?"

Alan shrugged. "I didn't force you in the same way he did, but would you really have refused me? I know that you were grateful to me, that you would have done anything to repay the favor you feel I did you in allowing you to stay here."

"Grateful! I don't understand you. Is that the kind of woman you think I am, that I would sleep with a man just because I was grateful to him? That I'm the sort who would use her body to repay a man for a favor?"

Alan looked startled. "Opal . . . no, wait. I didn't think anything bad about you. I didn't mean that you were bartering yourself."

But Opal plowed ahead, bright red spots of fury tinting her cheekbones. "You think I would actually go to a man's room and strip off my clothes for him, let him touch me and kiss me and do those things to me if I didn't love him? Well, I wouldn't, I'm not that kind of woman. I loved you; that's why I went with you. I still love you."

He stared at her. "You can't be serious."

"Why not? I am. I love you. I understand why you wouldn't want anything with me. I mean, you're such a good man and all; you wouldn't want to lead a woman on, to make her think that you would marry her some-day if you knew you couldn't. I know that you want to have more than . . . more than just passion. You want to love a woman, someone equal to yourself, someone you can marry." She flung herself down on her knees beside his chair and grasped his hands, gazing up earnestly into his eyes. "I'm not good enough for you; I know that. I'm . . . damaged. Soiled by that horrible man. It would be a terrible scandal if anyone knew that you had anything to do with me. But no one has to know. I'd never let on; I wouldn't act like I had a claim on you. Please, Alan, let me stay with you. Let me be your mistress."

Alan could not speak, stunned by her words.

"I've been thinking about it a lot the last few weeks. Ever since that night. I want you so much, Alan. I'd like to be with you; I'd like to feel what I did that night. It was wonderful. Maybe it's wrong and wicked of me to want it, but I do. It'd be so good to lie with you again. You did desire me that night; I know you did. I wouldn't expect you to love me, but don't you think you would enjoy doing what we did that night? Couldn't we have just that? I don't know very much; maybe I was a disappointment to you, but—"

"No! God, no, you were no disappointment. It was I who was a fumbling fool." His fingers closed tightly around hers. "I haven't stopped thinking about it, wishing it could happen again. That was the most beautiful night of my life."

"Really?" Joy spread across her face. "Oh, Alan, I'm so glad! Then wouldn't you like to feel it again? Surely it wouldn't be too much of a sin. Do you think? I promise that I would never expect anything of you, and I wouldn't make a fuss if you decided to marry a girl your own class. I'd just leave. I swear. I wouldn't make any trouble for you and her."

"A girl my own class! Stop talking that way. You're as good as any woman here. You are my class; no, you're higher than I am. I would never marry someone else; I don't want anyone else. You're the only woman I want, the only woman I love. You aren't beneath me. My God, that's not the reason I didn't ask you to marry me. I'd marry you in a second. I love you. Nothing in the world would make me happier."

A glow started on Opal's face and spread, transforming her. "Do you mean that? You'd actually like to marry me? You aren't just saying it, trying to make me feel good?"

"No! How can you think that? I love you."

"Honestly?" A giggle escaped her. "Then what are we talking about? What have we been doing the last couple of months?"

"You're saying you want to marry me?"

Opal nodded, catching her lower lip between her teeth in an endearing nervous gesture. "Yes. Of course I want to marry you, but I'm not sure it'd be right for you."

"Right! My God, Opal, I'd be the happiest man in the world." He paused, suddenly trembling on the threshold of a life he had never dreamed he could have, a great and unbelievable possibility. All he had to do to have everything in the world he wanted was to say yes, to ask Opal to marry him. Bravely he turned from the possibility. "You don't know what you're suggesting. You may think you want to marry me now, but you're still so young. You think I'm some kind of wonderful man, and I'm not. After a while, that image you have of me would tarnish. You'd realize what I am. Or you'd meet a man you could really love. You don't want to be tied down to me. You can't throw your life away on me."

"I'm not throwing my life away! You are all I want. Alan, I love you! Isn't that enough? Isn't that clear? There will never be any other man for me. That night, when you touched me, it was the most wonderful feeling in the world. I—it wiped out the bad things that Johnston did to me. You made me feel clean and whole and . . . and cherished! I could never feel that way again with anyone else. I love you. Please, Alan, let me love you."

He held out for an instant longer, looking at her with frustration and a hope he had tried for so long to subdue. Then he moved, as if something inside him had broken, and he grasped her hand tightly. "I love you. And if you're serious about wanting to stay with me . . ."

"I am! I am!"

A grin spread across his face. "All right then." He took her hand and pulled her over to the railing with him. He looked out at the people gathered in the yard below him and raised his voice, "Everybody! Everybody! I have an important announcement to make."

Gradually everyone within hearing distance turned

toward him, quieting down, their curiosity overriding all else.

"Alan! What are you doing?" Opal hissed.

Alan ignored her. "I want to announce an engagement. Opal Wilkins has agreed to become my wife. It looks like the Hayes family is going to have another wedding very soon."

Everyone began to chatter excitedly.

"Alan! Why did you come right out and say it like that?" Opal asked. "Now you can't change your mind. You should have thought about it first."

"I won't change my mind. I want to marry you, and I will. Hush!" He raised a finger to her lips. "Don't you dare say that you're not good enough. You're more than good enough. You are the most admirable woman I know, the best, the sweetest, and the kindest. I'd be the luckiest man in the world if you were to marry me. Why do you think I announced our engagement like that? Because I knew you'd say this, and I wanted to trap you into it, where you couldn't wriggle out. I intend to marry you."

Tears started in Opal's eyes. "I love you," she whispered.

"Alan!" Millicent came flying up the steps, Jonathan and Betsy not far behind her. She bent and hugged him fiercely. "This is the most wonderful thing! Why didn't you tell me a while ago? Why did you let me go on worrying and telling you to marry her?"

"I just now decided. I didn't realize until a moment ago that Opal was actually foolish enough to marry me."

"Oh, you." Millicent gave him a little push on the

shoulder. "I'm so happy! This is absolutely, without question, the most wonderful day of my life." She turned to Opal and hugged her tightly.

Jonathan shook Alan's hand in congratulations, and Betsy hugged and kissed Alan and Opal, babbling that she had the most wonderful family in the world now. Jonathan looked at his wife and took her hand in his, raising it to his lips. He turned back toward Alan and Opal. "I can only hope that you'll be as happy in your marriage as I am in mine."

Millicent laughed. "You've been married only two hours. We haven't even had time for a small argument."

Jonathan chuckled. "Oh, I'll enjoy those, too, large or small, as long as they're with you." He smiled down into her eyes and said softly, "Don't you think it's time we left this gathering?"

Millicent colored a little and stepped back from Opal and her brother and the relatives crowding around him. "If you want . . ."

"Oh, I want," Jonathan assured her, and his eyes left no doubt of his intentions.

"Me, too," Millicent agreed inelegantly.

Jonathan took her hand, and they started toward the backyard. Betsy came bounding after them. "Papa! Millicent! Can't I come, too? I want to go, too."

"Not tonight," Jonathan told her firmly. "You're going to stay with your friend Annabeth, remember?"

Betsy frowned. "I know. But I want to be with you-all."

"You will be. Don't worry. You'll be with us for years and years, until you get married yourself. But tonight, and the next few nights, I want to have Millicent to myself."

"Oh, all right," Betsy gave in grudgingly.

He bent down and gave her a kiss on the head, and Millicent hugged her. They turned and strolled into the backyard. When they came to the gap in the hedges between the two backyards, Jonathan stopped. He glanced at the pyracantha bush, where it had all started, and then at Millicent, his eyes twinkling. Millicent raised a haughty eyebrow, but she couldn't maintain the pose. She smiled. They began to laugh.

Jonathan curled his arm around her shoulders. "Come along, Mrs. Lawrence. Let me take you home."

Mike fears what may happen to Kelly during the winter, but even more he fears losing her. . .forever.

Mike's heart clenched. "Please don't take a job that might put you in danger. I couldn't stand it if something were to happen to you, Kelly."

She gave him a questioning look.

"I love you, and I—" Mike never finished his sentence. Instead, he took Kelly in his arms and kissed her upturned mouth. Her lips tasted sweet as honey, and it felt so right to hold her.

When Kelly slipped her hands around his neck and returned his kiss, Mike thought he was going to drown in the love he felt for her.

Kelly was the first to pull away. Her face was bright pink, and her eyes were cloudy with obvious emotion. Had she enjoyed the kiss as much as he?

She placed her trembling hands against her rosy cheeks. "I–I think it's time to go."

"But we haven't picked any wildflowers for you to use as watercolors yet," Mike argued.

She stood and dropped her art supplies into the pocket of her skirt. "I shouldn't have let you kiss me. It wasn't right."

Mike jumped to his feet. "It felt right to me."

She hung her head. "It wasn't, and it can never happen again."

WANDA E. BRUNSTETTER lives in Central Washington with her husband, who is a pastor. She has two grown children and six grandchildren. Besides writing, Wanda enjoys making Amish dolls, ventriloquism, stamping, reading, and gardening. Wanda and her husband have a puppet ministry, which they often share at other churches, Bible camps, and Bible schools. Wanda invites you to visit her website: www.wandabrunstetter.com

Books by Wanda E. Brunstetter

HEARTSONG PRESENTS

HP254—A Merry Heart
HP421—Looking for a Miracle
HP465—Talking for Two
HP478—Plain and Fancy
HP486—The Hope Chest
HP517—The Neighborly Thing
HP542—Clowning Around

Kelly's Chance

Wanda E. Brunstetter

Heartsong Presents

To my husband, Richard, born and raised in Easton,
Pennsylvania, near the Lehigh Canal.
Thanks for your love, support, and research help.

To Char and Mim,
my brother-in-law and sister-in-law.
Thanks for your warm hospitality
as we researched this book.

A note from the Author:
I love to hear from my readers! You may correspond with me by writing:

Wanda E. Brunstetter
Author Relations
PO Box 719
Uhrichsville, OH 44683

ISBN 1-59310-055-8

KELLY'S CHANCE

Our mission is to publish and distribute inspirational products offering exceptional value and biblical encouragement to the masses.

All Scripture quotations are taken from the King James Version of the Bible.

one

Lehigh Valley, Pennsylvania
Spring 1891

Kelly McGregor trudged wearily along the towpath, kicking up a cloud of dust with the tips of her worn work boots. A size too small and pinching her toes, they were still preferable to walking barefoot. Besides the fact that the path was dirty, water moccasins from the canal sometimes slithered across the trail. Kelly had been bitten once when she was twelve years old. She shuddered and groaned as the memory came back to her. . . Papa cutting her foot with a knife, then sucking the venom out. Mama following that up with a poultice of comfrey leaves to take the swelling down, then giving Kelly some willow bark tea for the pain. Ever since that day, Kelly had worn boots while she worked, and even though she could swim quite well, she rarely did so anymore.

As Kelly continued her walk, she glanced over her shoulder and smiled. Sure enough, Herman and Hector were dutifully following, and the rope connected to their harnesses was still held taut.

"Good boys," she called to the mules. "Keep on comin'."

Kelly knew most mule drivers walked behind their animals in order to keep them going, but Papa's mules were usually dependable and didn't need much prodding. Herman, the lead mule, was especially obedient and docile. So Kelly walked in front, or sometimes alongside the team, and they followed with rarely a problem.

Herman and Hector had been pulling Papa's canal boat since Kelly was eight years old, and she'd been leading them for the last nine years. Six days a week, nine months of the year, sometimes eighteen hours a day, they trudged up and down the towpath that ran alongside the Lehigh Navigation System. The waterway, which included the Lehigh Canal and parts of the Lehigh River, was owned by a Quaker named Josiah White. Due to his religious views, he would not allow anyone working for him to labor on the Sabbath. That was fine with Kelly. She needed at least one day of rest.

"If it weren't for the boatmen's children, the canal wouldn't run a day," she mumbled. "Little ones who can't wait to grow up so they can make their own way."

Until two years ago, Kelly's older sister Sarah had helped with the mules. Then she ran off with Sam Turner, one of the lock tenders' boys who had lived along their route. Sarah and Sam had been making eyes at each other for some time, and one day shortly after Sarah's eighteenth birthday, they ran away together. Several weeks later, Sarah sent the family a letter saying she and Sam were married and living in Phillipsburg, New Jersey. Sam had gotten a job at Warren Soapstone, and Sarah was still looking for work. Kelly and her folks hadn't seen or heard a word from either of them since that time. Such a shame! She sure did miss that sister of hers.

Kelly moaned as she glanced down at her long, gray cotton skirt, covered with a thick layer of dust. She supposed the sifting dirt was preferable to globs of gritty, slippery mud, which she often encountered in early spring. "Long skirts are such a bother. Sure wish Mama would allow me to wear pants like all the mule boys do."

Sometimes, when the wind was blowing real hard, Kelly's skirt would billow, and she hated that. She'd solved the problem when she got the bright idea to sew several small stones into the hemline, weighing it down so the wind couldn't lift her skirt anymore.

Kelly looked over her shoulder again, past the mules. Her gaze came to rest on her father's flat-roofed, nearly square, wooden boat. They were hauling another load of dark, dirty anthracite coal from the town of Mauch Chunk, the pickup spot, on down to Easton, where it would be delivered.

Kelly's thoughts returned to her sister, and a knot rose in her throat. She missed Sarah for more than just her help. Sometimes, when they'd walked the mules together, Kelly and Sarah had shared their deepest desires and secret thoughts. Sarah admitted how much she hated life on the canal. She'd made it clear that she would do about anything to get away from Papa and his harsh, stingy ways.

Kelly groaned inwardly. She understood why Sarah had taken off and was sure her older sister had only married Sam so she could get away from the mundane, difficult life on the Lehigh Navigation System. It didn't help any that Kelly and Sarah had been forced to work as mule drivers without earning one penny of their own. Some mule drivers earned as much as a dollar per day, but not Kelly and her sister. All the money they should have made went straight into Papa's pocket, even if Mama and the girls had done more than their share of the work.

In all fairness, Kelly had to admit that even though Papa yelled a lot, he did take pretty good care of them. He wasn't like some of the canal boatmen, who drank and gambled whenever they had the chance, wasting away their earnings before the month was half over.

Kelly was nearing her own eighteenth birthday, and even though she was forced to work without pay, there was nothing on earth that would make her marry someone simply so she could get away. In fact, the idea of marriage was like vinegar in her mouth. From what she'd seen in her own folks' lives, getting hitched wasn't so great anyway. All Mama ever did was work, and all Papa did was take charge of the boat and yell at her and Mama.

Tears burned in Kelly's eyes, but she held them in check. "Sure wish I could make enough money to support myself. And I don't give a hoot nor a holler 'bout findin' no man to call husband, neither."

Kelly lifted her chin and began to sing softly, "Hunks-a-go

pudding and pieces of pie; my mother gave me when I was knee-high. . . And if you don't believe it, just drop in and see—the hunks-a-go pudding my mother gave me."

The tension in Kelly's neck muscles eased as she began to relax. Singing the silly canaler's tune always made her feel a bit better. Especially when she was getting hungry and could have eaten at least three helpings of Mama's hunks-a-go pudding. The fried batter, made with eggs, milk, and flour, went right well with a slab of roast beef. Just thinking about how good it tasted made Kelly's mouth water.

Mama would serve supper when they stopped for the night, but that wouldn't be 'til sundown, several hours from now. When Papa hollered, "Hold up there, Girl!" and secured the boat to a tree or near one of the locks, Kelly would have to care for the mules. There was always currying and cleaning of the animals to do, in particular around Herman and Hector's collars where their sweaty hair often came loose. Kelly never took any chances with the mules, for she didn't want either of them to get sores or infections that would end up needing to be treated with medicine.

When the grooming was done each night, Kelly fed the animals and bedded them down in fresh straw spread along the floor in one of the lock stables or in their special compartment on the boat. Only when all that was done could Kelly climb on board, wash up, and sit down to Mama's hot meal of salt pork and beans or potato-and-onion soup. Roast beef and hunks-a-go pudding were reserved for a special Sunday dinner when there was more time for cooking.

After supper, when all the dishes had been washed, dried, and put away, Kelly would read, draw, or maybe play a game. Mama and Papa amused themselves with an occasional game of checkers, and sometimes they lined up a row of dominoes and competed to see who could acquire the most points. That was fine with Kelly. She much preferred to retire to her bunk in the deck below and draw by candlelight until her eyes became too heavy to focus. Most often she'd sketch something she'd seen along the canal, but many times her charcoal pictures were of things she'd never seen before. Things she'd read about and could only dream of seeing.

On days like today, when Kelly was dog-eared tired and covered from head to toe with dust, she wished for a couple of strong brothers to take her place as driver of the mules. It was unfortunate for both Kelly and her folks, but Mama wasn't capable of having any more children. She'd prayed for it; Kelly had heard her do so many times. The good Lord must have thought two daughters were all Amos and Dorrie McGregor needed. God must have decided Kelly could do the work of two sons. Maybe the Lord believed she should learn to be content with being poor.

Contentment. That was something Kelly didn't think she could ever manage. Not until she had money in her pockets. She couldn't help but wonder if God cared about her needs at all.

Herman nuzzled the back of Kelly's neck, interrupting her musings and nearly knocking her wide-brimmed straw hat to the ground. She shivered and giggled. "What do ya want, ol' boy? You think I have some carrots for you today? Is that what you're thinkin'?"

The mule answered with a loud bray, and Hector followed suit.

"All right, you two," Kelly said, reaching into her roomy apron pocket. "I'll give ya both a carrot, but you must show your appreciation by pullin' real good for a few more hours." She shook her finger. "And I want ya to do it without one word of complaint."

Another nuzzle with his wet nose, and Kelly knew Herman had agreed to her terms. Now she needed confirmation from Hector.

❧

Mike Cooper didn't have much use for some of the new-fangled things he was being encouraged to sell in his general store, but this pure white soap that actually floated might be a real good seller. Especially to the boatmen, who seemed to have a way of losing bars of soap over the side of their vessels. If Mike offered them a product for cleaning that could easily be seen and would bob like a cork instead of sinking to the bottom of the murky canal, he could have a best-seller that would keep his customers coming back and placing orders for "the incredible soap that floats."

Becoming a successful businessman might help him pursue his goal of finding a suitable wife. Ever since Pa died, leaving him to run the store by himself, Mike had a terrible ache in his heart. Ma had gone to heaven a few years before Pa, and his two brothers, Alvin and John, had relocated a short time later, planning to start a fishing business off the coast of New Jersey. That left Mike to keep the store going, but it also left him alone, wishing for a helpmate and a brood of children. In fact, Mike prayed for this every day. He felt he was perfectly within God's will to make such a request. After all, in the Book of Genesis, God said it wasn't good for a man to be alone, so He created Eve to be a helper and to keep Adam company. At twenty-four years old, Mike thought it was past time he settled down with a mate.

Mike's biggest concern was the fact that there weren't too many unattached ladies living along the canal. Most of the women who shopped at his store were either married or adolescent girls. There was one young woman—Sarah McGregor— but word had it she'd up and run off with the son of a lock tender from up the canal a ways. Sarah had a younger sister, but the last time Mike saw Kelly, she was only a freckle-faced kid in pigtails.

Then there was Betsy Nelson, daughter of the minister who lived in nearby Walnutport and regularly traveled along the canal in hopes of winning folks to the Lord. Betsy wasn't beautiful, but she wasn't as ugly as the muddy waters in Lehigh Canal either. Of course, Mike wasn't nearly as concerned over a woman's looks as he was with her temperament. Betsy should have been sweet as apple pie, her being a pastor's daughter and all, but she could cut a body right in two with that sharp tongue of hers. Why, he'd never forget the day Betsy raked old Ross Spivey up one side and down the other for spitting out a wad of tobacco in the middle of one of her daddy's sermons. By the time she'd finished with Ross, the poor man was down on his knees, begging forgiveness for being so rude.

Mike grabbed a broom from the storage closet, shook his head, and muttered, "A fellow would have to be hard of hearin' or just plain dumb-witted to put up with the likes of Miss Betsy Nelson. It's no wonder she's not married yet."

He pushed the straw broom across the wooden floor, visualizing with each stroke a beautiful, sweet-spirited woman who'd be more than happy to become his wife. After a few seconds, Mike shook his head and murmured, "I'll have to wait, that's all. Wait and keep on prayin'."

Mike quoted Genesis 2:18, a verse of Scripture that had become one of his favorites since he'd decided he wanted a wife: "'And the LORD God said, It is not good that the man should be alone; I will make him an help meet for him.'"

"I know the perfect woman is out there somewhere, Lord," he whispered. "All I need is for You to send her my way, and I can take it from there."

two

Kelly awoke feeling tired and out of sorts. She'd stayed up late the night before, working on another charcoal drawing. It was an ocean scene, with lots of fishing boats on the water. Not that Kelly had ever seen the ocean. Her only experience with water involved the Lehigh, Morris, and Delaware Rivers and Canals. She'd only seen the ocean in her mind—from stories she'd read in books or from the tales of those who had personally been to the coast.

If she could ever figure out a way to earn enough money of her own, Kelly might like to take a trip to the shore. Maybe she would open an art gallery there, to show and sell some of her work. She had seen such a place in the town of Easton, although Papa would never let her go inside. Kelly wondered if her drawings were good enough to sell. If only she could afford to buy a store-bought tablet, along with some oil paints, watercolors, or sticks of charcoal. She was getting tired of making her own pieces of charcoal, using hunks left over in the cooking stove or from campfires that had been set along the canal. Kelly would let the chunks cool, and then whittle them down to the proper size. It wasn't what she would have liked, but at least it allowed her to draw.

Kelly swung her legs over the edge of the bunk and stretched her aching limbs. If a young woman of seventeen could hurt this much from long hours of walking and caring for mules, she could only imagine how older folks must feel. She knew Papa worked plenty hard steering the boat and helping load and unload the coal they hauled, which might account for his usual crabby attitude. Mama labored from sunup to sunset as well. Besides cooking and cleaning, there was always laundry and mending to do. At times, Mama even steered the boat while Papa rested or took care of chores only he could do. Kelly's mother also helped by watching up ahead and letting Papa know where to direct the boat.

Stifling a yawn, Kelly reached for a plain brown skirt and white long-sleeved blouse lying on a straight-backed chair near the bed. She glanced around the small cabin and studied her meager furnishings. The room wasn't much bigger than a storage closet, and it was several steps below the main deck. Her only pieces of furniture were the bunk, a small desk, a chair, and the trunk she kept at the foot of her bed.

I wonder what it would be like to have a roomy bedroom in a real house, Kelly mused. The canal boat had been her primary home as far back as she could remember. The only time they lived elsewhere was in the winter, when the canal was drained due to freezing temperatures and couldn't be navigated. It was during those days that Kelly's dad worked at one of the factories in the town of Easton. Leaving the few pieces of furniture they owned on their boat, the McGregor family settled into Flannigan's Boardinghouse until the spring thaw came and Papa could resume work on the canal. During the winter months, Kelly and her sister had gone to school when they were younger, but the rest of the year Mama taught them reading and sums whenever they had a free moment.

Kelly's nose twitched and her stomach rumbled, as the distinctive aroma of cooked oatmeal and cinnamon wafted down the stairs, calling her to breakfast. A new day was about to begin, and she would need a hearty meal to help get her started.

"We'll be stoppin' by Cooper's General Store this afternoon, 'cause we need some supplies," Papa announced when Kelly arrived at the breakfast table. He glanced over at Mama, then at Kelly, his green eyes looking ever so serious. "Don't know when we'll take time out for another supply stop, so if either of you needs anything, you'd better plan on gettin' it today." He slid his fingers across the auburn-colored handlebar mustache that filled the space between his nose and upper lip.

"I could use a few more bars of that newfangled soap I

bought last time we came through," Mama spoke up. "It's a wonder to me the way that stuff floats!"

Kelly couldn't help but smile at her mother's enthusiasm over something as simple as a bar of white soap that floated when it was dropped in water. *I guess things like that are important to a woman with a family. Mama doesn't have much else to get excited about.*

Kelly ate a spoonful of oatmeal as she studied her mother, a large-boned woman of Italian descent. She had dark brown hair like Kelly's; only Mama didn't wear hers hanging down. She pulled it up into a tight bun at the back of her head. Mama's eyes, the color of chestnuts, were her best feature.

Mama could be real pretty if she was able to have nice, new clothes and keep herself fixed up. Instead, she's growing old before her time—slavin' over a hot stove and scrubbin' clothes in canal water, with only a washboard and a bar of soap that bobs like a cork—poor Mama!

Papa's chair scraped across the wooden planks as he pulled his wiry frame away from the table. "It's time to get rollin'." He nodded toward Kelly. "Better get them mules ready, Girl."

Kelly finished the rest of her breakfast and jumped up. When Papa said it was time to roll, he meant business. In fact, when Papa said anything at all, she knew she'd better listen.

❧

It was noon when the McGregors tied their boat to a tree not far from the town of Walnutport and stopped for lunch. Normally they would have eaten a quick bite, then started back up the canal, but today they were heading to Cooper's General Store. After a bowl of vegetable soup and some of Mama's sweet cornbread, they would be shopping for needed supplies and more food staples.

Kelly welcomed the stop. Not only because she was hungry and needed to eat, but also because Papa had promised to buy her a new pair of boots. She'd been wearing the same ones for more than a year, and they were much too tight. Besides, the laces were missing, and the soles were nearly worn clear through. Kelly had thought by the time she turned sixteen her feet would have quit growing. But here she was only ten months from her eighteenth birthday, and her long toes were still stretching the boots she wore. At this rate she feared she'd be wearing a size nine when her feet finally stopped growing.

Kelly ate hurriedly, anxious to head over to the general store. She hadn't been inside Cooper's in well over a year because she usually chose to wait outside while her folks did the shopping. Today Kelly planned to check the mules over and offer them a bit of feed, then hurry into the store. If she found new boots in short order, there might even be enough time to sit on a log and draw awhile. There were always interesting things along the canal—other boats, people fishing, and plenty of waterfowl.

Too bad I can't buy some oil paints or a set of watercolors, Kelly thought as she hooked the mules to a post and began to check them over for harness sores, fly bites, or hornet stings. *Guess I should be happy Papa has agreed to buy me new boots, but I'd sure like to have somethin' just for fun once in awhile.*

Kelly released a groan and scratched Hector behind his ear. "If I ever make any money of my own, I might just buy you a big, juicy apple." She patted Herman's neck. "You too, Old Boy."

❧

Mike whistled a familiar hymn as he dusted off the candy counter, always a favorite with the children who stopped by his store. He was running low on horehound drops but still had plenty of licorice, lemon drops, and taffy chews. He knew he'd have to order more of everything soon, since summer was not far off, and there would be a lot more little ones coming by in hopes of finding something to satisfy their sweet tooth.

Many boats were being pulled up the Lehigh Navigation System already, and it was still early spring. Mike figured by this time next month his store would have even more customers. Last winter, when he'd had plenty of time on his hands, Mike had decided to order some Bibles to either sell or give away. If someone showed an interest and didn't have the money to buy one, he'd gladly offer it to them for free. Anything to see that folks learned about Jesus. Too many of the boatmen were uneducated in spiritual matters, and Mike wanted to do his part to teach them God's ways.

Mike leaned on the glass counter and let his mind wander back to when he was a boy of ten and had first heard about the Lord. Grandma Cooper, a proper Englishwoman, had told him about Jesus. Mike's family had lived with her and Grandpa for several years, when Mike's pa was helping out on the farm in upstate New York, where Mike had been born. Ellis Cooper had no mind to stay on the farm, though, and as soon as he had enough money, he moved his wife and three sons to Pennsylvania, where he'd opened the general store along the Lehigh Canal.

Mike's father didn't hold much to religious things. He used to say the Bible was a bunch of stories made up to help folks get through life with some measure of hope.

"There's hope, all right," Mike whispered as he brought his mind back to the present. "And thanks to Grandma's teachings, I'd like to help prove that hope never has to die."

When he heard a familiar creak, Mike glanced at the front door. Enough daydreaming and reflecting on the past. He had customers to satisfy, and as always, he'd do his best to see that their needs were met.

As he moved toward the front of the store, Mike's heart slammed into his chest. Coming through the doorway was the most beautiful young woman he'd ever laid eyes on. *Don't reckon I've seen her before. She must be new. . .just passing through. Maybe she's a passenger on one of the packet boats that hauls tourists. Maybe. . .*

Mike blinked a couple of times. He recognized the man and woman entering the store behind the young woman: Amos and Dorrie McGregor. It wasn't until Amos called her by name that Mike realized the little beauty was none other than the McGregors' youngest daughter, Kelly.

Mike shook his head as amazement swept though his

body. It couldn't be. Kelly had pigtails, freckles, and was all arms and legs. This stunning creature had long brown hair that reached clear down to her waist, and from where he stood, there wasn't one freckle on her lovely face. She looked his way, and he gasped at the intensity of her dark brown eyes. *A man could lose himself in those eyes. A man could. . .*

"Howdy, Mike Cooper," Amos said, extending his hand. "How's business these days?"

Mike forced himself to breathe, and with even more resolve, he kept his focus on Amos and not the man's appealing daughter. "Business is fine, Sir." He shook Mr. McGregor's hand. "How are you and the family doing?"

Amos shrugged. "Fair to middlin'. I'd be a sight better if I hadn't hit one of the locks and put a hole in my boat the first week back to work." He gave his handlebar mustache a tug. "In order to get my repairs done, I had to use most of what I made this winter workin' at a shoe factory in Easton."

"Sorry to hear that," Mike said sincerely. He glanced back at Kelly, offering her what he hoped was a friendly smile. "Can this be the same Kelly McGregor who used to come runnin' in here begging her pa to buy a few lemon drops?"

Kelly's face turned slightly pink as she nodded. "Guess I've grown a bit since you last saw me."

"I'll say!" Mike felt a trickle of sweat roll down his forehead, and he quickly pulled a handkerchief out of his pant's pocket and wiped it away. Kelly McGregor was certainly no child. She was a desirable woman, even if she did have a few layers of dirt on her cotton skirt and wore a tattered straw hat and a pair of boots that looked like they were ready for burial. *Could she be the one I've been waiting for, Lord?*

Mike cleared his throat a few times. "So, what can I help you good folks with today?"

Amos gave his wife a little nudge. "Now don't be shy, Dorrie. Tell the man what you're needin'. I'll just poke around the store and see what I can find, while you and Kelly stock up on food items and the like."

Kelly cast her father a pleading look. "I'm still gettin' new boots, right, Papa?"

Her dad nodded and grunted. "Yeah, sure. See if Mike has somethin' that'll fit your big feet."

Mike felt sorry for Kelly, whose face was now red as a tomato. She shifted from one foot to the other, and never once did she look Mike right in the eye.

"I got a new shipment of boots in not long ago," he said quickly, hoping to help her feel a bit more at ease. "They're right over there." He pointed to a shelf across the room. "Would you like me to see if I have any your size?"

Dorrie McGregor spoke up for the first time. "Why don't you help my husband find what he's needin'? Me and Kelly can manage fine on our own."

Mike shrugged. "Whatever you think best." He offered Kelly the briefest of smiles, and then headed across the room to help her pa.

◆

Kelly didn't know why, but she felt as jittery as one of the mules when they were being forced to walk through standing water. Was it her imagination, or was Mike Cooper staring at her? Ever since they'd first entered the store, he seemed to be watching her, and now, while she was squatted down on the floor trying on a pair of size-nine boots, the man was actually gawking.

Maybe he's never seen a woman with such big feet. Probably thinks I should have been born a boy. Kelly swallowed hard and forced the threatening tears to stay put. *Truth be told, Papa probably wishes I was a boy.* Most boys were able to work longer and harder than she could. And a boy wasn't as apt to run off with the first person who offered him freedom from canal work, the way Sarah had.

Kelly glanced around the room, feeling an urgency to escape. She stood on shaky legs and forced herself to march around the store a few times in order to see if the boots were going to work out okay. When she was sure they were acceptable, she pulled the price tag off the laces and handed it to

Mama. "If ya don't mind, I'd like to wait outside. It's kinda stuffy in here, and since it's such a nice day, maybe I can get in a bit of sketchin' while you and Papa finish your shopping."

Mama nodded, and Kelly scooted quickly out the front door. The sooner she got away from Mike Cooper and those funny looks he kept giving her, the better it would be!

three

Kelly's heart was pounding like a hammer as she exited the store, but it nearly stopped beating altogether when Mike Cooper opened the door behind her and called, "Hey, Kelly, don't you want a bag of lemon drops?"

She skidded to a stop on the bottom step, heat flooding her face like it did whenever Mama lit the cook stove. She turned slowly to face him. *Why does he have to be so handsome?* Mike's medium-brown hair, parted on the side and cut just below his ears, curled around his neck like kitten fur. His neatly trimmed mustache jiggled up and down, as though he might be hiding a grin. The man's hazel-colored eyes seemed to bore right through her, and Kelly was forced to swallow several times before she could answer his question.

"I–uh–don't have money to spend on candy just now. New boots are more important than satisfyin' my sweet tooth." She turned away, withdrawing her homemade tablet and a piece of charcoal from the extra-large pocket of the apron covering her skirt.

Kelly was almost to the boat when she felt Mike's hand touch her shoulder. "Hold up there. What's your hurry?" His voice was deep, yet mellow and kind of soothing. Kelly thought she could find pleasure in listening to him talk awhile—if she had a mind to.

"I was plannin' to do a bit of drawing." She stared at the ground, her fingers kneading the folds in her skirt.

Mike moved so he was standing beside her. "You're an artist?"

She felt her face flush even more. "I like to draw, but that don't make me an artist."

"It does if you're any good. Can you draw something for me right now?"

She shrugged her shoulders. "I suppose I could, but don't you have customers to wait on?"

Mike chuckled. "You've got me there. How about if you draw something while I see what your folks might need? When they're done, I'll come back outside and you can show me what you've made. How's that sound?"

It sounded fair enough. There was only one problem. Kelly was feeling so flustered, she wasn't sure she could even write her own name, much less draw any kind of picture worthy to be shown.

"Guess I can try," she mumbled.

Unexpectedly, he reached out and patted her arm, and she felt a warm tingle shoot all the way up to her neck. Except for Papa's infrequent hugs, no man had ever touched her before. It felt kind of nice, in a funny sort of way. *Could this be why Sarah ran off with Sam Turner? Did Sam look at my sister in a manner that made her mouth go dry and her hands feel all sweaty?* If that's what happened to Sarah, then Kelly knew she had better run as far away from Mike Cooper as she possibly could, for he sure enough was making her feel giddy. She couldn't have that, no way!

Kelly took a few steps back, hoping the distance between them might get her thinking straight again. "See you later," she mumbled.

"Sure thing!" he called as he headed back to the store.

Kelly drew in a deep breath and flopped down on a nearby log. The few minutes she'd spent alone with Mike had rattled her so much, she wondered if she still knew how to draw.

In all the times they'd stopped by Cooper's General store, never once had Mike looked at her the way he had today—like she was someone special, maybe even pretty. *Of course*, she reminded herself, *I usually wait outside, so he hasn't seen me in awhile.* The time it took for her folks to shop was a good chance for Kelly to sketch, feed and water the mules, or simply rest her weary bones. Truth be told, it had probably been more than a year since she'd seen Mike face-to-face.

Forcing her thoughts off the handsome storekeeper, Kelly focused her attention on a pair of mallard ducks floating in the canal. The whisper of the wind sang softly as it played with the ends of Kelly's hair. A fat bullfrog was posed on the bank nearby. It seemed to be studying a dragonfly hovering above the water. It was a peaceful scene, and Kelly felt one with her surroundings. In no time, she'd filled several pages of the simple drawing pad she usually kept inside the pocket of either her skirt or apron.

Kelly was pulled from her reverie when Papa and Mama walked up, each carrying a wooden box. She rolled up her artwork and slipped it, along with the hunk of charcoal, inside her pocket. Then she wiped her messy hands on her dusty skirt and jumped to her feet. "Need some help?"

"I could probably use another pair of hands puttin' stuff away in the kitchen," Mama replied.

"Will we be leavin' soon?" Kelly asked, glancing at Cooper's General Store and wondering if Mike would come back to see her drawings as he'd promised.

"Soon as we get everything loaded," Papa mumbled. "Sure would help if we had a few more hands. Got things done a whole lot quicker when Sarah was here."

Kelly watched her dad climb on board his boat. She knew he'd been traveling the canal ever since he was a small boy. Except for times during winter when he worked in town, running the boat was Papa's whole life. Even though he had a fiery Irish temper, once in awhile she caught him whistling, singing some silly tune, or blowing on his mouth harp. Kelly figured he must really enjoy his life on the canal. Too bad he was so cheap and wouldn't hire another person to help out. Most of the canalers had a hired hand to steer the boat while the captain stood at the front and shouted directions.

I wish God had blessed Papa and Mama with a whole passel of boys. Sarah's gone, and I'm hoping to leave someday. Then what will Papa do? Kelly shrugged. *Guess he'll have to break down and hire a mule driver, 'cause Mama sure can't do everything she does now and drive the mules too.*

As Kelly followed her mother into the cabin, she set her thoughts aside. They had a long day ahead, with much to be done.

❧

Mike hoisted a box to his shoulders and started out the door. He had offered to help Amos McGregor haul his supplies on board the boat. It was the least he could do, considering the fact that Amos had no boys to help. Besides, it would give him a good excuse to talk to Kelly again and see what she'd drawn.

Mike met Amos as the older man was stepping off the boat. "Didn't realize you'd be bringing a box clean out here," Amos commented, tipping his head and offering Mike something akin to a smile.

"I said I'd help, and I thought it would save you a few steps." Mike nodded toward the boat. "Where shall I put this one?"

Amos extended his arms. "Just give it to me."

Taken aback by the man's abruptness, Mike shrugged and handed over the box. Amos turned, mumbled his thanks, and stepped onto the boat.

"Is Kelly on board?" Mike called, surprising himself at his sudden boldness. "I'd like to speak with her a moment."

Kelly's dad whirled around. "What business would ya have with my daughter?"

"She was planning to show me some of her artwork."

Amos shook his head. "Her and them stupid drawings! She's a hard enough worker when it comes to drivin' the mules, but for the life of me, I can't see why she wastes any time scratchin' away on a piece of paper with a stick of dirty, black charcoal."

"We all need an escape from our work, Mr. McGregor," Mike asserted. "Some read, fish, or hunt. Others, like me, choose to whittle." He smiled. "Some, such as your daughter, enjoy drawing."

"Humph! Makes no sense a'tall!" Amos spun around. "I'll tell Kelly you're out here waitin'. Don't take up too much of her time, though. We're about ready to shove off."

Mike smiled to himself. Maybe Amos wasn't such a tough fellow after all. He could have said Kelly wasn't receiving any visitors. Or he could have told Mike to take a leap right into the canal.

Mike waited on the dock, and a few minutes later Kelly showed up. She looked kind of flustered, and he hoped it wasn't on account of him. It could be that Kelly's pa had given her a lecture about wasting time with her sketches. Or maybe he'd made it clear he wanted no one calling on the only daughter he had left. It might be that Amos was afraid his youngest child would run off with some fellow, the way his eldest had done.

He needn't worry. While I'm clearly attracted to Kelly McGregor, I don't think she's given me more than a second thought today.

✦

Kelly's legs were shaking as she lifted one foot over the side of the boat and stepped onto dry ground. She could hardly believe Mike Cooper had really come looking for her. She knew Papa was none too happy about it because he'd told her she wasn't to take much time talking to the young owner of the general store. Kelly figured it was probably because Papa was anxious to be on his way, but from the way her father had said Mike's name, she had to wonder if there might be more to his reason for telling her to hurry. Maybe Papa thought she had eyes for Mike Cooper. Maybe he was afraid Kelly would run off and get married, the way Sarah had done. Well, he needn't worry about that happening!

Mike smiled as Kelly moved toward him. "Did you bring your drawings?"

She averted his gaze. "I only have a few with me, and they're done up on scraps of paper sack so they're probably not so good." She blinked a couple of times. "I got some free newsprint from the *Sunday Call* while we were livin' in Easton, and some of my pictures have a white background. Those are in my room on the boat and might be some better."

"Why not let me be the judge of how good your pictures

are? Can I take a peek at what you've got with you?"

Kelly reached inside her ample apron pocket and retrieved the tablet she'd put together from cutup pieces of paper sack the size of her Bible. She handed it to Mike and waited for his response.

He studied the drawings several seconds, flipping back and forth through the pages and murmuring an occasional "ah. . . so. . .hmm. . ."

She shifted her weight from one foot to the other, wondering what he thought. Did Mike like the sketches? Was he surprised to see her crude tablet? The papers were held in place by strings she'd pushed through with one of Mama's darning needles. Then she'd tied the strings in a knot to hold everything in place. Did Mike's opinion of her artwork and tablet even matter? After all, he was nothing to her—just a man who ran a general store along the Lehigh Navigation System.

"These are very good," Mike said. "I especially like the one of the bullfrog ready to pounce on the green dragonfly." He chuckled. "Who won, anyway?"

Kelly blinked. "What?"

"Did the bullfrog get his lunch, or did the dragonfly lure the old toad into the water, then flit away before the croaker knew what happened?"

She grinned. "The dragonfly won."

"That's what I expected."

Kelly pressed a hand to her chest, hoping to still a heart that was beating much too fast. If only Papa or Mama would call her back to the boat. As much as she was enjoying this little chat with Mike, she felt jittery and unsure of herself.

"Have you ever sold any of your work?" Mike asked.

She shook her head. "I doubt anyone would buy a plain old charcoal drawing."

He touched her arm. "There's nothin' *plain* about these, Kelly. I have an inkling some of the folks who travel our canal or live in the nearby communities might be willing to pay a fair price for one of your pictures."

Her face heated with embarrassment. She got so few

compliments and didn't know how to respond. "You. . .you really think so?"

He nodded. "In fact, the other day there was a packet boat that came through, transporting a group of people up to Allentown. Two of the men were authors, and they seemed real interested in the landscape and natural beauty growing along our canal."

Kelly sucked in her lower lip as she thought about the prospect. This might be the chance she'd been hoping for. If she could make some money selling a few of her charcoal drawings, maybe she'd have enough to purchase a store-bought writing tablet, a good set of watercolors, or perchance some oil paints. Then she could do up some *real* pictures, and if she could sell those. . .

"How about I take two or three of these sketches and see if I can sell them in my store?" Mike asked. "I would keep ten percent and give you the rest. How's that sound?"

Ten percent of the profits for him? Had she heard Mike right? That meant she'd get ninety percent. The offer was more than generous, and it seemed too good to be true.

"Sounds fair, but since I've never sold anything before, I don't know how much of a price to put on the drawings," Kelly said.

"Why not leave that up to me?" Mike winked at her, and she felt like his gentle gaze had caught and held her in a trap. "I've been selling things for several years now, so I think I can figure out a fair price," he said with the voice of assurance.

She nodded. "All right, we have us a deal, but since these pictures aren't really my best, I'll have to go back on the boat and get ya three other pictures."

"That's fine," Mike said as he handed her the drawings.

"The next time we come by your store, I'll ask Papa to stop; then I can check and see if you've sold anything."

Mike reached out his hand. "Partners?"

They shook on it. "Partners."

four

Shaking hands with Mike Cooper had almost been Kelly's undoing. When Mike released her hand, she was trembling and had to clench her fists at her sides in order to keep him from seeing how much his touch affected her.

Mike opened his mouth, as if to say something, but he was cut off by a woman's shrill voice.

"Yoo-hoo! Mr. Cooper, I need you!"

Kelly and Mike both turned around. Betsy Nelson, the local preacher's daughter, was heading their way, her long, green skirt swishing this way and that.

Kelly cringed, remembering how overbearing Betsy could be. She didn't simply share the good news, the way Rev. Nelson did. No, Betsy tried to cram it down folks' throats by insisting they come to Sunday school at the little church in Walnutport, where her father served as pastor.

One time, when Kelly was about seven years old, Betsy had actually told Kelly and her sister, Sarah, that they were going to the devil if they didn't come to Sunday school and learn about Jesus. Papa overheard the conversation and blew up, telling sixteen-year-old Betsy what he thought of her pushy ways. He'd sent her home in tears and told Kelly and Sarah there was no need for either of them to go to church. He said he'd gotten along fine all these years without God, so he didn't think his daughters needed religion.

Mama thought otherwise, and while the girls were young, she often read them a Bible story before going to bed. When Kelly turned twelve, Mama gave her an old Bible that had belonged to Grandma Minnotti, who'd died and gone to heaven. It was during the reading of the Bible story about Jesus' death on the cross that Kelly confessed her sins in the quiet of her room one night. She'd felt a sense of hope, realizing Jesus was her personal Savior and would walk with her wherever she went—even up and down the dirty towpath.

What had happened to her childlike faith since then? Had she become discouraged after Sarah ran away with Sam, leaving her with the responsibility of leading the mules? Or had her faith in God slipped because Papa was so mean and wouldn't give Kelly any money for the hard work she did every day?

Kelly's thoughts came to a halt when Betsy Nelson stepped between her and Mike and announced, "I need to buy material for some new kitchen curtains I plan to make."

"Go on up to the store and choose what you want. I'll be there in a minute," Mike answered with a nod.

Betsy stood grounded to her spot, and Mike motioned toward Kelly. "Betsy, in case you didn't recognize her, this is Kelly McGregor, all grown up."

Kelly felt her face flame, and she opened her mouth to offer a greeting, but Betsy interrupted.

"Sure, I remember you—the skinny little girl in pigtails who refused to go to Sunday school."

Kelly knew that wasn't entirely true, as it had been Papa's decision, not hers. She figured it would be best not to say anything in her own defense, however.

Betsy squinted her gray blue eyes and reached up to pat the tight bun she wore at the back of her head. Kelly wondered if the young woman ever allowed her dingy blond hair to hang down her back. Or did the prim and proper preacher's daughter even sleep with her hair pulled back so tightly her cheeks looked drawn?

"I was hoping you would help me choose the material," Betsy said, offering Mike a pinched-looking smile.

Mike fingered his mustache and rocked back on his heels. Kelly thought he looked uncomfortable. "I'm kinda busy right now," he said, nodding at Kelly.

"It's all right," she was quick to say. "Papa's about ready to go, and I think we've finished with our business."

"But you haven't given me any pictures," Mike reminded her.

"Oh. . .oh, you're right." Kelly's voice wavered when she spoke. She was feeling more flustered by the minute.

"Kelly, you got them mules ready yet?" Papa shouted from the bow of the boat.

Kelly turned to her father and called, "In a minute, Papa." She faced Mike again. "I'll be right back with the drawings." She whirled around, sprinted toward the boat, and leaped over the side, nearly catching her long skirt in the process.

A few minutes later, Kelly came back, carrying three drawings done on newsprint and neatly pressed between two pieces of cardboard. Two were of children fishing along the canal, and the third was a picture of Hector and Herman standing in the middle of the towpath. She handed them to Mike. "I'll have more to show you the next time we stop by."

Mike lifted the top piece of cardboard and studied the drawings. "Nicely done, Kelly. Very nice."

Heat rushed to Kelly's face, but she appreciated his compliment. "Thanks. I hope the others will be as good."

"I don't see why they wouldn't be." Mike held up the picture of Kelly's mules. "Look, Betsy. See what Kelly's drawn."

"Uh-huh. Nice." Betsy barely took notice as she grabbed hold of Mike's arm. "Can we go see about that material now?"

"I guess so." Mike turned to Kelly. "See you in a few days."

She nodded. "If Papa decides to stop. If not, then soon, I hope."

"Kelly McGregor!" Papa's voice had grown even louder, and Kelly knew he was running out of patience.

"Ready in a minute," she hollered back. "See you, Mike. See you, Betsy." Kelly grabbed hold of the towline and then hurried off toward the mules waiting patiently under a maple tree. A few minutes later she was trudging up the towpath, wishing she could have visited with Mike a bit longer.

Kelly glanced over her shoulder and saw Betsy hanging onto Mike's arm. A pang of jealousy stabbed her heart, but she couldn't explain it. She had no claims on Mike Cooper, nor did she wish to have any. Betsy Nelson was more than welcome to the storekeeper.

❧

Mike headed for the store, wishing it were Kelly and not Betsy clinging to his arm. As he reached the front door, he glanced over his shoulder and saw the McGregors' canal boat disappear around the bend. He'd wanted to spend more time with Kelly, but Betsy's interruption had stolen what precious moments they might have had.

As he stepped into the store, Mike shot a quick prayer heavenward. *Is Kelly the one, Lord? Might she make me a good wife?*

"Mr. Cooper, are you listening to me?" Betsy gave his shirtsleeve a good tug.

Mike refocused his thoughts and turned to look at Betsy, still clinging to his arm.

"The material's on that shelf, and please feel free to call me Mike." He pulled his arm free and pointed to the wall along the left side of his store. "Give me a minute to put Kelly's drawings in a safe place, and I'll join you over there."

Mike could see by the pucker of Betsy's lips that she wasn't happy, but she headed in the direction he had pointed.

Did Betsy think he would drop everything just because she wanted his opinion on the material she wished to buy? Mike doubted his advice counted for much. Truth of the matter, he knew little about kitchen curtains. His mother had decorated the house he lived in, which was connected to the back of the store. Since Ma's death, he hadn't given much thought to her choice of colors, fabric, or even furniture. If it had been good enough for Ma and Pa, then it was good enough for him.

Mike placed Kelly's drawings on a shelf under the counter and headed across the room to where Betsy stood holding a bolt of yellow-and-white calico material.

She smiled at him. "What do you think of this color?"

He shrugged. "Guess it would work fine."

For the next half hour, Mike looked at bolts of material,

nodded his head, and tried to show an interest in Betsy's curtain-making project. He felt a sense of relief when another customer entered the store, but much to his disappointment, Betsy was still looking at material when he finished up with Hank Summers' order.

"Have you made a decision yet?" Mike called to Betsy from where he stood behind the counter.

"I suppose the yellow-and-white calico will work best." Betsy marched across the room and plunked the bolt of material on the wooden counter. "I'll take ten yards."

Ten yards? Mike thought Betsy was only making curtains for the kitchen, not every window in the house. *Guess women are prone to changing their minds.*

Betsy grinned at him and fluttered her pale eyelashes. "I'm thinking of making a dress from the leftover material, and I want to be sure I have plenty. Do you think this color will look good on me?"

Mike groaned inwardly. He didn't want to offend the preacher's daughter, so he merely smiled and nodded in response.

As soon as Betsy left the store, Mike withdrew Kelly's pictures from under the counter, took a seat on his wooden stool, and studied the charcoal drawings.

Kelly McGregor had talent; there was no doubt about it. The question was, would he be able to sell her artwork?

five

Over the next couple days, Kelly daydreamed a lot while she walked the towpath. Was it possible that Mike Cooper might be able to sell some of her drawings? Were they as good as he'd said, or had Mike been trying to be polite when he told Kelly she had talent?

"Sure wish he wasn't so handsome," Kelly muttered as she neared the changing bridge where she and the mules would cross to the other side of the canal. A vision of Mike's face crept into her mind, and she began to sing her favorite canal song, hoping to block out all thoughts of the storekeeper.

"Hunks-a-go pudding and pieces of pie; my mother gave me when I was knee-high. . . . And if you don't believe it, just drop in and see—the hunks-a-go pudding my mother gave me."

Kelly found herself thinking about food and how good supper would taste when they stopped for the night. Mama had bought a hunk of dried beef at Mike Cooper's store, so they would be having savory stew later on.

Up ahead was the changing bridge, and Kelly knew it time to get the mules ready to cross over to the towpath on the other side of the canal. Soon they were going up and over the bridge, as Kelly lifted the towrope over the railing. Obediently, Hector and Herman followed. In no time they were on the other side, and Papa was able to steer his boat farther down the canal.

Kelly was relieved it had gone well and that the towline hadn't become snagged. Whenever that happened, they were held up while Papa fixed things again. Then he was angry the rest of the day because they'd lost precious time. Every load of anthracite coal was important, and payment was made only when it was delivered to the city of Easton, where it was weighed and unloaded. The trip back up the navigation system to Mauch Chunk was with an empty boat, and Papa never wanted to waste a single moment.

Today they were heading to Easton and would arrive by late afternoon if all went well. Kelly knew there was no way Papa would agree to stop by Cooper's General Store on the way to deliver their coal, but coming back again, he might.

Maybe we'll get there early enough so I'll have time to get some drawing done, Kelly told herself. If there was any possibility of Mike selling her artwork, she needed to have more pictures ready to give him.

Kelly didn't realize she'd stopped walking until she felt Hector's wet nose nudge the back of her neck. She whirled around. "Hey there, Boy. Are ya that anxious to get to Easton?"

The mule snorted in response, and she laughed and reached out to stroke him behind the ear. Not to be left out, Herman bumped her hand.

"All right, Herman the Determined, I'll give you some attention too." Kelly stroked the other mule's ear for a few seconds, and then she clicked her tongue. "Now giddy-up, you two. There's no more time to dawdle. Papa will be worse than a snappin' turtle if we make him late tonight."

The day wore on, and every few miles they came to another lock where they would wait while it filled with water to match the level of the canal. Then their boat entered the lock, and the gates enclosed the boat in a damp, wooden receptacle. Right ahead, the water came sizzling and streaming down from above, and gradually the boat would rise again, finally coming to a respectable elevation. The gates swung open, Kelly hooked the mules back to the towrope, and they resumed their voyage.

Ahead was another lock, and Papa blew on his conch shell, letting the lock tender know he was coming. When they approached the lock, Kelly saw another boat ahead of them. They would have to wait their turn.

Suddenly, a third boat came alongside Papa's. "Move outta

my way!" the captain shouted. "I'm runnin' behind schedule and should've had this load delivered by now."

"I was here first," Papa hollered in response. "You'll have to wait your turn."

"Oh, yeah? Who's gonna make me?" The burly looking man with a long, full beard shook his fist at Papa.

Standing on the bank next to the mules, Kelly watched as Mama stepped up beside Papa. She touched his arm and leaned close to Papa's ear. Kelly was sure Mama was trying to get Papa calmed down, like she always did whenever he got riled.

Kelly took a few steps closer to the canal and strained to hear what Mama was saying.

"Don't tell me what to do, Woman!" Papa yelled as he leaned over the side of his boat. The other craft was right alongside him, and the driver of the mules pulling that boat stood next to Kelly.

The young boy, not much more than twelve or thirteen years old, gave Kelly a wide grin. His teeth were yellow and stained. Probably from smoking or chewing tobacco, Kelly figured. "Looks like my pa is gonna beat the stuffin's outa your old man," he taunted.

Kelly glanced back at the two boat captains. They were face-to-face, each leaning as far over the rails as possible. She sent up a quick prayer. *Not this time, Lord. Please help Papa calm down.*

"Move aside, or I'm comin' over there to clean your clock," the burly man bellowed.

"Amos, please!" Mama begged as she gripped Papa's arm again. "Just let the man pass through the lock first. This ain't worth gettin' into a skirmish over."

Papa shot the man a look of contempt and grabbed hold of the tiller in order to steer the boat. "I'll let it go this time, but you'd better never try to ace me out again."

Kelly breathed a sigh of relief as Papa steered the boat aside and the other vessel passed through the lock. She'd seen her hot-tempered father use his fists to settle many disagreements in the past. It was always humiliating, and what did it prove—that

Papa was tougher, meaner, or more aggressive than someone else? As far as Kelly could tell, nothing good had ever come from any of Papa's fistfights. He was a hotheaded Irishman, who'd grown up on the water. His dad had been one of the men who'd helped dig the Lehigh Canal, and Papa had said many times that he'd seen or been part of a good many fights throughout his growing-up days. If only he would give his heart to Jesus and confess his sins, the way Kelly and Mama had done.

Herman nuzzled Kelly's shoulder, and she turned to face her mule friends. *If God really loves me, then why doesn't He change Papa's heart?*

&

Mike had been busier than usual the last couple days, and that was good. It kept him from thinking too much about Kelly McGregor. How soon would she and her family stop at his store again? Could he manage to sell any of her drawings before they came? Was Kelly the least bit interested in him? All these thoughts tumbled around in Mike's head whenever he had a free moment to look at Kelly's artwork, which he'd displayed on one wall of the store. The young woman had been gifted with a talent so great that even a simple, home-made charcoal drawing looked like an intricate work of art. At least Mike thought it did. He just hoped some of his customers would agree and decide to buy one of Kelly's pictures.

As Mike wiped off the glass on the candy counter, where little children had left fingerprint smudges, a vision of Kelly came to mind. With her long, dark hair hanging freely down her back, and those huge brown eyes reminding him of a baby deer, she was sure easy to look at. Nothing like Betsy Nelson, the preacher's daughter, who had a bird-like nose, squinty gray blue eyes, and a prim-and-proper bun for her dingy blond hair.

Kelly's personality seemed different too. She wasn't pushy and opinionated, the way Betsy was. Kelly, though a bit shy, seemed to have a zest for life that showed itself in her drawings. She was a hard worker too—trudging up and down the towpath six days a week, from sunup to sunset. Mike was well aware of the way the canal boatmen pushed to get their loads picked up and delivered. The responsibility put upon the mule drivers was heavy, yet it was often delegated to women and children.

I wonder if Amos McGregor appreciates his daughter and pays her well enough. Mike doubted it, seeing the way the man barked orders at Kelly. And why, if she was paid a decent wage, would Kelly be using crude sticks of charcoal instead of store-bought paints or pencils, not to mention her homemade tablet?

Mike's thoughts were halted when the front door of his store opened and banged shut.

"Good morning, Mike Cooper," Preacher Nelson said as he sauntered into the room.

"Mornin'," Mike answered with a smile and a nod.

"How's business?"

"Been kind of busy the last couple of days. Now that the weather's warmed and the canal is full of water again, the boatmen are back in full swing."

The preacher raked his long fingers through the ends of his curly, dark hair. His gray blue eyes were small and beady, like his daughter's. "You still keeping the same hours?" the man questioned.

Mike nodded. "Yep. . .Monday to Saturday, nine o'clock in the morning 'til six at night."

Hiram Nelson smiled, revealing a prominent dimple in his clean-shaven chin. "Sure glad to hear you're still closing the store on Sundays."

Mike moved over to the wooden counter where he waited on customers. "Sunday's a day of rest."

"That's how God wants it, but there's sure a lot of folks who think otherwise."

Not knowing what else to say, Mike merely shrugged. "Anything I can help you with, Reverend Nelson?"

The older man leaned on the edge of the counter. "Actually, there is."

"What are you in need of?"

"You."

"Me?"

The preacher's head bobbed up and down. "This Friday's my daughter's twenty-sixth birthday, and I thought it would be nice for Betsy if someone her age joined us for supper." He chuckled. "She sees enough of her old papa, and since her mama died a few years ago, Betsy's been kind of lonely."

Mike was tempted to remind the preacher that his daughter was two years older than he but decided not to mention their age difference—or the fact that most women Betsy's age were already married and raising a family. "Isn't there someone from your church you could invite?" he asked.

Pastor Nelson's face turned slightly red. "It's you Betsy thought of when she said she'd like to have a guest on her birthday." He tapped the edge of the counter.

Mike wasn't sure how to respond. Was it possible that Betsy Nelson was romantically interested in him? If so, he had to figure out a way to discourage her.

"So, what do you say, Son? Will you come to supper on Friday evening?"

Remembering that the Nelsons' home was next to the church and several miles away, Mike knew he would have to close the store early in order to make it in time for supper. This would be the excuse he needed to decline the invitation. Besides, what if the McGregors came by while he was gone? He didn't want to miss an opportunity to see Kelly again.

"I—I'm afraid I can't make it," Mike said.

The preacher pursed his lips. "Why not? You got other plans?"

Mike shook his head. "Not exactly, but I'd have to close the store early."

Rev. Nelson held up his hand. "No need for that, Son. We'll have a late supper. How's seven o'clock sound?"

"Well, I—"

"I won't take no for an answer, so you may as well say you'll come. Betsy would be impossible to live with if I came home and told her you'd turned down my invitation."

Mike didn't want to hurt Betsy's feelings, and the thought of eating someone else's cooking did have some appeal. "Okay," he finally conceded. "Tell Betsy I'll be there."

six

Kelly hummed to herself as she kicked the stones beneath her feet. They had made it to Easton by six o'clock last night, and after they dropped off their load of coal and had eaten supper, she'd had a few hours to spend in her room, working on her drawings.

Now it was the following day, and they were heading back to Mauch Chunk for another load. By five or six o'clock they should be passing Mike Cooper's store. Kelly hoped she could talk Papa into stopping, for she had three more drawings she wanted to give Mike. One was of a canal boat going through the locks, another of an elderly boatman standing at the bow of his boat playing a fiddle, and the third picture was the skyline of Easton, with its many tall buildings.

Kelly was pretty sure her pictures were well-done, although she knew they could have been better if they'd been drawn on better paper, in color instead of black and white.

She stopped humming. *Someday I hope to have enough money to buy all kinds of paints and fancy paper.* Even as the words popped into her mind, Kelly wondered if they could ever come true. Unless Papa changed his mind about paying her wages, she might never earn any money of her own. Maybe her dream of owning an art gallery wasn't even possible.

"At least I can keep on drawing," she mumbled. "Nobody can take that away from me."

Kelly's stomach rumbled, reminding her it was almost noon. Since they had no load, they would be stopping to eat soon. If Papa was hurrying to get to Easton with a boatload of coal, Kelly might be forced to eat a hunk of bread or some fruit and keep on walking. Today, Mama was fixing a pot of vegetable and bean soup. Kelly could smell the delicious aroma as it

39

wafted across the space between the boat and towpath.

A short while later, Kelly was on board the boat, sitting at the small wooden table. A bowl of steaming soup had been placed in front of her, a chunk of rye bread to her left, and her drawing pad was on the right. She'd decided to sketch a bit while her soup cooled.

Kelly had just picked up her piece of charcoal to begin drawing when Papa sat down across from her. "You ain't got time to dawdle. Get your lunch eaten and go tend to the mules."

Tears stung the backs of Kelly's eyes. She should be used to the way her dad shot orders, but his harsh tone and angry scowl always upset her.

"My soup's too hot to eat yet," she said. "I thought I might get some drawin' done while I wait for it to cool."

Papa snorted. "Humph! Fiddlin' with a dirty stick of charcoal is a waste of time!" He grabbed the loaf of bread from the wooden bowl in the center of the table and tore off a piece. Then he dipped the bread into his bowl of soup and popped it into his mouth.

Kelly wasn't sure how she should respond to his grumbling, so she leaned over and blew on her soup instead of saying anything.

Mama, who was dishing up her own bowl of soup at the stove, spoke up. "I don't see what harm there'd be in the girl drawin' while her soup cools, Amos."

Papa slammed his fist down on the table so hard, Kelly's piece of bread flew up and landed on the floor. "If I want your opinion, Dorrie, I'll ask for it!"

Kelly gulped. She hated it when Papa yelled at Mama. It wasn't right, but she didn't know what she could do about it. Only God could change Papa's heart, and she was growing weary of praying for such.

"Well, what are ya sittin' there lollygaggin' for?" Papa bellowed. "Start eatin', or I'm gonna pitch your writing tablet into the stove."

Kelly grabbed her spoon. No way could she let her dad

carry through with his threat. She'd eat all her soup in a hurry, even if she burned her tongue in the process.

Awhile later, she was back on the towpath. She'd given the mules some oats in their feedbags, and they were munching away as they plodded dutifully along. Kelly knew they were making good time, and they'd probably pass Mike Cooper's sometime early this evening. She'd hoped to ask Papa about stopping by the store, but he'd been so cross during lunch, she'd lost her nerve.

Besides, what reason would she give for stopping? She sure couldn't tell her dad she wanted to make a few more drawings so Mike could try to sell them in his store. Papa had made it clear the way he felt about Kelly wasting time on her artwork. If she told him her plans, Papa might make good on his threat and pitch her tablet into the stove.

"If he ever does that, I'll make another one or find some old pieces of cardboard to draw on," Kelly fumed.

A young boy about eight years old crossed Kelly's path. He carried a fishing pole in one hand and a metal bucket in the other. The child stopped on the path and looked at Kelly as though she was daft. Had he overheard her talking to herself?

Kelly stopped walking. "Goin' fishin'?" *What a dumb question. Of course he's goin' fishin'. Why else would he be carryin' a pole?*

The freckle-faced, red-haired lad offered Kelly a huge grin, revealing a missing front tooth. "Thought I'd try to catch myself a few catfish. They was bitin' real good yesterday afternoon."

"You live around here?" Kelly questioned.

"Yep. Up the canal a ways."

Kelly's forehead wrinkled. She didn't remember seeing the boy before, and she wondered why he wasn't in school. The youngster's overalls were torn and dirty, and when Kelly glanced down at his bare feet, she shuddered. It was too cold yet to be going without shoes. Maybe the child was so poor his folks couldn't afford to buy him any decent footwear.

"My pap's workin' up at Mauch Chunk, loadin' coal," the

boy said before Kelly could voice any questions.

"But I thought you said you lived nearby."

He nodded. "For the last couple months we've been livin' in an old shanty halfway up the canal." He frowned. "Don't see Pap much these days."

"Do you live with your mother?" Kelly asked.

The boy offered her another toothless grin. "Me, Ma, and little Ted. He's my baby brother. Pap was outa work for a spell, but things will be better now that he's got a job loadin' dirty coal."

Kelly's heart went out to the young child, since she could relate to being poor. Of course, Papa had always worked, and they'd never done without the basic necessities. Still, she had no money of her own, and that bothered Kelly a lot.

"Kelly McGregor, why have you stopped?"

Kelly whirled around at the sound of her dad's angry-sounding voice. He was leaning over the side of the boat, shaking his fist at her.

"Sorry, Papa," she hollered back. "Nice chattin' with you," Kelly said to the child. "Hope you catch plenty of fish today." She gave the boy a quick wave and started off.

As Kelly led her mules down the rutted path, she found herself envying the freckle-faced boy with the holes in his britches. At least he wasn't being forced to work all day.

❧

Mike pulled a pocket watch from his pant's pocket. It was almost six o'clock. He needed to close up the store and head on over to the preacher's place for supper. All day long he'd hoped the McGregors would stop by, but they hadn't, and he'd seen no sign of their boat. Of course, they could have gone by without him seeing, as there were many times throughout the day when he'd been busy with customers. As tempting as it had been, Mike knew he couldn't stand at the window all day and watch for Amos McGregor's canal boat. He had a store to run, and that took precedence over daydreaming about Kelly or watching for her dad's boat to come around the bend.

Mike put the "closed" sign in the store window and grabbed his jacket from a wall peg near the door. He was almost ready to leave when he remembered that tonight was Betsy's birthday and he should take her a gift.

He glanced around the store, looking for something appropriate. Mike noticed the stack of Bibles he had displayed on a shelf near the front of his store. He'd given plenty of them away, but he guessed Betsy, being a preacher's daughter, probably had at least one Bible in her possession.

As he continued to survey his goods, Mike's gaze came to rest on Kelly's drawings, tacked up on one wall. What better gift to give someone than something made by one of the locals? He chose the picture that showed two children fishing along the canal. He thought Betsy would like it. This would be Kelly's first sale, and he would give her the money she had coming as soon as he saw her again.

Since it was a pleasant spring evening with no sign of rain, Mike decided to walk to the Nelsons' rather than ride his horse or hitch up the buggy. He scanned the canal, looking for any sign of the McGregors' boat, but the only movement on the water was a pair of mallard ducks.

Mike filled his lungs with fresh air as he trudged off toward Walnutport. Sometime later, he arrived at the Nelsons' front door.

Betsy greeted him, looking prim and proper in a crisp white blouse and long blue skirt. Her hair was pulled into its usual tight bun at the back of her head.

"Come in, Mr. Cooper—I mean, Mike," she said sweetly. "Supper is ready, so let me take your coat."

Mike stepped inside the small, cozy parsonage and slipped off his jacket. He was about to hand it to Betsy when he remembered the picture he'd rolled up and put inside his pocket. He retrieved it and handed the drawing to Betsy. "Happy birthday."

Betsy smiled and unrolled the picture. She studied it a few seconds, and her forehead creased as she squinted her eyes. "This isn't one of those drawings young Kelly McGregor drew, is it?"

Mike nodded. "I thought you might like it, seeing as how there are children in the picture."

Her frown deepened. "What makes you think I have a fondness for children?"

"Well, I. . .that is, doesn't everyone have a soft spot for little ones?" Mike thought about his desire to have a large family, and he remembered reading how Jesus had taken time to visit with children. It only seemed natural for a preacher's daughter to like kids.

Betsy scrunched up her nose, as though some foul odor had permeated the room. "Children are sometimes hard to handle, and I don't envy anyone who's a parent." She batted her eyelashes a few times. "I get along better with adults."

Mike wondered if there was something in Betsy's eye. Or maybe she had trouble seeing and needed a pair of spectacles.

"Do you like Kelly's charcoal drawing or not?" he asked.

Betsy glanced at the picture in her hand. "I'll find a place for it, since you were thoughtful enough to bring me a present."

Mike drew in a deep breath and followed Betsy into the next room, where a table was set for three. Preacher Nelson stood in front of the fireplace, and he smiled at Mike.

"Good to see you, Son. Glad you could make it tonight."

Mike nodded and forced a smile in return. He had a feeling it was going to be a long evening, and he could hardly wait for it to come to an end.

seven

Kelly plodded along the towpath, tired from another long day, and feeling frustrated because they'd passed Mike's store without stopping. It was getting dark by the time they got to that section of the navigation system, and she hadn't seen any lights in the store windows. Maybe Mike was closed for the day.

It had been less than a week since Kelly had left three of her drawings with him. Chances were none of them had sold yet. By the time they did stop at Cooper's General Store, Kelly thought she would have a few more drawings to give Mike, and hopefully he'd have good news about the ones he was trying to sell. In the meantime, Kelly knew she needed to be patient.

"Patient and determined," she muttered into the night air. The moon was full this evening, and Kelly could see some distance ahead. They were coming to another lock, and Papa was already blowing on his conch shell to announce their arrival to the lock tender.

Kelly looked forward to each lock they went through. It gave her a chance to rest, tend to the mules, or draw.

She patted her apron pocket. *That's why I keep my tablet and a hunk of charcoal with me most of the time.*

Tonight, however, there were no boats ahead of them, and they went through the lock rather quickly. Kelly wasn't disappointed. It was too dark to draw anyway, and getting through the lock meant they would soon be on their way.

Kelly was hungry and tired. She could hardly wait to stop for the night. She didn't smell the usual aroma of cooking food coming from the boat, however. It made her wonder if Mama was tired and had decided to serve a cold meal. Maybe cheese and bread, with a piece of fruit or some carrot sticks. At this moment, anything would have tasted good.

When Kelly thought she'd die of hunger and couldn't take another step, Papa hollered for her to stop. With her dad's help, Kelly loaded the mules onto the boat, where they would be bedded down in the enclosed area reserved for them. If they'd been at a place where they could have stabled the mules, they wouldn't have to go through this procedure.

Kelly stretched her limbs with a weary sigh. "What's Mama got planned for supper, do ya know?"

Papa shook his head. "Your mama ain't feelin' well, and she's taken to her bed. You'll have to see about supper tonight."

Kelly felt immediate concern. "Mama's sick? What's wrong, and why didn't you tell me sooner?"

Papa shrugged. "Saw no need."

"But I could've come aboard and started supper. Maybe seen if there was somethin' I could do to make Mama more comfortable."

Papa grunted. "It's best you kept on walkin'. I don't wanna be late picking up my load of coal in Mauch Chunk tomorrow."

Kelly stared down at her clenched hands as anger churned in her stomach. All Papa cared about was hauling coal and making money he never shared. Didn't he give a hoot that Mama was sick in bed?

Feeling as though she carried the weight of the world on her shoulders, Kelly headed for their small kitchen. She would get some soup heating on the stove, then go below to see how Mama was doing.

A short time later, Kelly and her dad sat at the kitchen table, eating soup and bread—leftovers from their afternoon meal. Kelly had checked on her mother awhile ago, and she'd found her sleeping. She didn't have the heart to wake her, so she tiptoed out of her parents' cubicle with the intention of offering Mama a bowl of soup later on.

"You'd better get to sleep right after ya clean up the dishes," Papa said. "I'm planning to head out at the first light of day tomorrow mornin'." He wiped his mouth on the edge of his shirtsleeve. "If your mama's still feelin' poorly, you'll need to get breakfast made before we go."

Kelly watched the flame flicker from the candle in the center of the table. More chores to do. Just what she didn't need. She'd better pray extra hard for Mama tonight.

❧

Mike was never so glad to see his humble home as he was tonight. The time he'd spent at the Nelsons' place had left him feeling irritable and exhausted. Didn't Betsy ever stop talking or batting her eyelashes? Reverend Nelson had acted a bit strange all evening too. He kept dropping hints about his daughter needing a God-fearing husband, and he'd even asked Mike to sit on the sofa beside Betsy as they drank their coffee after dinner. Maybe the preacher was trying to link Mike up with his daughter, but it wasn't going to work. Mike had other ideas about who was the right woman for him.

Mike hung his jacket on a wall peg near the door, sank into an overstuffed chair by the stone fireplace, and looked around the room. He really did need someone to help fill his lonely evening hours. He'd been praying for a wife for some time now, but surely Betsy Nelson wasn't the one God had in mind for him. The woman got on his nerves, with her constant jabbering and opinionated remarks.

"It doesn't seem as if she likes children either," Mike murmured. He didn't see any way he could be happily married to a woman who didn't share his desire for a family. Mike saw children as a gift from God, not a nuisance, the way some folks did. He'd had customers come into his store who'd done nothing but yell at their kids, shouting orders or scolding them for every little thing.

Mike's thoughts went immediately to Kelly McGregor. Did she like children? Would Kelly make a good wife? Was she a believer in Christ? Mike knew so little about the young woman. The only thing he was sure of was that he was attracted to her.

I need to figure out some way for us to become better acquainted. With the McGregors' canal boat coming by every few days, there ought to be a chance to see Kelly more and get to know her.

Mike closed his eyes, and a few minutes later he fell asleep, dreaming about Kelly McGregor.

~

Kelly stretched her aching limbs and forced herself to sit up. Inky darkness enveloped her room, but Papa was hollering at her to get up. She needed to see if Mama was still ailing, and if so, fix some breakfast. Then she'd have to feed the mules, lead them off the boat, and get ready to head for Mauch Chunk. She hadn't slept well the night before, and she'd had several dreams—one that involved Mike Cooper.

Why do I think about him so often? Kelly fumed. *Probably because he has my drawings, and I'm anxious to see if he's sold any. Yep, that's all there is to it—nothin' more.*

After Kelly washed up and got dressed, she rolled up her finished drawings and placed them inside her apron pocket, just in case they made a stop at Cooper's store today. Then she tiptoed over to her folks' room to check on Mama.

Her mother was awake, but she looked terrible. Dark circles lay beneath her eyes, her skin was pasty white, and her forehead glistened with sweat.

"How are ya feelin' this mornin'?" Kelly whispered.

Mama lifted her head off the pillow and offered Kelly a weak smile. "I'll be back on my feet in no time a'tall. It's just a sore throat, and my body aches some too."

Kelly adjusted the patchwork quilt covering her mother's bed. "I'll bring you a cup of hot tea and a bowl of cornmeal mush as soon as I get Papa fed. He might be less crabby if his belly is full."

Mama nodded, coughed, and relaxed against the pillow. "I'm sorry you're havin' to do more chores than usual. If Sarah were still here, your load would be a bit lighter."

Kelly shrugged. She didn't want to think about her runaway sister. "I'll manage. You just get well." She patted the quilt where Mama's feet were hidden. "I'll be back soon."

A short while later, Kelly was in the kitchen preparing breakfast.

"What about lunch and supper?" she asked her dad when she handed him a bowl of mush.

His forehead wrinkled. "What about it?"

"If I'm gonna be leadin' the mules all day, and Mama's still sick in bed—"

Papa grunted and pulled on the end of his mustache. "Guess that means I'll be stuck with the cookin'."

"But how will you do that, watch up ahead, and steer the boat too?" she questioned.

"I'll manage somehow. Don't guess I've got much other choice." He snorted. "If that renegade sister of yours hadn't run off with Sam Turner, we wouldn't be shorthanded right now."

Kelly drew in a deep breath, feeling a bit put out with her sister too.

Things seemed to go from bad to worse as the day progressed. Kelly kept an eye on the boat, and a couple times she spotted her dad racing back and forth between the woodstove sitting on the open deck and the stern of the boat. He would lift the pot lid and take a look at the beans she knew he was cooking, run back to the stern and give the tiller a twist, and do it all over again. Kelly wondered if he might collapse or run the boat aground from all that rushing around.

When it came time for lunch, Papa gulped down a hasty meal, leaped from the boat to the towpath, and took over leading the mules so Kelly could eat. She did all right getting into the boat, but when she jumped over the side again, she missed her mark and landed in the canal with a splash.

Now she was walking the towpath in a sopping wet skirt that stuck to her legs like a tick on a mule. She'd been forced to remove her boots because they were waterlogged, and she sure hoped no snakes came slithering across the path and nailed her bare feet.

To make matters worse, the drawings she'd put in her pocket that morning had gotten ruined when she fell in the water.

Now she had nothing to give Mike if she saw him today.

The only bright spot in Kelly's day was when Papa told her they would be stopping by Cooper's General Store later on. He wanted to see if Mike had any cough syrup in stock. Papa thought it might make Mama sleep better if they could get her cough calmed down. Stopping at the store would be good for Mama as well as Kelly. She only hoped her dress would be dry by the time they got there.

eight

For the past couple of days Mike had tried unsuccessfully to sell some of Kelly's drawings. "Isn't there anyone in the area who can see her talent and needs something special to give as a gift?" he muttered as he studied the two remaining pictures displayed on the wall of his store. Was it possible that Kelly wasn't as talented as Mike thought? Maybe folks were put off by the simplicity of the paper she used. Maybe he was too caught up in his unexplained feelings for the young woman. He might have been thinking with his heart instead of his head when he'd agreed to try to sell some of her artwork.

Mike clicked his tongue against the roof of his mouth. Now he was going to have to face Kelly when she stopped by the store again and tell her nothing had sold.

That's not entirely true, he reminded himself. *I took one of her pictures to give Betsy Nelson, and I plan to pay Kelly her share for it. Maybe I should buy a second picture, then frame and hang it in my house.* Mike smiled, feeling a sense of satisfaction because of his idea. Kelly wouldn't have to know who'd bought the drawings. She'd probably be happy just getting the money.

With that decided, Mike removed the picture of Kelly's two mules and stuck it under the front counter. He would take it home when he was done for the day.

Mike pulled an envelope out of a drawer underneath the counter and wrote Kelly's name on the front. Then he withdrew some money from the cash box and tucked it inside. Hopefully he'd be able to sell her other drawing before Kelly came by the store again.

"I need to get busy and quit thinking about Kelly McGregor," Mike muttered as he grabbed a broom and started sweeping the floor. Thoughts of the young woman with dark brown eyes and long, coffee-colored hair were consuming too much of his time.

Mike had just put the broom away in the storage closet when the front door opened. He pivoted, and his heartbeat quickened. Kelly McGregor stood there, her straw hat askew, and her long, gray skirt, wrinkled, dirty, and damp. She looked a mess, yet he thought she was beautiful.

Mike swallowed hard and moved toward her. "Kelly. It's good to see you again."

&

"Hello, Mike Cooper," Kelly said, feeling timid and unsure of herself.

He smiled, and the dimple in his chin seemed to be winking at her.

She took a tentative step forward. "Mama's sick and needs some cough syrup. Have ya got any on hand?"

"I think there's still several bottles on the back shelf." Mike pointed to the other end of the store. "Would you like me to get one for you?"

She nodded. "If ya don't mind."

"Not at all." Mike headed in the direction he'd pointed, and Kelly turned her attention to the wall nearest the door. One of her drawings of children playing along the canal was there, but the other two were nowhere in sight. A feeling of excitement coursed through her veins. Had Mike sold them? Did she have some money coming now? Dare she ask?

When Mike returned a few minutes later, she was still studying her drawing. She glanced over at him. He held a bottle of cough syrup and stood so close she could smell the aroma of soap, which indicated that he at least was wearing clean clothes. Mike's hair was nicely combed too. She, on the other hand, looked terrible. He probably thought she was a filthy pig. Should she explain about falling into the canal? Would he even care?

"You're quite talented," Mike said, bringing Kelly's thoughts to a halt. "Have you done any more pictures lately?"

"I did have three more ready, but Mama's been sick, so Papa and me have had to share all the chores." She glanced down at her soiled skirt and frowned. "As you can probably see, I fell in the canal earlier today, trying to jump from the boat back to the towpath. My drawings were in my pocket, and they got ruined."

Mike shook his head slowly. "Sorry to hear that. I did wonder why your skirt was so rumpled and wet." He moved toward the counter, and Kelly followed. "Sorry you're having to do double duty, but maybe this will make you feel better." He set the cough syrup down, pulled open a drawer beneath the counter, withdrew an envelope, and handed it to Kelly.

She took the envelope and studied it a few seconds. Her name was written on the front. "What's this?"

"It's your share of the money for two of the drawings you left with me."

She smiled up at him. "You really sold two of my pictures?"

Mike's ears turned slightly red, and he looked a little flustered. Was he embarrassed because he hadn't sold all three?

"I—uh—found someone who really appreciates your talent," he said, staring down at the wooden counter.

Kelly's smile widened. "I'm so glad. Once Mama gets better, I'll have a bit more time to draw, and maybe when we stop by here again I'll have a few more pictures to give you."

Mike's smile seemed to be forced, and his face had turned red like his ears. Something seemed to be troubling him, and Kelly aimed to find out what it was.

"Is everything all right? You look kinda upset."

Mike lifted his gaze. "Everything's fine. Feel free to bring me as many drawings as you like."

Kelly felt a sense of relief wash over her. If she could get Mama back on her feet, she'd have more time to draw. Mike wanted her to bring more pictures, she'd already sold two, and things were looking hopeful. She slipped the envelope into her apron pocket and turned toward the door.

"Aren't you forgetting something?" Mike called after her.

Kelly whirled around and felt the heat of a blush spread

over her face when Mike held up the bottle of cough syrup. She giggled self-consciously and fished in her pocket for the coins to pay for her purchase.

Mike's fingers brushed hers as she dropped the money into his hand, and Kelly felt an unexpected shiver tickle her spine. What was there about Mike Cooper that made her feel so giddy and out of breath? Was it the crooked smile beneath his perfectly shaped moustache? Those hazel-colored eyes that seemed capable of looking into her soul? The lock of sandy brown hair that fell across his forehead?

Kelly snatched up the bottle of cough syrup, mumbled a quick thanks, and fled from the store.

❧

Mike couldn't believe the way Kelly had run out of the store. Had he said or done something to upset her? He'd thought they were getting along pretty well, and Kelly had seemed pleased about her drawings being sold.

Maybe she suspects I'm the one who bought the pictures. But how could she know that? He'd been careful not to give her too much information, so she couldn't have guessed he was the one. He hadn't actually lied to her, but he didn't see the need to tell Kelly he was the one either. She might have taken it the wrong way.

Seeing Kelly again had only reinforced the strong feelings Mike was having for her. When their hands touched briefly during the money exchange, he had felt as though he'd been struck by a bolt of lightning. Had Kelly felt it too? Could that have been the reason for her sudden departure? Or maybe she just needed to get back to work. The canal boaters always seemed to be in a hurry to get to and from their pickup and delivery points. That was probably all it was. Kelly's dad had no doubt told her to hurry, and she was only complying with his wishes.

How am I going to get to know Kelly better if she only stops by the store once in awhile, then stays just long enough to buy something and hurries off again? Mike closed his eyes, folded his hands, and placed them on the counter. *Lord, would You please work it out so Kelly and I can spend more time together?*

Mike was still standing behind the counter, mulling things over, when Amos McGregor entered the store.

"Mr. McGregor, your daughter was just here buying some cough syrup for your wife."

"Don'tcha think I know that?" the boatman snapped. His bright red hair stuck out at odd angles, like he hadn't combed it in a couple of days, and there were dark circles under both eyes.

Mike's only response to Amos's comment was a shrug of his shoulders. It was obvious by the scowl on the man's face that he wasn't in a good mood, and there was no point in saying anything that might rile him further.

"The wife's been sick for a couple of days," Amos mumbled. "That left me stuck doin' most of her chores." He stuffed his hands inside the pocket of his dark blue jacket and started for the back of the store.

"Can I help you find something?" Mike called after him.

"Need some of that newfangled soap that floats," came the muffled reply. "I told Kelly to get some, but as usual, she had her head in the clouds and forgot."

Mike skirted around the counter and went straight to the shelf where he kept the cleaning supplies and personal toiletries. "Here's what you're looking for, Sir," he said, lifting a bar of soap for the man's inspection.

"Yep. That's it, all right." Amos shook his head slowly. "I dropped our last bar overboard by mistake and didn't wanna take the time to stop and fish it outa the canal." He grabbed another bar of soap off the shelf and marched back to the counter. "Better to have a spare," he muttered.

Mike nodded and slipped the cakes of soap into a paper sack. "Good idea." He handed the bag to Amos. "Need anything else?"

"Nope." Amos plunked some coins on the counter and started for the front door.

"Feel free to stop by anytime," Mike called after him. "And

if you ever need a place to spend the night, I'll gladly let you stable your mules in my barn."

The boatman mumbled something under his breath and shut the door.

Mike shook his head. "I wonder why that man's such a grouch? No wonder Kelly acts like a scared rabbit much of the time. Guess I'd better pray for the both of them."

nine

On Saturday evening, much to Mike's surprise, Kelly and her mother stopped by the store.

"That cough syrup you sold Kelly a few days ago sure helped me sleep," Dorrie said as she stepped up beside Mike, who'd been stocking some shelves near the front of the store.

Mike smiled. "I'm glad to hear that, Mrs. McGregor. Are you feeling better?"

She nodded. "I'm back to doin' most of my own chores now too."

Mike glanced at Kelly out of the corner of his eye. She was standing by the candy counter, eyeing something she was obviously interested in. He started to move toward the young woman, but Dorrie's next words stopped him.

"Amos is feelin' poorly now, so we need more medicine." Her forehead wrinkled, and she blinked a couple of times. "Sure hope you've got some, 'cause I used up the bottle of cough syrup Kelly bought."

Mike nodded toward the back of the store. "There's a couple bottles on the second shelf to the right. Want me to get one for you?"

Dorrie glanced over at Kelly, still peering inside the candy counter, and she shook her head. "Why don'tcha see what kind of sweet treat my daughter would like, while I fetch the medicine?"

Mike didn't have to be asked twice. He'd been holding a tin of canned peaches, which he promptly set on the shelf, and then he hurried over to Kelly.

"How are you?" he asked. "Sure hope you're not gettin' sick too."

"Nope. I'm healthy as a mule."

"Glad to hear it, but I'm sorry about your dad. Is he able to keep on working?"

"He made it through the day, even with his fits of coughing and fever. I think he's plannin' to tie up here and spend the night. We'll stay all day Sunday, so he can rest." Kelly's gaze went to her mother, who was at the back of the store. "Mama doesn't have all her strength back yet either, so a good day's rest should do 'em both some good."

And you, Kelly, Mike thought as he studied her face. There were dark circles under her eyes, which gave evidence to the fact that she too was tired and probably needed a break.

"The last time your dad was in the store, I told him I'd be glad to stable your mules in my barn anytime he wanted to dock here for the night."

"That's right nice of you." Kelly gazed at the candy counter with a look of longing on her face.

Mike wondered how long it had been since she had eaten any candy. Without hesitation, he opened the hinged lid on the glass case. "Help yourself to whatever you like—my treat."

Kelly stiffened. "Oh, no. I couldn't let you do that. Thanks to you sellin' a couple of my charcoal drawings, I've got money of my own now." She shrugged. "Although, it's safely hidden in my room on the boat, and I'd have to go back and get it."

"Wouldn't you rather spend it on something more useful than candy?"

She pursed her lips. "Probably should be savin' my money, but I've sure got a hankerin' for some lemon drops."

Mike reached down and grabbed the glass jar filled with sugar-coated lemon drops. "Take as many as you like, and please consider it a present from me to you."

Kelly tipped her head to one side, and he knew she was contemplating his offer. Finally with a nervous giggle, she agreed.

He filled a small paper bag half full of candy and handed it to her, hoping she wouldn't change her mind.

She took the sack and stuffed it in her apron pocket. "Thank you."

"You're welcome."

Kelly shuffled her feet, and her boots scraped nosily against the wooden planks. Why did she seem so nervous? Was it because her mother was nearby and might be listening in on their conversation?

Hoping to put her at ease, Mike reached out and touched Kelly's arm. She recoiled like she'd been bitten by a snake, and he quickly withdrew his hand.

"Sorry, I didn't mean to startle you."

Kelly's only reply was a slight shrug of her shoulders. What was wrong? They'd had such a pleasant visit the last time she'd come by the store.

"Did you bring me any more drawings?" Mike asked, hoping the change of subject might ease the tension he felt filling up the space between them.

She shook her head. "I'm out of charcoal, and for the last couple days Papa's been burnin' coal instead of wood in our cook stove. I haven't come across any cold campfires along the canal lately neither."

So that was the problem. Kelly was feeling bad because she hadn't been able to draw, and she'd promised Mike she would have more pictures the next time she came by.

Mike had a brand new set of sketching pencils for sale, along with some tubes of oil paints. He would have gladly given them to her but was sure she would say no. It had taken some persuasion to get her to take a few lemon drops, and they weren't worth half as much as the art supplies. Since Kelly did have some money of her own, she could probably purchase a box of pencils, but she might be saving up for something more important.

Suddenly, Mike had an idea. "I've got some burned charcoal chips in my home fireplace at the back of the store," he announced. "How 'bout I run in there and get them for you?"

Kelly hesitated a moment but finally nodded. "That would be right nice."

Before she had a chance to change her mind, Mike hurried

to the back of the store. He passed Kelly's mother on his way to the door leading to his attached house.

"I'll be right back, Mrs. McGregor. Take your time looking around for anything you might need."

&

Kelly watched Mike's retreating form as he disappeared behind the door at the back of his store. He seemed like such a caring young man. Probably would make someone a mighty fine husband. Maybe he and the preacher's daughter would link up. Betsy had seemed pretty friendly to him the last time Kelly saw the two of them together.

She frowned. Why did the idea of Mike and Betsy Nelson together make her feel so squeamish? She reached into the sack inside her pocket and withdrew a lemon drop, then popped the piece of candy into her mouth.

"We'll head on back to the boat as soon as the storekeeper returns and I pay for the cough syrup and a few other things I found," Mama said, driving Kelly's thoughts to the back of her mind.

Kelly's response was a slow nod of her head.

"Mike Cooper seems like a nice young man," Mama remarked.

Kelly nodded again. "He offered to let us stable Herman and Hector in his barn for the night."

Mama's dark eyebrows lifted. "For free?"

"I think so. He never said a word about money."

"Hmm. . .guess as soon as we leave the store, you should get the mules fed and ready to bed down then."

"I'd be happy to," Kelly readily agreed. "I'm sure Hector and Herman will be right glad to have a bigger place to stay tonight than they have on board our boat."

"You're probably right." Mama smiled. "Say, I was thinkin'—since tomorrow's Sunday, and we won't be movin' on 'til early Monday morning, why don't the two of us head into town and go to church?"

Kelly opened her mouth to respond, but Mama rushed on.

"It's been a good while since I've sat inside a real church and worshiped God with other Christian folks."

"Well, I. . .uh. . ." Kelly swallowed against the urge to say what was really on her mind. Being in church would make her feel uncomfortable—like others were looking down their noses at the poor boatman's daughter who wore men's boots and smelled like a dirty mule. Kelly had seen the way Betsy Nelson turned her nose up whenever the two of them met along the towpath. She wasn't good enough to sit inside a pretty church building; it was just that simple.

"I'm waitin' for your answer," Mama said, giving Kelly's shoulder a gentle tap.

"I was kinda hoping to get rested up tomorrow. Maybe do a bit of drawin'."

Mama's squinted eyes and furrowed brow revealed her obvious concern. "You ain't feelin' poorly too, I hope."

Kelly shook her head. "Just tired is all."

"And well you should be," Mama agreed. "The last few days, you and your dad have been workin' real hard trying to do all my chores plus keeping up with your own jobs as well." She gave Kelly a hug. "I think you're right. It might be good for us all to spend the day restin'."

Kelly felt bad about not being willing to attend church with her mother. She could tell by Mama's wistful expression that she really did miss Sunday services inside a church building. Reading the Bible every night after supper was a good thing, but it wasn't the same as being in fellowship with other believers.

She and her mother moved away from the candy counter and went to wait for Mike by the wooden counter where customers paid for their purchases.

A few seconds later, Mike entered the store, carrying a large paper sack. He handed it to Kelly and grinned. "This should get you by for awhile."

She peered inside the bag. Several large clumps of charcoal, as well as some smaller ones, completely filled it. Mike was right. These would last a good while, and tonight she planned to start putting them to use. "Thanks," she murmured.

He winked at her. "You're more than welcome."

Kelly cleared her throat, feeling kind of warm and jittery inside. Maybe she was coming down with whatever had been ailing her folks. A day of rest might do her more good than she realized.

ten

Sunday morning dawned with a blue, cloudless sky. It would be the perfect day for Kelly to enjoy the warm sun and draw. She hurried through her breakfast and morning chores, anxious for some time alone. Mama would be tending to Papa's needs for the next little while, and after that, she would probably take a rest herself.

Papa had taken to his bed last night and not even shown his face at the breakfast table. Kelly figured he must be pretty sick if he wasn't interested in food, for her dad usually had a ravenous appetite. She had taken him a tray with a cup of tea and bowl of oatmeal a little while ago, but Papa turned his nose up at both and said he wanted to be left alone—needed some sleep, that was all.

It seemed strange for Kelly to see her dad, who was usually up early and raring to go, curled up in a fetal position with a patchwork quilt pulled up to his ears. His breathing sounded labored, and he wheezed and coughed like the steam train that ran beside the canal, despite the medicine Mama had been spoon-feeding him since their visit to Mike's store last evening.

Thinking about Mike Cooper made Kelly remember their mules had been sleeping in his barn all night. She needed to feed and groom the animals, then take them outdoors for some fresh air and exercise. Wouldn't do for the mules to get lazy because they'd stopped for a bit. As soon as she was finished tending the critters, Kelly hoped to finally have some free time.

As she headed for the barn, which sat directly behind Mike's house, Kelly hummed her favorite song—"Hunks-a-go Pudding." Would Mama feel up to fixing a big meal today? Would it include a roast with some yummy hunks-a-go pudding? Kelly sure hoped so. It had been a good long while since she'd enjoyed the succulent taste of roast with beef and hunks-a-go pudding, where the batter was put in the fat left over from the meat and then fried in a pan on top of the stove.

Forcing thoughts of food to the back of her mind, Kelly opened the barn door and peered inside. Except for the gentle braying of the mules, all was quiet. The sweet smell of hay wafted up to her nose, and she sniffed deeply. She stepped inside and was almost to the stall where Hector and Herman were stabled when she heard another sound. Someone was singing.

"Sweet hour of prayer, sweet hour of prayer, that calls me from a world of care."

Kelly plodded across the dirt floor, and the sound of the clear, masculine voice grew closer. She recognized it as belonging to Mike Cooper.

"And bids me at my Father's throne, make all my wants and wishes known."

Kelly halted, feeling like an intruder on Mike's quiet time alone with God. He must be deeply religious, for not only was he kindhearted, but he sang praises to God. Whenever Kelly sang, it was some silly canaler's song like "Hunks-a-go Pudding" or "You Rusty Canaler, You'll Never Get Rich." As a young child she would often sing "Jesus Loves Me," but she'd been a lot happier back then. Sarah was still living with them, helping share the burden of walking the mules and visiting with Kelly for hours on end. Papa expected twice as much from Kelly now that Sarah was gone. But was that any excuse to quit worshiping the Lord in song?

Kelly knew the answer deep in her soul. She was angry with God for not changing Papa's heart. She was angry with Papa for being so stubborn and hot-tempered and angry with Sarah for running off and leaving her to face Papa's temper while she did all the work.

I'll show them. I'll show everyone that Kelly McGregor doesn't need anyone to get along in this world. I'm gonna make it on my own someday.

When Mike's song ended, Kelly moved forward again. She could see him sitting on a small wooden stool, milking a fat brown-and-white cow.

She cleared her throat real loud to make her presence known and stepped into the stall where Herman and Hector had bedded down for the night.

"Good morning," Mike called to her.

" Mornin'," she responded.

"Looks like it's gonna be a beautiful day."

"Yep. Right nice."

"What plans have you made for this Lord's Day?" he asked.

Kelly patted Herman's flank and leaned into the sturdy mule. "As soon as I get these two ready, I plan to take 'em outside for some exercise and fresh air."

Mike didn't say anything in reply, and Kelly could hear the steady *plunk, plink, plunk,* as the cow's milk dropped into the bucket. It was a soothing sound, and she found herself wishing she had a real, honest-to-goodness home with a barn, chicken coop, and maybe a bit of land. For nine months out of the year, her home was the inside of a canal boat, and then during the winter, it was a cramped, dingy flat at a boardinghouse in Easton. Papa seemed to like their vagabond life, but Kelly hated it—more and more the older she got. Someday she hoped to leave it all behind. Oh, for the chance to fulfill her dreams.

❧

Mike grabbed the bucket of milk and headed for the stall where Kelly's mules had been stabled. He was finally being given the chance to spend a few minutes alone with Kelly, and he aimed to take full advantage. If things went as he hoped, he would have the pleasure of her company for several hours today.

Mike leaned against the wooden beam outside the mules' stall and watched Kelly as she fed and groomed her beasts of burden. She wasn't wearing her usual straw hat this morning, and her lustrous brown hair hung down her back in long, loose waves. His fingers itched to reach out and touch those silky tresses.

"You're good with the mules," he murmured.

Kelly jumped, apparently startled and unaware that he'd been watching her. "Hector and Herman are easy to work with."

Mike drew in a deep breath. *May as well get this over with.* "I. . .uh. . .was wondering if you'd like to go on a picnic with me later today."

Kelly turned her head to look directly at him, and she blinked a couple of times. "A picnic? You and me?"

He nodded, then chuckled. "That's what I had in mind."

"Well, I was plannin' to spend some time drawin', and—"

"No reason you can't draw after we share our picnic lunch."

She hesitated a few seconds. "Mama may need my help with somethin', and my folks might not approve of me goin' on a picnic."

Mike smiled. At least she hadn't said no. He took that as a good sign. "While you finish up with the mules, how about I go talk to your parents?"

Kelly's forehead wrinkled. "I don't know if that's such a good idea."

"If they say it's all right, would you be willing to eat a picnic lunch with me?"

She nodded, but made no verbal reply. It was enough affirmation for Mike, and he grinned at her. "Great! I'll take this milk into the house, get cleaned up a bit, and run down to the boat to speak with your folks."

"Papa's still in bed," Kelly said. "He ain't feelin' much better today than he was last night."

"Sorry to hear it. I'll ask your mother." Mike hurried out of the barn before Kelly had a chance to say anything more, and he hummed "Sweet Hour of Prayer" all the way. God was already answering his prayer for the day, and he felt like he was ten feet tall.

❧

Kelly couldn't believe her mother had actually given permission for Mike Cooper to take her on a picnic. Maybe she felt bad because Kelly worked so hard and rarely got a day off. Or it might be that Mama needed some quiet time by herself today, so she thought it would be good if Kelly were gone awhile.

The idea of a picnic did seem kind of nice. It would be a chance for Kelly to relax and enjoy Mike's company, as well as the good food he'd promised to prepare. On the other hand, spending time alone with the fine-looking storekeeper might not be such a good thing. What if he got the notion she was interested in him? Would Mike expect her to do more things with him when she was in the area? In some ways, she hoped they could. Life along the canal was lonely, especially for Kelly, whose only companions were a pair of mules.

Kelly stood in her tiny room below the boat's main deck and studied her reflection in the mirror that she kept in the trunk at the foot of her bed. Did she look presentable enough to accompany Mike Cooper on a picnic? Mike always smelled so clean, and he wore crisp trousers and shirts without holes or wrinkles. It was hard to believe he had no mother or wife caring for his needs. He must be very capable, she decided.

Mike had said he would meet Kelly out in front of his store, a little before noon. This gave her plenty of time to get ready, and she'd even taken a bath in the galvanized tub and washed her hair, using that new floating soap Mama liked so well.

Kelly grabbed a lock of hair, swung it over her shoulder, and sniffed deeply. "Smells clean enough to me." She glanced down at her dark green skirt and long-sleeved white blouse with puffy sleeves. Both were plain and unfashionable, but Kelly didn't care a hoot about fashion, only comfort and looking presentable enough to be seen in public. Her clothes were clean; Mama had washed them yesterday. At least today she wasn't likely to offend Mike by smelling like one of her mules.

Kelly took out her drawing tablet and a piece of charcoal and stuffed them in her oversized skirt pocket. Then she grabbed her straw hat and one of Mama's old quilts. At least they would have something soft to sit on during their picnic lunch. She left the room and tiptoed quietly past her parents' bedroom. It wouldn't be good to wake Papa. He'd probably be furious if he knew she was taking the day off to go on a picnic—especially with a man. If Papa got wind of her spending time with Mike Cooper, he might think she was going to up and run off, the way Sarah had. Well, that would never happen!

As Kelly stepped off the boat, she caught a glimpse of Reverend Nelson and his daughter, Betsy. They were standing in front of Mike's store, and several boatmen and their families had gathered around.

It made no sense to Kelly. Shouldn't the preacher have been at his church, pounding the wooden pulpit and shouting at the congregation to repent and turn from their wicked ways? Instead, he was leading the group of people in song, and his daughter was playing along with her zither.

Kelly hoped to avoid the throng entirely, but Mike, who stood on the fringes, motioned her to join him. He was holding a wicker basket, and Kelly figured he was probably ready to head out on their picnic. If she hung back until the church service was over, it would mean they would lose some of their time together. If she joined Mike, he might say he was ready to go now.

Mike crooked his finger at Kelly again, and she inched her way forward. *Guess I may as well see what he's plannin' to do.*

eleven

Mike smiled at Kelly when she stepped up beside him.

"What's goin' on?" she whispered.

"Reverend Nelson finished his worship service early today, so he and Betsy decided to bring a bit of revival to the boatmen and their families who stayed in the area for the night."

"Do you attend their church in town?" Kelly asked.

Mike shrugged his shoulders. "Sometimes." The truth was, he used to go every Sunday, but here of late he'd been feeling mighty uncomfortable around Betsy Nelson. He'd stayed home the last couple weeks, praying and reading his Bible in solitude. He knew he shouldn't be using Betsy's overbearing, flirtatious ways as an excuse to stay away from church, but it was getting harder to deal with his troubling emotions where she was concerned. Especially since Kelly McGregor had come into his life.

He stared down at her, small and delicate, yet strong and reliable. Where did Kelly stand as far as spiritual things were concerned? He needed to find out soon, before he lost his heart to the beautiful young woman.

"Ready to head out on our picnic?" Kelly questioned.

Now was as good a time as any to see how interested she was in church.

"I thought maybe we'd stick around until Rev. Nelson is done preaching," Mike said. "It's been awhile since I've heard a good sermon." He studied Kelly's face to gauge her reaction. She looked a bit hesitant, but agreeably she nodded. He breathed a sigh of relief.

"Should we take a seat on the grass?" he asked, motioning to a spot a few feet away.

She followed him there and spread out the quilt she'd been holding so tightly.

Mike set the picnic basket down, and they both took a seat on the blanket. Leaning back on his elbows, Mike joined the group singing "Amazing Grace." His spirits soared as the music washed over him like gentle waves lapping against the shore. He loved to sing praises to God, and when the mood hit, he enjoyed blowing on the old mouth harp that had belonged to Grandpa Cooper.

He glanced over at Kelly. She wasn't singing, but her eyes were closed, and her face was lifted toward the sun. *She must be praying. That's a good indication that she knows the Lord personally.*

He smiled to himself. The day had started out even better than he'd expected.

❧

Kelly opened her eyes and looked around. A couple dozen people were seated on the ground. Some were singing, some lifted their hands in praise, and others quietly listened. She couldn't believe she'd let Mike talk her into staying around for this outdoor church service. It was a beautiful spring day, and she wanted to be away from the crowd, where she could listen to the sounds of nature and draw to her heart's content. When she'd agreed to accompany Mike on a picnic, the plan hadn't included church.

Kelly knew her attitude was wrong. She'd asked Jesus to forgive her sins several years ago. She should take pleasure in worshiping God. Besides, out here among the other boatmen and their families, Kelly didn't stick out like a sore thumb. Nobody but the preacher and his daughter were dressed in fine clothes, so Kelly blended right in with her unfashionable long cotton skirt and plain white blouse.

The singing was over now, and the Reverend had begun to preach. Kelly's gaze wandered until she noticed a young boy who sat several feet away. He had bright red hair, and his face and arms were covered with freckles. The child's looks weren't what captured Kelly's attention, though. It was the small green toad he was holding in his grubby hands. He stroked the critter's head as though it were a pet.

He's probably poor and doesn't own many toys. If his papa's a boatman, they travel up and down the canal most of the year, so the little guy can't have any real pets.

Kelly knew that wasn't entirely true. Many canalers owned dogs that either walked along the towpath or rode in the boat. She figured the little red-haired boy's dad was probably too cranky or too stingy to let his son own a dog or a cat. *Kind of like my dad. He'd never allow me to have a pet.*

Kelly's thoughts were halted as Preacher Nelson shouted, "God wants you to turn from your sins and repent!"

She sat up a little straighter and tried to look attentive when she noticed Mike look over at her. Had he caught her daydreaming? Did he think she was a sinner who needed to repent?

After the pastor's final prayer, he announced, "My daughter, Betsy, will now close our service with a solo."

Betsy stood up and began to strum her zither as she belted out the first verse of "Sweet By and By." As the young woman came to the last note, her voice cracked, and her faced turned redder than a radish.

Kelly stifled a chuckle behind her hand. *Serves the snooty woman right for thinkin' she's better'n me.*

"He that is without sin among you, let him cast a stone at her." Kelly gulped as she remembered that verse of Scripture from the Book of John. Mama had quoted it many times over the years.

The preacher's daughter might be uppity and kind of pushy at times, but truth be told, Kelly knew she was no better in God's eyes. Fact of the matter, Kelly felt that she was probably worse, for she often harbored resentment in her heart toward Papa. She resolved to try to do better.

When the service was over, Mike stood and grabbed their picnic basket. Kelly gathered up her quilt and tucked it under one arm. She'd thought they would head right off for their picnic, but Mike moved toward Preacher Nelson. Not knowing what else to do, Kelly followed.

"That was a fine sermon you preached," Mike said, shaking Reverend Nelson's hand.

The older man beamed. "Thank you, Mike. I'm glad you enjoyed it."

Betsy, who stood next to her father, smiled at Mike and fluttered her eyelashes. "How about the singing? Did you enjoy that too?"

Mike nodded. It was downright sickening the way Betsy kept eyeing him, as though she wanted to kiss the man, of all things.

Kelly nudged Mike in the ribs with her elbow. "Are we goin' on that picnic or not?"

"Yes. . .yes, of course," he stammered.

Why was Mike acting so nervous all of a sudden? Did being around Betsy Nelson do this to him? Kelly opened her mouth to say something, but Betsy cut her right off.

"You're going on a picnic, Mike?" Her eyelids fluttered again. "It's such a beautiful day, and I haven't been on a picnic since early last fall. Would you mind if I tag along?"

"Well, uh. . ." Mike turned to Kelly, as though he expected her to say something.

When she made no response, Betsy said, "You wouldn't mind if I joined you and Mike, would you, Kelly?"

Kelly's irritation flared up like fireflies buzzing on a muggy summer day. She didn't want to make an issue, so she merely shrugged her shoulders and made circles in the dirt with the toe of her boot.

"Great! It's all settled then." Betsy grinned like an eager child. "Have you got enough food for three, Mike?"

"Sure, I made plenty of fried chicken and biscuits."

Betsy turned to her father then. "I won't be gone long, Papa."

He smiled. "You go on with the young people and have yourself a good time. I want to visit with several folks, and if I'm fortunate enough to be invited to join one of the families for a meal, I probably won't be home until evening."

"Everything is perfect then. I'll see you at home later on." Betsy handed her father the zither and slipped her hand through the crook of Mike's arm. "So, where should we have this picnic?"

"Guess we'll look for a nice spot up the canal a bit." When Mike looked at Kelly, she noticed his face was a deep shade of red. Was he wondering why he'd invited her on a picnic? Did he wish he could spend time alone with Betsy Nelson? Should Kelly make up some excuse as to why she couldn't go? Maybe it would be best if she went off by herself for the day.

She had made up her mind to do just that, when Mike pulled away from Betsy and grabbed hold of Kelly's hand. "Let's be off," he announced. "I'm hungry as a bear!"

twelve

Kelly, Mike, and Betsy sat in silence on the quilt. The picnic basket was empty now, and everyone admitted to being full. There had been plenty of food to go around.

Kelly leaned back on her elbows, soaking up the sun's warming rays and listening to the canal waters lapping against the bank. She felt relaxed and content and had almost forgotten her irritation over the preacher's daughter joining their picnic.

Seeing a couple of ducks on the water reminded Kelly that she'd brought along her drawing tablet and a piece of charcoal. She sat up and withdrew both from her skirt pocket and then quickly began to sketch. A flash of green on the mallard's head made her once again wish she could work with colored paints. Folks might be apt to buy a picture with color, as it looked more like the real thing.

"In another month or so the canal will be filled with swimmers," Betsy said, her high-pitched voice cutting into the serenely quiet moment.

"You're right about that," Mike agreed. "It scares me the way some youngsters swim so close to the canal boats. It's a wonder one of them doesn't get killed."

"I hear there's plenty of accidents on the canal," Betsy put in.

"Kelly could probably tell us a lot of stories in that regard," Mike said.

Kelly's mind took her back to a couple years ago, when she'd witnessed one of the lock tender's children fall between a boat and the lock. The little boy had been killed instantly— crushed to death. It was a pitiful sight to see the child's mother weeping and wailing for all she was worth.

Kelly had seen a few small children fall overboard and drown. Most folks who had little ones kept them tied to a rope so that wouldn't happen, but some who'd been careless paid the price with the loss of a child.

"Yep," Kelly murmured, "there's been quite a few deaths on the Lehigh Navigation System."

Mike groaned. "I was afraid of the water when I was a boy, so I never learned to swim as well as I probably should have. That means I don't often go in the canal except to wade or do a couple of dives off the locks now and then."

"If you can't swim too good, aren't you afraid to dive?" Kelly asked.

He shrugged his shoulders. "I can manage to kick my way to the surface of the water, then paddle like a dog back to the lock."

"Hmm. . .I see."

"What about you?" Betsy asked, looking directly at Kelly. "As dirty as you get trudging up and down the dusty towpath, I imagine you must jump into the canal quite frequently in order to get cleaned off."

Kelly sniffed deeply, feeling a sudden need to defend herself. "I learned to swim when I was a little girl, so I have no fear of drowning." *Just scared to death of water snakes,* her inner voice reminded. She saw no need to reveal her reservations about swimming in the canal, however. No use giving the preacher's daughter one more thing to look down her nose about.

Mike shifted on the quilt and leaned closer to Kelly. She could feel his warm breath against her neck and found it to be a distraction.

"That's a nice picture you're making," Mike whispered. "Is the charcoal I gave you working out okay?"

"It's fine," she answered as she kept on drawing.

"Maybe you can get a few pictures done today so I can take them back to the store and try to sell them."

She nodded. "Maybe so."

"How about you and me going for a walk, Mike?" Betsy asked, cutting into their conversation.

Mike moved away from Kelly, and she felt a keen sense of

disappointment, which made no sense, since she wasn't the least bit interested in the storekeeper. She'd already decided Betsy Nelson would make a better match for Mike than someone like herself.

"Kelly, would you like to walk with me and Betsy?" Mike asked.

She shook her head. "I'd rather stay here with my tablet and charcoal. You two go ahead. I'll be fine."

Betsy stood up and held her hand out to Mike. "I'm ready if you are."

He made a grunting sound as he clambered to his feet. "We'll be back soon, Kelly."

Keeping her focus on the ducks swimming directly in front of her, Kelly mumbled, "Sure, okay."

❧

Mike wasn't the least bit happy about leaving Kelly alone while he and Betsy went for a walk. This was supposed to be his and Kelly's picnic—a chance for them to get better acquainted. It should have been Kelly he was walking with, not the preacher's daughter.

Betsy clung to his arm like they were a courting couple, and she chattered a mile a minute. If only he could figure out some way to discourage her without being rude. Mike didn't want to hurt Betsy's feelings, but he didn't want to lead her on either.

"Maybe we should head back," he said, when Betsy stopped talking long enough for him to get in a word.

She squeezed his arm a little tighter and kept on walking. "Why would you want to head back? It's a beautiful day, and the fresh air and exercise will do us both some good."

Mike opened his mouth to reply, but she cut him right off.

"I missed seeing you in church this morning."

He cleared his throat a few times, feeling like a little boy who was about to be reprimanded for being naughty. "Well, I—"

"Papa says we need young men like yourself as active members in the church," Betsy said, chopping him off again.

Mike shrugged as a feeling of guilt slid over him. He knew

what the Bible said about men being the spiritual leaders. He also was aware that he needed to take a more active part in evangelizing the world. Maybe he would speak to Reverend Nelson about holding regular church services along the canal. Mike could donate some of his Bibles for people who didn't have one of their own. As far as attending the Nelsons' church, Mike wasn't sure that was such a good idea. It would mean spending more time with Betsy. It wasn't that he disliked the woman, but her chattering and pushiness got on his nerves.

"Mike, are you listening to me?"

He pushed his thoughts aside and focused on the woman who was tugging on his shirtsleeve. "What were you saying?"

"I was talking about mission work," Betsy replied in an exasperated tone. "I said we have a mission opportunity right here along the canal."

He nodded. "I agree. In fact, I was just thinking that if your father wanted to hold regular Sunday services out in front of my store, I'd be happy to furnish folks with Bibles."

Betsy's thin lips curled into a smile. "That sounds like a wonderful idea. I'll speak to Papa about it this evening."

Mike was amazed at Betsy's exuberance. She either shared his desire to tell others about Jesus or was merely looking forward to spending more time with him.

He grimaced. *I shouldn't be thinking the worst.* Mike knew he was going to have to work on his attitude. Especially where the preacher's daughter was concerned. She did have some good points, but she wasn't the kind of woman Mike was looking for.

A vision of Kelly flashed into his mind. Dark eyes that bore right through him; long dark hair cascading down her back; a smile that could light up any room. But it was more than Kelly's good looks and winning smile that had captured Mike's attention. There was a tenderness and vulnerability about Kelly McGregor that drew Mike to her like a thirsty horse heads for water. Sometimes she seemed like an innocent child needing to be rescued from something that was causing her pain. Other times Kelly appeared confident and self-assured. She was like a jigsaw puzzle, and he wanted to put all the complicated pieces of her together.

"Mike, you're not listening to me again."

He turned his head in Betsy's direction. "What were you saying?"

"I was wondering if you would like to come over for supper one night next week."

He groped for words that wouldn't be a lie. "I. . .uh. . .am expecting a shipment of goods soon, and I need to clean off some shelves and get the place organized before the load arrives."

Betsy's lower lip jutted out. "Surely you won't be working every evening."

Mike nodded. "I could be."

Her eyebrows drew together, nearly meeting at the middle. "I was hoping to tempt you with my chicken and dumplings. Papa says they're the best he's ever tasted."

"I'm sure they are." Mike gave Betsy's arm a gentle pat. "Maybe some other time."

"I hope so," she replied.

Should I be frank and tell her I'm not interested in pursuing a personal relationship? Mike stopped walking and swung around, taking Betsy with him, since she still held onto his arm. "We'd better head back now."

"Why so soon?"

"We left Kelly alone, and I don't feel right about that."

"I'm sure she's fine. She's not a little girl, you know."

Mike knew all right. Every time Kelly smiled at him or tipped her head to one side as she spoke his name, he was fully aware that she was a desirable young woman, not the child who used to drop by his store with her parents. He was anxious to get back to their picnic spot and see what Kelly had drawn.

"Mike, please slow down. I can barely keep up with you," Betsy panted.

"Sorry, but I invited Kelly to join me for a picnic today, and she probably thinks I've abandoned her."

Betsy moaned. "I didn't realize you two were courting.

Why didn't you say so? If I'd known, I certainly would not have intruded on your time together."

Mike's ears were burning, and he knew they had probably turned bright red, the way they always did whenever he felt nervous or got flustered about something.

"Kelly and I are not officially courting," he mumbled. *Though I sure wish we were.*

Betsy opened her mouth as if to say something, but he spoke first.

"Even though we're not courting, I did invite her on a picnic. So, it's only right that I spend some time with her, don't you think?"

Betsy let out a deep sigh, but she nodded her head. "Far be it from me to keep you from your Christian duty."

"Thanks for understanding." Mike hurried up the towpath, with Betsy still clutching his arm. Soon Kelly came into view, and Mike halted his footsteps at the sight before him. Stretched out on the quilt, her dark hair fanned out like a pillow, Kelly had fallen asleep. The sketching tablet was in one hand, and a chunk of charcoal was in the other. She looked like an angel. Would she be his angel someday?

thirteen

The following day, Mike was surprised when Kelly's dad entered his store shortly after he'd opened for business.

"Mr. McGregor, how are you feeling this morning?" Mike asked.

"I'll live," came the curt reply.

"I hope the days you spent docked here gave you ample time to rest up and get that cough under control."

Amos coughed and grunted in response. "I'll live, but it looks like we'll be stuck here another day or so, 'cause thanks to you, one of my mules came up lame this mornin'."

Mike frowned. "Really? They both seemed fine yesterday."

"Herman's not fine now. He went and got his leg cut up on a bale of wire you carelessly left layin' around." Kelly's dad leveled Mike with a challenging look.

Feeling a headache coming on, Mike massaged his forehead with his fingertips. "Weren't your mules in their stalls last night?"

"Yeah, in your barn."

"Then I don't understand how one of them could have gotten cut with the wire, which was nowhere near the stalls."

"Guess the door wasn't latched tight and they got out. At least Herman did, for he's the one with the cut leg."

Mike opened his mouth to respond, but Amos rushed on. "You got any liniment for me to put on the poor critter?"

"I'm sure I do." Mike hurried to the area of the store where he kept all the medicinal supplies, and Amos stayed right on his heels. The man seemed grumpier than usual today. Was it because he was so upset about the mule's injury and blamed Mike for the mishap?

Mike had no more than taken the medicine off the shelf,

when Amos snatched it out of his hands. The older man stomped up to the counter and demanded, "How much do I owe ya for this?"

"I normally charge a quarter for that liniment, but since you feel the accident was my fault, there'll be no charge," Mike answered as he moved to the other side of the counter. He knew the McGregors weren't financially well off, and now that they couldn't travel because of a lame mule, they would be set back even further.

Amos slapped a quarter down. "I won't be beholdin' to no man, so I'll pay ya what the stuff is worth." He grimaced. "I'm losin' money with each passing day. First I got slowed down when Dorrie was sick and I was tryin' to cook, clean, and steer the boat. Then I came down with the bug and was laid up for a couple of days. Now I've got me a lame mule, and it should never have happened!"

"I'm sorry for your inconvenience, Mr. McGregor," Mike said apologetically.

"Yeah, well, at the rate things are goin', it'll be the end of the week before I can get back up to Mauch Chunk for another load of coal."

"Could you go on ahead with just one mule? I'd be happy to stable Herman until you come back this way."

Amos scowled at Mike. "Hector might be strong enough to pull the boat when it's empty, but not with a load of coal. Don'tcha know anything, Boy?"

Mike clenched his teeth. Even though he didn't know everything about canal boating, he wasn't stupid. Should he defend himself to Kelly's dad or ignore the discourteous remark? After a few seconds deliberation, Mike opted for the second choice. "I hope your mule's leg heals quickly, Mr. McGregor, and I'm sorry about the wire. If you need anything else, please don't hesitate to ask."

Amos coughed, blew his nose on the hanky he'd withdrawn from the pocket of his overalls, and sauntered out the door, slamming it behind him.

Mike sank to the wooden stool behind the counter and shook his head. At least one good thing would come from the McGregors being waylaid another day or two. It would give him a chance to see Kelly again. Yesterday's picnic had been a big disappointment to Mike. First Betsy invited herself to join them, and then she'd hung on him most of the day. Kelly had fallen asleep while she was waiting for him and Betsy to return from their walk. He'd wakened her when they got back to the picnic site, but Kelly seemed distant after that and said she needed to head for the boat. Mike offered to walk with her, but she handed him her finished picture of two ducks on the water and said she could find her own way. She'd even insisted that Mike see the preacher's daughter safely home.

Mike reached up to scratch the back of his head. He had to let Kelly know he wasn't interested in Betsy. It was Kelly he cared about, and he wanted her to realize that. He just had to figure out how to go about revealing his true feelings without scaring her off.

❧

Kelly couldn't believe they were stranded in front of Mike's store yet another day, possibly more. And as she followed Papa's curt instructions to get off the boat and put some medicine on Herman's leg, she shook her head over Papa's refusal to let the mules be stabled in Mike's barn any longer. It wasn't Mike's fault Herman had broken free from his stall and cut his leg on a roll of wire that had been sitting near the barn door. Now Herman and Hector were both tied to a maple tree growing several feet off the towpath, not far from where their boat was docked. Tonight they would be bedded down in the compartment set aside for them in the bow of the boat.

Kelly squatted beside Herman's right front leg and slathered some of the medicine on. "I don't see why I have to do this," she muttered under her breath. "I'd planned to get some drawin' done today, but Papa will probably find more chores for me to do when I return to the boat."

Immediately, Kelly felt a sense of guilt for her selfish

thoughts. She knew her dad still wasn't feeling well, and he had a right to get some rest while they were laid over. Trouble was, she wanted to draw. At the rate she was going, she would never have anything to give Mike to try to sell in his store. She had given him the picture of the ducks she'd drawn during yesterday's picnic, but that was all.

Thinking about the picnic caused an ache in Kelly's soul. She didn't understand why Mike had invited her, then asked Becky Nelson to join them.

Well, not asked, exactly, she reminded herself. If Kelly's memory served her right, it was Betsy who had done the asking. Mike only agreed she could accompany them on the picnic. Might could be that he had no real interest in Betsy at all.

" 'Course I don't care if he does," she murmured.

Herman brayed, and Hector followed suit, as if in answer to her complaints.

When Kelly stood up, Herman nuzzled her arm with his nose. She chuckled and patted his neck. "You should be good as new in a day or so, Herman the Determined. Then we can be on our way again."

On impulse, Kelly reached into her apron pocket and withdrew the drawing pad and piece of charcoal she often carried with her. She flopped onto the ground and began to sketch the two mules as they grazed on the green grass.

Some time later, she stood up. She had drawn two pictures of Herman and Hector, and now she planned to take them over to Mike's.

When she entered the store, Kelly was pleased to see that Mike had no customers, and he seemed genuinely glad to see her.

"I was sorry to hear about Herman's leg," he said, moving toward Kelly. "Your dad thinks it's my fault because there was a roll of wire by the barn door."

She pursed her lips. "Papa always looks for someone to blame. Don't fret about it, 'cause it sure wasn't your doin'. If anyone's to blame, it's Papa. He's the one who fed and watered the mules last night, so he probably didn't see that the door to their stall was shut tight." She frowned. "Of course, he'd never admit it."

Mike grinned at Kelly, and her stomach did a little flip-flop. She licked her lips and took a step forward. "I. . .uh. . .brought you a couple more drawings."

She held the pictures out to Mike, and he took them. "Thanks, these are nice. I'll get them put on display right away."

"Sure wish they had a little color to 'em. Herman and Hector are brown, not black, but my picture don't show it."

"Maybe you could buy a set of watercolors or oil paints," Mike suggested.

She shook her head. "Don't have enough money for that yet." Kelly knew she needed to save all her money if she was ever going to earn enough to be on her own or open an art gallery.

"Have you considered making your own watercolors?"

Her forehead wrinkled. "How could I do that?"

"I noticed some coffee stains on my tablecloth this morning," Mike said. "Funny thing was, they were all a different shade of brown."

"Hmm. . .guess it all depends on the strength of the coffee how dark the stain might be."

He nodded. "Exactly. So, I was thinkin' maybe you could try using old coffee to paint with. I've got some brushes I could let you have."

Kelly considered his offer carefully. It did sound feasible, but she wouldn't feel right about taking the brushes without paying something for them. If Papa had taught her anything, it was not to accept charity.

"How much would the brushes cost?" she asked Mike.

"I just said I'd be happy to give them to you."

She shook her head. "I either pay, or I don't take the brushes."

He shrugged. "I'll let you have three for a nickel. How's that sound?"

She nodded. "It's a deal."

A few minutes later, Kelly was walking out the door with

three small paintbrushes, a jar of cold coffee, and an apple for each mule. Mike had insisted the coffee was a day old and he would only have to throw it out if she didn't accept it. Kelly decided stale coffee didn't have much value, so she agreed to take it off his hands. The apples she paid for.

"Come back tomorrow and let me know how your new watercolors work out," Mike said.

She smiled and called over her shoulder, "I may have more pictures for you in the mornin'."

fourteen

That night, after Kelly went to her room, she worked with the coffee watercolors. It was the first time she'd ever used a paintbrush, and it took awhile to get the hang of it. But once she did, Kelly found it to be thoroughly enjoyable. In fact, she decided to try a little experiment.

In her bare feet, she crept upstairs to the small kitchen area. She knew her folks were both asleep. She could hear Mama's heavy breathing and Papa's deep snoring.

Kelly lifted the lid from the wooden bin where Mama kept a stash of root vegetables. She pulled out a few carrots, two onions, and a large beet. Next, she heated water in the cast-iron kettle on the cook stove. When it reached the boiling point, she placed her vegetables in three separate bowls and poured scalding water over all. One by one Kelly carried the bowls back to her room. She would let them set overnight, and by tomorrow morning she hoped to have colored water in three different shades.

The following day, Herman's leg was no better, and Papa was fit to be tied.

"I'm losin' money just sittin' here," he hollered as he examined the cut on Herman's leg.

Kelly stood by his side, wishing she had some idea what to say.

"Do you know how many boats I've seen goin' up and down the canal?" he bellowed. "Everyone but me is makin' money this week!"

Kelly thought of the little bit of cash she'd made when Mike paid her for those first few drawings. If Papa were really destitute she would have offered to turn the money over to him. That wasn't the case, though. She knew her dad was tightfisted with his money, and truth be told, he probably had more stashed away than Kelly would ever see in her lifetime. Besides, she didn't want Papa to know she had any money of her own. If he found out, he would most likely demand that she give it all to him—and any future money she made as well.

So Kelly quietly listened to her father's tirade. He would soon calm down. He always did.

"Should I check with Mike Cooper and see if he has any other medicine that might work better on Herman's cut?" she asked when Papa finally quit blustering.

His face turned bright red, and his forehead wrinkled. "I ain't givin' that man one more dime to take care of an injury that he caused in the first place. We'll sit tight another day and see how Herman's doin' come morning." Papa turned and stomped off toward the boat.

Kelly reached up to stroke Herman behind his ear. "He's a stubborn one, that Papa of mine," she mumbled. Truth of the matter, Kelly knew they were losing time and money by waiting for the mule's leg to heal, but didn't Papa realize if he spent a little more on medicine, Herman's leg would probably heal faster? Then they could be on their way to Mauch Chunk and be making money that much sooner. Kelly thought her dad was just being mulish, refusing to see if Mike had any other medicine.

Kelly dipped her hand into the deep apron pocket where she kept her drawing tablet. At least one good thing had happened this morning. She'd gotten up early and painted a couple of pictures, using her new homemade watercolors. The first one was another pose of the mules; only now they were coffee-colored, not black. The second picture was of a sunset, with pink, orange, and yellow hues, all because of her vegetable watercolors. She was proud of her accomplishment and could hardly wait to show the pictures to Mike.

"I think I'll head over to his store right now," Kelly said, giving Hector a pat, so he wouldn't feel left out. The mule brayed and nudged her affectionately. Herman and Hector really were her best friends.

A short time later, Kelly entered Mike's store. He was busy waiting on a customer—Mrs. Harris, one of the lock tenders' wives. Kelly waited patiently over by the candy counter. It was tempting to spend some of her money on more lemon drops, but she reminded herself that she still had a few pieces of candy tucked safely away inside the trunk at the foot of her bed. She would wait until those were gone before she considered buying any more.

"Can I help you with something?" Lost in her thoughts, Kelly hadn't realized Mike had finished with his customer and now stood at her side. She drew in a deep breath as the fresh scent of soap reminded her of Mike's presence. He always smelled so clean and unsullied. His nearness sent unwanted tingles along her spine, and she forced herself to keep from trembling.

"I wanted to see what you thought of these." Kelly held out her drawing tablet to Mike.

He studied the first painting of Herman and Hector, done with coffee water. "Hmm. . .not bad. Not bad at all." Then he turned to the next page, and his mouth fell open. "Kelly, how did you make such beautiful colors?"

She giggled, feeling suddenly self-conscious. "I poured boiling water over some carrots, onions, and a beet; then I let it stand all night. This mornin' I had some colored water to paint with."

Mike grinned from ear to ear. "That's really impressive. I'm proud of you, Kelly."

Proud of me? Had she heard Mike right? In all her seventeen years, Kelly didn't remember anyone ever saying they were proud of anything she'd done. She felt the heat of a blush creep up her neck and flood her entire face. "It was nothin' so special."

"Oh, but it was," Mike insisted. "My idea of using coffee water was okay, and your picture of the mules is good, but you took it even further by comin' up with a way to make more colors." He lifted the drawing tablet. "You've captured a sunset beautifully."

She smiled, basking in his praise. If only Mama and Papa would say things to encourage her, the way Mike did. Mama said very little, and Papa either yelled or criticized.

"I think I'll come up with a better way to display your art-work," Mike announced.

"Oh? What's that?"

"I'm going to make a wooden frame for each of your pic-tures, and then I'll hang them right there." He pointed to the wall directly behind the counter where he waited on cus-tomers. "Nobody will leave my store without first seeing your talented creations."

Talented creations? First Mike had said he was proud of her, and now he'd called her talented. It was almost too much for Kelly to accept. Did he really mean those things, or was he only trying to be nice because he felt sorry for her? She hoped it wasn't the latter, for she didn't want anyone's pity.

"Kelly, did you hear what I said?"

She jerked her head toward Mike. "What did ya say?"

"I asked if you thought framing the pictures would be a good idea."

She nodded. "I suppose so. It's worth a try, if you want to go to all that trouble."

"I like workin' with my hands, so it won't be any trouble at all." Mike looked down at the tablet he still held. "Mind if I take the two colored pictures out now?"

"It's fine by me," she replied, feeling a sense of excitement. "If we stay around here another day or so, maybe I can get a few more drawings done."

He smiled and moved toward the counter. Kelly followed. "That would be great. I hope you do stay around a bit longer—for more reasons than one."

❧

Mike felt such exuberance over Kelly's new pictures, done on newsprint, not to mention the news of her staying for another day or so. He'd been asking God to give him the chance to get to know Kelly better, and it looked as if he might get that opportunity. He did feel bad that her father was losing money because of the mule's leg, however. If there was some way he could offer financial assistance, he would, but Mike knew it wouldn't be appreciated. Amos McGregor was a proud man. He'd made that abundantly clear on several occasions.

"Guess I should get goin'," Kelly announced. "Papa left me to tend Herman's leg, and that was some time ago. He'll probably come a-lookin' for me if I don't get back to the boat pretty soon."

Mike carefully removed Kelly's finished pictures and handed her the tablet. "Keep up the good work, and when you get more paintings done, bring them into the store." He chuckled. "If you give me enough, I'll line every wall with your artwork. Then folks won't have any choice but to notice. And if they notice, they're bound to buy."

Kelly snickered, and her face turned crimson. "I like you, Mike Cooper." With that, she turned around and bounded out the door.

Mike flopped down on his wooden stool. "She likes me. Kelly actually said she likes me."

fifteen

It took three days before Herman's leg was well enough so he could walk without limping. Even then, Papa had said at breakfast that they'd be taking it slow and easy. "No use pushin' things," he told Kelly and her mother. "Wouldn't want Herman to reinjure his leg."

As Kelly connected the towline to the mules' harnesses, she felt a sense of sadness wash over her soul. These last few days had been so nice, being in one place all the time, visiting with Mike Cooper whenever she had the chance, and painting pictures. She'd used up all her homemade watercolors and would need to make more soon. Kelly figured as she journeyed up the towpath she might come across some plants, tree bark, or leaves she could steep in hot water to make other colors. It would be an adventure to see how many hues she could come up with.

"You all set?" Papa called from the boat.

Kelly waved in response, her signal that she was ready to go. She'd only taken a few steps when she heard someone holler, "Kelly, hold up a minute, would you?"

She whirled around. Mike Cooper was heading her way, holding something in his hands.

Kelly stopped the mules, but Papa shouted at her to get them going again. She knew she'd better keep on walking or suffer the consequences. "I've gotta go," she announced when Mike caught up to her. "Papa's anxious to head out."

"I'll walk with you a ways," he said.

"What about your store?"

"I haven't opened for the day yet."

Kelly clicked her tongue, and the mules moved forward. Then she turned to face Mike as she moved along. The item he held in his hand was a wooden picture frame, and inside was her sunset watercolor.

"What do you think?" Mike asked as she looked at the piece of artwork.

"You did a fine job makin' that frame."

He laughed. "The frame's nothing compared to the beauty of your picture, but it does show off your work really well, don't you think?"

Kelly nodded but kept on walking. If she stopped, the mules would too.

"When do you think you'll be coming by my store again?" Mike asked.

She shrugged her shoulders. "Can't say for sure. Since Papa lost so much time because of his cough and Herman's leg gettin' cut, he probably won't make any stops that aren't absolutely necessary."

"Guess we could always pray he knocks a few more bars of soap overboard."

Kelly snickered. "With the way things have been goin' these days, Papa would probably expect me to jump in the canal and fetch 'em back out."

Mike reached out and touched Kelly's arm. She felt a jolt with the contact of his fingers and wondered if he had too.

"I'm sorry you have to work so hard, Kelly," he murmured.

She nodded and kept moving forward. "I'm used to it, but someday, when I make enough money of my own, I won't be Papa's slave no more."

"I'm sure he doesn't see you as his slave."

She snorted. "I don't get paid for walkin' the mules. Not one single penny had I ever made 'til you sold my two drawings." She glanced at Mike out of the corner of her eye and noticed his shocked expression.

"That will change," he said with a note of conviction. "By the time you stop at my store again, I'm sure several more of your pictures will be gone."

They were coming to a bend in the canal, and Kelly and the

mules would be tromping across the changing bridge soon. Kelly knew it was time to tell Mike good-bye, although she hated to see him go. She was beginning to see Mike Cooper as a friend.

"Guess I'd better head back and open up the store," Mike said, "but I wanted to ask you something before you crossed to the other side."

"Oh? What's that?"

"I was wondering if you've ever accepted Christ as your personal Savior. You know—asked Him to forgive your sins and come live in your heart?"

"I did that when I was twelve years old," she said as a lump formed in her throat. Why was Mike asking about her relationship to God, and why was she getting all choked up over a simple good-bye? She'd be seeing Mike again; she just didn't know when.

Mike took hold of Kelly's hand and gave it a gentle squeeze. She glanced back at the boat, hoping Papa couldn't see what was going on.

"I'm awful glad to hear you're a believer. See you soon, Kelly," he whispered.

"I hope so," Kelly said; then she hurried on.

&

Mike stood watching Kelly until she and the mules disappeared around the bend. She looked so forlorn when they parted. Was she going to miss him as much as he would miss her? He hoped so. These last few days had been wonderful, with her popping into the store a couple times, and the two of them meeting outside on several occasions. Mike felt as though he were beginning to know Kelly better, and he liked what he'd discovered. Not only was the young woman a talented artist, she was clever. She had figured out how to make her own watercolors, and Mike had a hunch she would probably have come up with even more colors by the time he saw her again.

"Sure hope I've sold some of her artwork by then," he muttered as he turned toward his store. "I can't keep buying them myself, and I wouldn't want Kelly to find out about the two I did pay for."

An image of Kelly lying on the patchwork quilt they'd used at the Sunday picnic flashed across Mike's mind. If Betsy hadn't been there, he might have taken a chance and kissed his sleeping beauty, for he was quickly losing his heart to Kelly McGregor.

a

Kelly had to hold up the mules at the changing bridge, as two other boats passed and their mules went over. While she waited, she decided to take advantage of the time, so she reached into her apron pocket and pulled out her drawing pad and a stick of charcoal. Kelly had just begun to sketch the boat ahead of her when Reverend Nelson and his daughter came walking up the towpath.

"Good morning," the preacher said. "It's a fine day, wouldn't you say?"

Kelly nodded in reply.

"Daddy and I are walking a stretch of the towpath today," Betsy remarked. "We're calling at people's homes who live near the canal, as well as visiting with those we meet along the way." She stuck out her hand and waved a piece of paper in front of Kelly's face. "We are handing these out too. Would you like one?"

"What is it?" Kelly asked.

"It's a verse of Scripture," Rev. Nelson answered before his daughter could respond.

Kelly took the Bible verse with a mumbled thanks, then stuffed it into her apron pocket. She would look at it later.

"What's that you're drawing?" the pastor asked.

"One of the canal boats."

Reverend Nelson glanced at her tablet and smiled. "It's a good likeness."

Kelly shrugged her shoulders. "I've only just begun."

"Betsy has one of your drawings. It's quite well done, considering what you have to work with."

Kelly's mouth dropped open. Betsy had one of her drawings?

But how? A light suddenly dawned. The preacher's daughter must have gone into Mike's store and purchased one of Kelly's pictures. She smiled at Betsy and asked, "Which one did you buy?"

Betsy's pale eyebrows drew together as she frowned. "The picture is of a couple children fishing on the canal, but I didn't buy it."

"You didn't?"

Betsy shook her head. "Mike Cooper gave it to me as a birthday present. A few weeks ago he came over to our house for supper and to help me celebrate. He presented it to me then."

Kelly felt as though someone had punched her in the stomach. If Mike had given one of the drawings away, then he must have bought it himself. Her fingers coiled tightly around the piece of charcoal she still held in her hand. Who had bought the other picture Mike had paid her for? Was it him? He'd led her to believe he'd sold the pictures to some customers who'd come into the store. He hadn't actually said so, but that was the impression she'd gotten from their conversation.

The ground beneath her feet began to rumble, as a steam train lumbered past. Billows of smoke from the burning coal poured into the sky, leaving a dark, sooty trail.

"Guess we'd better be moving on," the preacher said with a wave of his hand.

Kelly only nodded in response. Her heart was hammering in her chest like the *clickety-clack* of the train's wheels against the track.

Just wait until I drop by Mike's store again, she fumed. *I'm gonna give that man a piece of my mind, and that's for certain sure!*

༜

For the rest of the day Kelly fretted about the pictures Mike had supposedly sold. At supper that night she was in a sour mood and didn't feel much like eating, even though Mama had made Irish stew, a favorite with both Kelly and her dad.

"What was that storekeeper doing, walkin' along the towpath

with you this mornin'?" Papa asked, sending Kelly a disgruntled look.

She shrugged and switched her focus to the bowl of stew in front of her. "He was showin' me something he made and plans to sell in his store."

"What did he make?" Mama questioned.

Kelly had hoped neither of her parents would question her further. She didn't want them to know she'd given Mike some of her drawings and paintings to sell in his store. And she sure wasn't about to tell them the storekeeper had been the only person to buy any of her work.

"It was a picture frame," she said, her mind searching for anything she could say to change the subject. She took a bite of stew and smacked her lips. "This is delicious, Mama. Good as always."

Her mother smiled from ear to ear. She was a good cook; there was no denying it. Mama could take a few vegetables and a slab of dried meat and turn it into a nutritious, tasty meal.

"I don't want that storekeeper hangin' around you, Kelly. Is that understood?"

At the sound of her dad's threatening voice, Kelly dropped the spoon, and it landed in her bowl, splashing stew broth all over the oilcloth table covering.

"You don't have to shout, Amos," Mama said in her usual soft-spoken tone.

"I'll shout whenever I feel like it," he shot back, giving Kelly's mother a mind-your-own-business look.

Mama quickly lowered her gaze, but Kelly, feeling braver than usual, spoke her mind. "Mike and I are just friends. I don't see what harm there is in us havin' a conversation once in awhile."

"Humph!" Papa sputtered. "From what I could see, the two of you was havin' more than a little talk."

So he had seen Mike take her hand. Kelly trembled, but she couldn't let her father know how flustered she felt. She was glad Mama hadn't said anything about her and Mike going on a picnic together, for that would surely get Papa riled.

Mama touched Kelly's arm. "I think your dad is concerned that you'll run off with some man, the way Sarah did."

"You needn't worry about that," Kelly was quick to say. "I don't plan on ever gettin' married." *Besides, Mike Cooper's not interested in me. It's Betsy Nelson he's set his cap for.*

"I'm glad to hear that." Papa tapped his knife along the edge of the table. "Just so you know. . . If I catch that store-keeper with his hands on you again, I'll knock his block off. Is that clear enough?"

Kelly nodded, as her eyes filled with tears. She might be mad as all get-out at Mike, but she couldn't stand to think of him getting beat up by her dad. She would have to make sure Mike never touched her when Papa was around. Not that she wanted him to, of course.

She reached into her pocket for a hanky and found the slip of paper Betsy Nelson had given her instead. Holding it in her lap, so Papa couldn't see it, Kelly silently read the verse of Scripture: *"Jesus said, 'If ye forgive men their trespasses, your heavenly Father will also forgive you.'" Matthew 6:14*

Kelly swallowed hard. She knew she needed to forgive Papa for the way he acted toward her. It sure wouldn't be easy, though.

sixteen

On Thursday morning a sack of mail was delivered to Mike's store, brought in by one of the canal boats. This was a weekly occurrence, as Mike's place of business also served as the area's post office.

While sorting through the pile of letters and packages, Mike discovered one addressed to him. He recognized his brother Alvin's handwriting and quickly tore open the envelope.

Mike hadn't heard from either Alvin or John in several months, so he was anxious to see what the letter had to say:

> *Dear Mike,*
>   *John and me are both fine, and our fishing business is doing right well. I wanted to let you know that I've found myself a girlfriend, and we plan to be married in December, when we'll be done fishing for the season.*
>   *Hope things are good for you there at the store.*
>
>

Your brother,
Alvin

Mike was happy for his brother, but he couldn't help feeling a pang of envy. He wanted so much to have a wife and children, and he wasn't any closer to it now than he had been several weeks before, when he'd prayed earnestly for God to send him a wife. He was still hoping Kelly McGregor might be that woman, but so far she'd given him no indication that she was interested in anything beyond friendship. At least he knew she'd had a personal relationship with Christ, even though she had been in a hurry when he'd asked her, so they couldn't really discuss it.

Mike turned and glanced at the wall directly behind the counter. He'd framed all of Kelly's pictures and hung them there. One had sold yesterday, and the man who'd bought it seemed interested in the others. Kelly had talent, there was no doubt about it, but she was also young and probably insecure when it came to men. Maybe she didn't know how to show her feelings. Maybe she was afraid. Mike had noticed how Amos McGregor often yelled at Kelly and his wife. Kelly might think all men were like her dad.

"I'll go slow with Kelly and win her heart over time," Mike murmured as he continued to study her artwork. "And while I'm waiting, I'll try even harder to get some of these pictures sold."

❧

Papa had kept true to his word and taken it slow and easy on the trip to Mauch Chunk. On a normal run they would have been there by Wednesday night, since they'd left from Mike's store, and it was near the halfway point. Instead, they'd spent Wednesday night outside the small town of Parryville.

They arrived in Mauch Chunk on Thursday afternoon, with Herman doing well and his leg in good shape. Then they loaded the boat with coal from the loading chutes, which descended 250 feet to the river. They spent the night in Mauch Chunk, surrounded by hills that were covered with birch, maple, oak, and wild locust trees.

Now it was Friday, and they were heading back toward the town of Easton to deliver their load. They'd be passing Mike's store either this evening or tomorrow morning, depending on how hard Papa pushed Kelly today. Since Herman was doing well, she suspected they would move faster than they had on Wednesday and Thursday.

"Probably won't be stopping at Mike's store this time," Kelly mumbled. "Sure wish we were, though. I need to talk to him about the picture he gave Betsy Nelson."

As the wind whipped against her long skirt, Kelly glanced up at the darkening sky. They were in for a storm, sure as anything. She hoped it would hold off until they stopped for the night. She hated walking the towpath during a rainstorm.

Hector's ears twitched, as though he sensed the impending

danger a torrential downpour could cause—fallen trees, a muddy towpath, rising canal waters. Then there was always the threat of being hit by lightning. Especially with so many trees lining the path. A few years back a young boy leading his dad's mules had been struck by a bolt of lightning and was killed instantly. Such a shame!

Kelly shivered. Just thinking about what was to come made her feel jumpy as a frog. The mules would be harder to handle once the rain started, for she reminded herself that they had no depth perception and hated walking through water, even small puddles. If they came to a stretch of puddles on the path, they would tromp clear around them. There was no fear of the mules jumping into the canal to get cooled off on a hot day either—the way a horse would have done. Kelly's mules liked water for drinking, but that was all.

Forcing her mind off the impending storm, Kelly thought about how glad she was that Papa had chosen mules, not horses, to pull his boats. It was a proven fact that mules, with their brute strength and surefooted agility, were much less skittish and far more reliable than any horse could be. If horses weren't stopped in time, they would keep on pulling until they fell over dead. Mules, if they were overly tired or had fallen sick, would stop in the middle of the path and refuse to budge. A mule ate one-third less food than a horse did as well, making the beast of burden far more economical to own.

By noon the rain began falling. First it arrived in tiny droplets, splattering the end of Kelly's nose. Then the lightning and thunder came, bringing a downpour of chilling rain.

Kelly cupped her hands around her mouth and leaned into the wind. "Are we gonna stop soon?" she hollered to Papa, who stood at the stern of the boat, already dripping wet. He was just getting over a bad cold and shouldn't even be out in this weather.

"Keep movin'!" Papa shouted back to her. "We won't stop unless it gets any worse."

Worse? Kelly didn't see how it could get much worse.

Thunder rumbled across the sky, and black clouds hung so low, she felt as if she could reach out and touch them. "I—I'm cold and wet," she yelled, wondering if he could hear her. The wind was howling fiercely, and she could barely hear herself. Then Kelly's straw hat flew off her head, causing long strands of hair to blow across her face. She ran up ahead, retrieved the hat, and pushed it down on her head, hoping it would stay in place.

Papa leaned over the edge of the boat and tossed a jacket over the side. Kelly lunged forward and barely caught it in time. If it had fallen into the canal, it would have been lost forever, as the murky brown water was swirling and gurgling something awful.

Kelly slipped her arms into the oversized wool jacket and buttoned it up to her neck. It helped some to keep out the wind, but she knew it was only a matter of time until the rain leaked through and soaked her clean to the skin.

On and on Kelly and the mules trudged, through the driving rain, pushing against the wind, tromping in and out of mud puddles, murk, and mire. Several times the mules balked and refused to move forward. Kelly coaxed, pushed, pleaded, and pulled, until she finally got them moving again.

By the time Papa signaled her to stop, Kelly felt like a limp dishrag. She glanced around and realized they were directly in front of Mike's store. Lifting her gaze to the thunderous sky, Kelly prayed, "Thank You, God, for keepin' us safe and for givin' Papa the good sense to stop."

"We're stayin' here for the night," Papa shouted. "Help me get the mules on board the boat."

"Can't they bed down in Mike Cooper's barn tonight?" Kelly asked. "I could care for 'em better there."

"Guess it wouldn't hurt for one night," Papa surprised her by saying.

≥∙

Mike was about to close up his store, figuring no one in their right mind would be out in this terrible weather, when the door flew open, and Kelly practically fell into the room. She looked like a drowned rat. Her hair, wet and tangled, hung in her face. Her clothes were soaked with rainwater, and her boots were covered in mud. Her straw hat, pushed far over her forehead, resembled a hunk of soggy cardboard.

Mike grabbed hold of Kelly as a gust of wind pushed her forward. The door slammed shut with so much force that the broom, lying against one wall, toppled over, while several pieces of paper blew off the counter and sailed to the floor.

"Kelly, what are you doin' here?" he questioned.

"We've stopped for the day because of the storm." She leaned into him, and he had the sudden desire to kiss her. Why was it that every time they were together anymore, Mike wanted to find out what her lips would feel like against his own?

He drew in a deep breath and gently stroked her back. "Are you okay? You look miserable."

She pulled away suddenly. "I'm fine, but we were wonderin' if we could stable the mules in your barn tonight."

He nodded. "Of course. I'll put on my jacket and help you get them settled in."

"I can manage," she said in a brisk tone of voice. She'd been so friendly a few minutes ago. What had happened to make her change?

Mike studied Kelly's face. It was pinched, and there were tears streaming down her face. At least he thought they were tears. They might have been raindrops, he supposed.

"Kelly, what's wrong?" Mike touched her arm, and she recoiled as if some pesky insect had bitten her.

As she moved toward the door, her gaze swung to the pictures on the wall.

"How do you like the way I've got your artwork displayed?" he questioned.

She squinted her eyes at him. "How could you, Mike?"

"How could I what?"

"Buy my drawing and give it to Betsy Nelson for her birthday?"

"Her dad invited me to their house for supper to help her

celebrate. I wanted to take something, and I thought Betsy would like one of your wonderful charcoal drawings."

She continued to stare at him, and Mike felt his face heat up. Why was she looking at him as though he'd done something wrong? He'd paid her for the picture; same as if someone else had bought it.

"And the other drawing?"

"Huh?"

"You gave me money for two drawings and said you'd sold them both."

The heat Mike felt on his face had now spread to his ears. "I. . . that is. . .I bought both of the pictures," he admitted. "One for Betsy's birthday and the other to hang in my living room."

She shook her head slowly. "I figured as much."

"How did you find out about the picture I gave the preacher's daughter?"

"Reverend Nelson told me when I ran into him and Betsy on the towpath the other day." Kelly bit down on her lower lip, like she might be about to cry. "Why did you lead me to believe you'd sold my pictures, Mike?"

"I did sell them," he defended. "I don't see what difference it makes who bought them."

"It makes a lot of difference," Kelly shouted before she turned toward the front door. "I'm not a poor little girl who needs charity from you or anyone else!"

He couldn't let her leave like this. Not without making her understand he wasn't trying to hurt her. Mike grabbed Kelly's arm and turned her around. "Please forgive me. I never meant to upset you, and I really did want those drawings." He pointed to the wall where her other paintings hung. "I sold one of your watercolors this morning to a man who lives in Walnutport."

She squinted her dark eyes at him. "Really?"

"Yes. He was impressed with your work and said he may be back to buy more."

Kelly's eyes were swimming with tears. "I—I can't believe it."

"It's true. Mr. Porter knows talent when he sees it, and so do I." Mike reached for her hand and gave it a gentle squeeze. "Am I forgiven for misleading you?"

She hesitated a moment, then her lips curved up. "Yes."

"Good. Now will you let me help you stable the mules?"

She nodded.

Mike grabbed his jacket off the wall peg by the door. "You lead one mule, and I'll take the other."

A moment later, they stepped into the driving rain, but Mike paid it no mind. All he could think about was spending the next hour or so in the company of Kelly McGregor.

seventeen

During the next half hour, Kelly and Mike got the mules fed and bedded down for the night. Kelly was grateful for his help and the loan of the barn. It meant Herman and Hector had a warm, dry place to rest, without cramped quarters, and no bouncing or swaying from the rough waters caused by the storm.

Truth be told, Kelly dreaded going to her own room. It would be hard to sleep with the boat bobbing all over the place. She'd probably have to tie herself in bed in order to keep from being tossed onto the floor.

"I was wondering if you and your folks would like to stay at my place tonight," Mike said, as he rubbed Herman down with an old towel.

"Your place?"

"My house. I've got plenty of room."

Kelly wondered if Mike had been able to read her mind, or was he smart enough to figure out how difficult it would be to spend the night on a boat riding the waves of a storm?

"I'd have to ask Papa and Mama," she said. "They might agree, but I'm not sure."

"Would you prefer it if I asked them instead?"

"That probably would be best. Papa's usually more open to things if it comes from someone other than me."

Mike hung the towel on a nail and moved toward Kelly, who'd been drying Hector off with another piece of heavy cloth. "I take it you and your dad don't get along."

Kelly lowered her gaze to the wooden floor. "I used to think he liked me well enough, but ever since Sarah left, he's been actin' meaner than ever."

Mike's heart clenched. He hated to see the way Kelly's

shoulders drooped or hear the resignation in her voice. "Are you afraid of him, Kelly?"

She nodded slowly. "Sometimes."

"Has he ever hit you?"

"Not since I was little. Then it was only a swat on the backside." Kelly's eyes filled with tears, and it was all Mike could do to keep from kissing her. "Papa mostly yells, but sometimes he makes me do things I know are wrong."

"Like what?"

She sucked in her lower lip. "The other day there was a bunch of chickens runnin' around near the towpath. He insisted I grab hold of one and give it to Mama to cook for our supper that night."

Mike drew in a deep breath and let it out in a rush. "But that's stealing. Doesn't your dad know taking things that don't belong to you is breaking one of God's commandments?"

"Papa don't care about God. He thinks Mama is plain silly for readin' her Bible every night."

"What do you think would have happened if you'd refused to do what your dad asked?"

"I don't know, but I didn't think I should find out."

Mike could hardly believe Kelly's dad had asked her to do something so wrong, but it was equally hard to understand why she wouldn't stand up to him. If he wasn't physically abusive, then what kind of hold did the man have on her?

"Does your dad refuse your pay if you don't do what he asks?" Mike questioned.

Kelly planted her hands on her hips. "I told you the other day, Papa has never paid me a single penny for leadin' the mules."

Mike reached up to scratch the side of his head. He'd forgotten about their conversation about Kelly's lack of money. That was why she wanted to sell some of her artwork. And it was one more reason Mike had to help make it happen.

"It's all Sarah's fault for runnin' off with one of the lock tender's sons. She made Papa angry and left me with all the work." Kelly balled her fingers into tight fists, and Mike wondered if she might want to punch someone. He took a few steps back, just in case.

Before he had a chance to respond to her tirade, Kelly announced, "I'm afraid men are all the same, and I ain't never gettin' married, that's for certain sure!"

Mike felt like he'd been kicked in the gut. Never marry? Had he heard her right? If Kelly was dead set against marriage, then what hope did he have of winning her hand? About all he could do was try to be her friend, but he sure wished he could figure out some way to prove to her that all men weren't like her dad.

❧

Kelly felt the heat of embarrassment flood her face. What had possessed her to spout off like that in front of Mike? He'd been helping her with the mules and sure didn't deserve such wrath. She knew she should apologize, but the words stuck in her throat like a wad of chewing gum.

She grabbed a hunk of hay and fed it to Hector. Maybe if she kept her hands busy, she wouldn't have to think about anything else.

"Why don't you finish up with the mules while I go talk to your folks and see if they'd like to spend the night at my place?" Mike suggested.

Kelly nodded. "Sounds good to me."

A few seconds later, she heard the barn door close behind Mike, and she dropped to her knees. "Oh, Lord, I'm sorry for bein' such a grouch. Guess I'm just tired and out of sorts tonight 'cause of the storm and all."

Tears streamed down Kelly's cheeks. Mike thought she was a sinner for taking that chicken. He didn't understand how things were with Papa either. To make matters worse, Mike had been kind to her, and she'd yelled at him in return. What must he think of her now?

"I'm sorry for stealin' the chicken, Lord. Give me the courage to tell Papa no from now on."

Kelly dried her eyes with the backs of her hands and was

about to leave the barn when Mike showed up with Mama.

"Where's Papa?" Kelly questioned.

Her mother sighed deeply. "He's bound and determined to stay on the boat tonight. Never mind that it's rockin' back and forth like a bucking mule." She wrinkled her nose. "And now the roof's leaking as well."

"So are you and me gonna stay at Mike's house?" Kelly asked.

"Yes, and it was a very kind offer, wouldn'tcha say?"

Kelly nodded in response and smiled at Mike. "Sorry for snappin' like a turtle."

He winked at her. "Apology accepted."

❧

For the next two days, the storm continued, and Papa still refused to leave the boat. He said he might lose it if he did, but Kelly knew the truth. Her dad didn't want to appear needy in front of Mike. He'd rather sit on his vessel and be tossed about like a chunk of wood thrown into a raging river than accept anyone's charity.

Sitting at Mike's kitchen table with her drawing tablet, Kelly thought about a verse of Scripture she'd learned as a child: *The substance of a diligent man is precious—Proverbs 12:27.* Papa was diligent, that was for sure. Too bad he wasn't kinder or more concerned about his family.

The last two nights she and Mama had shared a bed inside a real home, and Kelly found herself wishing even more that she could leave the life of mule driver behind.

"Aren't you gonna eat some breakfast?" Mama asked, pushing a bowl of oatmeal in front of Kelly.

"I will, after I finish this drawing."

Mama leaned forward with her elbows on the table. "What are you makin'?"

"It's a picture of our boat bein' tossed by the rising waters. I took a walk down to the canal this morning so I could see how things were lookin'." Kelly frowned. "The rain hasn't let up one little bit, and I figure God must be awful angry with someone."

Mama looked at Kelly as if she'd taken leave of her senses.

"What would make ya say somethin' like that?"

"Doesn't God cause the rain and winds to come whenever He's mad?"

Reaching across the table, Mama took hold of Kelly's hand. "Storms are part of the world we live in, but I don't believe God sends 'em to make us pay for our sins."

"Really?"

Mama nodded. "The Bible tells us in Psalm 34:19, 'Many are the afflictions of the righteous: but the LORD delivereth him out of them all.' Everyone goes through trials, and some of those come in the form of storms, sickness, or other such things. That don't mean we're bein' punished, but we can have the assurance that even though we'll have afflictions, God will deliver us in His time."

Kelly tried to concentrate on her drawing, but Mama's words kept rolling around in her head. *When's my time comin' to be delivered, Lord? When are You gonna give me enough money so I can leave this terrible way of life?*

She grabbed the hunk of charcoal and continued to draw, not wanting to think about her situation. It was bad enough that the storm wasn't letting up and Papa refused to get off the boat. She didn't wish to spend the rest of the day worried about God's direction for her life. If more of her drawings didn't sell soon, she'd have to figure out some other way to make money on her own. When they wintered in Easton, Kelly might get a job in one of the factories. Then she'd have plenty of money, and Papa could find someone else to lead the mules.

A few minutes later the door flew open, and Papa lumbered into the room. Mama jumped up and moved quickly toward him.

"Oh, Amos, it's so good to see you. Can I fix ya a bowl of oatmeal, or maybe some flapjacks?"

He stormed right past Mama as though she hadn't said a word about food. "Stupid weather! It ain't bad enough we lost so much time with sickness and mule problems; now we're stuck here 'til the storm passes by. I'm gettin' sick of sittin' around doin' nothin', and I can't believe my family abandoned me to come get all cozy-like over here at the storekeeper's place!"

Kelly tried to ignore her dad's outburst, but it was hard, especially with him breathing down her neck, as he was now. She could feel his hot breath against her cheek, as he leaned his head close to the table. "What's that you're doin'?" he snarled.

"I'm drawin' a picture of our boat in the storm."

"Humph! Ain't it bad enough I have to endure the torment of bein' tossed around like a cork? Do ya have to rub salt in the wounds by makin' a dumb picture to remind me of my plight?"

Kelly opened her mouth to reply, but Papa jerked the piece of paper right off the table. "This is trash and deserves to be treated as such!" With that, he marched across the room, flung open the door on the wood stove, and tossed Kelly's picture into the fire.

She shot out of her seat, but it was too late. Angry flames of red had already engulfed her precious drawing.

"How could you, Papa?" she cried. "How could you be so cruel?" Kelly rushed from the house, not caring that she wasn't wearing a jacket.

eighteen

Mike glanced out the store window and was surprised to see Kelly run past. She wasn't wearing a jacket, and the rain was still pouring down. She would be drenched within seconds.

He yanked the door open and hurried out after her. A few minutes later she entered the barn, and Mike was right behind her.

"Kelly, what are you doin' out here without a coat?" he hollered as he followed her into the mules' stall.

She kept her head down, and he could see her shoulders shaking.

Mike rushed over to her. "What's wrong? Why are you crying?"

She lifted her gaze to his, and he noticed her dark eyes were filled with tears. He ached to hold her in his arms—to kiss away those tears. He might have, too, if he hadn't been afraid of her response.

"I was working on a drawing of our boat this mornin', and Papa got mad and threw it into the fire," she sobbed.

Mike took hold of Kelly's arms. "Why would he do such a thing?"

"He stormed into your kitchen, yelled about the weather, and said I was rubbin' salt into his wounds by makin' a picture of the boat in the storm. Then he said my picture was trash and deserved to be treated as such. That's when he turned it to ashes." Tears streamed down Kelly's face, and Mike instinctively reached up to wipe them away with the back of his hand.

"I'm so sorry, Kelly. I promise someday things will be better for you."

"How can you say that? Are you able to see into the future and know what's ahead?" she wailed.

111

Mike shook his head slowly. Kelly was right; he couldn't be sure what the future held for either of them. He wanted things to be better and wished she would allow him to love her and help her. If Kelly were to marry him, Mike would gladly spend the rest of his life taking care of her. If only he felt free to tell her that.

"God loves you, Kelly, and He wants only the best for you."

She glared up at him. "If God loves me so much, then why do I have to work long hours with no pay? And why's Papa so mean?"

"God gives each of us a free will, and your dad is the way he is by his own choosing. We can pray for him and set a good example, but nobody can make him change until he's ready."

Kelly sniffed deeply. "I don't care if he ever changes. All I care about is earnin' enough money to make it on my own. I need that chance, so if you want to pray about somethin', then ask God to help *me.*"

Mike's hand rested comfortably on her shoulder. With only a slight pull, she would be close enough for him to kiss. The urge was nearly overwhelming, and he moved away, fighting for control. Kelly had made clear how she felt about marriage. Even if she were attracted to him—and he suspected she was—they had no hope of a future together. He wanted marriage and children so much. All she seemed to care about was drawing pictures and making money so she could support herself. Didn't Kelly realize he was more than willing to care for her needs? As long as he was able to draw breath, Mike would never let his wife or children do without.

"I'll be praying, Kelly," he mumbled. "Praying for both you and your dad."

❧

On Monday of the following week, the rain finally stopped, and the canal waters had receded enough so the McGregors could move on. Kelly felt a deep sense of sadness as she said good-bye to Mike. He truly was her friend, and as much as she hated to admit it, she was attracted to him. She would miss their daily chats as she cared for the mules. She would miss his kind words and caring attitude. As the days of summer continued, she hoped they would stop by his store on a regular basis. Not only to see if any of her paintings had sold, but also so she could spend more time with Mike.

Over the last few days she'd done several more charcoal drawings, always out of Papa's sight, and with Mike's encouragement.

"Get up there," Kelly said as she coaxed the mules to get going. They moved forward, and she turned to wave at Mike one last time. She didn't know why she should feel so sad. She'd see him again, probably on their return trip from Easton.

They'd only traveled a short ways when Papa signaled her to stop. They were between towns, and there were no other boats around. She had a sinking feeling her dad was up to something. Something he'd done a few times before, when he'd lost time due to bad weather or some kind of mishap along the way.

Sure enough, within minutes of their stopping, Papa had begun to shovel coal out of the compartment where it was stored and was dumping it into the canal. He did this to lighten their load, which in turn would help the boat move faster. Of course, it also meant Kelly would be expected to keep the mules moving at a quicker pace.

She shook her head in disgust. "I don't see why Papa has to be so dishonest."

Hector brayed loudly, as though he agreed.

"It's not fair for him to expect the three of us to walk faster," she continued to fume. "It's hard enough to walk at a regular pace, what with the mud and all, but now we'll practically have to run."

Kelly's thoughts took her back to what Mike had told her the other morning in his barn. He'd said they needed to pray for Kelly's dad and set him a good example. That was a tall order—especially since Papa seemed determined to be ornery, and he didn't think twice about cheating someone. She knew from times before that shortly before they arrived in Easton to deliver their load, Papa would wet the coal down, which made it weigh more. Since he was paid by weight and not by the amount, no one would be any the wiser.

She sighed deeply and turned her head away from the canal. There was no use watching what she couldn't prevent happening. Someday maybe she wouldn't have to watch it at all.

&

For the next several weeks, Kelly trudged up and down the towpath between Easton and Mauch Chunk, but they made no stops that weren't absolutely necessary. Papa said they'd lost enough time, and he didn't think they needed to dally. When Mama complained about needing fresh vegetables, Papa solved the problem by turning the tiller over to her. Then he jumped off the boat and helped himself to some carrots and beets growing near the towpath. The garden belonged to someone who lived nearby, but Papa didn't care. He said if the people who'd planted the vegetables so close to the canal didn't want folks helping themselves, they ought to have fenced in their crops.

Kelly had been praying for Papa, like Mike suggested, but it seemed the more she prayed, the worse he became. The effort appeared to be futile, and she had about decided to give up praying or even hoping Papa might ever change.

That morning at breakfast, Mama had asked Papa if they could stop at Mike's store later in the afternoon. She needed more washing soap, some thread, flour for baking, and a few other things she couldn't get by without. After a few choice words, Papa had finally agreed, but now, as they neared the spot in front of Cooper's General Store, Kelly wondered if he might change his mind. His face was a mask of anger, but he signaled her to stop.

She breathed a sigh of relief and halted the mules. At last she could see Mike again and ask if any of her pictures had sold. She didn't have more to give him, as she'd been too busy during the days to draw, and at night she was too tuckered out. At the rate things were going, Kelly doubted she'd ever get the chance to earn enough money to buy any store-bought paint, much less to open an art gallery.

"A dream. That's all it is," she mumbled under her breath a few moments before Mama joined her to head for the store.

ﾗﾟ

Mike stood behind the front counter, praying and hoping Kelly would stop by his store soon. He'd just sold another one of her paintings, and he could hardly wait to tell her the good news. It had been two whole weeks since he'd spoken with her, although he had seen the McGregors' boat go by on several occasions. Each time he'd had customers in the store, or else he would have dashed outside and tried to speak with Kelly—although it probably would have meant running along the towpath as they conversed, for that's pretty much what it looked like Kelly had been doing. Her dad was most likely trying to make up for all the time he'd lost during the storm, but Mike hated to see Kelly being pushed so hard. It wasn't right for a young woman to work from sunup to sunset without getting paid.

Mike was pleasantly surprised when the front door opened and in walked Dorrie and Kelly McGregor. They both looked tired, but Kelly's face showed more than fatigue. Her dark eyes had lost their sparkle, and her shoulders were slumped. She looked defeated.

Mike smiled at the two women. "It's good to see you. Is there something I can help you with?"

Dorrie waved a hand. "Don't trouble yourself. I can get whatever I'm needin'." She marched off in the direction of the sewing notions.

Kelly hung back, and she lifted her gaze to the wall where her artwork was displayed.

"I sold another picture this morning," Mike announced.

"That's good," she said with little feeling. "Sorry I don't have anymore to give you right now. There's been no time for drawin' or paintin' here of late."

"It's all right," he assured her. "I'm sure you'll find some free time soon."

She scowled at him. "Why do you always say things like that?"

"Like what?"

"You try to make me think things are gonna get better when they're not."

"How do you know they're not?"

"I just do, that's all."

Mike blew out his breath. It was obvious nothing he said would penetrate her negative attitude this afternoon. He offered up a quick prayer. *Lord, give me the right words.*

"Would it help if I had a talk with your dad?"

Kelly looked horrified. "Don't you dare! Papa would be furious if he knew I'd been complaining." She squared her shoulders. "I'll be fine, so there's no reason to concern yourself."

"But I am concerned. I'm in—" Mike stopped himself before he blurted out that he was in love with her. He knew it would be the worst thing he could say to Kelly right now. Besides the fact that she was in a sour mood and would probably not appreciate his declaration of love, her mother was in the store and might be listening to his every word.

Mike moved over to the candy counter. "How about a bag of lemon drops? I'm sure you're out of them by now."

Kelly's frown faded, and she joined him at the counter. "Since I sold a painting and have some money comin', I'll take two bags of candy—one lemon drops, and the other horehounds."

"I didn't know you fancied horehounds."

"I don't, but Papa likes 'em. Maybe it'll help put him in a better mood."

So she was trying to set a good example for her dad. That pleased Mike so much. At least one of his prayers was being answered. If Kelly's dad found the Lord, then Kelly might be more receptive to the idea of marriage.

Mike reached into the container of horehound drops with a wooden scoop. "You think you might be stopping over come Sunday?"

She shrugged her shoulders. "If we make it to Mauch Chunk in good time, Papa might be willin' to stop on our way back. Why do you ask?"

"I'd like to take you on another picnic." He grinned at her. "Only this time it'll be just you and me."

She tipped her head to one side. "No Betsy Nelson?"

"Nope."

She smiled for the first time since she'd come into the store. "We'll have to wait and see."

nineteen

When Mike asked Kelly about going on another picnic, she never expected her family's canal boat would be stopped in front of his store the next Sunday. In fact, they'd arrived the evening before, and Papa had decided to spend the night so he could work on the boat the following morning. He'd accidentally run into one of the other canal boats and put a hole in the bow of his boat. It wasn't a huge hole and was high enough that no water had leaked in, but it still needed to be repaired before it got any worse. Papa would be busy with that all day, which meant Kelly could head off with Mike and probably go unnoticed.

Not wishing to run into Betsy again, Kelly waited until the crowd had dispersed from Reverend Nelson's outdoor preaching service before she walked to Mike's store. They'd talked briefly the night before and had agreed to meet sometime after noon in front of his place.

It was a hot summer day late in the month of August, and Kelly wished she and Mike could go swimming in the canal to get cooled off. She dismissed the idea as quickly as it popped into her mind when she remembered Mike had said he didn't swim well, and she, though able to swim, was afraid of water snakes. They would have to find some other way to find solace from the oppressive heat and humidity.

Mike was waiting for her in front of the store, a picnic basket in one hand and a blanket in the other. "Did you bring along your drawing tablet?" he asked.

She nodded and patted the pocket of her long, gingham skirt.

"I thought we'd have our picnic at the pond behind Zach Miller's house. There's lots of wildflowers growing there, and maybe we can find some to brew into watercolors," he said, offering Kelly a smile that made her skin tingle despite the heat of the day.

"That would be good. Mama's runnin' low on carrots and beets, so I haven't been able to make any colors for a spell, other than the shades I've gotten from leftover coffee and some tree bark."

Mike whistled as they walked up the towpath, heading in the direction of the lock tender's house.

"You seem to be in an awful good mood this afternoon," Kelly noted.

He turned his head and grinned at her. "I'm always in fine spirits on the Lord's day. I looked for you at the preaching service but didn't see you anywhere."

"Mama needed my help with some bakin'." Kelly felt a prick of her conscience. She had helped her mother bake oatmeal bread, but truth be told, that wasn't the real reason she hadn't attended the church service. She didn't want to hear God's Word and be reminded that her prayers weren't being answered where Papa was concerned. Besides, Mama hadn't attended church either, and if she didn't feel the need to go, why should Kelly?

"Sure wish you could have heard the great message the reverend delivered this morning. It was a real inspiration."

"I'm sure it was."

"Summer will be over soon," Mike said, changing the subject. "Won't be long until the leaves begin to turn and drop from the trees."

Kelly nodded, feeling suddenly sad. When fall came, they'd only have a few months left to make coal deliveries. Winter often hit quickly, and Papa always moored the boat for the winter and moved them to Flannigan's Boardinghouse in Easton, where they would live until the spring thaw. That meant Kelly wouldn't be seeing Mike for several months. She would miss his smiling face and their long talks.

A lot could happen in three months. Mike and Betsy might start courting and could even be married by the time they returned to the canal. And Kelly was acutely aware that lots of coal was now being hauled via steam train, which meant fewer boats were working the canals in eastern Pennsylvania. How long would it be before Papa gave up canaling altogether and took a job in the city full-time?

"A lemon drop for your thoughts," Mike said.

"What?"

"I brought along a bag of your favorite candy, and I'd gladly give you one if you're willin' to share your thoughts with me."

She snickered. "I doubt anything I'd be thinkin' would be worth even one lemon drop."

Mike stopped walking and turned to face her. "Don't say that, Kelly. You're a talented, intelligent woman, and I value anything you might have to say."

She pursed her lips. "I'm not sure 'bout my talents, but one thing I do know—I'm not smart. I've only gone through the eighth grade, and that took me longer than most, 'cause I just attended school during the winter months."

"A lack of education doesn't mean you're stupid," Mike said with a note of conviction. "My dad used to say he graduated from the school of life and that all the things he learned helped him become a better man. We grow from our experiences, so if we learn from our mistakes, then we're smart."

Kelly contemplated Mike's words a few seconds. "Hmm. . .I've never thought about it that way before."

"I hope to have a whole passel of kids someday, and when I do, I want to teach them responsibility, so they can work hard and be smart where it really counts."

Kelly wasn't sure she liked the sound of that, but she chose not to comment.

Mike started walking again, and Kelly did as well. Soon they were at the pond behind the Millers' house. Nobody else was around, so Kelly figured they weren't likely to be interrupted, and she might even get some serious drawing done.

Sitting on the blanket next to Kelly, his belly full of fried chicken and buttermilk biscuits, Mike felt content. He could spend the rest of his life with this woman—watching her draw, listening to the hum of her sweet voice, and kissing away all her worries and cares. Should he tell her what he was feeling? Would it scare her off? He drew in a deep breath and plunged ahead. "Kelly, I was wondering—"

"Yes?" she murmured as she continued to draw the outline of a clump of wildflowers.

"Would it be all right if I wrote to you while you're living in the city this winter?"

She turned her head to look at him. Her dark eyes looked ever so serious, but she was smiling. "I'd like that."

"And will you write me in return?" he asked hopefully.

She nodded. "If I'm not kept too busy with my factory job."

"Do you know where you'll be working?"

"Not yet, but I'll be eighteen on January fifth, and I'm gettin' stronger every year. I can probably get a job at most any of the factories. Even the ones where the work is heavy or dangerous."

Mike's heart clenched. "Please don't take a job that might put you in danger. I couldn't stand it if something were to happen to you, Kelly."

She gave him a questioning look.

"I love you, and I—" Mike never finished his sentence. Instead, he took Kelly in his arms and kissed her upturned mouth. Her lips tasted sweet as honey, and it felt so right to hold her.

When Kelly slipped her hands around his neck and returned his kiss, Mike thought he was going to drown in the love he felt for her.

Kelly was the first to pull away. Her face was bright pink, and her eyes were cloudy with obvious emotion. Had she enjoyed the kiss as much as he?

She placed her trembling hands against her rosy cheeks. "I–I think it's time to go."

"But we haven't picked any wildflowers for you to use as watercolors yet," Mike argued.

She stood and dropped her art supplies into the pocket of her skirt. "I shouldn't have let you kiss me. It wasn't right."

Mike jumped to his feet. "It felt right to me."

She hung her head. "It wasn't, and it can never happen again."

Mike's previous elation plummeted clear to his toes. "I'm sorry you didn't enjoy the kiss."

"I did," she surprised him by saying. "But we can never be more than friends, and I don't think friends should go around kissin' each other."

So that's how it was. Kelly only saw him as a friend. Mike felt like a fool. He'd read more into her physical response than there was. He'd decided awhile back to take it slow and easy with Kelly—be sure of her feelings before he made a move. He'd really messed things up, and it was too late to take back the kiss or his declaration of love.

"Forgive me for taking liberties that weren't mine," he said, forcing her to look him in the eye, even though it pained him to see there were tears running down her cheeks.

When she didn't say anything, Mike bent to retrieve the picnic basket and blanket. "I think you're right. It's time to go."

❧

All the way back to the boat, Kelly chided herself for being foolish enough to allow Mike to kiss her. Now she'd hurt his feelings. It was obvious by the slump of his shoulders and the silence that covered the distance between them. On the way to the pond he'd been talkative and whistled. Now the only sounds were the call of a dove and the canal waters lapping against the bank.

I was wrong to let him kiss me, but was I wrong to tell him we could only be friends? Should I have let him believe I might feel more for him than friendship? Do I feel more?

Kelly's disconcerting thoughts came to a halt when they rounded the bend where the canal boats could be seen. In the middle of the grassy area between Mike's store and the boats that had stopped for the day, two men were fist fighting. One was Patrick O'Malley. The other was Kelly's dad. Several other men stood on the sidelines, shouting, clapping, and cheering them on. What was the scuffle about, and why wasn't someone trying to stop it?

As though Mike could read her thoughts, he set the picnic basket and blanket on the ground, then stepped forward. "Please, no fighting on the Sabbath. Can't you two men solve your differences without the use of your knuckles?"

Pow! Papa's fist connected on the left side of Patrick's chin. "You stay outa this, Boy!" he shouted at Mike.

Smack! Patrick gave Papa a head butt that sent him sprawling on the grass.

"Stop it! Stop it!" Kelly shouted. Tears were stinging the backs of her eyes, and she felt herself tremble. Why must Papa make such a spectacle of himself? What did Mike and the others who were watching think of her dad?

The men were hitting each other lickety-split now, apparently oblivious to anything that was being said. Closer and closer to the canal they went, and when Papa slammed his fist into Patrick's chest, the man lost his footing and fell over backwards. He grabbed Papa's shirtsleeve, and both men landed in the water with a splash.

Mortified, Kelly covered her face with her hands. How could a day that started out with such promise end on such a sour note?

After the fight was over and the two men settled down, Kelly learned the reason behind the scuffle. It had all started over something as simple as whose boat would be leaving first come Monday morning.

After the way her dad caused such a scene, Kelly didn't think she could show her face to Mike or anyone else without suspecting they were talking behind her back. It was embarrassing the way her dad could fly off the handle and punch a man for no reason at all. Men didn't make a lick of sense!

twenty

As summer moved into fall, Kelly saw less of Mike. Papa kept them moving, wanting to make as many loads as possible before the bad weather. He refused to stop for anything that wasn't necessary.

It was just as well she wasn't spending time with Mike, Kelly decided as she sat upon Hector's back, bone tired and unable to take another step. After Mike's unexpected kiss the day they'd had a picnic by the Millers' pond, Kelly hadn't wanted to do or say anything that might cause Mike to believe they had anything more than a casual friendship. What if Mike was thinking about marriage? What if he only felt sorry for her because she worked so hard? Kelly wasn't about to marry someone just to get away from Papa.

"I wish I didn't like Mike so much," Kelly murmured against the mule's ear.

❧

It had been a long day, and Mike was about ready to close up his store when Betsy Nelson showed up. She seemed to have such good timing. Mike had just finished going through a stack of mail brought in by the last boat that had come through before dark, and he was feeling lower than the canal waters after a break. He'd gotten another letter from his brother Alvin. This one said his other brother John had also found himself a girlfriend. There was even mention of a double wedding come December.

"Sorry to be coming by so late in the day," Betsy panted, "but Papa's real sick, and I need some medicine to help quiet his cough." Her cheeks were red, and it was obvious by her heavy breathing that she'd probably run all the way to Mike's store. Mike knew Preacher Nelson didn't own a horse, preferring to make all his calls on foot.

"Come inside, and I'll see what kind of cough syrup I've got left in stock." Mike stepped aside so Betsy could enter, and she followed him to the back of the store.

"I haven't seen you for awhile," Betsy said as Mike handed her a bottle of his best-selling cough syrup.

"I've been kinda busy."

Her eyelids fluttered. "I've missed you."

Mike swallowed hard. Betsy was flirting again, and it made him real nervous. He didn't want to hurt her feelings, but the simple fact was, he didn't love Betsy. Even though Kelly had spurned his kiss, he was hoping someday she would come to love him as much as he did her.

As lonely as Mike was, and as much as he desired a wife, he knew it couldn't be the preacher's daughter. She was too self-centered and a bit short-tempered, which probably meant she wouldn't be a patient mother. Kelly, on the other hand, would make a good wife and mother. It wasn't just her lovely face or long, brown hair that had captured Mike's heart. Kelly had a gentle spirit. He'd witnessed it several times when she tended the mules. If only she seemed more willing.

Maybe I should quit praying for a wife and get a dog instead.

"Mike? Did you hear what I said?"

Betsy's high-pitched voice drove Mike's musings to the back of his mind. "What was that?"

"I said, 'I've missed you.'"

Mike felt his ears begin to warm, which meant they were probably bright red. "Thank you, Betsy. It's nice to know I've been missed."

She looked at him with pleading eyes. No doubt she was hoping he would respond by saying he missed her too. Mike couldn't lie. It wouldn't be right to lead Betsy on.

He moved quickly to the front of the store and placed the bottle of medicine on the counter. "Is there anything else you'll be needin'?"

Betsy's lower lip protruded as she shook her head.

He slipped the bottle into a brown paper sack, took her money, and handed Betsy her purchase. "I hope your dad is feeling better soon. Give him my regards, will you?"

She gave him a curt nod, lifted her head high, and pranced out the door. Mike let out a sigh of relief. At least she hadn't invited him to supper again.

~

The last day of November arrived, and Kelly couldn't believe it was time to leave the Lehigh Navigation System until spring. When Mama said she needed a few things, Papa had agreed to stop by Cooper's General Store. Kelly felt a mixture of relief and anxiety. Even though she wanted the chance to say good-bye, she dreaded seeing Mike again. Ever since the day he'd kissed her, things had been strained between them. She was afraid Mike wanted more from her than she was able to give. He'd said once that he wanted a whole passel of children so he could teach them responsibility. Did he think making children work would make them smart?

"I wonder if he wants kids so he can force 'em to labor with no pay," Kelly fumed to the mules. All the men she knew who put their kids to work paid them little or nothing. It wasn't fair! No wonder Sarah ran away and got married.

" 'Course if Sarah hadn't run off, I wouldn't have been left with all the work. Maybe the two of us could have come up with a plan to make money of our own."

They were in front of Mike's store now, so Kelly secured the mules to a tree while she waited for her parents to get off the boat. A short time later, Mama disembarked.

"Where's Papa?" Kelly asked her mother.

Mama shrugged her shoulders. "He said he thought he'd take a nap while we do our shoppin'. He gave me a list of things he needs and said for us not to take all day."

Kelly followed her mother inside the store. She was glad to see Mike was busy with a customer. At least she wouldn't have to speak with him right away. It would give her time to think of something sensible to say. Should she ask if he still planned to write her while she was living in Easton? Should she promise to write him in return?

She thought about the paintings she had in her drawing tablet, which she hoped to give Mike before she left. Trouble was, she didn't want Mama to see. Could she find some way of speaking to Mike alone?

As if by divine intervention, the man Mike had been waiting on left the store, and about the same time, Mama decided to go back to the boat. She said something about needing to get Papa's opinion on the material she planned to use for a shirt she'd be making him soon.

Kelly knew she didn't have much time, so when the door closed behind her mother, she moved over to the counter where Mike stood.

"Hello, Kelly," he said, offering her a pleasant smile. "It's good to see you."

She moistened her lips with the tip of her tongue. "We're on our way to Easton for the winter and decided to stop by your store for a few items."

When Mike made no comment, Kelly rushed on before she lost her nerve. "I've got a few more paintings to give you. That is, if you're interested in tryin' to sell them." She reached into her pocket and withdrew the tablet, then placed it on the counter.

Mike thumbed through the pages. "These are great, Kelly. I especially like the one of the two children playing in a pile of fallen leaves."

Kelly smiled. That was her favorite picture too. She'd drawn it in charcoal, then used a mixture of coffee shades, as well as some carrot, onion, and beet water for the colored leaves.

"I've sold a couple more pictures since you were last here," Mike said, reaching into his cash box and producing a few bills, which he handed to Kelly.

"What about your share of the profits?" she asked. "Did ya keep out some of the money?"

Mike gave her a sheepish grin. "I thought with you going to the big city and all, you'd probably need a little extra cash.

I'll take my share out of the next batch of pictures I sell."

Kelly was tempted to argue, but the thought of having more money made her think twice about refusing. She nodded instead and slipped the bills into her pocket.

"When do you think you'll be back?" Mike asked.

"Sometime in March, whenever the ice and snow are gone."

"Is there an address where I can write to you?"

"We'll be staying at Mable Flannigan's Boardinghouse. It's on the corner of Front Street in the eight hundred block."

"And you can write me here at Cooper's General Store, Walnutport, Pennsylvania."

"I'll try to write if there's time." That was all Kelly could promise. She had no idea where she might be working or how many hours she'd be putting in each day.

"Mind if I give you a hug good-bye?" Mike asked. "Just as friends?"

Kelly wasn't sure what to say. She didn't want to encourage Mike, yet she didn't want to be rude either. She guessed one little hug wouldn't hurt. He did say it was just as friends. She nodded and held out her arms.

Mike skirted around the counter and pulled her into an embrace.

Kelly's heart pounded against her chest, and she feared it might burst wide open. What if Mama came back and saw the two of them? What if Mike decided to kiss her again?

Her fears were relieved when Mike pulled away. "Take care, Kelly McGregor. I'll see you next spring."

twenty-one

Winter came quickly to the Lehigh Valley, and a thick layer of snow soon covered the ground. Mike missed Kelly terribly, and several times a week he would walk the towpath, as he was now, thinking about her and praying for her safety. He knew she cared for him, but only as a friend. If he just hadn't allowed himself to fall in love with her. If only she loved him in return.

Kelly had been gone a little over a month, and still not one letter had he received. He'd written to her several times, but no response. Was she too busy to write? Had she found a man and fallen in love? All sorts of things flitted through Mike's mind as he trudged along, his boots crunching through the fresh-fallen snow.

God would need to heal his heart if Kelly never returned, because Mike was in love with her, and there didn't seem to be a thing he could do about it.

I shouldn't have let myself fall for her, Lord, he prayed. *What I thought was Your will might have only been my own selfish desires. Maybe You want me to remain single.*

Shivering against the cold, Mike headed back to his house. There was no point in going over this again and again. If Kelly came back to the canal in the spring with a different attitude toward him, Mike would be glad. If she didn't, then he would have to accept it as God's will.

When Mike stepped inside the house a short time later, a blast of warm air hit him in the face. It was a welcome relief from the cold. As he hung his coat on a wall peg, he noticed the calendar hanging nearby. Today was January 5, Kelly's eighteenth birthday. He remembered her mentioning it before she left for the city. He'd sent her a package several days ago and hoped she would receive it on time. Even more than that,

Mike hoped she liked the birthday present he'd chosen.

❧

Kelly couldn't believe how bad her feet hurt. She was used to walking the towpath every day, but trudging through the hilly city of Easton was an entirely different matter. Papa had insisted Kelly get a job to help with expenses, and she'd been out looking almost every day since they had arrived at the boardinghouse in Easton. No one seemed to be hiring right before Christmas, and after the holidays, she was either told there was no work or that she wasn't qualified for any of the available positions. Kelly kept looking every day, and in the evenings and on weekends, she helped Mama sew and clean their small, three-room flat.

Kelly hated to spend her days looking for work and longed to be with their mules that had been left at Morgan's Stables just outside of town. It wasn't cheap to keep them there, but Papa said they had no choice. Needing money for the mules' care was one of the reasons he'd taken a job at Glendon Iron Furnace, which overlooked the canal and Lehigh Valley Railroad. The work was hard and heavy but pay was better than at many other manual jobs.

Every chance she got, Kelly went to see her animal friends. Today was her eighteenth birthday, and she'd decided to celebrate with a trip to the stables right after breakfast. It might be the only thing special about her birthday, since neither Mama nor Papa had made any mention of it. They'd been sitting around the breakfast table for ten minutes, and no one had said a word about what day it was. Papa had his nose in the Easton newspaper, *The Sunday Call,* and Mama seemed preoccupied with the scrambled eggs on her plate.

Kelly sighed deeply and took a drink from her cup of tea. It didn't matter. She'd never had much of a fuss made on her birthday anyway. Why should this year be any different?

Maybe I'll take some of the money I earned sellin' paintings and buy something today. Kelly grimaced. She knew she should save all her cash for that art gallery she hoped to open some day. Even as the idea popped into her mind, Kelly felt it was futile.

She'd only sold a few paintings so far, and even if she sold more, it would take years before she'd have enough to open any kind of gallery. She would need to pay rent for a building, and then there was the cost of all the supplies. It wouldn't be enough to simply sell her paintings and drawings; she'd want to offer her customers the chance to purchase paper, paints, charcoal pencils, and maybe some fancy frames. All that would cost a lot of money. Money Kelly would probably never see in her lifetime.

I may as well give up my dream. If I can find a job in the city, it would probably be best if I stay here and work. Papa can hire a mule driver to take my place. It would serve him right if I never went back to the canal again.

A loud knock drove Kelly's thoughts to the back of her mind. She looked at Papa, then Mama. Neither one seemed interested in answering the door.

Kelly sighed deeply and pushed her chair away from the table. Why was she always expected to do everything? She shuffled across the room, feeling as though she had the weight of the world on her shoulders.

She opened the door and was greeted by their landlord, Mable Flannigan. A heavyset, middle-aged woman with bright red hair and sparking blue eyes, Mable had told them that her husband was killed in the War Between the States, and she'd been on her own ever since. The woman had no children to care for and had opened her home to boarders shortly after the war ended nearly twenty-seven years ago. Kelly always wondered why Mrs. Flannigan had never remarried. Could be that she was still pining for her dead husband, or maybe the woman thought she could get along better without a man.

"This came for you in the mornin's mail," Mrs. Flannigan said, holding out a package wrapped in brown paper.

Kelly's forehead wrinkled. "For me?" She couldn't imagine who would be sending her anything.

The older woman nodded. "It has your name and the address of my boardinghouse right here on the front."

Kelly took the package and studied the handwriting. Her

name was there all right, in big, bold letters. Her heart began
to pound, and her hands shook when she saw the return
address. It was from Mike Cooper.

Remembering her manners, Kelly opened the door wider.
"Would ya like to come in and have a cup of coffee or some tea?"

Mrs. Flannigan shook her head. "Thanks, but I'd better
not. I've got me some washin' to do today, and it sure won't
get done if I lollygag over a cup of hot coffee."

The woman turned to go, and Kelly called, "Thanks for
deliverin' the package."

A few seconds later, Kelly sat on the sofa, tearing the brown
paper away from the box. With trembling hands she lifted the
lid. She let out a little gasp when she saw what the box contained. Her eyes feasted on a tin of store-bought watercolor
paints, a real artist's tablet, and three brushes in various sizes.
There was also a note:

> *Dear Kelly,*
>   *I wanted you to have this paint set for your eighteenth*
> *birthday. I only wish I could be with you to help celebrate.*
> *I hope you're doing all right, and I'm real anxious for you to*
> *return to the canal.*
>
> > *Fondly, your friend,*
> > *Mike Cooper*
>
> *P.S. Please write soon.*

Kelly sat for several seconds, trying to understand how
Mike could have known today was her birthday and relishing
in the joy of owning a real set of watercolors, not to mention a
store-bought tablet that she'd hadn't put together herself. She
would be able to paint anything she wanted now, using nearly
every shade imaginable.

An image of Mike's friendly face flashed into Kelly's mind.
She might have mentioned something to him about her
birthday being on January the fifth. The fact that he'd
remembered and cared enough to send her a present was

almost overwhelming. No one had ever given her a gift like the one she held in her hands.

"Kelly, who was at the door?" Papa hollered from the next room.

She swallowed hard and stood up. Her dad might be mad when he saw the present Mike had sent her, but she wouldn't lie or hide it from him. While Papa was at work, and after Kelly got home from searching for a job every day, Mama had been reading the Bible out loud, and Kelly had fallen under deep conviction. She'd strayed from God and knew she needed to make things right. It was wrong to lie, or even hide the truth from her parents. It had been a sin to harbor resentment toward Papa, and with the Lord's help, she was doing much better in that regard.

Grasping the box with her birthday present inside, Kelly walked back to the kitchen. "Mrs. Flannigan was at the door with a package for me." Kelly placed the box on the table.

"Who would be sendin' you anything?" Papa asked, his eyebrows drawing together.

"It's from Mike Cooper."

"The storekeeper along the canal?" Mama questioned as she peered into the box.

Kelly nodded. "It's for my birthday." She sank into her chair, wondering when the explosion would come.

Mama pulled the tin of watercolors out of the box and held it up. Papa frowned, but he never said a word. Kelly held her breath.

"What a thoughtful gift," Mama said. "Now you'll be able to paint with real colors instead of makin' colored water out of my vegetables."

Kelly felt her face heat up. So her mother had known all the time that she was taking carrots, beets, and onions out of the bin. Funny thing, Mama had never said a word about it until now.

"Humph!" Papa snorted. "I hope that man don't think his gift is gonna buy him my daughter's hand in marriage."

"Mike and I are just friends, Papa," Kelly was quick to say. She turned to face her dad. "Can I keep it? I promise not to paint when I'm supposed to be workin'."

"You've gotta find a job first," her dad grumbled. "We've been in the city for a whole month already, and not one red cent have you brought in."

"I'll look again on Monday," Kelly promised.

"Why don'tcha try over at the Simon Silk Mill on Bushkill Creek?" Mama suggested. "I hear tell they're lookin' to hire a few people there."

Kelly nodded. "I'll go first thing on Monday morning."

Papa took a long drink from his cup of coffee, wiped his mouth with the back of his hand, and stood up. "I need to get to work."

"But it's Saturday," Mama reminded.

He leveled her with a disgruntled look. "Don'tcha think I know that, Woman? They're operatin' the plant six days a week now, and I volunteered to come in today." His gaze swung over to Kelly. "You can keep the birthday present, but I'd better not find you paintin' when ya should be out lookin' for work."

"Thank you, Papa, and I promise I won't paint until all my chores are done for the day neither." Kelly felt like she could kiss her dad. She didn't, though. Papa had never been very affectionate, and truth be told, until this moment, Kelly had never felt like kissing him.

Papa grunted, grabbed his jacket off the wall peg, and sauntered out the door.

Mama patted Kelly's hand. "Tonight I'm fixin' your favorite supper, in honor of your birthday."

"Hunks-a-go pudding and roast beef?" Kelly asked hopefully.

Mama nodded and grinned. "Might make a chocolate cake for dessert too."

Kelly smiled in return, feeling better than she had in weeks. Today turned out to be a better birthday than she'd ever imagined. Now if she could only find a job.

twenty-two

As Kelly stood in front of the brick building that housed the Simon Silk Mill, she whispered a prayer, petitioning God to give her a job. She didn't know any other kind of work besides leading the mules, but Mama had taught her to sew, and she figured that's what she would be doing if she were hired here. All the other times they'd wintered in Easton, Papa had never demanded Kelly find a job. That was probably because Mama insisted Kelly go to school. She was older now and done with book learning, so it was time to make some money. If only she didn't have to give it all to Papa. If she could keep the money she earned, Kelly would probably have enough to open her art gallery in no time at all. Of course, she didn't think she would have the nerve to tell Papa she wasn't going back to the canal in the spring.

Pushing the door open, Kelly stepped inside the factory and located the main office. She entered the room and told the receptionist she needed a job. Disappointment flooded Kelly's soul when she was told all the positions at the mill had been taken.

Kelly left the office feeling a sense of frustration. What if she never found a job? Papa would be furious and might make her throw out her art supplies. She couldn't let that happen. There had to be something she could do.

Kelly was almost to the front door when she bumped into someone. Her mouth dropped open, and she took a step back. "Sarah?"

The young woman with dark brown hair piled high on her head looked at Kelly as if she'd seen a ghost. "Kelly, is that you?"

"It's me, Sarah. I'm so surprised to see you."

"And I, you," her sister replied.

"Do you work here?"

Sarah nodded. "Have been for the last couple of months. Before that I was home takin' care of little Sam."

"Little Sam?"

"Sam Jr."

"You have a son?" Kelly could hardly believe her sister had a baby they knew nothing about. For that matter, they hadn't heard anything from Sarah since that one letter, telling the family she and Sam had gotten married and were living in New Jersey.

"The baby was born six months ago," Sarah explained. "Sam was workin' at Warren Soapstone, but one day he lost his temper with the boss and got fired. So I had to find work, and he's been home takin' care of the baby ever since."

Kelly stood there for several seconds, studying her sister and trying to let all she'd said sink into her brain. Sarah was dressed in a beige-colored cotton blouse and plain brown skirt covered with a black apron. Her shoulders were slumped, and she looked awful tired.

The fact that Sam Turner would allow his wife to work while he stayed home was one more proof for Kelly that men only used women. Sam was no better than Papa. Sarah had run off with Sam to get away from working, and now she was being forced to support not only herself, but her husband and baby as well. It made Kelly sick to the pit of her stomach.

"Are you and the folks stayin' at the boardinghouse like before?" Sarah's question drove Kelly's thoughts to the back of her mind.

"Yes, we've been there since early December." Kelly gave her sister a hug. "I'm sure Mama and Papa would like to see you and the baby. . .Sam Sr. too."

When Sarah pulled away, tears stood in her dark eyes. "Oh, please don't say anything to the folks about seein' me today."

"Why not?"

"Papa always hated Sam, and when we tried to tell him we were in love and wanted to get married, he blew up and said if we did, he'd punch Sam in the nose."

Kelly flinched at the memory. She'd been there when Papa had gotten all red in the face and shouted at Sam and Sarah. She could understand why her sister might be afraid to confront their dad now.

"I won't say a word," Kelly promised, "but I would sure like to see my nephew. You think there's any way that could be arranged?"

Sarah gave a tired yet sincere smile. "I'd like you to meet little Sam. Mama too, for that matter. Maybe the two of you can come by our apartment sometime soon. Let me talk it over with my husband first, though."

"How will we get in touch with you?"

Sarah looked thoughtful. "Is Papa workin' every day?"

Kelly nodded. "Over at Glendon Iron Furnace, even Saturdays now."

"Then how about if the baby and I come by the boarding-house next Saturday?"

"That would be great. Should I tell Mama ahead, or do you want to surprise her?"

"Let's make it our little surprise." Sarah squeezed Kelly's arm. "I need to get back up to the second floor where I work on one of the weavin' looms."

Kelly gave her sister another hug. "Sure is good to see you, Sarah."

"Same here." Sarah started for the stairs, and Kelly headed for the front door, feeling more cheerful than she had all morning. Even if she didn't have a job, at least she'd been reunited with her sister. That was something to be grateful for.

❧

For the third time that morning, Mike sorted through the stack of mail he'd dumped on the counter after it arrived by canal boat. There was nothing from Kelly. Wasn't she ever going to respond? Had she received his birthday present? Did she like the watercolor set, sketching pad, and paintbrushes, or was she mad at him for giving them to her? If only she'd written a note to let him know the package had arrived.

"I've got to get busy and quit thinkin' about Kelly." Mike slipped each letter into the cubbyholes he'd made for his postal customers. The packages were kept in a box underneath. As local people dropped by the store, he would hand out their mail and be glad he'd taken the time to organize it so well. Any mail that came for the boatmen who were working in the city and wanted their parcels to be held until they returned to the canal was stored safely in a wooden box under the front counter. Most canalers lived in homes nearby, and those, like Amos McGregor, would be getting their mail forwarded to their temporary address during the winter months.

Thinking about Amos caused Mike's mind to wander back to Kelly. Whenever he closed his eyes at night he could see her smiling face, hear her joyous laughter, and feel her sweet lips against his own. Had it been wrong to kiss her? He hadn't thought so at the time, but after she'd pulled away and cooled off toward him, Mike figured he'd done a terrible thing.

"I kept telling myself I would go slow with Kelly, but I moved too fast," Mike moaned. "Why must I always rush ahead of God?" He reached for one of the Bibles he had stacked near the end of the counter and opened it to the Book of Hebrews. He found chapter 10 and read verses 35 and 36: *"Cast not away. . .your confidence, which hath great recompense of reward. For ye have need of patience, that, after ye have done the will of God, ye might receive the promise."*

Mike closed his eyes and quoted from Genesis, chapter 2, verse 18: *"And the LORD God said, It is not good that the man should be alone; I will make him an help meet for him."* He dropped to his knees behind the counter. "Oh, Lord, if I have patience and continue to do Your will, might I receive the promise of an help meet?"

Except for the eerie howling of the wind against the eaves of the store, there was no sound. Patience. Mike knew he needed to be more patient. With God's help he would try, but it wouldn't be easy.

twenty-three

On Saturday afternoon Sarah, with baby Sam tucked under one arm, came by the boardinghouse. Kelly was shocked at her sister's haggard appearance. Sarah had looked tired the other day, but it was nothing like this. Puffiness surrounded her sister's red-rimmed eyes, indicating she had been crying. Something was wrong. Kelly could feel it in her bones.

Mama, who hadn't been told about Sarah's surprise visit, rushed to her oldest daughter's side when Kelly stepped away and closed the door. "Sarah!" Mama exclaimed. "I can't believe it's you. Where have you been livin'? How did you know we'd be here?" She reached out to touch the baby's chubby hand. "And who is this cute little fellow?"

Sarah emitted a small laugh, even though her expression was strained. "Too many questions at once, Mama. Can I come in and be seated before I answer each one?"

Mama's hands went to her flushed cheeks. "Yes, yes. Please, let me have your coats, then go into the livin' room and get comfortable."

Sarah turned to Kelly, who so far hadn't uttered a word. "Would ya mind holdin' Sam while I take off my coat?"

Kelly held out her arms to the child, but little Sam buried his head against his mother's chest and whimpered.

"He's a bit shy around strangers," Sarah said. "I'm sure he'll warm up to you soon." She handed the baby over to Kelly despite the child's protests.

Feeling awkward and unsure of herself, Kelly stepped into the living room and took a seat on the sofa. Baby Sam squirmed restlessly, but he didn't cry.

A few minutes later, Sarah and their mother entered the room. Mama sat beside Kelly on the sofa, and Sarah took a seat in the rocking chair across from them.

"Mama, meet your grandson, Sam Jr.," Sarah announced.

Mama's lips curved into a smile, and she reached out to take the infant from Kelly. He went willingly, obviously drawn to his grandma.

"I can't believe you have a baby, Sarah. How old is he, and why didn't ya write and tell us about him?"

Sarah hung her head, and Kelly noticed tears dripping onto her sister's skirt, leaving dark spots in the gray-colored fabric. "I–I knew you and Papa were angry with me for runnin' off with Sam, so I figured you wouldn't want to know anything about what I was doin'."

Kelly closed her eyes and offered up a prayer on her sister's behalf as she waited for her mother's reply.

Mama's eyes filled with tears, and she hugged the baby to her breast. "I could never turn my back on one of my own, Sarah. I love both my girls." She glanced over at Kelly, who was also close to tears.

"I love you too, Mama," Kelly murmured.

"So do I," Sarah agreed. "Now as to your questions. . . Sam is six months old, and we've all been livin' in a flat across the bridge in Phillipsburg. Up until a few weeks ago, Sam worked at Warren Soapstone, but he got fired for shootin' off his mouth to the boss." Sarah paused and drew in a deep breath. "I've been workin' at the Simon Silk Mill ever since, and Sam *was* takin' care of the baby."

Was? What did Sarah mean by that? Before Kelly could voice the question, her sister rushed on.

"Sam's been drinkin' here of late, and actin' real funny. Last night when I got home from work, he had his bags packed and said he was leavin' me and the baby." Sarah's eyes clouded with fresh tears, and she choked on a sob. "I've got no place to leave Sam Jr. while I'm at work now, and I can't afford to hire a babysitter and pay the rent on my flat too."

"I could watch the baby for you," Kelly spoke up. "I haven't been able to find work anywhere yet, so I have nothin' else to do with my time." *Except paint and dream impossible dreams,* she added mentally.

Sarah shot Mama an imploring look. "Would ya allow Kelly to come live with me?"

"I'm not sure that would set well with your papa." Mama pursed her lips. "Why don't you and the baby move in here with us?"

Sarah glanced around the room. "This is the same place you've always rented from Mable Flannigan, right?"

Their mother nodded.

"Mama, it's so small. There's not nearly enough room for two extra people." She nodded at Kelly. "If you could come stay with me and Sam Jr., I couldn't pay you, but I could offer free room and board. You'd also have a small room, which you'd need to share with the baby."

As sorry as Kelly was to hear the news that Sarah's husband had left, the idea of moving in with her sister sounded rather pleasant. It would give her more time to paint without Papa breathing down her neck or hollering because she still hadn't found a job. She touched her mother's arm gently. "Please, Mama. I'd like to help Sarah out in her time of need."

Mama shrugged her shoulders. "If Papa says it's all right, then I'll agree to it as well."

❧

The next few months were like none Kelly had ever known. Much to her surprise, Papa had given permission for her to move in with Sarah. Kelly now spent five days a week taking care of little Sam while Sarah was at work. This gave her some time to use her new watercolor set, since she could paint or draw whenever the baby slept.

Besides babysitting, Kelly cleaned the apartment, did most of the cooking, and even sewed new clothes for her fast-growing nephew. She and little Sam had become good friends, and Kelly discovered she was more capable with children than she'd ever imagined.

As Kelly sat in the rocking chair, trying to get the baby to sleep, she let her mind wander back to the general store outside of Walnutport, along the Lehigh Navigation System. A vision of Mike Cooper flashed into her mind. He was good with children. Kelly had witnessed him giving out free candy to several of the kids who played along the canal and to many who visited his store as well. Mike wanted a whole houseful of children; he'd told her so.

"I never did write and thank Mike for the birthday gift," Kelly whispered against little Sam's downy blond head. The baby looked a lot like his papa, but Kelly hoped he didn't grow up to be anything like the man. How could Sam Turner have left his wife and child? Just thinking about it made Kelly's blood boil. Was Mike Cooper any different than Papa or Sam? Could he be trusted not to hurt her the way Papa often did or the way Sam had done to Sarah?

Mike had promised to write, and he'd done so several times. He'd also sent her a wonderful present. He might not be the same as other men she knew. Kelly guessed she'd have to make up her mind about Mike when they returned to the canal sometime in March.

She bent her head and kissed the tip of little Sam's nose. "You and your mama might be goin' with us this spring. I don't rightly see how the two of you can stay on here by yourselves." She giggled at the baby's response to her kiss. He'd scrunched up his nose and wiggled his lips, almost as if he was trying to kiss her back.

"Of course, I could always stay on here, I suppose. Papa can't make me return to the canal if I don't want to." Even as the words slipped off her tongue, Kelly knew what she would do when Papa said it was time to return to their boat. She would go along willingly because she missed her mule friends, missed the smell of fresh air, and yes, even missed Mike Cooper.

৯

Mike stared at his empty coffee cup. He should clear away the breakfast dishes and get his horse hitched to the buckboard. He was expecting a load of supplies to be delivered to

Walnutport today by train, and it would be good if he were there when it came in. Mike knew that Gus Stevens, the man who ran the livery stable next to the train station, would be happy to take the supplies to his place and hold them for him. Gus had done that a time or two, but Mike didn't like to take advantage of the older man's good nature.

With that thought in mind, Mike scooped the dishes off the table and set them in the sink. He'd pour warm water over them and take care of the washing part when he returned from town.

A short time later, Mike climbed into his wagon, clucked to the horse, and headed in the direction of Walnutport. During the first part of the trip, he sang favorite hymns and played his mouth harp. It made the time go quicker and caused Mike to feel a bit closer to his Maker. It also made him feel less lonely.

As the days had turned into weeks, and the weeks into months, Mike's yearning for a wife had not diminished. In fact, he'd been feeling so lonely here of late, he'd actually considered accepting one of Betsy Nelson's frequent supper invitations. The woman was persistent, he'd give her that much. Persistent and pushy. Nothing like Kelly McGregor.

"I've got to quit thinkin' about Kelly," Mike berated himself. "She obviously feels nothing for me. If she did, she would have written by now." Mike wasn't sure he'd ever see Kelly again. For all he knew, she'd decided to stay in the city of Easton. She'd probably found a job and a boyfriend by now. She could even be married.

By the time Mike arrived at his destination, he was sweating worse than his horse. He'd let the gelding run and had enjoyed the exhilarating ride. It helped clear his thinking. Nothing else had mattered but the wind blowing against his face. Tomorrow would be a new day. Another time to reflect on God's will for Mike's life.

twenty-four

On Monday morning, the third week of March, the McGregors boarded their boat. The canal was full of water again, and Papa was most anxious to get started hauling coal. Sarah and baby Sam had come along, since Sarah didn't want to stay in Easton by herself and couldn't talk Kelly into staying on. Besides, Mama could use Sarah's help on the boat and would be available to watch the baby whenever Kelly's sister took over walking the mules.

Kelly felt bad that Sarah was returning to the canal she'd hated so much in the past, but it would be nice to have her sister's help, as well as her companionship.

Kelly looked forward to stopping by Mike's store, and she knew they would because Papa had said so. They'd picked up some supplies at Dull's Grocery Store in Easton, but Papa forgot to get a couple of things. Kelly planned to give Mike several more pictures to try to sell, as she'd been able to paint many during her stay in the city. She was also anxious to see whether he'd sold any of her other pieces. Kelly hoped she could continue her friendship with Mike without his expecting anything more. They should arrive at his store sometime tomorrow, late afternoon or early evening.

Kelly pulled the collar of her jacket tightly against her chin as she tromped along the towpath, singing her favorite song, and not even minding the chilly March winds.

"Hunks-a-go pudding and pieces of pie; my mother gave me when I was knee-high. . . . And if you don't believe it, just drop in and see—the hunks-a-go pudding my mother gave me."

Mike felt better than he had in weeks. He'd had several customers and given away a couple of Bibles to some rough and tumble canalers who were desperately in need of God. Mike had witnessed these two men fighting on more than one occasion, and the fact that they'd willingly taken a Bible gave him hope that others might also be receptive to the gospel.

As Mike washed the store windows with a rag and some diluted ammonia, he thought about Kelly's dad. Now there was a man badly in need of the Lord. Mike had witnessed Amos McGregor's temper several times. If Amos found forgiveness for his sins and turned his life around, maybe Kelly would be more receptive to Mike's attentions. Mike was sure the main reason Kelly was so standoffish was because she was afraid of men.

He glanced at the wall behind his front counter. Only two of Kelly's pictures had sold since she'd left for Easton, and those had both been bought before Christmas. No one had shown any interest in her work since then, even though Mike often pointed the pictures out to his customers, hoping they would take the hint and buy one.

Mike studied the window he'd been washing, checking for any spots or streaks. To his surprise, he noticed Amos McGregor's boat docked out front, and the man was heading toward the store. Trudging alongside of Amos was his wife, Dorrie, Kelly, and another woman carrying a young child.

Mike climbed off his ladder and hurried to the front of the store. Kelly had returned to the canal! He opened the door and greeted his customers with a smile and a sense of excitement. "It's sure nice to see you folks again."

Amos only grunted in reply, but Kelly returned his smile. "It's good to be back," she said.

"And who might this little guy be?" Mike asked, reaching out to clasp the chubby fingers of the little boy who was held by the other young woman.

"That's baby Sam," Kelly said. "In case you don't remember, this is my sister, Sarah. She and Sam Jr. are gonna be livin' with us for awhile."

"Yes, I remember Sarah." Mike nodded and smiled at Kelly's sister. He didn't ask for details. From the pathetic look on Sarah's face, he figured her marriage to Sam Turner was probably over.

"Do you have any soft material I might use for diapers?" Sarah asked. "Sam seems to go through them pretty fast, and I don't have time to be washin' every day."

Mike pointed to the shelf where he kept bolts of material. "I'm sure you'll find something to your liking over there."

Sarah moved away, and her mother followed. Amos was across the room looking at some new shovels Mike had recently gotten in, so apparently Kelly felt free to stare up at her paintings.

Mike positioned himself so he was standing beside Kelly. "How have you been? I've missed you," he whispered.

Her gaze darted from her dad, to the paintings, and back to Mike. "I'm fine, and I've brought you more pictures." She frowned. "But from the looks of it, you still have quite a few of my old ones."

He nodded. "Sorry to say I only sold two while you were gone." He leaned his head close to her ear. "Did you get the birthday present I sent? I'd hoped you would write and let me know."

"Yes, I got the package and put it to good use." Kelly averted his gaze. "Sorry for not writing to say thank you. I kept meaning to write, but I got busy takin' care of little Sam while Sarah went to work each day."

"That's okay. I understand." Mike touched her arm briefly, but then he pulled his hand away. "Do you have the new pictures with you now?"

She nodded, reached into her pocket, retrieved the drawing tablet he'd sent her, and handed it to him. "I was able to make things look more real usin' things you sent me."

Mike thumbed quickly through the tablet. Pictures of row housing, tall buildings, and statues in the city of Easton covered the first pages. There were also some paintings of the bridge that spanned the river between Easton, Pennsylvania, and Phillipsburg, New Jersey, as well as a few pictures of people. They were all done well, and Mike was glad he'd sent

Kelly the paint set, even if she hadn't chosen to write and tell him she'd received it. He was even happier that she'd accepted the gift and put it to good use.

"These are wonderful," he said. "Would you mind leaving them with me to try and sell?"

Kelly's eyebrows furrowed. "But you still have most of my other pictures. Why would ya be wantin' more?"

"Because they're good—really good," he asserted. "I've always admired your artwork, and I believe you've actually gotten better."

Her expression turned hopeful. "You really think so?"

"I do."

She pointed to the tablet. "And you think you can sell these?"

"I'd like to try."

She nodded her consent. "Do as you like then."

"Will you be spending the night in the area?" Mike asked.

Kelly opened her mouth, but her dad spoke up before she could say anything. "We'll be headin' on up the canal. Won't be back this way 'til probably late Saturday."

Mike turned his head to the left. He hadn't realized Kelly's dad was standing beside him, holding a shovel in one hand.

"You think you might stay over on Saturday night?"

"Could be," was all Amos said.

Mike smiled to himself. If the McGregors were here on Sunday, then he might get the chance to spend some time alone with Kelly. Even though the weather was still a bit chilly, it was possible that they'd be able to go on another picnic.

❧

Kelly left Mike's store with mixed feelings. It was wonderful to see him again, but her spirits had been dampened when he'd told her he'd only sold two pictures during her absence. Mike had given her the money for those paintings as she was on her way out the door. He'd also whispered that he wanted to take her on another picnic and hoped it would be this Sunday, if they were near his store.

"Mind if I walk with you a ways?" Sarah asked, breaking

into Kelly's musings. "Sam's ready for a nap, and Mama doesn't need me for anything. I thought the fresh air and exercise might do me some good."

Kelly was always glad for her sister's company. "You wanna be in charge of the mules or just offer me companionship?"

"You can tend the mules," Sarah was quick to say. "I think they like you better than they do me, anyway."

"They're just used to me, that's all." Kelly adjusted the brim of her straw hat, which seemed to have a mind of its own. "Truth be told, I think old Herman kinda likes it when I sing silly canal songs."

"You sing to the mules?"

Kelly nodded. "Guess it's really for me, but if they enjoy it, then that makes it all the better."

Sarah chuckled. It was good to see her smile. She'd been so sad since her husband had run off, and Kelly couldn't blame her. She would be melancholy too if the man she'd married had chosen not to stay around and help out. Sam Turner ought to be tarred and feathered for walking out on his wife and baby. He probably never loved Sarah in the first place. Most likely he only married her just to show her folks that he could take their daughter away.

"Tell me about Mike Cooper," Sarah said.

Kelly jerked her head. "What about him?"

"Have you and him been courtin'?"

"What would make you ask that?"

Sarah gave Kelly a nudge in the ribs with her bony elbow. "He couldn't take his eyes off you the whole time we were in the store." She eyed Kelly curiously. "I'd say it's as plain as the nose on your face that you're smitten with him as well."

What could Kelly say in response? She couldn't deny her feelings for Mike. She enjoyed his company, and he was the best-looking man she'd ever laid eyes on. That didn't mean they were courting, though. And it sure didn't mean she was smitten with him.

"Mike and me have gone on a few picnics, but we're not a

courtin' couple," Kelly said, shrugging her shoulders.

"But you'd like to be, right?" her sister prodded.

"We're just friends; nothin' more."

Sarah wiggled her dark eyebrows, then winked. "Whatever you say, little sister. Whatever you say."

twenty-five

Early Saturday afternoon Mike went outside to help one of the local boatmen load the supplies he had purchased onto his boat. They had no more than placed the last one on deck when Mike saw the McGregors' boat heading their way.

His heart did a little flip-flop. Would they be stopping for the night? Mike stepped onto the towpath, anxious for Kelly to arrive. While he waited, he slicked back his hair, finger-combed his mustache, and made sure his flannel shirt was tucked inside his trousers.

A few minutes later Kelly and her mules were alongside him. The animals brayed and snorted, as if they expected him to give them a handout, as he'd done a few times before.

"Sorry, fellows, but I didn't know you were comin', so there aren't any apples or carrots in my pockets today." Mike gave each mule a pat on its flank, then he turned and smiled at Kelly. "I'm glad you're here. Are you planning to stay overnight?"

She shook her head. "Now that Sarah's here to help, Papa has us movin' twice as fast as before. He says there's no time to waste. Especially when we never know if there's gonna be trouble ahead that might slow us down."

Mike felt his anticipation slip to the toes of his boots. He'd been waiting so long to be with Kelly again, and now they weren't stopping? How was he ever going to tell her what was on his mind if they couldn't spend any time together?

"I'm sorry to hear you're not staying over," he muttered. "I was really hoping we'd be able to go on a picnic tomorrow afternoon."

"Isn't it a mite chilly for a picnic?"

Mike shrugged his shoulders. "I figured we could build a fire and snuggle beneath a blanket if it got too cold."

When Kelly smiled at him, he wanted to take her into his arms and proclaim his intentions. He knew now wasn't the time or the place, so he pulled from his inner strength and took a step back. "When do you think you might be stoppin' long enough so we can spend a few minutes together?"

She turned her palms upwards. "Don't know. That's entirely up to Papa."

Mike groaned. "Guess I'll just have to wait and ask God to give me more patience."

"Get a move on, would ya, Girl?"

Kelly and Mike both turned their heads. Amos McGregor was leaning over the side of the boat, and he wasn't smiling.

"I need to get the mules movin' again," Kelly said to Mike.

He stepped aside but touched her arm as she passed by. "See you soon, Kelly."

"I hope so," she murmured.

❧

The next few weeks sped by, as Kelly and Sarah took turns leading the mules, and Papa kept the boat moving as fast as the animals would pull. They stopped only once for supplies, and that was at a store in Mauch Chunk. Kelly was beginning to think she'd never get the chance to see Mike Cooper again or find out if any of her paintings had sold. On days like today, when the sky was cloudy and threatened rain, Kelly's spirits plummeted, and she didn't feel much like praying. All the while they'd been living in Easton, she'd felt closer to God, reading her Bible every day and offering prayers on behalf of her family and her future. It didn't seem as if any of her prayers were going to be answered, and she wondered if she should continue to ask God for things He probably wouldn't provide.

She'd prayed for her sister, and look how that had turned out. She had prayed for Papa's salvation, yet he was still as moody and cantankerous as ever. She'd asked God to allow her to make enough money to support herself and open an art gallery, but that wasn't working out either. So far she'd only made a few dollars, which was a long ways from what she would need. It was an impossible dream, and with each passing day Kelly became more convinced it was never going to happen.

She looked up at the darkening sky and prayed, "Lord, if walkin' the mules is the only job You have in mind for me, then help me learn to be content."

&

It was the end of April before Kelly saw Mike again. They'd arrived in front of his store at dusk on Saturday evening, so Papa decided to stay for the night. Since the next day was Sunday and the boatmen were not allowed to pull their loads up the canal, they would be around for the whole day.

Kelly settled into her bed, feeling a sense of joy she hadn't felt in weeks. Tomorrow she planned to attend the church service on the grassy area in front of Mike's store. Afterward she hoped to see Mike and talk to him about her artwork. She'd managed to do a few more paintings—mostly of little Sam—so she would give those to Mike as well.

Sam was growing so much, and soon he'd be toddling all over the place. Then they would have to be sure he was tied securely to something, or else he might end up falling overboard. Canal life could be dangerous, and precautions had to be taken in order to protect everyone on board. Even the mules needed safeguarding from bad weather, insects, freak accidents, and fatigue.

Kelly closed her eyes and drew in a deep breath as she snuggled into her feather pillow. She fell asleep dreaming about Mike Cooper.

&

The following day brought sunshine and blue skies. It was perfect spring weather, and Kelly had invited her sister and mother to join her for the church service that had just begun. Mama said she'd better stay on the boat with Papa, but Sarah left the baby behind with her parents and joined Kelly.

The two young women spread a blanket on the grass and took a seat just as Betsy Nelson began playing her zither, while her father led those who had gathered in singing "Holy Spirit, Light Divine."

Kelly lifted her voice with the others. The first verse spoke to her heart:

Holy Spirit, Light divine,
Shine upon this heart of mine.
Chase the shades of night away;
Turn my darkness into day.

The song gave Kelly exactly what she needed. A reminder that only God could turn her darkness into day. As difficult as it was, she knew she needed to keep praying and trusting Him to answer her prayers.

Kelly felt her sister's nudge in the ribs. "Psst. . .look who's watchin' you."

Kelly turned her head and noticed Mike sitting on a wooden box several feet away. He grinned and nodded at her, and she smiled in return.

"I told you he likes you."

Kelly put her fingers to her lips. "Shh. . .someone might hear."

Sarah snickered, but she stopped talking and began to sing. Kelly did the same.

A short time later, the preacher gave his message from the Book of Romans.

" 'For we know that all things work together for good to them that love God, to them who are the called according to his purpose,' " Rev. Nelson read in his booming voice.

All things. For them that love God and are called according to His purpose. Kelly was sure that meant her. The preacher was saying all things in her life would work together for good because she loved God. Surely He wanted to give her good things. The question was, would those good things be what she'd been praying for?

Kelly hadn't realized the service was over until Sarah touched her arm. "You gonna sit there all day, or did ya plan to go speak to that storekeeper who hasn't taken his eyes off you since we sat down?"

Kelly wrinkled her nose. "You're makin' that up."

"Am not." Sarah stood up. "I'd better get back to the boat and check on little Sam. Got any messages you want me to give the folks?"

Kelly got to her feet as well. "What makes you think I'm not returnin' to the boat with you?"

"Call it a hunch." Sarah bent down and grabbed the blanket. She gave it a good shake, then folded it and tucked it under Kelly's arm. "Should I tell Mama you won't be joinin' us for the noon meal?"

Kelly felt her face heat up. Was Sarah able to read her mind these days?

"Well, I. . .uh. . .thought I might speak to Mike about my paintings. See if any more have sold."

"And if he invites you to join him for lunch?"

Kelly chewed on her lower lip. "You think I should say yes?"

Sarah swatted Kelly's arm playfully. "Of course, silly."

"What about the folks? Shouldn't I check with them first?"

"Leave that up to me."

"Okay, then. If I don't return to the boat in the next half hour, you can figure I'm havin' a picnic lunch with Mike. He did mention wantin' to do that the last time we talked."

Sarah gave Kelly a quick hug, hoisted her long skirt, and trudged off in the direction of the boat. Kelly turned toward the spot where Mike had been sitting, but disappointment flooded her soul when she realized he was gone. With a deep sigh, she whirled around and headed the same way Sarah had gone. There was no point in sticking around now.

Kelly had only taken a few steps when she felt someone touch her shoulder. She whirled around, and her throat closed with emotion. Mike was standing so close she could feel his warm breath on her neck. She stared up at him, her heart thumping hard like the mules' hooves plodding along the hard-packed trail.

"Kelly." Mike's voice was soft and sweet.

She slid her tongue across her lower lip, feeling jittery as a june bug. "I came to hear the preaching."

"Reverend Nelson delivered a good message today, didn't he?"

Kelly nodded in response. It was hard to speak. Hard to think with him standing there watching her every move.

"Can you join me for a picnic?" Mike asked. "It will only take me a few minutes to throw something in the picnic basket, and it's the perfect day for it, don't you think?"

"Yes, yes, it is," she replied, glad she'd found her voice again.

"Then you'll join me?"

"I'd be happy to. Is there anything I can bring?"

"Just a hearty appetite and that blanket you're holding."

Kelly glanced down at the woolen covering still tucked under her arm. Sarah must have given it to her because she'd been pretty certain Mike would be taking her on a picnic. "Where should I meet you?"

"How about at the pond by the lock tender's house again? That way you won't have to worry about anyone seeing us walk there together."

Kelly knew Mike was probably referring to her dad, and he was right. It would be much better if Papa didn't know she was going on a picnic with the storekeeper.

"Okay, I'll head there now, and maybe even get a bit of sketching done while I'm waitin' for you."

Mike winked at her. "See you soon then."

"Yes, soon."

twenty-six

The warmth of the sun beating down on her head and shoulders felt like healing balm as Kelly reclined on her blanket a few feet from the pond. She always enjoyed springtime, with its gentle breezes, pleasantly warm temperatures, and flowers blooming abundantly along the towpath. Summer would be here soon, and that meant hot, humid days, which made it more difficult to walk the mules. So she would enjoy each day of spring, and try to be content when the sweltering days of summer came upon them.

"Are you taking a nap?"

Kelly bolted upright at the sound of Mike's voice. "I. . .uh . . .was just resting and enjoyin' the warmth of the sun."

He took a seat beside her and placed the picnic basket in the center of the blanket. "It's a beautiful Lord's day, isn't it?"

She nodded and smiled.

"I hope you're hungry, because I packed us a big lunch."

Kelly eyed the basket curiously. "What did ya fix?"

Mike opened the lid and withdrew a loaf of bread, along with a hunk of cheese and some roast beef slices. "For sandwiches," he announced.

Kelly licked her lips as her mouth began to water. She hadn't realized how hungry she was until she saw the food.

"I also brought some canned peaches, a bottle of goat's milk, and a chocolate cake for dessert."

"Where did you get all this?" Surely the man hadn't baked the cake and bread, canned the peaches, and milked a goat. When would he have had the time? Papa always said cooking and baking were women's work, although he had been forced to do some of it when Mama had taken sick last year.

Mike fingered his mustache as a smile spread across his face.

"I must confess, I bought the bread and cake from Mrs. Harris, the lock tender's wife. I often buy her baked goods and sell them in my store. The peaches came from Mrs. Wilson, who lives in Walnutport."

"And the goat's milk?"

He wiggled his eyebrows. "I recently traded one of my customers a couple of kerosene lamps for the goat."

"Couldn't they have paid for the lamps, or were you actually wantin' a goat?"

He chuckled. "Truth of the matter, they didn't have any cash, and even though I offered them credit, they preferred to do a bit of bartering." He poured some of the goat's milk into a cup and handed it to Kelly. "I enjoy animals, so Henrietta is a nice addition to the little barnyard family I adopted this winter."

"Your barnyard family? How many other animals do you have?"

"Besides Blaze, my horse, and Henrietta the goat, I also own a cat, a dozen chickens, and I'm thinkin' about getting a pig or two."

Kelly shook her head. "Sounds like a lot of work to me."

"Maybe so, but a man can get lonely living all by himself, and taking care of the critters gives me something to do when I'm not minding the store."

Kelly was about to take a sip of her goat's milk, when Mike took hold of her hand. "Shall we pray?"

"Of course."

After Mike's simple prayer, he sliced the bread and handed Kelly a plate with a hunk of cheese, some meat, and two thick pieces of bread. She made quick work out of eating it, savoring every bite.

When they finished their sandwiches, Mike opened the jar of peaches and placed two chunks on each of their plates.

"Don't you ever get lonely walking the towpath by yourself?"

"I'm not really alone," Kelly replied. "Herman and Hector are good company, and of course, now that Sarah's back, she sometimes walks with me."

His eyebrows drew together. "Mind if I ask where Sarah's husband is?"

Kelly felt her stomach tighten. She didn't want to think of the way Sam had run off and left his family, much less talk about it.

"I guess it's none of my business," Mike said, before she could make a reply. "Forget I even asked."

Kelly reached out and touched the sleeve of his shirt. "It's all right. Others will no doubt be askin', so I may as well start by telling you the facts." She swallowed hard, searching for the right words. "Shortly after we arrived in Easton, I ran into my sister at the Simon Silk Mill, where I'd gone looking for a job."

Mike nodded but didn't say anything.

"That day Sarah told me Sam had lost his job at Warren Soapstone. Said it was because he'd gotten mad at his boss and talked back." Kelly paused a moment and was surprised when Mike reached for her hand. She didn't pull it away. It felt good, and his hand was warm and comforting.

"Sarah said Sam had been staying home with the baby while she worked," Kelly continued. "I invited her to drop by the boardinghouse where we were staying, so Mama and me could meet Sam Jr."

"And did she stop by?" Mike asked.

"Yes, the next Saturday. But as soon as I laid eyes on my sister, I knew somethin' was wrong."

"What happened?"

"She said Sam up and left her, which meant she had no one to watch the baby." Kelly's eyes filled with tears, just thinking about how terribly her sister had been treated. "I agreed to move in with Sarah and watch the little guy while she was at work."

"So that's how you were able to get so many paintings done." Mike squeezed Kelly's hand. "That was a fine thing you did, agreeing to help care for your sister's child." He frowned. "I'm sorry to hear Sam Turner couldn't face up to his responsibilities. Guess maybe he wasn't ready to be a husband or father."

Kelly snorted. "I'd say most men aren't ready."

"That's not true," Mike said, shaking his head. "I'm more than ready. Have been for a couple of years." He eyed Kelly in a curious sort of way. What was he thinking? Why was he smiling at her like that?

She didn't know what to say, so she withdrew her hand and popped a hunk of peach into her mouth.

"Ever since my folks passed away, I've felt an emptiness in my heart," Mike went on to say. "And after Alvin and John left home to start up their fishin' business in New Jersey, I've had a hankering for a wife and a houseful of kids." He stared down at his plate. "I've been praying for some time that God would give me a Christian wife, and later some children who'd take over the store some day." His gaze lifted to her face, and she swallowed hard. "I feel confident that God has answered my prayer and sent the perfect woman for my needs."

Kelly's heart began to pound. Surely Mike couldn't mean her. He must be referring to someone else. . .maybe Betsy Nelson, the preacher's daughter. It was obvious that the woman had eyes for Mike. Maybe the two of them had begun courting while Kelly was away for the winter months.

"I think the preacher's daughter would make any man a fine wife," Kelly mumbled.

"The preacher's daughter?" Mike's furrowed brows showed his obvious confusion.

"Betsy Nelson. I believe she likes you."

Mike set his plate on the blanket, then took hold of Kelly's and did the same with it. He leaned forward, placed his hands on her shoulders, and kissed her lips so tenderly she thought she might swoon. When the kiss ended, he whispered, "It's you I plan to marry, and it has been all along."

Kelly's mouth dropped open, but before she could find her voice, he spoke again. "Ever since that day you and your folks came into my store so you could buy a pair of boots, I've had an interest in you. I thought you might feel the same."

"I–I—" she sputtered.

"We can be married by Preacher Nelson whenever you feel

ready," Mike continued, as though the matter was entirely settled. "I'm hoping we can start a family right away, and—"

Kelly jumped up so quickly she knocked over the jar still half-full of peaches. "I won't be anyone's wife!" she shouted. "Especially not someone who only wants a woman so he can have children he can put to work and never pay!"

Mike scrambled to his feet, but before he had a chance to say one word, she turned on her heel and bounded away, not even caring that she'd left her blanket behind.

❧

Mike stood staring at Kelly's retreating form and feeling like his breath had been snatched away. What had gone wrong? What had he said to upset her so?

Taking in a deep breath of air, Mike tried to sort out his tangled emotions. Kelly had to be the one for him. After all, she'd appeared at his store last year only moments after his prayer for a wife. He'd thought they'd been drawing closer with each time they spent alone. She'd allowed him to kiss her. Had Kelly really believed he was interested in Betsy Nelson? And what had she meant by shouting that she didn't want to be anyone's wife—especially not someone who only wanted a woman so he could have children he could put to work and never pay?

"I would never do such a thing," Mike muttered. "I can't imagine why she would think so either."

An image of Amos McGregor popped into Mike's mind. The man was a tyrant, and he remembered Kelly saying on several occasions that her dad had refused to pay her any money for leading the mules. That was the reason her sister, Sarah, had run off with Sam Turner a couple years ago.

Mike slapped the side of his head and moaned. "How could I have been so stupid and insensitive? I should have realized Kelly might misunderstand my intentions."

He closed his eyes and lifted his face toward the sky. "Father in heaven, please guide me. I love Kelly, and I thought by her actions she might have come to love me now. Help me convince her, Lord."

twenty-seven

Kelly knew her face must be red and tear-stained, and she also knew her parents would want to know where she'd gone after the church service. She couldn't face anyone now or answer any questions. She just wanted to be alone in her room, to cry and sort out her feelings.

Kelly climbed onto the boat and hurried to her bedroom, relieved that nobody was in sight. They were probably all taking naps, which is what Mama and Papa usually did on a Sunday afternoon.

She flung the door of her room open and flopped onto the bed, hoping she too might be able to nap. But sleep eluded her as she thought about the things that had transpired on her picnic with Mike.

Did the man really expect her to marry him and bear his children, just so they could work in his store? Mike hadn't really said it would be without pay, but then she'd run off so fast there hadn't been a chance for him to say anything more. Maybe she should have asked him to explain his intentions. Maybe she should have admitted that she'd come to care for him in a special way.

A fresh set of tears coursed down Kelly's cheeks, and she sniffed deeply while she swiped at them with the back of her hand. *I can never tell Mike how he makes me feel. If I did, he would think I wanted to get married and raise his children. I won't marry a man just to get away from Papa's mean temper or the hard work I'm expected to do. I want the opportunity to support myself. I need the chance to prove I can make money of my own.*

She squeezed her eyes shut. "Dear God, please show me what to do. Help me learn to be content with my life, and help me forget how much I enjoyed Mike's kiss."

❧

For the next several weeks, Kelly avoided Mike's store. Even when they stopped for supplies, she stayed outside with the mules. She couldn't face Mike. He probably thought she was an idiot for running out on their picnic, and it was too difficult for her to explain the way she'd been thinking. She was pretty sure she loved him, but she couldn't give in to her feelings. No way did she want to end up like Mama, who had to endure Papa's harsh tongue and controlling ways. Nor did Kelly wish to be like her sister, raising a baby alone and continuing to work for their father with no pay.

Today was hotter than usual, especially since it was only the end of May. Kelly looked longingly at the canal as she plodded along the towpath, wishing she could stop and take a dip in the cooling waters. Even though she was leery of water moccasins, Kelly would have set her fears aside and gone swimming if they'd stopped for any length of time.

A short time later, Kelly's wish was granted. A long line of boats waited at the lock just a short way past Mike's store. No telling how long they might be held up. Kelly decided she would take off her boots and go wading. No point in getting her whole body wet when all she needed was a bit of chilly water on her legs to get cooled off.

She made sure both mules had been given a drink of water, then secured them to a nearby tree. She thought about asking Sarah to join her in the water, but the baby was down for a nap, and Sarah and Mama had taken advantage of the stop and begun washing clothes.

Kelly plunked herself on the ground, slipped off her boots and socks, and then stood up again. It was time to get cooled off.

❧

Mike closed the door behind a group of tourists from New York who were traveling by boat up the canal. They'd dropped by his store in search of food supplies, but to his surprise, they'd been favorably impressed with Kelly's artwork. So much so that Mike had sold all of Kelly's paintings, and two of the travelers had asked if he would be getting anymore, saying they would stop by the store on their return trip.

Mike promised to try to get more, but after the customers left he wondered how it would be possible. He hadn't seen Kelly since their picnic, when he'd been dumb enough to announce that he wanted to make her his wife. Her folks had stopped by a couple of times, but Kelly never came inside.

He'd been tempted to seek her out, but after a time of prayer, Mike decided to leave their relationship in God's hands. He had tried to take control of the matter before, and it only left him with an ache in his heart. From now on he'd let God decide if Kelly McGregor was meant for him. If she showed an interest, he would know she was the one. If not, then he needed to move on with his life. Maybe it wasn't meant for him to have a wife.

Feeling a headache coming on, Mike closed his store a bit early and went outside for some air. He hoped it would be fresher than what was inside his store on this hot, muggy day. Even though Mike had never learned to swim well and couldn't do much more than dive in the water and paddle back to the lock, today seemed like the perfect day for getting wet. Wearing only a pair of trousers he'd rolled up to the knees, Mike jumped into the canal near the stop gate.

❧

With her skirt held up, Kelly plodded back and forth along the bank by the lock tender's house. Several swimmers had been there earlier, but most had gone for the day. It would be awhile until Papa was ready to go, as there had been a break in the lock and all the boats were still held up. Kelly decided to take advantage of this free time to get some sketching done. She'd left her drawing tablet on the grass next to her boots and was about to reclaim it when she noticed Mike Cooper in the water. He dove from one dock, then crossed the gates and grabbed hold of the dock on the other side. She was surprised to see him, as she remembered Mike saying once that he wasn't a good swimmer and didn't go into the canal very often.

Kelly stood still, watching in fascination as Mike took

another dive. She waited for him to resurface on the other side, but he didn't come up where he should have.

A sense of alarm shot through her body when she noticed small bubbles on top of the water. They seemed to be coming from a large roll of moss about ten feet above the gates. With no thought for her own safety, Kelly jerked off her skirt, and wearing only her white pantalets and cotton blouse, she dove into the water and swam toward the spot where she'd seen the bubbles. Her scream echoed over the water. "Hold on, Mike! I'm comin'!"

A few seconds later, Kelly dove under the water and spotted Mike, thrashing about while he tried to free his hands and feet from the twisted moss. Visions of them both being drowned flashed through her mind as Kelly tried to untangle the mess. Mike wouldn't hold still. He was obviously in a state of panic. At one point, he grabbed Kelly around the neck, nearly choking her to death.

. Her lungs began to burn, and she knew she needed air quickly. Desperation surged within. Her insides felt as if they would burst. She knew they were in a tough spot, so she sent up a prayer and did the only thing that came to mind.

Pop! Kelly smacked Mike right in the nose. Blood shot out in every direction, but Mike loosened his grip on her neck. Using all her strength and inner resolve, Kelly managed to get his hands and feet free from the moss, and she kicked her way to the surface, pulling Mike along.

When Mike's face cleared the water, she breathed a sigh of relief. Gasping for breath, Kelly propelled them through the murky water, until at last they were both on the shore. Mike lay there, white as a sheet, and Kelly worried that he might be dead. She rolled him over and began to push down on his back. A short time later, he started coughing and sputtering.

A great sense of relief flooded Kelly's soul. She grabbed hold of the skirt she'd left on the grass, ripped off a piece, and held it against Mike's bleeding nose. How close she'd come to losing the man she loved. The realization sent shivers up

Kelly's spine, and she trembled and let out a little sob.

Mike opened his eyes and stared up at her, a look of confusion on his face. "What happened? Where am I?"

"You were trapped in a wad of moss," she rasped. "I'm awful sorry, but I had to punch you in the nose to get you to stop fightin'."

He blinked several times. "You hit me?"

She nodded. "Sorry, but I didn't know what else to do."

Mike reached up and touched her hand where she held the piece of material against his nose. "Is it broken?"

She pulled the cloth back and studied the damage. "I don't think so. The bleedin' seems to be almost stopped."

"You saved my life."

"I guess I did, but it was God who gave me the strength to do it."

He clutched her hand. "Why would you do that if you don't care about me?"

She frowned. "Who says I don't care?"

"Do you?" Mike's eyes were seeking, his voice imploring her to tell the truth.

Kelly's heart was beating so hard she thought it might burst wide open. She'd been fighting her feelings for Mike all these months, yet seeing him almost drown made her realize she wouldn't know what to do if he wasn't part of her life. But was love enough? If she were to marry Mike, would he expect her and their children to work for free at his store?

"Kelly, my love," Mike murmured. "You're the answer to my prayers."

"You were prayin' someone would find you in the moss and save your life?"

He laughed, coughed, and tried to sit up.

"You'd better lie still a few more minutes," she instructed. "That was quite an ordeal you came through."

"I'm okay," he insisted as he pulled himself to a sitting position in front of her.

"Are you sure?"

"I'm sure about one thing."

"What's that?"

He pulled her into his arms. "I'm sure I love you, and I believe God brought us together. Will you marry me, Kelly McGregor?"

Before Kelly could answer, Mike leaned over and kissed her upturned mouth. When the kiss was over, he said, "I promise never to treat you harshly, and I won't ask you or any children we may be blessed with to work for free. If you help me run the store, you'll earn half the money, same as me. If our kids help out, they'll get paid something too."

She opened her mouth, but he cut her off. "There's more."

"More?" she echoed.

He nodded. "This morning a group of tourists came by the store, and they bought the rest of your paintings."

"All of them?"

"Yes, and they said they'd be stopping by the store on their return trip to New York, so if you have any more pictures, they'll probably buy those as well."

Kelly could hardly believe it. All her pictures sold? It was too much to digest at once. And Mike asking her to be his wife and help run the store, agreeing to give her half of what they made? She pinched herself on the arm.

"What are you doing?" Mike asked with a little scowl.

"Makin' sure I'm not dreaming."

He kissed her again. "Does this feel like a dream?"

She nodded and giggled. "It sure does."

"Kelly, I've been thinking that I could add on to the store. Make a sort of gallery for you to paint and display your pictures. Maybe you could sell some art supplies to customers as well."

Her mouth fell open. She'd been dreaming about an art gallery for such a long time, and it didn't seem possible that her dream could be realized if she married Mike. "I'd love to have my own art gallery," she murmured, "but I won't marry you for that reason."

"You won't? Does that mean you don't love me?"

Mike's dejected expression was almost her undoing, and Kelly placed both her hands on his bare shoulders. "I do love you, and I will marry you, but not because of the promise of a gallery."

"What then?"

"I'll agree to become your wife for one reason and only one." Kelly leaned over and gently kissed the tip of Mike's nose. "I love you, Mike Cooper—with all my heart and soul. This is finally my chance for real happiness, and I'm not about to let it go."

Mike looked upwards and closed his eyes. "Thank You, Lord, for such a special woman."

epilogue

It was a pleasant morning on the last Saturday of September. So much had happened in the last four months that Kelly could hardly believe it. From her spot in front of an easel, she glanced across the room where her husband of three months stood waiting on a customer.

Mike must have guessed Kelly was watching him, for he looked over at her and winked.

She smiled and lifted her hand in response. Being married to Mike was better than she ever could have imagined. Not only was he a kind, Christian man, but he'd been true to his word and had added onto the store so Kelly could have her art gallery. Whenever she wasn't helping him in the store, she painted pictures, always adding a verse of Scripture above her signature. This was Kelly's way of telling others about God, who had been so good to her and the family.

Sam Turner had returned to the canal a few weeks ago, apologizing to Sarah and begging her to give him the chance to prove his love for her. Rather than going back to the city, the couple and the baby were living with Sam's parents. Sam assisted his dad with the lock chores, and Sarah helped her mother-in-law make bread and other baked goods, which they sold to many of the boaters who came through. They'd also begun to take in some washing, since many of the boatmen were either single or didn't bring their wives along to care for that need.

Kelly had finally seen the seashore along the coast of New Jersey, where Mike's brothers lived. They'd gone there for their honeymoon, and she'd been able to meet Alvin, John, and their wives.

The most surprising thing that had happened in the last few months was the change that had come over Kelly's dad. He'd accepted one of Reverend Nelson's cards with a Bible verse written on it, and Papa's heart was beginning to change. Not only was he no longer so ill-tempered, but Papa had given money to Kelly and Sarah, saying they'd both worked hard and deserved it. Since neither of them was available to work for him any longer, their dad had willingly hired two young men—one to drive the mules, the other to help steer the boat. Kelly figured if she kept praying, in time Papa would turn his life completely over to the Lord.

When the front door opened and Betsy Nelson walked in, Kelly smiled and waved. What had happened in the life of the preacher's daughter was the biggest surprise of all.

"That's a beautiful sunset you're working on," Betsy said, stepping up beside Kelly.

"Thanks. Would ya like to have it?"

Betsy shook her head. "I'm afraid where I'm going, there will be no use for pretty pictures."

Kelly nodded, knowing Betsy was talking about South America, where she'd recently decided to go as a missionary. "No, I suppose not."

"I'm leaving tomorrow morning for Easton, and then I'll ride the train to New York. From there I'll board a boat for South America," Betsy said.

"Everyone will miss your zither playin' on Sunday mornings," Kelly commented.

Betsy gave her a quick hug. "Thanks, but I'll be back someday, and when I return, I expect you and Mike will have a whole houseful of little ones."

Kelly smiled and placed one hand against her stomach. In about eight months the first of the Cooper children would make an appearance, and she couldn't wait to become a mother. God had given her a wonderful, Christian man to share the rest of her life with, and she knew he would be an amazing father.

As soon as Betsy and the other customer left, Mike moved across the room and took Kelly into his arms. "I sure love you, Mrs. Cooper."

"And I love you," she murmured against his chest.

Mike bent his head to capture her lips, and Kelly thanked the Lord for giving her the chance to find such happiness. She could hardly wait to see what the future held for Cooper's General Store on the Lehigh Canal.

&

Recipe for Hunks-A-Go Pudding

Make a batter with the following ingredients:

1 cup flour
1 tsp. salt
1 cup milk
2 eggs

Pour the batter into hot grease left over from cooked roast beef. Cover with a lid and cook on top of the stove until done.

A Letter To Our Readers

Dear Reader:

In order that we might better contribute to your reading enjoyment, we would appreciate your taking a few minutes to respond to the following questions. We welcome your comments and read each form and letter we receive. When completed, please return to the following:

Fiction Editor
Heartsong Presents
PO Box 719
Uhrichsville, Ohio 44683

1. Did you enjoy reading *Kelly's Chance* by Wanda E. Brunstetter?
❏ Very much! I would like to see more books by this author!
❏ Moderately. I would have enjoyed it more if

_____

_____

_____

2. Are you a member of **Heartsong Presents**? ❏ Yes ❏ No
If no, where did you purchase this book? _____

_____

3. How would you rate, on a scale from 1 (poor) to 5 (superior), the cover design? _____

4. On a scale from 1 (poor) to 10 (superior), please rate the following elements.

_____	Heroine	_____	Plot
_____	Hero	_____	Inspirational theme
_____	Setting	_____	Secondary characters

5. These characters were special because?_____
_____
_____

6. How has this book inspired your life?_____
_____
_____

7. What settings would you like to see covered in future
   Heartsong Presents books? _____
_____
_____

8. What are some inspirational themes you would like to see
   treated in future books? _____
_____
_____

9. Would you be interested in reading other **Heartsong
   Presents** titles? ❑ Yes ❑ No

10. Please check your age range:
   ❑ Under 18   ❑ 18-24
   ❑ 25-34   ❑ 35-45
   ❑ 46-55   ❑ Over 55

Name _____
Occupation _____
Address _____
City_____ State_____ Zip_____

Castles

4 stories in 1

The "merrie old days" of the Middle Ages leave much to be desired for four women in England and France. None of them ever believed they'd be embroiled in such plots of devastation and danger. Can God rescue them from the emotional dungeons they face—and lower the drawbridges into the hearts of the men they love? Meet four memorable characters created by respected author Tracie Peterson, and see if they can turn cavernous medieval castles into heavenly havens.

Historical, paperback, 464 pages, 5 ³⁄₁₆"x 8"

Nov. 14, 2015.

------- Presents -------

Great Inspirational Romance at a Great Price!

Heartsong Presents books are inspirational romances in contemporary and historical settings, designed to give you an enjoyable, spirit-lifting reading experience. You can choose wonderfully written titles from some of today's best authors like Peggy Darty, Sally Laity, Tracie Peterson, Colleen L. Reece, Debra White Smith, and many others.

When ordering quantities less than twelve, above titles are $3.25 each.
Not all titles may be available at time of order.

HEARTSONG ❤ PRESENTS

Love Stories
Are Rated G!

That's for godly, gratifying, and of course, great! If you love a thrilling love story but don't appreciate the sordidness of some popular paperback romances, **Heartsong Presents** is for you. In fact, **Heartsong Presents** is the premiere inspirational romance book club featuring love stories where Christian faith is the primary ingredient in a marriage relationship.

Sign up today to receive your first set of four, never-before-published Christian romances. Send no money now; you will receive a bill with the first shipment. You may cancel at any time without obligation, and if you aren't completely satisfied with any selection, you may return the books for an immediate refund!

Imagine. . .four new romances every four weeks—two historical, two contemporary—with men and women like you who long to meet the one God has chosen as the love of their lives. . .all for the low price of $10.99 postpaid.

To join, simply complete the coupon below and mail to the address provided. **Heartsong Presents** romances are rated G for another reason: They'll arrive Godspeed!

YES! Sign me up for Hearts❤ng!

NEW MEMBERSHIPS WILL BE SHIPPED IMMEDIATELY!
Send no money now. We'll bill you only $10.99 post-paid with your first shipment of four books. Or for faster action, call toll free 1-800-847-8270.

NAME_____

ADDRESS_____

CITY_____ STATE_____ ZIP_____

MAIL TO: HEARTSONG PRESENTS, P.O. Box 721, Uhrichsville, Ohio 44683
or visit www.heartsongpresents.com